Lucky 13:
Thirteen Tales of Crime & Mayhem

Edited by

Edward J. McFadden III

Padwolf Publishing Books by Edward J. McFadden III:

Deconstructing Toiken: A Fundamental Analysis of The Lord of the Rings & The Hobbit

Anywhere But Here

Padwolf Publishing Books edited by Edward J. McFadden III:

The Best of Pirate Writings: Tales of Fantasy, Mystery & Science Fiction, Vol. I

The Second Coming: The Best of Pirate Writings, Vol. II

Time Capsule

Epitaphs

BOOKS IN THE PADWOLF 13 SERIES

APOCALYPSE 13
-edited by Diane Raetz

MERMAIDS 13
-edited by John L. French

FANTASTIC FUTURES 13
-edited by Robert E Waters & James R Stratton

Lucky 13:
Thirteen Tales of Crime & Mayhem

Edited by

Edward J. McFadden III

PADWOLF PUBLISHING

PADWOLF PUBLISHING INC.

WWW.PADWOLF.COM

Lucky 13: Thirteen Tales of Crime & Mayhem

Edited by Edward J. McFadden III

Padwolf 13 Series: Managing Editor Patrick Thomas
                    Art Director Roy Mauritsen

Cover Art © Roy Mauritsen

ISBN 13 digit 978-1-890096-53-3

Table of Contents

Introduction

Luck is relative. It's elusive, a mystery wrapped in an enigma. Am I lucky? Unlucky? People ask themselves this question on a regular basis. There are even different types of luck. Who knew?

1. Constitutional luck, that is, luck with factors that cannot be changed. Place of birth and genetic constitution are typical examples.

2. Circumstantial luck—with factors that are haphazardly brought on. Accidents and epidemics are typical examples.

3. Ignorant luck, that is, luck with factors one does not know about. Examples can be identified only in hindsight.

So can one be constitutionally lucky, but circumstantially unlucky? My guess is that most people would consider themselves unlucky, but are in fact, lucky. It all depends on perspective.

I don't consider myself a lucky person. In fact, I used say I'm unlucky. I've never won anything of substance. I've never gotten "the luck of the draw" when it comes to writing, or any professional endeavor. My life seems to be filled with one trial after another. However, when I look close, I am in fact lucky. Though the country I live in has many issues, it's still one of the better places on the planet to be born and to live. I was born healthy. No major problems during childhood. Neither of my parents were taken from me, and though I've had my share of accidents, I'm still in one piece, and I still have all my limbs, fingers and toes. I have a job. And it's not shoveling turd. I have medical benefits, a wonderful wife and a beautiful, successful daughter. Add all this up, and I'm pretty lucky when compared to others I know. My guess is most of you reading this could make a similar analysis of your lives, and come to a similar conclusion. We're lucky to be here. Whether you've survived cancer, some other terrible disease, or a broken heart, the loss of someone dear—you're here. Reading this book. And that makes you lucky.

The idea for this book came while I was writing a story called "Canceled". It's a tale about an old mobster who is having the day from hell. Nothing but bad luck. It made me think about what luck meant. Was it real? A random fart in the space time continuum? Did it occur in equal amounts of good and bad, like a coin landing heads or tails? Was it magic? Could it be controlled?

Read these thirteen tales of horror, fantasy, science fiction, and everything in between as talented writers from every conceivable genre do their best to weave tales of luck. What it means to them, and more importantly, the world at large. I was committed to having a strong female presence in the book—something I believe is often overlooked in genre publications—so I must give a special shout-out to the ladies of *Lucky 13* for agreeing to appear in the book: Jessica McHugh, Sarah A. Hoyt, Danielle Ackley-McPhail, Diane Raetz, and Georgina Morales. Thanks for trusting me. And thank you for creating such wonderful stories. Thank you: Trent Zelazny, Matt Schiariti, Brady Allen, Patrick Thomas, Robert E. Waters, g. Elmer Munson, John L. French, and Michael Laimo. Thanks also to the folks at Padwolf Publishing, Inc., who listen to my crazy ideas and encourage me to pursue them—just as they have for going on twenty years now. Thank you all for believing in me, and the project, and for making me look good. Please read on, and enjoy, and always be sure to remember if you're alive and healthy, you're lucky. Here endeth the lesson.

Quarter, Quarter, How I Wonder
Trent Zelazny

*E*very life story is a mystery. Life itself, story aside, is a mystery. At one time or another, thoughts on the subject cross every person's mind. Some people relentlessly harp on these thoughts, pursue them until the day they die, while for some they are only an occasional fleeting fancy.

Ted Howard did not spend his days questioning the meaning of life. Rarely did he wonder if things in life were controlled by fate, or destiny, or whether it was all the result of volition, or even the mystifying crisscross, which some call serendipity.

Ted was thirty-four years old, his height average and his weight proportionate. His physical health was unexceptional, his IQ middle of the road. His looks were neither attractive nor repulsive. He was single, owned a modest car and lived in a modest home. His job neither impressed nor caused ridicule or pity.

For all intents and purposes, Ted Howard was a complacent man. His skeleton, his flesh and blood were all assembled by contentment as he walked along San Francisco Street, the sky with more night than day in it. Being Sunday, even on this spring-like evening, the meanderers were sparse.

Every Sunday at eight he stopped at the Mesa Café, had a cup of chamomile tea, and spent an hour reading a book. His hip pocket contained a slim volume of poetry. By the face of the Easy Reader watch on his wrist, he saw that it was exactly eight o'clock when he reached the café's doorway. He pulled the door open and stepped inside.

As per usual eight o'clock Sunday, the café's business was slow. A few people here and there, immersed in their computers, or books, or quiet conversation—nothing obtrusive. Just how he liked it, he thought with an internal smile.

There was no line at the counter. Behind it were the two Sunday regulars, Jennifer and Hal.

"Evening, Ted, you want your usual?"

"Yes, please."

Jennifer dropped a teabag into a mug, filled the mug with hot water, set the mug on the counter then punched buttons on the register.

Ted knew the price: a dollar sixty-one, after tax. In addition, he always tipped a dollar. He removed two ones from his wallet, then reached into his pocket for his change, always making sure to have at least sixty-one cents when he came to the Mesa Café.

Pulling a small handful of change out, a few coins fell from his hand and clinked on the floor. He glanced quickly, then back to the change in his hand, from which he plucked two quarters, a dime, and a penny.

"Oh my God," someone behind him said.

Ted looked over his shoulder at a man, who sat at a table, eyes wide, mouth agape. He was pointing down near Ted's feet.

Ted looked down at his fallen coins: a couple of pennies, a nickel, and a quarter. With a slight tilt of his head, he got a slightly different perspective, and then understood why the man was so surprised.

It was a couple of pennies, a nickel, and *two* quarters. He hadn't seen the second quarter until the tilt of his head had changed the light. The second quarter stood upright, on its edge, rather than down, displaying heads or tails.

"That's incredible," the man at the table said. "What are the odds of that? I'm guessing at least a million to one. Maybe more."

Ted looked at the man, then back down to the quarter. He looked at Hal and then at Jennifer, who were both bent over the counter, looking down at the upright coin.

"That's amazing," Jennifer said.

"Yeah," Hal said. "You don't see that every day."

"Hang on to that quarter, man," the man behind him said. "If you don't have a good luck charm, then that's it, that's the one, right there."

Ted smiled. He looked down at the coins again, then crouched and picked them up, one by one, except for the upright quarter, which he stared at, George Washington's profile, from 1979, shining back at him.

The floor was perfectly flat. There were no nicks or crevices that could have caught and held it upright.

Rising, he dumped the rest of his change into the tip jar, then he crouched back down, laughed a little, and picked up the coin and stuffed it into his pocket, thus now making it the only coin he carried.

He smiled at Jennifer, smiled at Hal. "Maybe it's my lucky day," he said, then took his chamomile tea over to his favorite table. He sat down, and for an hour lost himself in poetry.

* * *

At nine o'clock he closed up the book. He carried his mug over to the bus bin, said goodnight to Hal and Jennifer, then left the Mesa Café. There were fewer people outside than there had been at eight. Apparently not a night for gallivanting.

His car was parked roughly two and a half blocks away, over at West Alameda and Ortiz Street. He walked down Don Gaspar, turned right on Water Street, then went left on Ortiz, a narrow, dimly-lit one-way, only one block in length, currently vacant of pedestrians. Without using his voice, he hummed to himself as he strolled along the sidewalk in the opposite direction of the one-way signs.

After a few dozen steps, the song in his head was interrupted by voices. Two of them, one malicious, one frantic. His feet slowed but kept moving. His ears listened and his eyes roamed and then he saw the shadows. The shadows became silhouettes, then developed into defined people with shaded features.

A woman struggled as a man overpowered her.

Without another thought, Ted raced forward, and tried to break it up. The man was larger than Ted, certainly stronger, and clearly had more experience in the realm of fighting.

The large man hit him once and Ted went down, his world spinning. No one had ever hit Ted before. For a time he remained on the pavement, head throbbing, listening to the ruckus of the man and woman roughhouse.

He got to his hands and knees, looked and saw that the woman was a shadow again, while a distant streetlight gave just enough to show that the man had his back to him.

Instinct, preservation, whatever it might have been, Ted thrust his arm up between the man's legs, rolled and pulled, whirling the man backwards, where he came down hard on the pavement, losing his wind and banging his head.

Timidly, Ted got to his feet. He watched the man gasp, roll over, then get up and stumble away, holding the back of his head.

"Thank you," the woman said, and Ted turned to see her come out of the shadows. "Thank you so much." She was weepy, frightened, grateful. And gorgeous. Fragile china doll beauty flanked and topped by silky brown hair, sultry eyes, a husky voice and an enticing figure.

"Thank you so much," she said again.

Ted searched for words, eventually found some, and said, "Are you all right?"

"I am now. A bit rattled, but I'm okay. Thank you. Are you okay?"

Ted felt the side of his head. The throb was there but fading. "Yeah, I'm okay."

"Good. Thank God."

"Should we call the police?" He reached for his cell phone.

"No. There's no point. He didn't get anything, and I never got a good look at him. Did you?"

"No, not really."

"So there's no point. Nothing they can really do but waste their time—and ours."

A fight. Ted had broken up a fight. He thought about the quarter, the almost impossible odds of how it landed. How the man had told him, *If you don't have a good luck charm, then that's it, that's the one, right there.*

He looked at the woman. "What happened?"

"That *man*. That crazy man. He was trying to mug me. I think he might have been planning to try raping me, too." She wiped tears from her beautiful eyes. "I honestly don't know what would've happened if you hadn't come along when you did."

Internal smile: it grew, spread to the external, and curved his lips.

It was subtle, but she smiled back at him.

"What's your name?" she asked.

"Ted."

"Thank you again, Ted. I'm Gwendolyn."

"Nice to meet you, Gwendolyn."

She shook her head. "Sorry, that came out so damn formal. Please, call me Gwen."

"Gwen," he said, and let the name resonate through him, chiming like an angel's song.

"You never think this part of town to be dangerous, you know?"

"No, you don't. But I guess danger can lurk anywhere."

"Isn't that the truth." She looked down at her clothes, brushed a bit of dust from them, then looked him up and down, hesitated, and finally said, "This may sound silly, but have you had dinner yet? Or could I maybe buy you a drink? You know, as a—as a thank you?"

"I actually don't drink, and I ate not long ago."

"I see." Her face donned a mask of disappointment.

"But," he said, "if you're hungry, or you want a drink, I'd be more than happy to join you."

The mask fell away and the smile that grew on her face was small, but real. "I *need* a drink, after what's just happened."

"Okay."

* * *

The lounge was beautiful. Dim, romantic lighting, gorgeous flowers everywhere, and leather chairs that were both luxurious *and* comfortable. They sat close to one another, separated only by a small wooden table.

"So what do you do?"

Ted laced his fingers in his lap, looked at his mug of tea. "Nothing impressive. I'm a receptionist for an insurance company."

Gwen picked up her scotch and soda. "A job's a job," she said, and drank. "I'm currently between jobs."

"What do you usually do? When you're not, uh… between?"

A gentle scoff, she rolled her eyes and drank again. "What *haven't* I done?" she said, then rattled off a list: waitress, bartender, retail, modeling, secretarial, housekeeping, data processing... "The list goes on and on," she said, then finished her drink.

"The modeling certainly doesn't surprise me," he said, and fought hard to keep from blushing. He'd never been good at flirting with women. "Modeling doesn't surprise me at all."

She smiled. "Thank you," she said, paused, then said, "Well, I could use another one of these. You don't mind, do you?"

"Not at all."

When her next drink came, she stared into it, stirred the swizzle stick.

"Work's hard to come by these days. Not just me. I know a lot of people who can't find anything. How long have you been working at the insurance company?"

"A little over six years."

She looked into her drink. "You're lucky, Ted. That sounds like job security. Or close to it." She removed the swizzle stick and set it aside.

Luck, Ted thought. That word had come up several times this evening. Maybe he *was* lucky, having a steady job. When he thought on it, really, he was lucky for lots of reasons. But he couldn't help thinking about how his luck had changed drastically tonight. He'd merely dropped a quarter, and it had landed on its edge. Bordering the impossible, but it had happened, and the next thing he knew, he'd saved a beautiful woman from being mugged—maybe worse. He fought and won the fight. And now, immediately after, he was sitting in an intimate lounge with the woman. Maybe the loveliest woman he'd ever seen in his life.

"Maybe I am lucky," he said. "I certainly consider myself fortunate."

"Life hasn't thrown you many curveballs, has it, Ted?"

"No. No, I guess it hasn't. I mean, my life's not perfect by any means, but, really, whose is?"

She sipped her scotch with a smile, eyes studying him over her glass.

"You're a very nice man, Ted. I mean it, you really are." She hesitated, then said, "Just curious, but is there a *Mrs.* Ted in your life?"

He laughed, a very joyless laugh. "No, nothing like that." He squirmed. "I do my best to be an overall nice guy... but you know the saying."

"Nice guys finish last?"

"That's the one."

Gwen sipped her scotch, quaked a tiny shrug. "In bed, I'd consider that a good thing."

Ted laughed again, this time out of a timid embarrassment. He stuck his hand into his pocket, found the lucky quarter, and gripped it.

When she finished her drink a few minutes later, she insisted on paying the bill, then together, the two of them left the lounge.

The night was clear and flecked with stars. They walked along the street, Gwen every so often gently bumping against him. Each time she did, warmth flowed from her body into his.

"So what do you do for fun?"

"I don't know. I have a few friends, we hang out from time to time."

"I bet you've got a lot of friends."

"Not really, no, just a few. What about you?"

"About the same, I guess."

"I imagine, you know, a nice, beautiful woman like you… I imagine you'd be rather popular."

"Beauty is only skin deep. And the adage about nice guys finishing last, I think that goes for women, too."

After a while Ted checked his watch. "It's getting late. I have to get up and go to work in the morning."

"All right."

"May I walk you to your car?"

"Oh, I walked downtown." She chuckled self-consciously at herself. "I don't actually have a car."

Ted didn't like this bit of information. "Well, I'd rather you not walk home tonight. Not alone, anyway. Not after what happened."

"You're sweet, Ted."

"I'd be happy to drive you home."

"No, I don't wanna put you out."

"You're not putting me out at all. I'd be more than happy to, and I'd feel better, too, knowing you got home safe."

She stopped, turned toward him, kissed him lightly on the cheek, then smiled. "Whoever said chivalry is dead?" She took his hand and squeezed it.

He couldn't help blushing this time.

They walked to Ted's car, taking a slightly longer route to avoid Ortiz Street. They drove six blocks and then she pointed to a house on the right, a dilapidated house with a dead yard.

"Thank you so much again—for everything."

"Glad I could help. Thank you for the tea."

She reached for the door handle then stopped, turned back to him. "I'd like to see you again," she said. "That is, I mean, if you don't mind."

"Are you kidding? I'd love to."

She opened her purse, took out a crumpled piece of paper and a pen. "What's your phone number?"

He gave it to her, then asked, "Could I get your number, too?"

"Well," she said, shying away. "I don't actually have a phone right now."

"Really?"

"Having a phone costs money."

"I'm sorry. I didn't realize it was so—"

"Don't worry about it, Ted. Are you free tomorrow night?"

"I'm free most every night."

"Tomorrow, then. I'll call you." She kissed him on the cheek again, paused, then kissed him quickly on the lips and then opened the door. "Thanks again. Sleep tight. I'll call you tomorrow."

The door closed and he watched her walk up to the doorway. She stopped at the door, opened her purse and rummaged through it.

Ted drove off. He licked his lips once, then smiled the whole drive home.

Lucky. Yes. Tonight he felt very lucky.

* * *

That night he sat on his couch before his coffee table. For nearly an hour he tried time and again to balance his lucky quarter on its edge. No matter what he did, no matter how careful he was, the coin inevitably tilted, wobbled, then dropped.

It wasn't an impossible feat. He knew it could be done. He'd seen people do it dozens of times, in bars and in restaurants; but no matter how hard he tried, he just couldn't get it to balance.

Still, when he looked at the coin, he smiled. A freak occurrence, luck—whatever it had been, it didn't matter; this was the best night of his life.

* * *

The next evening he took Gwen to an early movie, then out to dinner. It wasn't a fancy dinner, just a simple meal at a moderately upscale diner.

She placed her elbows on the table. "I'm glad you wanted to see me again."

A sensation that was half giddy and half nervous tingled through him as one of her legs found one of his, and slid up and down it a couple of times. Ted reached into his pocket, subtly adjusted himself, felt the quarter there, squeezed it, then removed his hand.

Ted paid the bill this time. Such a nice night, they took a stroll. There weren't a lot of stores around, but enough to do a little window-shopping. From time to time they stopped to look at this or that, but mostly they walked.

After a while they turned to head back to Ted's car. After only a few steps Gwen stopped, placed the back of her hand to her nose, and a whimpering sob escaped her.

Ted, who had walked a few steps past her, returned, and placed his hand on her shoulder.

"What's wrong?"

"Nothing. I'm sorry, it's not your problem." She wiped her nose on the back of her hand.

Ted squeezed her shoulder, trying to encourage her.

"I'm just scared," she said. "I'm scared of what's gonna happen, of what I'm gonna do." Her teary eyes looked at him, glistened like jewels in the streetlight. Then she looked away and shook her head.

"Talk to me, Gwen."

"Like I said, it's not your problem."

"But maybe I can help."

"You've helped me enough. All I want from you now... is you."

The sensation that oscillated through him was similar to the one he'd experienced at the diner, only this time it had a more serious, heavier weight to it.

"I'm being evicted," she said, and could no longer meet his eyes.

"What?"

"You run out of money when you don't have an income. I was given thirty days notice, yesterday." She sniffled. "That's why I was heading downtown last night. To get drunk. To drown my sorrows and feel sorry for myself. Then that—that *bastard attacked me*. He attacked me before I could even get started." She looked at him then looked away. "Shit, had you not come along, and he'd succeeded at... whatever it was he planned to do, I'd probably be in a bathtub full of red water right now."

Her sobs burst into full-on crying. Ted wrapped his arms around her and pulled her close. The feeling of her body against his was intoxicating. They stood that way for a while, a window display spraying light on them.

"How much is your rent?"

"No, Ted"—sniffle—"don't even go there."

"Too late, I already have. How much is your rent?"

She gripped him tighter, cried into his chest. "Nine hundred," she told him.

Ted thought for a minute. He had roughly fifteen thousand in his savings account, and about another twenty-two hundred in his checking. Nine hundred dollars would make a dent, but not a big enough one to put him at risk.

He did a little more number crunching, then said, "You think you'll be able to find work in, say, the next two months?"

"I don't know, Ted, I really don't. I try nearly every day and hope and pray that someone can find a use for me."

He kissed her silky brown hair, squeezed her tighter. "Okay," he said. "Here's what's gonna happen. I'm gonna give you a check—"

"No!"

"I'm gonna give you a check for two thousand dollars. That's two months' rent plus a tiny bit extra."

"I can't let you do that."

"You can and you will. It's not gonna solve all your problems, but at least it'll give you a little breathing room."

"Please, Ted, no."

"I'm not about to let the best thing that's happened to me go homeless and starve."

She pulled away from him, gently, and looked into his eyes. "The best thing that's happened to you?"

He smiled at her. Then the distance between their faces closed, and they kissed for a long time, in the light of the window display.

When their lips finally parted, he said, "My checkbook's at home."

She placed her hands on his waist. Her voice was soft and filled with honey-like emotion when she said, "May I go home with you?"

* * *

That night they made love in Ted Howard's bed. Gwen clearly had more experience than he did. When they finished she fell asleep in his arms, and Ted stared up at the darkness of the ceiling, thinking about her, thinking about the check he'd written to Gwendolyn Cartwright, in the amount of two thousand dollars. Eight thousand quarters. He knew that if, one by one, he dropped eight thousand quarters on the floor, not a single one would land upright, on its edge.

Like the man at the café had said, one in a million. Maybe more.

He'd gotten that one in a million, and since then he'd become a hero, and had just made love to the most beautiful woman he'd ever seen in his life.

Because of a single quarter? Maybe, maybe not. Maybe the quarter had nothing to do with it. Maybe it was all him. Maybe the greatness he was feeling about himself, which seemed to increase with nearly every passing hour—maybe it had always been there, inside him. If the coin played any part, maybe it was a simple key. That night at the Mesa Café, maybe the key had finally fallen into place, unlocking the greatness that was inside him.

He thought about it for well over an hour. How lucky he was. How blessed. How great, how truly great. But as he drifted off, something else entered his mind: as wonderful as luck could be, if indeed it was luck, there was also such thing as bad luck; and if luck really existed, then couldn't it easily go from good to bad in the blink of an eye?

His eventual sleep was swathed in an abstract uncertainty.

* * *

In the morning, before work, Ted drove Gwen to the bank. After she deposited the check, he drove her to the dilapidated house with the dead yard, which looked deader in daylight.

She kissed him hard on the mouth, told him to have a nice day at work.

"What are your plans this evening?" he asked her, and before she could say anything he said, "You're going out with me." He enjoyed the confidence in his voice when he told her that.

He smiled at her, said, "Kiss me."

A discombobulated look crossed her face, but she kissed him, then got out of the car. He drove off just as the passenger door closed.

"One in a million," he said, and caught a glimpse of himself in the rearview mirror.

He smiled all the way to work.

* * *

At seven-thirty he pulled along the curb in front of her house, tapped the horn twice, then sat and waited. She looked radiant as she crossed the walkway, flanked by chaparral death, and then climbed into his car.

He sat there behind the wheel, staring at her.

"What?"

He smiled, put the car in gear and drove.

On San Francisco Street, the Lensic Performing Arts Center was showing a play called *Nice Work If You Can Get It*, which was also a current Broadway show. The paper said it was a twenties-era feel-good musical, with laughter, romance, and high-stepping musical magic, featuring old songs by George and Ira Gershwin.

After the play they walked four blocks up the street, to the Mesa Café. Being Tuesday rather than Sunday, Ted saw Hal, but didn't recognize the other person working. It was also busier than usual, what with the play just letting out.

"Hey there, Ted. You have company tonight."

"Yes, this is Gwen."

"Hi, Gwen, I'm Hal."

"Nice to meet you."

"You want your usual, Ted?"

Ted nodded, turned to Gwen. "What do you want?"

"A decaf latte?"

"You got it," Hal said.

"Find us a table," Ted told her.

Gwen nodded and turned away.

"She's a looker," Hal said, when Gwen was out of earshot. "Where'd you manage to find her?"

"I met her Sunday. Remember when I dropped my change and that quarter landed upright?"

"Sure, that was unbelievable."

"I met her right after leaving here that night."

"No kidding?"

Ted shook his head and smiled. "Guess that guy was right, about that quarter being a lucky charm."

"Apparently didn't hurt things any, that's for sure. She's gorgeous."

"She is, isn't she?"

"But don't get too cocky," Hal told him with a chuckle. "You don't wanna press your luck and come up with a Whammy."

Ted laughed, but didn't much care for the insinuation. He paid for the drinks, skipped leaving a tip, then took the drinks over to the table Gwen had selected.

"Thank you, Ted. Not just for the latte. Thank you for everything." She wrapped both hands around her cup. "Not only have you saved my life, a couple of times, in different ways, but also, just being who you are, you've been a burst of sunshine on my otherwise cloudy days." She sipped her latte and blushed a little.

"What?" he asked her.

"It's gonna sound ridiculous."

He smiled. "I think get it. You're falling in love with me."

The words were cause for serious silence and consideration. It seemed awfully fast for something like that. Maybe too fast. Too fast to be real... or true. But it was true. It had to be true, didn't it?

"Ted, I—p..."

"You're sure it's not something else?" he said. "The Florence Nightingale affect, or something?"

"What, because you've been my savior?" She shook her head. There was strain in her voice now, and hesitation. "No, nothing like that, and you have that situation backwards. The Florence Nightingale effect is when the caregiver falls for his or her patient...or dependent."

"So then maybe *I* have the Florence Nightingale effect."

She smiled and reached her hand out.

He took her hand and squeezed it, smiled back at her smile, then said, "My luck has been incomprehensible."

"What do you mean?"

Ted almost told her about the quarter. Instead he gave a dismissive headshake and said, "I've just been very lucky." He looked at her, half of his mouth smiling, the other half straight. "My lucky has been... implausible. Or maybe...maybe implausibly phenomenal."

***

That night they made love again. This time, however, it was as though Ted had popped a handful of Viagra. This time he was a relentless machine, and he kept going, even when Gwen yelped, and pleaded for him to stop.

He continued thrusting, a pounding piston.

"Stop. Ted, please, *please* stop it!"

Finally, when he was satisfied, he did.

"That was really starting to hurt," she told him.

"You'll get over it," he said. "No reason to whine, you'll be okay."

Clouds of silence converged in the room.

Then after several minutes:

"Ted?"

"Yeah?"

"I'm not entirely sure I'm comfortable here tonight."

"What'd you mean?" He turned toward her, propped himself up on one elbow.

She drew a deep breath. "You hurt me, Ted."

"I didn't hurt you."

"Yes you did."

"You wanted it."

"That hurt, Ted. It really hurt. You hurt me, and then you told me to get over it and not to whine, as if your actions have no consequence."

He sighed. "I'm sorry, Sweetie." He reached out and touched her shoulder. "I'm sorry, Gwen. I didn't mean to. I didn't mean for any of that. Okay, maybe—*maybe*—I got a tiny bit carried away."

She propped up on her own elbow. "Would you take me home?"

"What, now?"

"I don't wanna be a wet blanket, but—"

"Oh, Gwen, I'm sorry," he said. But when he said it, something inside him shifted. In his mind he saw a spinning coin, heads and tails rapidly flashing, too quick to comprehend one or the other.

"So you don't mind?" she asked.

"No, I don't... I don't think I'm gonna take you home."

He heard her moving on the bed, then the bedside lamp switched on and she looked at him in disbelief. "You're not gonna take me home?"

He smirked, shook his head.

"Why not?"

A quick glance at her then he looked at the ceiling. "I was very lucky the night I found you. The situation was harrowing, and I was fantastic, but I was also very lucky." He looked at her again. "How much do you believe in fate?"

"What?"

"Fate, luck, karma. Any of that stuff. How much do you believe in those kinds of things?"

"Ted, you're acting strange. What's gotten into you?"

"Thing is," Ted said, not listening, "there's a degree of chance involved with virtually anything and everything that happens in life. I've only really thought about this over the last few days. Sometimes the odds are incredible, sometimes about fifty-fifty, give or take, and sometimes the odds are a million to one. Maybe more. Twice—*twice* Sunday night, I beat a million to one odds, Gwen. *Twice.* Think about that for a minute. *Twice.*"

"I don't know what you're talking about."

"A freak occurrence, a million to one chance, and it happened to me just an hour before I met you." He sat up. "*You*, Gwen. *You're* the other one in a million. You're the other miracle that happened that night."

Gwen shook her head, baffled. "I don't really know what you're saying. I don't know what you're trying to get at here, Ted, but—"

"What I'm saying is, there are two types of luck, Gwen. Good and bad. For me, it's been a few days of very good luck. *Very* good. But if you flip a coin and it keeps coming up heads, you know that, eventually, it'll come up tails." He shook his head. "If I take you home now, what's to keep you from running off with the two thousand dollars I gave you? What's to keep you from disappearing and never looking me up again? What's to keep you from being the coin flip that turns up tails?"

"Are you out of your mind? I don't understand this, Ted. Not at all. I could've done that this morning, after you took me to the bank and then dropped me off back at home. Why would I have stuck around, if that had been my plan?"

"On one hand I feel like I'm invincible these days, Gwen, but that doesn't mean I don't have vulnerabilities. I'm a happy, very contented man, but it's been a long time since I've been with a woman, and that second million-to-one chance—meeting Gwendolyn Cartwright— rekindled something in me I'd completely forgotten existed. My complete and utter lack of trust."

"Ted, this is nuts. I mean, I really don't know where any of this is coming from." She drew a breath, said, "How about this. First thing tomorrow, we go back to the bank. I'll withdraw all the money and give it right back to you."

"To build trust?"

"I thought we *had* trust."

"We did, until I remembered that *I* don't actually have it. Me and trust, we parted ways a long, long time ago. You're the best thing that's ever happened to me. So much so that I'm not entirely sure I believe it. I mean, if it happened to you, would you believe it?

"It *did* happen to me!"

"Not the same way," he told her. "No, not at all. Not the same way. You're the best thing that's ever happened to me, Gwen, yet I'm not quite sure that I truly believe it… but I'm also not about to simply let it go."

"I don't *want* to go. I just wanna go home for the night."

He glanced around the room, picked at his nose, then looked at her again. "I'm sorry, no. Not tonight. Trust will be impossible if you go home tonight."

In an instant Gwen flung the covers off her naked body and began dressing.

"What are you doing?"

"What does it look like? I'm getting out of here."

He laughed. "How?"

"Don't worry about me, Ted. I'm a big girl. I'll walk."

"No, you can't walk," he said, pulling on his boxers. "What if something happens?" Putting on his shirt. "Something like what happened on Sunday?" He struggled to pull on his pants.

"Right now I'd take that over staying here."

"You don't mean that."

"You bet your ass I mean it." Fully dressed, she rounded the bed and headed for the door. "Psycho," she said. "All of a sudden, Ted, you're psycho. You've fucking gone psycho."

Pants wrapped around one ankle, Ted rushed and blocked the doorway.

"Move, Ted."

"Be reasonable, Gwen."

"You're the one being unreasonable." She grabbed his arm and flung it.

The momentum caused him to stumble, which caused his feet to get snarled in his pants. He fell against the bed.

Gwen opened the bedroom door and walked out.

"Gwen, wait!" He yanked up his pants as quickly as he could. A faint metallic clink sounded as he rushed from the bedroom after her.

She was at the front door, opening it.

"Gwen, wait!"

"Goodbye, Ted." She walked out and slammed the door.

Barefoot, Ted raced out after her. She was already on the sidewalk, moving at something between a walk and a run. When he called her name she moved faster.

"Gwen!"

"Leave me alone!" she shouted, and lights began turning on in houses.

Ted picked up his pace, closed the distance between them, and a moment later he grabbed her arm and she screamed.

"Calm down," he said.

"Get off me!"

People were coming out of their houses now. Voices and audible commotion.

As the two of them struggled, someone raced in to break it up. Ted swung and hit the man in the head, then reached back and seized Gwen, telling her to calm down, calm down, *please* just *calm the fuck down*!

An arm shot up between Ted's legs. It pulled him, and he went whirling backwards. He came down hard, heard the crack of his skull as it smacked the pavement. Crackles of black and crimson spidered in his eyes. Then they spread out and filled his head and he could no longer see. He was aware that his head hurt, and that he couldn't move. Then he wasn't aware of anything at all.

* * *

The converged clouds of silence expanded in Ted Howard's bedroom. On one of the two nightstands that flanked the bed, a '79 quarter stood upright, on its edge.

The Riddled Heart
Jessica McHugh

Drake Ulster left his smile on the shoulder of Queenstown Boulevard. Crouching beside the road, Pierce Gordon wondered if the scarlet smear was a testament to Drake's persistent joy in life, or the strength of his killer's tires. The Chevrolet that mowed him down had been abandoned just up the road with no indication of the driver's motivations, but Pierce felt it safe to say that his friend's death wasn't an accident. He hadn't been a private investigator for over six months, but he couldn't resist contemplating why the nicest man in Queenstown would be a target for murder.

Unfortunately, the mere thought stirred up sour memories of Pierce's old life. There hadn't been much to remind him of his past since leaving Los Angeles, but staring at the crime scene he realized the sad truth: once a PI, always a PI. Whether the crime was as dull as a missing cat or as heartbreaking as a friend's face on the highway, Pierce's instincts made it impossible for him to ignore an unsolved mystery.

Drake Ulster had been his only friend. Pierce wasn't ill tempered or solitary by nature, but after the death of his wife Natalia he'd become afraid to let anyone close. He'd come to Queenstown a used tissue of a man. Grief allowed him to do little besides cry and obsess over the ways in which he'd failed her, which kept him awake most of the night. The town seemed content to let him alone—until Ulster knocked on his door.

"You should let me in," he'd said. "You need someone to talk to."

Pierce scoffed. "How do you know?"

"It doesn't take a genius to see you're in pain, son. You don't talk to anyone. You're in and out of the market without eye contact, no conversation. As far as I can tell, you just sit alone in this house all day. That can't be how you want to live."

Pierce hadn't considered needing a friend. Yet faced with the notion, he decided to let Drake Ulster inside. He hadn't been forthcoming in their first conversations, but he couldn't deny the comfort Ulster provided. When Pierce offered nothing, Drake told his own stories. Speaking of his life as the owner of the nearby Queenstown Orchard, his face became animated, his eyebrows bouncing high on his forehead, his laugh so powerful it tilted his head. It was hard for Pierce not to catch a spark from such a firecracker.

It wasn't long before he told some of his own stories. In opening up to Drake about elements of his past, he felt a peace he hadn't expected. He still didn't sleep—not since his wife was murdered—but his relationship with Ulster helped him cope. Sometimes the smell of Drake's hand-rolled cigars lingering in his screened-in porch was enough to usher a shallow sleep.

Realizing his best friend was truly gone, Pierce's progress dropped away. As hard as he'd tried to ditch the gray days of LA, they'd found their way back to him, to the sleepy town where he'd been born. He hoped even the happiest days wouldn't follow him to Queenstown, which disheartened in its own right. How could he wish to forget joyful nights in Natalia's arms?

In five years of marriage, Natalia's loveliness hadn't fallen an inch. He attributed it less to fitness and her monthly shipments of fresh fruit, and more to a natural, tireless beauty. He had taken that, and so much more, for granted.

Despite the sorrow of remembrance, she was the only thing from that world worth holding onto. He just wished she were more substantial than the ghost she'd become, haunting Pierce nightly with the memory of his unhappiest day.

Would Ulster leave such a ghost behind? He'd seemed too cheerful for midnight moans and rattling chains. But he'd seemed too cheerful to wind up as road kill, too. He'd had friendly dealings with everyone in town. Even on frustrated nights when he would sit at Pierce's table and grumble over complications in the orchard, he never spoke an ill word against anyone. His powers of restraint must've helped him tolerate Pierce's bouts of depression. Looking back, he couldn't imagine how Drake had suffered through those first few months. Pierce knew he'd never be the robust man from the old days, but Drake Ulster had made him believe it was possible, that he might one day recover a smile to rival his friend's.

As the ambulance carted Ulster's body away, Pierce realized it was now highly unlikely.

* * *

"Are you Pierce Gordon?"

He nodded, tears welling as he turned to the police officer.

"I know this is difficult for you, Mr. Gordon. We've heard how close you were to the victim."

Victim. It was a common word in Pierce's former profession, but he hadn't heard it aloud in months. It made a harsh, dry sound when the officer's tongue stabbed his teeth.

"Who's *we*?" Pierce asked.

He'd been so preoccupied by his devastation he hadn't noticed how many cops speckled the scene. The boys in blue were exactly that—not one of the cobalt-clad men appeared older than forty. He recognized a few of them from around town, including Jeffrey Dimes, the officer standing opposite. But the person who stood out amongst the cops was someone Pierce didn't know.

She was a tall drink of water with a gin kicker. Closing her notepad, the woman in a cinched pea coat turned. While most of her face was a warm welcome, her eyes were warnings. Nearly as dark as her raven hair, they studied him too closely to be civilian eyes. That, paired with her austere wardrobe, led Pierce to believe she was more cop than woman today.

"That's Detective Leon," the officer said. He called Pierce's eyes back with a wave. "I know I'm not as nice to look at, Mr. Gordon, but I hoped you'd answer some questions for me. You work at the orchard, yes? Did Mr. Ulster mention anything about where he was headed after work tonight?"

"Not that I recall. I assumed he'd go home."

"Nothing about meeting with a friend—maybe an enemy?"

He shook his head. "As far as I knew, Drake didn't have any enemies."

"You're fairly new in town, aren't you?"

"It's been about six months," he replied. "Since you didn't know, I guess it means I've stayed out of trouble."

A stiff breath shot from the man's nose. Pierce supposed it could have been considered a laugh in certain circles.

"Is there anything else?" he asked.

"That's all for now, but don't leave town, okay? We might have more questions."

"Where would I go? Tragedy follows me everywhere," he muttered.

Wiping his eyes with his sleeve, he realized his shirt smelled of cigars. The tears came harder. Officer Dimes flipped his notebook closed and patted Pierce's shoulder.

"You sure you're okay to drive? I can have someone follow you if you want. Are you headed home?"

"My best friend just died, Officer. I'm headed to the nearest bar."

"Are you sure that's wise?"

"Except for befriending Drake Ulster, I think it's the wisest decision I've made since moving to Queenstown."

"It's just that—well, you look tired."

"I'd look this way no matter what. I haven't had a good night's sleep in over six months." Seeing his continued concern, Pierce added, "I walked here from work, Officer Dimes. I was on my way home when I found him."

"Oh. Right." Dimes leaned in, whispering, "In that case, I don't think anyone would blame you for getting obliterated tonight."

"I'm not much of a drinker, so I don't see that being a problem."

"Just be careful," he said, shaking Pierce's hand. "I'm sorry for your loss."

Pierce watched him walk back to the gaggle of police, but his gaze soon moved to Detective Leon, who gave him a sympathetic nod. The officers mimicked her, nodding in unison before returning to their conversation. It seemed rude to have so many officers chatting leisurely onsite. He even noticed a few chomping on apples. It was too much for him to handle.

Nauseated, he shuffled away from the scene. The bar was only three miles away, but foreseeing the pain in his stroll past Queenstown Orchard, he wished it were closer.

*   *   *

There's nothing a man can't say to a cold beer. When life is at its stillest and troubles are tripled by the quiet, the greatest of all liars is the best conversationalist around.

Hunched over a corner table of the Apple Core Tavern, Pierce's worries emptied glass after glass. He longed to think of anything but Drake Ulster, but blocking those thoughts resurrected ones of Natalia, prompting him to drink faster.

Work was Pierce's poison in the old days. The more he worked, the further it spread, gumming up every vein in his life. He was incapable of seeing past the blockage, forgetting to eat and sleep and, too often, that he had a wife at home, waiting.

When Natalia complained about his obsession, he would coolly reply, "At least I'm not a drunk," and she would always nod. Pierce saw the exchange as a loving joke between them, something they could enjoy into old age. He didn't realize until their last year together that Natalia never found it amusing. She suffered in silence. Having a big house and wealth entertained her for a few years, but she'd wanted more. She'd wanted Pierce.

Diving into a new beer, he remembered how he'd taken her hands in his, more mechanical than comforting. *Soothe her, put the argument to bed, and get back to work.* In only five years, he'd stopped appreciating her baby-soft skin, her firm body, her lips as sweet as fresh fruit. He was a goddamn fool.

The beer slipped out of his hand, splashing on the table. Harry the bartender dropped a stack of napkins by the spill as he collected the empty glasses. Pierce was already drunk, but he had no intention of stopping. Sometimes a lump of grief dammed the beer, and he had to think of Natalia's voice to soften his gullet: shower songs, her musical laughter, or the silly things she whispered as she watered the garden:

"Eat, little buds. Be beautiful forever."

Pierce trembled. Natalia would be beautiful forever, too.

He suddenly felt her beside him, running her hands over his chest like she had on their last night together.

"Let's go away," she'd purred. "Just for a short time. You, me, and an ocean breeze. I'll get the plane tickets, you pack, and let's head south tonight. We can wake up in Cancun."

He hadn't hated the idea. It sounded like just the thing they needed to revitalize their relationship, to remind Pierce that there were better, more magical things in the world than work.

It was too bad he'd already taken the Simmons case.

"I'm sorry" was as far as she let him get. By the "but," she was on the stairs, leaving him to sleep alone.

After the argument, Pierce stayed at his office. He'd begged for her forgiveness, but she refused all efforts to reconcile. Apologetic chocolates went uneaten, gift cards unspent, and bouquets withered in front of their home.

Three days later, Natalia was dead, and Pierce would have to remember forever that the last words he said to his wife were "I'm sorry, but."

Sad as it was, it epitomized the last year of their relationship.

"Another beer?" Harry asked.

"Yes, and a shot of whiskey. Doesn't matter what kind," Pierce said, forcing the words through a shaky slur.

"Okay, but it's last call. I didn't know if you heard me announce it."

He hadn't. Nor had Pierce Gordon noticed he was the only customer left in the Apple Core Tavern. "A beer and a shot, please."

Harry groaned, stomping back to the bar. He delivered the drinks with a check. Pierce took a large swig and slapped down his credit card. When Harry returned, he signed his name in minimalist loops and scratches, and was left alone to sip his beer. His head was a heavy cyclone of angst. It was the first time he'd had that much alcohol since he was eighteen years old. His heart begged his brain not to revisit that night, but drenched in beer, his brain did not obey.

* * *

Pierce Gordon was the son of shitty parents. Growing up in the care of an aunt and uncle who never argued the contrary, how could he think otherwise? He remembered living in Queenstown for a millisecond before being shipped to Los Angeles, but no details remained—and he couldn't care less. He loved being a Gordon; his aunt, uncle, and cousins were the only family he knew or wanted—until he turned eighteen.

On the night of his eighteenth birthday, Pierce's family gave him a letter written by his birth mother. By the time he reached the part about having zero blood relation to the Gordons, that "family" was gone, never to return to the house Pierce had called home all those years.

Despite the revelations about his "relatives," the letter revealed little about his birth mother—only that she felt unfit to be a mother, which confirmed his assumptions. No matter how many times she claimed he deserved better than her, he refused to think of that woman as anything but a coward. And he hoped the broken hunk of silver molded into half a heart locket that accompanied the letter wasn't meant to change his opinion. Why had she waited so long? And what was the "better" he deserved? A past riddled with lies and an incomplete heart?

He'd wanted to drive to the nearest ocean and throw her heart into the waves. He had no reason to keep it. And he certainly had no reason to carry it with him. But he did. Every day, the broken pendant rested against his chest, cradled between his clavicles.

Pierce threw back the shot of whiskey, tugging on the chain around his neck as he grumbled, "So why the hell did you come back here, you idiot?"

Harry looked up from his phone. Once he realized Pierce was talking to himself, he shook his head and disappeared into the kitchen.

Alone again, in the silence. He'd spent weeks that way when he first came to Queenstown. Even with Natalia's ghost hounding him nightly, he spoke only once to say, "I should've gone to Cancun."

"Ah, but then you wouldn't have your precious torment, would you?" she'd replied, her voice more vicious in death. "You wouldn't have the mystery of how to cure it, either. And what would Pierce Gordon be without a mystery to solve?

She'd had him there. But at least he wasn't compelled to solve *every* mystery. He'd made it thirty-nine years without searching for his real family. If his mother was the kind of person who'd dispose of him, send him across the country to live with strangers, he assumed she wouldn't be the kind to stick around Queenstown hoping for her bastard son to return.

No, Pierce believed that mystery was already solved. She was a spineless woman with no heart—or half of one, he supposed.

He tucked the locket under his shirt, feeling the booth spin under him. His stomach lurched, and bile crawled up his throat. Exhaling slowly, the nausea faded. He tried to stand, but he only gained an inch before his rubbery legs buckled beneath him. He crumpled under the table, his ass aching from the fall and head lolling. The struggle to stay awake was futile. His eyes closed, and he slumped to the floor. Curled into a ball beneath the table, Pierce passed out, clutching his broken heart.

* * *

"What happened to Ulster?"

"Run down, backed over, squished to nothing."

"Nasty way to go."

"Made an impression, though. And not just on the side of Queenstown Boulevard."

Pierce awoke with pain cracking through his brain. Even the faraway voices were too loud, each one a hammer missing its nail. The Apple Core Tavern was dark, the "open" sign switched off. Pierce crawled out from under the table, a cocktail napkin stuck to his face, and gripping his head, he groaned at how low he'd sunk.

A beam of light broke through the blackness, accompanying the voices. He stood, but the men following their flashlights beams didn't see him. They crossed behind the bar and ducked down. He waited for them to stand back up, but it never happened.

After a few minutes, Pierce thought he'd imagined them: a byproduct of his inebriation. Thirsty, he stumbled through the darkness, gripping the sticky bar to steady himself as he made his way to the cooler. Grabbing a bottle of water, he sat down and gulped. That's when he saw the door in the floor—and the light shining between the cracks.

Pressing his ear to the floor, Pierce heard faint music, laughter, and several people saying Drake Ulster's name. Crazy as it was, it sounded like people were celebrating the death of the nicest man in town.

Pierce opened the door. His head pounded with each cheer charging up the ladder, but he leaned into the din.

"Did you see his face? It was priceless. For a moment, I thought he'd lose it right there. He almost cried over rabbit meat on the road," a man chuckled.

"He didn't know it was a rabbit," another said. "Still, he was almost too pathetic to watch. I'm not sure Gordon's even worthy of the Aeterna Cor."

Pierce didn't understand the last few words, but he did recognize the voice of Harry the bartender. The other was still a mystery—but not for long.

He hung his head over the opening, scooting forward until he could see into the chamber below. The spacious room had no furniture or adornment, save the pipes and tubing affixed to the chamber walls. Robed individuals gathered near one of two catty-corner doors, conversing as they sipped drinks. While scarlet hoods obstructed many faces, some of the folks were less formal, boasting their identities. Next to Harry stood Marvin Driscoll, the president of Queenstown Bank, and Samantha Hook, the town veterinarian. He spotted postal workers and waitresses and nearly every police officer in town.

The music stopped, the conversation faded, and the people pulled up their hoods. As they stood in a circle, one person distributed candles while another lit the wicks. Once the room was aglow, the group chanted in a language Pierce couldn't understand.

When one of the doors creaked open, another figure emerged, cloaked in white. He stood at the center of their circle, the indecipherable chants growing louder. When the words stopped, the man threw back his hood.

Pierce gasped at the face, too loudly. Several people turned, seeing his head dangling from the opening. He tried to retreat, but dizziness and shock stole his balance. Standing, Pierce tripped over the door in the floor and fell backwards—down the ladder, into the secret chamber, and to the floor, where he writhed in screaming pain. The hooded people of Queenstown stood over him, but he only saw one. Before succumbing to unconsciousness, Pierce focused on the familiar face of the man in the white robe. His best friend, Drake Ulster, was alive.

* * *

His head felt like pitted fruit. Shivering, Pierce Gordon detected the aroma of coffee and iron. The pain was too great to open his eyes, but he'd spent enough time in police stations to know he was in a jail cell.

"You're awake. Excellent."

He squinted to see the beautiful woman standing opposite him. Detective Leon's hair was coiffed into raven waves, curling over one of her eyes. A high-waisted pencil skirt granted her the dangerous curves of a cliff-side road, racing upward to ample peaks glowing beneath the noisy fluorescents of Queenstown jail.

Marian dimmed the lights and dropped the shades. After handing him a bottle of water, she sat in front of his cell.

"There's a bucket under the bench if you need it," she said.

He belched. "I'd rather have a porcelain one, if you don't mind."

"I do mind, Mr. Gordon. You're in that cell for a reason. I can't let you out until I'm certain you aren't a threat." She stood, reaching out to shake his hand. "My name is Detective Marian Leon. I don't believe we've been properly introduced."

"If I'm a threat, why would you risk getting so close?"

"Because I don't think you are one. And since we've never met, you don't know the kind of threat *I* am either."

"You're a woman. I could take a guess." Wincing, he shook her hand. "Pierce Gordon, Hangover King of 2013."

"Are you sure it's all a hangover, Mr. Gordon? You have a sizable lump on your head. According to witnesses at the Apple Core Tavern, you took a nasty tumble," she said, returning to her chair.

"Considering what I saw last night..." Wringing the bars of his cell, Pierce sighed. "Detective Leon, Drake Ulster is alive."

"As someone who claimed to be Mr. Ulster's best friend, I didn't think you'd make such a sick joke."

"It's not a joke. And after last night, I don't know what Drake was to me. To fake his death, to lie like this..."

She stared at him like he'd sworn up and down the world's flatness. "I know it sounds crazy, but Drake Ulster is alive, and he's involved in something weird."

"Weird how?"

"I don't know what it was. Some kind of cult, a religious thing maybe. There was chanting and robes, and—" Marian Leon's forehead furrowed, her lips in a tight frown. "I swear I'm not crazy, Detective Leon."

"But you were drunk," she said. "Do you deny that?"

"Can you blame me? I thought my friend was murdered."

She tilted her head forward. "But you don't think that anymore."

Pierce groaned, slumping onto the bench. "Look, I know this game. I played it for fifteen years. Not with murder, but I played my fair share of Good Cop, Bad Cop."

"What kind of cop do you think I'm playing, Mr. Gordon?"

"You're a detective. That's worse than either."

Marian chuckled. "And you were a private investigator in Los Angeles."

It was Pierce's turn to furrow.

"By your expression, I gather you haven't shared that information with many people," she said. "I know a lot about you, Mr. Gordon. Your background wasn't hard to uncover. I suppose most people don't feel compelled to dig into those details, but when a man gets intoxicated in public, turns over tables, smashes bottles, and threatens to shoot a bartender, I find myself compelled to dig. Especially when he's killed a man before."

Pierce sputtered while sipping the water. Marian handed him a tissue to dry his face.

"I'm sorry, Detective, but I don't know what you're talking about."

"I just told you I did my research, Mr. Gordon. Don't lie to me."

Pierce lowered his head, nodding.

"I'm glad you're willing to work together. I know none of this is easy, especially considering how recently you lost your wife."

Pierce's body shook as tears fell to the jailhouse floor. When his cell door swung open, he lifted his head to see Marian Leon with the keys in one hand and cup of coffee in the other.

He faced her, the tissue balled in his fist. "Why would you let me out if you know I killed a man?"

"Because I also know you won't kill me, Mr. Gordon." She set the coffee on the desk and pushed a chair in front. "Sit. Talk with me."

He sat opposite her, cautious as he sipped the coffee.

"I'm sorry about last night, Detective. I was drunk, that's true, but I don't remember being as violent as you say. Just discovering the passage behind the bar, seeing the cult, and finding Drake alive."

"Tell me a different story, Pierce. May I call you 'Pierce'?" He nodded. "Tell me about your last assignment as a PI. I know the gist, but not from your side."

"I don't want to talk about it, if that's okay with you."

"It's not okay with me," Marian said. "I gave you water, coffee, I let you out of your cell. You should be locked up for public drunkenness, destruction of property, maybe even suspicion of Drake Ulster's murder."

"I would never—"

"Kill a man?" she chirped. Pierce fidgeted, tearing a chunk from the lip of his Styrofoam cup. "We're going around in circles, Pierce."

"Where's everyone else, the other officers?"

"I asked them to leave so I could speak with you alone."

She touched his hand. He flinched, but when Marian Leon's eyes fixed on his, Pierce found himself softening against her.

He sighed, leaning forward in his chair. "It was the Simmons case. A tough one," he started. "Kevin Simmons paid cash for his hookers and hotels. He had his rendezvouses out of town, even had alibis. He was a good adulterer."

"And he sounds like a terrible person."

"More than you know. He had a young son and a baby on the way. I understand people being unhappy in their marriages, but no one should screw over their kids like that."

"Was your marriage unhappy?" Detective Leon asked.

He gulped hard. The coffee was sweeter than he was used to, and it twisted his face. "Not on my end," he replied.

"I'm sorry, I shouldn't have interrupted. Continue."

"I followed Simmons and his hooker to a motel. All I needed were a couple of pictures of them in the act. After that, Sarah Simmons would pay me in full, and I'd be free to take my wife Natalia on vacation. Just us and an ocean breeze like she wanted. We could sip fruity drinks, go skinny dipping...God, just the thought of rubbing sunblock on her olive skin..."

Pierce turned away, pressing the tissue to his eyes. "I never got that chance. And it was all my fault."

"What happened?"

"I followed a Simmons, and a Simmons followed me. When I reached the motel, Kevin's wife pulled in behind me. I understand wanting to see her husband's infidelity with her own eyes, but to this day, I can't understand why she brought their son along."

It was the first time Marian Leon appeared sympathetic. She leaned forward, her head cocked to the side, eyelashes batting.

"I tried to stop her, but aside from punching her out, I didn't know what to do. She pounded the door of his room until he came out, his pants down and balance boozy. Seeing his wife was a shock, but seeing his son broke him, Detective Leon. He collapsed in shame, reaching out, but Sarah dragged the kid back to the car. From there he watched his father squirm in that motel parking lot, his half-naked hooker behind him." Pierce shook his head. "I should've done something, covered the boy's eyes or shoved his dad inside. But I didn't. I just collected my money and left."

"Your job was to gather evidence of the husband's infidelity, not to protect his son from it."

"I wish I could look at it like that," he said. "But guilt doesn't negotiate, Detective Leon. It doesn't bow to threats or indulge deception. It lords. And it roots. Job or not, the guilt remains."

He drank the rest of his coffee, his hands trembling as he set down the cup.

"After that, there was paperwork to do. A day or so of it. I stayed at my office because Natalia and I had gotten into a fight. We weren't speaking." He shook his head sadly. "But she called my cell phone a dozen times that night. I missed some of the calls, but I ignored some on purpose."

"I thought you said the marriage was happy on your end."

"I said I wasn't *unhappy*," he replied. "I was still nervous about facing her after a fight. I'm only human, Detective."

"Yes, of course."

Pierce massaged his temples. The memory bloomed with the same putrid stench of rotten bouquets that had greeted Pierce Gordon on the night of his wife's death.

"The house was silent when I entered—not surprising. But then I noticed the broken lock on the liquor cabinet. I went straight to the study for my gun. I never thought I'd have to use it…" He cleared his throat, but the grief stuck like a sideways needle. "Natalia was in the library. I saw her shadow first, stretching out to me. When I saw her face down on the floor, I thought she might have passed out. Even when I flipped her body over, the blood on the back of her head soaking my clothes, I thought she might be okay. I could stop the bleeding. I could save her. She wasn't breathing, but I could save her. I just had to get her breathing again.

I did CPR, but it was like pushing air into a busted balloon. She was dead. She'd been dead for hours," he said. "I was about to call the police when I spotted someone behind the desk. Past an overturned chair with frayed ropes, past a bloody liquor bottle, I looked down on my wife's killer—Kevin Simmons."

Pierce ran his fingers through his sweaty hair. "I saw red, Detective. When people say that, it's true. I recognized Simmons, I saw that he was alive. Everything after that was red death. One second, he was breathing. The next, a gunshot echoed through my house. I don't remember pulling the trigger, just seeing the bullet I'd put in Kevin Simmons' head."

Pierce met Marian's gaze. It was shaking, her eyes glazed with tears.

"I'm so sorry for you, Pierce. No one should have to experience something like that."

"Some people don't have that reaction to my story, Detective."

"*Marian*, please."

"Some people accuse me of murder, Marian, despite the acquittal. And I'm the loudest accuser of them all."

"Because of the footage?" she asked.

He clenched his jaw. "You *did* do your research. Yes, because of the footage," he replied. "I knew Simmons had killed her, but I needed to know what else he'd done. So, before I called 911, I watched the footage on my security cameras. I saw what he did."

"What did he do?"

"He tied her up and proceeded to get drunk. That's it. The only real interaction they had was when he forced her to call me. Those calls—if I'd picked up just one of those calls, Natalia might still be alive."

"You didn't know."

"And my ignorance got her killed. When I didn't pick up, he got drunker, angrier. But as he tore through the bottles, Natalia tore through her ropes. She had a nail file in her pocket, and when his back was turned, she used it on the ropes." Pierce looked away, his chin quivering. "It was stupid, but when I saw her break free, I got my hopes up. For a split second I thought she might get away, that I'd go downstairs to find only one corpse in my library," he said. "Obviously, that didn't happen. She jumped out of the chair and ran, but Simmons saw her. He lunged, swinging a full liquor bottle like a club. I don't know how he didn't see her hit the floor, or see her twitching as he strolled by, drinking the murder weapon. He talked to her like she was still in the chair. He told her she would be safe—"

Pierce choked on a sob, and Marian pushed over a box of tissues. He nodded in gratitude, dabbing his nose.

"I don't think Simmons wanted to kill her," he continued. "He was drunk, he saw her running, and he panicked. And I shot him in cold blood for it."

"Is that why you came to Queenstown? To punish yourself? To drink to excess and go crazy—like Kevin Simmons?"

Pierce gulped, the similarity becoming a knot in his throat.

"No, I came here because I was born here."

Her eyes widened. "In Queenstown? I didn't know."

"No one does. Not even Drake," he said. "I left when I was a baby, so I don't remember much. But that's what I wanted after everything that happened—a place with no memory."

"I feel sorry for you," Marian said. "All you want is someone who loves you."

"Isn't that what everyone wants?"

She nodded. "But some people don't realize they were loved all along until the end."

"And that's me?"

"I guess you won't know until the end." She opened a desk drawer and tossed a bag of clothes to Pierce. "The bathroom's behind you. Wash up, get changed, and be on your way."

"Just like that? What about everything I saw?"

"The cult in the basement, you mean?"

"I know it sounds stupid—"

"Yes, it does, very stupid. I inspected Ulster's body myself. If he's not dead, I'm a hell of a liar."

"I don't know you. Maybe you are."

Her face scrunched into a pitying frown. "I don't think it's in your best interest to go on about this cult nonsense, Mr. Gordon. I uncovered your history easily enough. How long do you think it will take everyone else?" she asked. "You came to Queenstown for a good reason. I'm afraid if you keep raving about Drake Ulster, Queenstown will become yet another place with bad memories. Do you understand, or do we have to speak further with iron bars between us?"

Pierce clenched his jaw, shook his head, and shuffled to the bathroom in silence. He didn't recognize his face in the mirror. He hadn't realized how bruised it was, or that his forehead was spotted with dried blood. His cheeks had been bloodied too, but tears had washed the patches away, leaving trails of pink to his chin. Filling his hands with warm water, he submerged his face until the liquid drained through his fingers. He wished he could drown that way, in the hands that had caused his downfall. From the seedy pictures they'd snapped to the trigger they'd pulled, his hands had been put to bad use over the years, buried in work when they should have been on Natalia. Stroking her skin, playing with her curls, giving her the pleasure deserved by such a beautiful woman. Standing before the mirror, tears pooled on Pierce's palms, but it wasn't nearly enough to drown him.

A pity, he thought.

Pierce changed into the clean shirt and khakis. When he returned to Marian Leon, her eyes fell to the exposed pendant around his neck.

She pinched the silver heart, humming, "I didn't think you were the type."

He tucked it under his shirt, eyes averted. "Thank you for the clothes. And for understanding."

"I'm just doing my job, Pierce. And you should probably get to yours. You work at the orchard, don't you? I suspect they'll need all the help they can today."

Pierce's lungs emptied with a burst of breath. "God, I hadn't thought about that. Who opened the shop? Who baked the apple pies? Who will monitor the honeybees in the afternoon? Drake did everything. He was the lifeblood of that orchard."

"Maybe you can fill that role now. I think Mr. Ulster would've liked that."

A tiny smile lifted his right cheek. "Maybe I can. Thank you, Detective Leon."

He opened the door, shielding his eyes from the sun as pain struck his skull. As the door to the Queenstown Police Station swung closed, he looked back to Marian Leon's smiling face. He doubted he'd ever seen a grin so large.

* * *

Queenstown Orchard had never been a laugh-riot, but Pierce never dreaded his shifts. As he arrived to work that day, he realized it might've been because his best friend had owned the place.

A somber milieu was to be expected after Ulster's death, but he hadn't expected such rampant hostility, especially not aimed squarely at him. Pierce cloistered himself in Drake's office under the guise of tallying the previous night's receipts. As convincing as Detective Leon had been about the incident at the tavern, skepticism devoured Pierce's mind. He acknowledged the likelihood that he'd imagined seeing Drake among the cult members, but deep down he couldn't accept that the entire thing had been a figment. Why would he imagine waitresses he'd only seen a handful of times, and why the cultish setting?

He pulled the shade closed on Drake Ulster's office door and turned the lock. Everything was as Drake had left it, the acme of order. He'd once used his office to teach Pierce organizational techniques, so he had a fair knowledge of the layout. The financial records were kept in the left hand drawers of Drake's desk, the employee records in the right. Money and valuables were kept in the safe, and personal effects were stored in a small drawer beside the mini-fridge. But there was one file cabinet Pierce had never seen inside, making it the first to investigate. The drawers were locked, but he found a ring of keys tucked into the back of the safe.

Once opened, he dug into the folders inside. Moments later, he wished he hadn't.

The pictures of Pierce at thirty-nine, sitting with Drake Ulster in his living room, were disturbing enough, but the pictures of him as a child were more so. There was even a set that showed Pierce Gordon standing in front of Queenstown Orchard, thirty-six years apart.

Pierce dove into the bottom drawers where he found photos of other people. Some he recognized, some he didn't. Drake Ulster was among them, looking how Pierce had always known him, which didn't mean anything until he saw the date on the back of the picture.

March 15th 1958, as crisp as any apple in the orchard. If that year was right, it would make Drake over eighty years old. He thought it had to have been labeled wrong, but delving deeper into the files, he found the other pictures just as baffling. Officer Jeffrey Dimes, who appeared to be in his thirties now, had looked the same in 1970. The teenager who delivered the morning news looked no younger than a preteen in 1982. None of the ages made sense, especially when he saw a photo of nearly everyone in Queenstown. Dressed in crimson cloaks, they stood in front of the orchard, proud to be so inexplicably young in 1914.

The office door shook in its frame, the knob twisting furiously.

"Who's in there?" someone barked. "No one's supposed to be in here during the day."

Pierce stuffed the files and photos into the drawers, locked them, and shoved the keys in his pocket. He opened the door to Frank Dale's sour expression. His eyebrows were bent and quivering, like caterpillars unsure about climbing a mountain.

"What are you doing in here, Gordon?"

"What do you think?" Pierce replied. "I'm dealing with last night's receipts."

Dale opened the folder in his hand and removed a stack of papers. "These receipts?"

"Why do you have them? That's my job."

"Not anymore," he said. "I'm in charge of the orchard now."

"Says who?"

Frank Dale's eyes were focused iron, but his lips remained soft, playful. They curled as he looked Pierce up and down.

"What the hell's so funny?" he asked.

"I just remembered what an idiot you made of yourself last night. I always thought you were the sober sort. Not dry, but sensible," Frank replied.

"Obviously you weren't as close to Drake as I was."

"You couldn't have been too close. Otherwise, he would have left you something in his will instead of firing you."

"Firing me? What are you talking about?"

Dale reached into the folder again, withdrew a letter, and handed it to Pierce. It was typed, but the bottom was marked with Drake's signature; it even smelled of his cigars. The will had the usual bequeathments, house and savings and music collection, but Pierce skimmed until he found his name.

"If Pierce Gordon is still in the orchard's employ, he is to be relieved of his position on account of his months of theft from my establishment," he read aloud. "Theft? I never stole anything. Not one cent, not one apple."

"Ulster saw it differently," Frank said. "And considering I practically caught you red-handed today, I don't think I'll dispute his claim."

"How did you get this? Why wouldn't he tell me? When was it written?"

"You can ask as many questions as you want, but I'm afraid you'll have to ask them off of orchard property."

Each breath hurt Pierce's chest. He shook his head, refusing to believe, or move until Dale called security to escort Gordon from the premises.

"I won't let this die," he declared to Dale from the road. "Something strange is going on here, and I will get to the bottom of it."

"Do what you want," Frank said. "But I recommend you don't get to the bottom by falling down a ladder like last night."

His heart raced. "What did you say?"

"You're not as clever as you think you are, Gordon. Continue to snoop around, and you'll only find trouble."

With that, Frank Dale turned his back and marched away.

"I knew it was real," Pierce shouted at him. "You and this whole damn town are going down! I won't stop until I've uncovered the truth."

For a moment, he could've sworn he heard Natalia's voice, pleading for him to turn away. He whispered, "I'm sorry, but…"And as usual, she was gone before he could finish.

Pierce stood alone beside the orchard, torn. He no longer had a job or friends, and he'd become a puppet for Queenstown's amusement. He had no reason to stay—except for the heaviest anchor of all: a mystery to solve.

* * *

The Apple Core Tavern had been closed for hours when Pierce Gordon tiptoed to the cellar door. Pressing his ear against it, he didn't hear anything, but the quiet didn't make him feel safer. Nor did his pistol. He didn't want to carry it, let alone use it—just to get inside, confirm the cult's existence, and leave town forever.

Opening the door cautiously, he entered the corridor adorned with gurgling pipes. The hall led to several chambers, but only one room appeared active. Light shone under the door at the end of the hall, and as Pierce crept closer, he heard chanting. Easing the door open a crack, he peered in. Seeing the cloaked citizens of Queenstown filled him with satisfaction, a confirmation that he wasn't crazy. But before he could leave, he needed to see one person in particular.

"The Aeterna Cor hungers, my friends," Frank Dale declared from the middle of their circle. "The fruits of our labor are ripe. We must only wait for the apple to drop and roll to our feet, which I suspect will be any time now."

Natalia said Pierce's name in a sensual whisper.

Great, he thought. I'm not hallucinating a cult, just my wife's ghost.

"Look at me, Pierce."

He exhaled, the grief shaking his voice. "I'm sorry, but I can't."

Pierce expected her to disappear like normal, but she drew her body closer. Her hand rested on his shoulder, the heat prompting him to face the shadowy visage of a cloaked woman. She dropped the hood and smiled, her skin the same olive velvet, pristine as the day they'd met. Her hair had the same onyx shine, and her warmth the same magic: one second on his skin drove it straight to his core.

Natalia Gordon was really there, in living flesh.

He collapsed to the floor, his hands shaking as he reached out to her. She squeezed them, and he desperately pressed her fingers to his lips.

"How is this possible?" he asked. "How long have you been here?"

"Since my death." A smirk bloomed on her cheek. "Well, since I *faked* my death. But in a way, I've always been here, just like you. Even when we were in LA, our hearts were in Queenstown."

"I don't understand," he said, rising.

"You will. But before that happens, I want you to know that I did care for you. Five years ago, it was easy to love you. I even wanted to save you."

Pierce backed away, but the passage was clogged with cloaked bodies.

"Natalia, what's going on?"

"I'm sorry," she said, "but that's not my name."

Dozens of hands latched on, pushing Pierce to the door as Natalia wrapped her arm around his neck. She forced him into the largest room, where more people waited with candles lit.

"I don't want any trouble," he stammered.

Natalia scoffed. "Don't be stupid, Pierce. That's exactly what you wanted."

When she squeezed him closer, his gun pressed into his hip. He flinched and Natalia met his peeled eyes, her head shaking a warning Pierce ignored.

He elbowed his mailman in the nose and kicked Eugena from the coffee shop in his struggle to break free. Tearing himself from their grasp, he pulled his gun. The people of Queenstown backed off, but they remained clustered around the exit.

"Calm down," Natalia said. "You know you don't want to hurt anyone. Think of Kevin Simmons."

"What about him? He's probably alive, too."

"No, he's dead. We're capable of ambitious orchestrations, but we can't control everything. The Aeterna Cor has you to thank for taking Simmons out."

"The *what*?"

Fingers clamped onto Pierce's shoulder. He jerked as he wheeled around, punctuated by the earsplitting sound of a gunshot. Pierce panted, his mind whirring as he looked upon the trembling face of Drake Ulster. The man stumbled backwards in shock and pain, his stomach pouring blood.

"Drake, oh my God..." Pierce dropped the gun as his friend sank to the floor.

Natalia sat beside Ulster and cradled his head as Frank Dale brought her an apple. She put it to Drake's mouth, but he turned his face away. While Pierce shook in shame, Dale collected his gun and tied the former PI's hands behind his back.

His whisper quaked. "Drake, I'm so sorry..."

"I'm the one who's sorry," he sputtered. "I never wanted to lie to you."

"Be quiet and eat," Natalia snapped, pressing the apple to his lips.

He took a large bite, chewing the fruit with grateful moans. Swallowing, he gritted his teeth and pushed himself up. Bracing himself on Natalia, he doubled over with a scream that ended in the clang of a bullet dropping to the floor. When Drake lifted his shirt, his stomach was drenched in blood but the skin unbroken.

"What the hell are you people? Why are you doing this to me?" Pierce growled. "Goddammit, Drake, you were supposed to be my friend!"

"I did what I had to do for the Aeterna Cor, no matter how much it hurt to deceive you," he said. "You were a good friend to me. You were—" He shook his head. "I'm sorry, Pierce, but I drew the short straw this time. I had to accept my role, and you have to accept your fate. That's why you came back to Queenstown: to face your destiny, and to face your mother."

Pierce's eyes widened. "I never told you I was born here. I never mentioned my mother."

"You didn't have to. She's talked about you every day since you were born," Natalia said. "She's here too, you know. She's waiting for you."

"I don't give a damn," he snarled, tugging at his restraints.

"No?" Natalia reached into his shirt and laid the heart locket on top. "You've worn this every day since we met. I assume longer. You might not care for her, but you've never forgotten her."

"And she's never forgotten you," the shadows replied. Stepping out of the adjoining room, the hooded woman revealed her face.

Marian Leon looked more beautiful than ever, her raven hair loose and her face flushed in triumph. Frank Dale dragged Piece to his mother and pushed him down at her feet. She touched his cheek, ran her fingers through his hair, and purred, "Hello, baby."

He pulled away. "You're not my mother. That's not possible."

She opened the top of her cloak. There, sparkling on her jugular notch, hung the other half of Pierce's heart.

"All things are possible in Queenstown," she said. "You are part of a centuries-long tradition. I send my children away to live, and my children return to die. My eternal heart binds us. It is that love which feeds my flock. As I live, they live. But as you die, we all live forever."

She ripped the locket from Pierce's neck and held it up for all to see. The people cheered as she headed back through the door and flipped on the light. A metallic throne with pivoting arms and restraints sat at the center, a menacing origin for every tube and pipe in the building. Pierce screamed as he was hauled into the room, past a barrel of apples, and thrown into the terrifying chair.

"Our forty year wait is over, my friends. The child has returned. Tonight, as the last sacrifice runs dry, we can rejoice anew. My son's blood will nourish the orchard, and the Aeterna Cor will nourish our eternity."

"You're going to eat me?"

She chuckled. "We're not monsters, Pierce."

"What about Drake? Only a monster can push a bullet from his body."

"Or an angel," she said, plucking an apple from the barrel. "There's magic here, my son. Good or evil, it's real, and we have to protect it. For the next forty years, your blood will help us do that." As Pierce was cuffed to the contraption, Marian said, "Thank the lost son of Queenstown, everyone," and the Aeterna Cor chanted, "Thank you, Pierce."

"Shut up," he screamed. "You're crazy. You're killers!"

"So are you," Frank Dale said. "If not for the Aeterna Cor, you'd be rotting in prison right now."

"He's right, Pierce. We lied to get you back here, but you killed a man on your own. You chose obsession and darkness *on your own*." She took a bite of an apple, catching the juice that spilled down her chin.

"I thought my wife was dead. I shot a man in the face. I could go deeper into my reasons for darkness."

"No need. I'm your mother, I would never judge you."

"But killing me is okay."

"You were dead at your first breath, son. Accept it."

Natalia grinned when Marian looked to her and said, "Start the machine."

She threw the lever, and Pierce's body convulsed with pain. Dozens of needles stabbed his limbs, neck, and belly, and his blood drained fast into the pipes. He fought against the machine, but the struggle made him weaker.

"You won't get away with this," he whimpered.

Dale exploded with laughter. "That's twelve for twelve. Pay up, Eugena." The clerk gagged as she slapped a twenty-dollar bill onto Frank's palm.

When Pierce's head lolled, Marian cradled his face in one hand and danced the other over the transfusion tubes.

"The Aeterna Cor is larger and more powerful than you can imagine. You remember the Gordons, don't you? They're one of many families I employ. From sea to shining sea, my orchards flourish."

Pierce's thoughts blurred. He had to fight to keep his eyes open, but only one person kept his focus. Through the death, through the plots riddled with betrayal, Pierce believed he'd really connected with Drake Ulster. He'd loved Natalia, but he'd trusted Drake more than anyone in the world.

"I should have left town," he said.

"You couldn't. Fate kept you here," Marian said.

"*He* kept me here," Pierce replied, staring at Drake. "I couldn't leave until I knew he was safe...or dead."

Drake shook his head, whispering, "This is wrong."

"Quiet, Ulster. You're too close to this."

"No, this is wrong, Marian. I can't let this happen."

"You never had a problem before. Three hundred years, and you've never said anything. You've laughed and lusted in the ritual like the rest of us."

"And I'm tired of it."

She snarled. "You don't get tired. You get younger, you live forever."

"It's different this time. He's different."

"Why? Because of—" Drake's gaze softened, and his head drooped. Marian grunted, "Oh, you weak, little man. If I'd known you'd react like this, I never would've invited you to my bed. You didn't deserve my love."

"Your love is death, Marian. Your fruit may give us external youth, but it rots everything else. There's nothing inside me. Just the black pulp of your so-called love. I've spent three hundred years playing this game. For what? I run the orchard, ration the blood of innocents, and lie to squeeze it from their veins."

"For eternity," she boomed.

"There is no joy in this eternity. There is no life in our lifeblood."

Natalia stomped up to him. "I knew you would be a problem. I should've left that bullet where it was."

The blood pumped from Pierce's body like stolen oil to feed a fire, and he could do nothing to stop it. As dizziness became normal, the world's light faded from Pierce Gordon's eyes. His body became a husk with voices vibrating throughout, screams and whispers the same volume. Even the gunshots that rang through the room were indistinguishable from human cries.

All at once, the needles withdrew from Pierce's flesh. The restraints retracted, and he slumped from the chair to the floor. Echoes of "Chew, chew, eat, eat" pounded his ears, and chunks of apple slid down his throat, hitting his belly with thankful thuds.

Pierce's eyes fluttered open, and he breathed deep for what felt like the first time. Drake Ulster was at his side, feeding him an apple while pointing the gun at his fellow citizens. Several were wounded, but Drake stood between them and the barrel of apples. The moment he looked to Pierce, Marian seized the opportunity to charge. She smacked the gun from Drake's hand, grabbed him by the neck, and pinned him to the wall. "Get Pierce back in the machine!" she screeched at her ailing flock.

Pierce's wounds closed as he stood to face Frank Dale and Officer Dimes. He had never felt so alive, so powerful. They lunged, and he threw his body against them, forcing them far enough through the door to close and lock it. He grabbed one of the pipes on the machine and snapped it free.

Swinging the pipe, Pierce Gordon advanced on his mother. But before he could strike, she spun around, holding Drake Ulster as a shield.

"Go on, son," Marian said. "You'll have to kill him first."

"Do it, Pierce. Kill her," Drake squeaked under Marian's grip.

"No, you saved my life…"

"Do it!"

With a grunt, Pierce drove the pipe into Drake's chest. It stabbed through, nailing Marian's heart to the wall behind her.

Her gasp was a shuddering collapse. Blood poured from the massive wound in her chest, and her cries spawned a din on the other side of the door, shaking the building with pain and terror.

Drake hung like a sopping towel on the pipe, scarlet torrents pooling at his feet. Pierce wrapped himself around his friend and pulled him free, tumbling backwards into crimson lakes. From the puddles, Pierce snatched an apple and pushed it to Drake's lips.

"There's no point," Ulster whispered. "Her blood is our blood. It's over."

Flopping on the pipe, Marian Leon screamed like an animal being gutted alive. Pierce watched in equal terror and satisfaction as her beauty retreated. Her skin yellowed and sagged. Her hair turned white and brittle, and her lips receded from her splintering teeth. Her shrieks deepened to gritty growls burbling from her throat while her chest sucked air. Her body dried to a shrunken kernel as cracks jutted from her wound, cutting her into fragments of fragile stone that crumbled to the floor.

Drake's body had started down a similar road, his skin withering to a mass of wrinkles.

"Leave me, Pierce. I'm done for."

"I'm not leaving you to die with these people. Doomed or not, we're getting out of here."

Draping Drake's withered body on his shoulder, Pierce noticed the change in his own. His hands were shrunken, the skin spotted and drooping.

He kicked open the door to a sea of gray bodies. Against the walls, across the floor, the people of Queenstown writhed with rotten fruit in their dusty hands. Their skeletons howled as Pierce rushed past, trying not to inhale the reeking death.

Natalia threw her brittle body against the door, hunched between Pierce and the exit.

"You won't escape," she hissed. "Marian's blood is in your veins. You will die with us."

"I might die," Pierce said, "but not with monsters like you."

He grabbed her by the hair, the former onyx mane tangled in his fist. But when he tried to tug her aside, the hair ripped from her scalp. Skull sludge slapped against his fingers before he dropped it to the floor, following the wet slap with one of his own. One firm smack took her out, her body folding and skull cracking on the concrete. Blood and ash spilled from the sunken bone as Natalia's emaciated face collapsed inward.

Immense pain boggled Pierce's thoughts and direction. As Drake deteriorated on his shoulder, Pierce's knees cracked so often he assumed they'd be reduce to grit, his thighbones grinding against his shins. He thought he might collapse, but a glint of salvation kept him moving. The glimpse of a free night was hope—even as Pierce died in every step to the exit. Pushing the door open, he gasped fresh air, cold in his rotting lungs.

Queenstown Orchard was drenched in blood. The trees sagged from the heft of dripping ebony fruit, and flies buzzed over the mush Pierce and Drake stumbled into with sighs. As they fell together, their bodies inconsequential to life, Drake's face was little more than paper stretched over bone, but his signature smile held strong.

Pierce's voice was a wheeze, softer with each word. "What's happening to us?"

"I'm getting what I deserve, and you're suffering the fate of many before you."

"If this was going to happen anyway, why did you help me?"

"So you could end it," Ulster said. Like shrunken sandpaper, his hand moved over Pierce's wrinkled cheek. "I've wanted to do this for years—put an end to it all—but all of the orchard's power didn't give me the courage to try. You did that. Marian Leon has had many children," Drake said, using his last strength to squeeze Pierce's hand. "But I've only had one."

His breath was shallow, but Pierce was able to use his last gasp.

"You're my father?"

"I'm sorry I couldn't tell you before. I wanted to, and Marian knew it. That's why she forced me to fake my death. I still thought I could save you, but she was too powerful. I failed, son."

"You did save my life. You were my friend. I don't care if you were told to be, you were the truest friend of my life, Drake… Dad."

As they clasped hands, their cracking fingers expelled dust, but Pierce was too weak to cry, too tired to curse his fate.

Soft apples dropped around them, the ground a mire of sweet death. With his final breath, Drake Ulster lifted his thin lips into a smile, and Pierce closed his own eyes. He didn't see Drake turn to soot. He didn't feel the moment his hand disintegrated. In his mind, his father held his hand until the end.

Pierce didn't try to fight. He lay down on Ulster's ashy clothes and inhaled his last moments. How beautiful it was at the end. No mysteries to solve. No last words to lament. Just him and an orchard breeze.

The smell of cigars overpowered the stench of rotten apples. Before the dark came, Pierce Gordon thought it was the friendliest perfume possible to herald a good night's sleep.

A Dollar and a $cream
Matt Schiariti

*T*he silver-haired bailiff approached the bench and handed Judge Adams a piece of paper. A bead of sweat worked its way down Mike Higgins's cheek. He dabbed at it with an expensive silk handkerchief. The man standing next to him swayed on the balls of his feet, a smile plastered on his plump face as if he didn't have a care in the world.

Silence reigned in the court, only broken by a muted cough and the creaking of a bench.

The judge adjusted black rimmed glasses higher onto her nose and read the decision. Her eyebrow rose for a split second before she addressed the lead juror.

"Has the jury reached a verdict?"

All eyes focused on the middle-aged man who stood in the jury box. All except for those that belonged to Higgins and his client, Anthony Fortunato. Their focus lay on a mousy young woman with coke bottle glasses, unkempt red hair, freckles, and a perpetually runny nose which she wiped at with a ratty tissue.

"We have, your honor," the juror said.

"And how do you find?"

"On the count of murder in the first degree, we the jury find the defendant…"

Higgins pulled at his shirt collar. If things didn't go their way, it wouldn't be a happy ending for the forty-year-old lawyer.

"…not guilty."

Fortunato clapped his hands as a combination of cheers, jeers, and gasps issued from the trial's attendees. The District Attorney's curse was swallowed by the commotion. The large mobster shook Mike's hand and slapped him on the back so hard it stung.

He leaned in and whispered in Mike's ear. "I told you, Mikey. Nothing to worry about. I gotta hit the head. I'll see you in a few."

Mike nodded and let out the breath he'd been holding. Judge Adams, pursed her lips, banged the gavel, and thanked the jury for their service. District Attorney Bennet walked his way.

Mike smiled. "Nice job, Susan. You put up a hell of a…"

She glared. "Save it, Higgins. Bad chain of evidence? What a crock. Your client's guilty as sin. I know jury tampering when I see it."

"Hey now." Mike held up his hands. "It's not my fault the cops didn't handle things properly. I don't know where you're getting this jury tampering idea from," he lied. "Making allegations you can't substantiate is a lawsuit waiting to happen. Don't be such a sore loser, Suzy."

"Don't call me that. You lost the right to call me that when I found out you were married." A wicked smile tugged at her lips, malice burning in her brown eyes. "I'm glad your ex got it all. How's life in that dump apartment of yours?"

"I win a few more of these and I'll be back in a penthouse in no time."

"I don't know how you sleep at night," she said, shaking her head.

"I sleep just fine. Everybody's entitled to a defense."

"Even the guilty?"

"Proven innocent. You know how this works."

"Bullshit. Fortunato's so slick he makes John Gotti look like Velcro. You'll get yours one of these days, Mike. Only a matter of time before defending the fantastically guilty catches up with you." She clenched her jaw and stormed out.

Gathering his head as well as his papers, Mike shut his briefcase as people filed out of the hot room.

"I could go for a drink," Fortunato said, approaching with a smile the size of a train spread across his moon-shaped face. "How's about you join me, counselor?"

Knowing that it was an order, not a request, Mike agreed.

Fortunato grabbed Mike's shoulder. "Good, good. We have a few financial matters to discuss."

The high from winning the case immediately dissipated, leaving a cold void in its place.

* * *

Mike replayed the conversation over in his head as he waited outside for his cab. A fine sheen of sweat clung to his skin, amplifying the chilliness of the dusk air.

After the trial, he'd met Fortunato at the criminal's Italian Bistro in the heart of the city, a known mob front and money laundering operation. Mike spent more than his fair share of hours working on defenses for Fortunato's various employees, each of whom was guiltier than the last.

"So you see," Fortunato said after he took a sip of Midori, "I'm a bit torn, Mikey. While I'm glad that you, once again, have shown that Lady Justice indeed favors the righteous and have restored my good name to its gleaming luster, it still doesn't get you off the hook. It just buys you time."

The room was small, smelled of rich coffee and garlic, and was kept in perpetual semi-darkness. Soft light thrown off from the candle at the center of the table flickered in the mobster's eyes, giving him a demonic appearance. Mike shifted in his seat and swallowed the lump in his throat.

"By my recollection," Forunato continued, "you're still in to us for about eighty grand. I like the ponies as much as the next guy, but Mikey, Mikey, Mikey!" He shook his head. "You really need to get that gambling problem under control. Your wife didn't exactly leave you with an overabundance of expendable income, know what I mean?"

"Tony, I mean…Anthony. Time. I need more time. Just a few more weeks. That's all I ask. How many of your hoods have I gotten off over the years? You owe—"

Fortunato's glare made Mike shrink farther into his seat. "Owe? I don't owe you shit, Mikey. You've been paid top dollar for your services. Is it my fault you couldn't keep it in your pants? Is it my fault you piss money away on horses?" He finished off his drink, placed the glass down with a slight clink. "I like you. I really do. But, even I got a boss. Eighty grand is a lotta cake. I can only cover for you for so long. You have two weeks. That's the best I can do. If my boss had his way? You'd be in a landfill in Staten Island right now, but I stuck up for ya. 'No no no, Monty' I says. 'Mikey's a good guy'." Fortunato sat back and burped. "Friendship and services rendered only go so far, know what I'm sayin'? Hey, it's nothing personal."

Naw, nothing personal, Mike thought. *It's just my goddamn life.* "Right, yeah. I understand, Anthony. Nothing personal."

Anthony led Mike to the front door, a large arm wrapped around his shoulders. "Business is business. Not a thing I can do about it. My words to God's ears," he said, making the sign of the cross. "Hey, there's always the lottery, right?"

Now, as the cab pulled up, the reality of the situation hit Mike in the chest. Where the hell was he going to come up with that much money in two weeks?

An old woman, fragile and small, was stepping out of the cab. She looked like a modern-day Gypsy in a loud, floral patterned frock. A matching scarf was wrapped tightly around her head. He bumped into her, trying to get into the cab before she'd managed to fully exit.

She yelled something in a language he didn't recognize, and pointed at him with a gnarled finger that sprouted from a misshapen hand. Mike reeled back in revulsion when he caught sight of her face. She was hideous. Lips the consistency of old paper moved in a blur, exposing jagged, green teeth. Her nose, crooked and hawkish, sat between a bizarre pair of eyes; one reduced to barely more than a squint, the other clouded over by a chalky white cataract.

He tore his eyes off of her and dumped himself into the cab, closing the door while she pawed at it. Mike began to give the cabby his address, but was interrupted by the woman's incessant tapping on the window.

"What?" Mike snapped.

She sputtered something in a guttural voice, her spit decorating the window, and pointed to the floor by the back seat.

"What are you going on about? God dammit!" Furious, impatient, and bigger concerns on his mind, he scanned the floor of the dark cab. A tattered purse lay haphazardly at his feet. He snapped it up, spilling some of its contents, and dangled it in front of the window like a child taunting a caged tiger at the zoo that had long outlived its usefulness. "Is this what you want? Is it?" He rolled down the window and tossed it into the wet, slimy gutter.

"Where to, buddy?" the cabbie asked for the third time.

Mike yelled to be heard over the woman's wailing. "Broad and Market. Just get me the hell outta here." He rolled up the window and flipped her the middle finger. The Gypsy's alabaster eye opened wide. She raised her hand, making a gesture with her index finger and pinky, spittle flying out of her mouth with each word she flung at him. "Yeah yeah. Good night to you too, lady."

Mike settled into the seat as the cab pulled away. Curious, he looked out the rear window and saw the stooped old lady stabbing fingers at him and shaking her purse over her head.

* * *

Hands trembling from the run-in with the woman, Mike dropped his wallet at his feet. Money and credit cards spilled out and mixed with the other papers that littered the cab's grimy floor. "Dammit." He fumbled in the dark, picking up everything he could get his hands on; bills, receipts, credit cards. He forked over the cabbie's fare, and stuffed the rest of the detritus into his coat pocket. The slammed door silenced the driver's complaint about the lack of a substantial tip.

Inside his apartment, Mike breathed in the scents of stale air and moldy carpet; a relief compared to the smog of piss and shit fumes he'd endured during the four flight walk up the dimly lit stairwell.

Emptying the contents of his pockets onto the worn coffee table, he fixed himself a stiff Wild Turkey, then sat on the couch and turned on the TV. He started organizing his wallet as coverage of the Fortunato verdict played on the evening news. As if he needed to be reminded that a prodigious axe loomed over his head.

For a time, Mike had been on the fast track to being one of the top defense attorneys in the city, representing some of the wealthiest people in town. So what if his clientele consisted of mobsters, thugs, rapists, and murderers? Like he'd told his frigid ex-mistress after the trial, everybody's entitled to a defense. Fortunato was as guilty as the day is long, but Mike's moral compass only pointed in one direction; directly to Mike Higgins. Despite what Susan had said, he slept just fine, thank you very much.

Mike could have had it all if only it weren't for his biggest vice, one that trumped his inability to stay faithful to his gorgeous trophy wife, a self-destructive weakness so bad it made the monetary fallout from his divorce seem a cakewalk in comparison.

Nothing compared to the adrenaline rush of betting horses. The smell of the clay, the early morning dew in the air, cigar smoke hanging around the place like a comfy blanket, the uncertainty of chance. He felt like he was in the hands of a higher power when he bet, the closest he'd ever come to a religious experience. He'd done OK for a while, but it didn't take long for him dig a hole he couldn't climb out from. Using one of Fortunato's 'constituents' as a bookie served to worsen matters, marrying the two like a pair of dysfunctional lovers. The more he lost, the more the mobster dug his claws into Mike's flesh.

"Oh how the mighty have fallen." He fired down the rest of his Wild Turkey, and stared at the empty glass. In a fit of rage, he threw it across the room where it hit the wall and shattered. He stood up and kicked the coffee table, scattering papers and knocking his wallet to the floor.

"Damn it." He scowled and began picking up the chaos. "Wait. What's this?" One piece of paper stood out from the rest, and it certainly wasn't trash or a receipt. "Well, hello," he said in a singsong voice, caressing the lottery ticket with his thumb. "Where did you come from, baby?"

The old lady. It had to have come from her purse. No wonder why she'd cursed him so much when the cab pulled away, holding her handbag up in the air as if it were the severed head of Medusa. *Screw her*, he thought. If anybody needed a change of luck, it was him. Still relatively young and able to get an erection without the aid of pharmaceuticals, he'd put a winning lottery ticket to much better use than a creepy old hag who was no doubt one step away from checking out of life for good.

As if reading his mind, the news broadcast switched over to the daily lottery drawing. Mike sat on the edge of the seat, hoping against hope that the unassuming, innocent, magical piece of paper held in his sweaty grip would get his fat out of the fryer.

The announcer drew the first number. Mike checked his ticket. A match.

He inched further onto the edge of the couch.

Another number, another check, another match.

Breathing heavy, Mike found himself standing inches from the TV.

Another number.

Another match.

"Holy shit."

Match.

Match.

Match.

Lightheaded and bordering on hyperventilation, the desperate lawyer double checked the numbers on the ticket against those displayed on his television. Identical from first to last.

"Amen, motherfucker," Mike screamed at the top of his lungs, dancing a goofy jig. Angry neighbors pounded on the thin walls. "Kiss my ass, people. I'm a winner, a goddamn winner. No more skid row!"

In a daze, Mike backed into a wall and slid down onto his rear end. Should he take the annuity? The hell with that. Lump sum was the way to go. Why wait for the fortune to accrue when he could be rich all at once? His mind ran through the quick and dirty math. A dollar figure popped in his head and he nearly shat himself at the implications. Not only would he be able to pay off his debt to that rotund kingpin Fortunato and get out of his current shit hole, but he now had fuck you money, even after Uncle Sam got his grubby mitts on his slice. And the best thing? His ex-wife wouldn't see squat, not a single dime. His alimony payments were based on his average annual income at the time of the divorce.

"Mine, all mine!"

Once the fits of hysterical laughter subsided, Mike picked up the phone and called Anthony Fortunato, informing the crook that he'd get his money in advance of the two week deadline. The news made Anthony a very happy man. The mobster once told Mike that if he didn't get his shit straight, he'd be forced to fit the lawyer for a wood chipper, something he'd 'hate to do.' Mike shuddered at the memory, but none of that mattered now. His pot of gold within reach, Mike could finally pull himself out from underneath the Italian's obese thumb.

After hanging up with Fortunato and drinking several more bourbons, Mike drunk dialed his ex-wife. Her stunned silence upon hearing the news was nearly as rewarding as knowing he could light cigars with hundred dollar bills for the rest of his natural life.

* * *

"This is a completely remodeled unit," the realtor said as she led Mike across the open floor to the kitchen. "The countertops are top of the line granite and the cabinets are teak. The appliances are…"

"Garbage." He looked around the penthouse apartment. Brand new bamboo flooring in every room, stylish exposed duct work…the place was huge, fantastic, and expensive. The kitchen was one of the few drawbacks. Although well laid out, it suffered from substandard hardware, stove, oven, and range. "This will all have to be replaced." Mike made a sweeping gesture. "And the locks on the door aren't exactly cutting edge."

The young realtor's face fell. Mike almost felt sorry for razzing the twenty-five-year-old brunette in the flattering black suit jacket, white collarless shirt, and gray miniskirt.

"Still," he said, running a finger along the kitchen counter. "It could work. How much did you say it was again?"

Her face became hopeful. "Per month, with association fees it's…"

"Not per month. How much is it to *buy*?"

Freckles deepened in direct proportion to the excited gleam in her eyes. She gave him a number. "The seller is very motivated."

"I'll take it."

"Oh, my…well, that's wonderful, Mr. Higgins! Do you have a lawyer? I recommend it when dealing with these types of dollar figures. I could refer you to one if you'd like?"

"Not necessary," Mike said, grinning. "I am a lawyer."

Her smile bordered on flirtatious. "Well then. Let's head back to my office and I'll get right to work drawing up the contracts."

"Excellent. After you." He held the door open for her. "You wouldn't happen to know a good locksmith and interior decorator in the area by any chance, would you?"

* * *

Closing on the apartment had been a fast process since Mike paid cash. He'd settled his debt with Anthony Fortunato early as promised, and with the specter of meeting his end via wood chipper no longer hovering over him, Mike felt as if the weight of the world had lifted from his shoulders. He spent with wild abandon but the number of zeroes in his bank account was assurance that he'd never go hungry.

True to her word, the realtor scheduled appointments with the locksmith and an interior decorator. The former installed a state-of-the art breach-proof door, complete with military grade locks and security panel; the latter helped Mike pick out the best of everything in both furniture and kitchen needs. The empty floor plan filled quickly with expensive rugs, a titan sized leather sectional complete with recliners at both ends. A massive 90 inch LED TV now sat on top of a free standing entertainment system. Everything chosen for the kitchen was stainless steel, from the double sized Sub-Zero refrigerator, to the new sink and its industrial strength garbage disposal. Even the toaster she'd picked out cost more than what a Wal-Mart greeter made in a week.

Life had finally seen fit to garnish Mike with a little luck. And the best part? He owed nothing. Not one solitary penny. Freedom was never having to say 'how much is the interest rate?'"

Now that he'd settled into his new home, he looked forward to some female company. The cute realtor was good for a quick screw in her office after the papers had been signed, but Mike wanted to sample all life had to offer. He wondered what kind of women he'd be able to pick up when he pulled in front of a club and handed the valet the keys to his 2013 Lamborghini.

Only one way to find out.

* * *

The valet pocketed the hundred dollar bill and assured Mike he would take extra special care of the black Murcielago. Satisfied that his car was in good hands, Mike sauntered into the club, drawing appreciative looks from a group of younger women, and feeling supremely confident. Thudding techno music sent vibrations from the soles of his Italian leather shoes straight to his balls. He smiled as he passed through the crowd of scantily clad women dancing to the beat, lights bathing them in a ballet of chaotic, multicolored hues. The scents of perfume, alcohol, and excitement comingled and saturated the air.

As he neared the bar, he noticed a woman in a skintight red dress sitting on a stool, engaged in conversation with an overeager guy who looked to be at least ten years her junior. Mike took a seat several stools down and observed them from his peripheral vision. He had to stifle a chuckle; it was obvious that the lovely blonde with the long legs was humoring the young buck.

After finishing the Evan Williams 23 Year Old Bourbon he'd ordered, Mike decided to make his move.

He situated himself in between them, his back to the man. "Stephanie? Oh my God, it really is you! How the hell have you been?"

The woman looked at him strangely at first, her nose crinkling, eyes narrowing. Mike winked and gave a slight shake of the head to indicate her would-be suitor. Realization dawned in her blue eyes. She winked back.

"Yes! I can't believe it. *So* good to see you. How many years has it been?"

"At least ten. No, twelve," Mike said with a conspiratorial smile.

Mumbling, the younger man excused himself and walked off toward the dance floor in search of other prey.

"Thank you for that," she laughed. "He's been chatting me up for a half hour and I couldn't figure out how to get rid of him."

"Glad to be of service…?"

"Tanya." She extended a delicate hand. "And you are?"

He brushed his lips against her knuckles. "Mike. Can I buy you a drink?"

"I don't know, can you?"

Mike's smile widened. *"May* I buy you a drink?"

"Tell you what. I'll buy you one for saving me from Studly McStudderson back there." She caught the bar tender's attention and ordered herself a whiskey sour and Mike another Evan Williams.

The two drank, making idle chit chat as the night wore on. Mike couldn't help but notice that Tanya flicked glances at his expensive tailor made suit and platinum Rolex.

"So," she said, plucking the cherry from her drink and licking it suggestively before wrapping her red lips around it. "It's getting a little late, wouldn't you say?"

"Is it? I hadn't noticed. The company's been exhilarating." He looked at his watch. "It's only quarter after nine."

"No it's not. It's nearly midnight."

"Really?" Mike looked at his watch again. The hands weren't moving. "Well, that's weird."

Tanya laughed. "You sure that's a Rolex? Maybe you should check and make sure it's not spelled R-O-L-E-C-K-S."

Mike tapped the watch face. "I'll be…do you know how much this thing cost me?" He gave her a sheepish grin and tapped until the hands started moving. Sluggish at first, they soon accelerated into a blur. "What the…"

The crystal face popped off and the hands shot out like a circular saw blade. They buzzed over Tanya's head and if she hadn't ducked, they would have embedded themselves into her forehead rather than in the wall across the room.

"Holy Hell!" She laughed, holding a hand over her cleavage. "Do you still have the receipt for that thing? That could have taken my eye out."

"I…I don't know what happened. I've never seen that happen before with *any* watch. Wait till I get my hands on that jeweler. Son of a bitch sold me something out of a James Bond movie."

She eyed him then doubled over in laughter. Mike's anger bled away and he laughed along with her.

"Jesus, that was spooky. Maybe that's a sign that we should head back to your place?" She made a sensual display of licking her full lips.

Mike stood up and took her hand in his. "I thought you'd never ask."

* * *

Tanya had her tongue in Mike's ear, her hand creeping agonizingly close to his growing hard-on. The two sat in the opalescent blue of the parking garage's halogen lights, making out and fogging up the windows.

She pulled away. "I love a romp in the car as much as the next girl, but how about we move this to your bedroom?"

"Your wish is my command." He gave her another kiss then pressed the power lock button. Nothing. He pressed it again. Still, nothing. Mike swore under his breath and slammed it with his palm. The doors unlocked just before the code alarm went off, the shrill klaxon echoing off of concrete and steel.

"Not having a good run of luck on your recent purchases, are you, sweetie," Tanya said.

"I don't know what's going on. This thing is brand new." He fumbled with the remote, stabbing the alarm button a half dozen times until it fell silent. "Sorry about that."

She leaned over and nibbled his ear. "That's OK. Damn Italians don't make them like they used to," she whispered. "Now, about that nightcap."

That was all Mike needed to hear to forget about the car alarm issue and spirit her up to his apartment. Five minutes and one quick elevator ride later, he shut the door, and Tanya pressed her body to his. "Nice place," she said between kisses, her hands playing through his hair. "I know who you are, by the way."

"Do you?" He grabbed her firm ass and thrust his hips against hers.

"Mmmm hmmm." She worked soft kisses from his mouth to his ear. Mike felt her hard nipples press to his chest. "You won the lottery."

"Is that why you came home with me, for my money? I should be insulted, but right now I can't seem to find a reason to care."

"I don't give a shit about that. You picked up a trust fund girl. I have my own money." Tanya bit his lower lip, and took a step back. She shed her silky red dress and let it fall to the floor, revealing a heavenly body concealed only by a sheer red bra, G-string, and high heels. "All I care about is this," she said, gently massaging his crotch, "and where the bedroom is."

* * *

Tanya lay next to Mike, her arm draped over his chest. She played with the hair around his nipple, close enough to make him hard again.

He moaned. "Keep doing that and we'll have to go for round three."

"I'm game if you are," she said, flicking his nipple with the tip of her tongue. "But I'm thirsty. Got any milk?"

He laughed. "Milk? Yeah. It's in the fridge. This isn't going to be some kind of weird lactation fantasy role play is it?"

She bit his nipple playfully. "No, silly. Milk does a body good. Stay right there. I'll be back in a minute." Mike's eyes locked onto her tight ass as she walked out of the room naked as the day she was born.

He clasped his hands behind his head and smiled. "This is the life."

"Oh, Jesus. That's *disgusting*!"

Mike bounded out of bed and ran to the kitchen. Tanya stood over the sink, rinsing out her mouth with handfuls of water from the tap.

"Hey, what's wrong? Everything OK?"

"No." She spat and held up a carton of milk. "This stuff's gone bad."

"Bad?" He took the milk and checked the date. "But I just bought it this morning." He brought the spout to his nose and took a deep sniff. The fetid stench of curdled milk made him gag. "Holy shit. You weren't kidding." He dumped the chunky contents in the sink and used the faucet to flush it down the drain.

"No wonder why," Tanya said, poking her head in the Sub-Zero. "This thing isn't working right."

"That can't be. It's top of the line." He felt inside the fridge. She was right. The interior was as warm as if he'd never plugged it in. "What the hell?" He opened up the freezer door and found melted ice cream mixed in with water trickling from the ice maker. He slammed the door. "Shit!"

"Maybe I should just go, Mike." Tanya picked up her discarded dress.

"No, please. It's just…one of those things?" Mike rested his hands on her shoulders. "Please. Just stay. I'll make you breakfast." Tanya grinned. "Is that a yes?"

"Yes," she said, wrapping her arms around his neck. "It's a yes."

"Great. How about some music?" He turned on the CD player, found some romantic light jazz, and made sure the volume was reasonable. "Care to dance?"

Tanya took his outstretched hand, smiling seductively. "Love to."

The naked couple swayed to the soothing, intimate music emanating from the well-hidden speakers within the elaborate entertainment center. Mike was glad the weirdness of the night hadn't scared her off. She was a wild, imaginative lover and he had a few rounds left in him before the sun came up.

"I think this bumping and grinding is making you ready for round three, sailor." Tanya looked down at Mike's arousal.

"What can I say? You have that effect on…"

The CD player skipped.

Mike groaned and rested his head on Tanya's shoulder. "Now what?"

The volume rose to ear-shattering levels. They both clasped hands over their ears. Tanya tried to say something, but 1,000 watts of jazz as replicated to perfection through ten thousand dollars' worth of high-end audio swallowed her words.

Mike fiddled with the player, holding up a finger. "I'll fix this in a second!"

"What?" Tanya yelled.

"I said I'll…"

Blue-white sparks of electricity flew from the display. They connected with Mike's hand, shocking him and sending him reeling back. He stumbled and fell on his ass between Tanya's feet. The music sped up to Alvin and the Chipmunk proportions for a moment then stopped.

"Mike, what is up with your stuff?" Tanya said, helping him up.

"I have no fucking clue."

Curiosity driving them and arms wrapped around one another, the pair approached the entertainment center.

The stereo sparked once more, shuddered, and jumped. Tanya shrieked.

"Don't touch it," she whispered.

Mike's hand was inches away from the stereo. Another crackle of electricity sparked from the unit. Mike pulled back, and Tanya hugged him around the waist. There was a crackling sound, then, with a puff of smoke, the CD tray sprung open. The unit burst into flame as it started hurling compact discs through the air.

"Holy shit!" Mike grabbed Tanya by the arm and pulled her into a run toward the couch, zigging and zagging to avoid the silver discs of death. "Move. Move!"

Tanya screamed as the couple vaulted over the leather sectional. Whizzing sounds zipped above their heads as the CDs sliced the air and embedded themselves in nearly every flat surface of the apartment.

Mike and Tanya huddled behind the couch, using it as a shield. "Son of a bitch! I should have stuck with my iPod," Mike said.

"That's it. I'm out of here." Tanya pressed herself close to the ground and army-crawled to the door. The hundred disc player exhausted its ammunition by the time she reached her things. She stood up, her eyes fixed on the stereo-cannon, and shimmied into her dress.

"Look, I'll make it up to you, Tanya," Mike said. She tore her arm from out of his firm grasp and stepped into her shoes.

"No way. No friggin' way!" Her eyes were the size of silver dollars, her chest heaving. "I've had enough crazy for one night. You were a great lay, but this?" She gestured around the apartment. "Uh-uh. Let me out." Mike hesitated. She stomped a heel on the hardwood and pointed at the door. "Let me out, dammit!"

Mike sighed and punched his security code into the panel.

"Good luck, Mike," Tanya said. She rushed through the door and trotted at a near-run down the hallway. "You're going to need it!"

* * *

Royally pissed off, Mike wrenched the courtesy phone from its cradle. The building manager was about to get a piece of his mind. Something had to be screwy with the power. Why else would his fridge die for no reason and his stereo suddenly become possessed?

There was no dial tone.

"Goddamn it." He hung up and tried again. Same result.

Mike considered visiting the manager in person and telling him where he could stick his shitty electrical system, but a wave of exhaustion hit him. He'd grab a snack, get some shut-eye, and handle things in the morning with a clear head.

Anything from the fridge was out of the question. He found some Pop Tarts in the cupboard and loaded them into the six-slot toaster. Standing at arm's length, he gently pushed down the plunger. No sparks, no fires. Mike breathed a sigh of relief. His nerves were shot. Whiskey was in order. He fixed himself a bourbon and drank it slouched over the sink, too tired and frayed to give a shit about much of anything.

Then he noticed a burning smell. Tendrils of smoke were coiling their way out of the toaster.

He set down the drink. "You have got to be kidding me."

Spring! Spring!

Two charcoal-coated Pop-Tarts launched out of the toaster as if propelled by a turbine. They shot up, dented a length of exposed duct work with a loud clang, ricocheted off, and came straight for him. He staggered back, eyes tracking the burning projectiles as they crashed at his feet and shattered into tiny, smoking-black bricks.

Mike's body trembled, his heart raced.

He was trying to catch his breath as a rumbling deep within the kitchen brought his attention to the stainless steel sink. Thinking it came from the pipes, he peered into the drain... A sound like bare metal-on-metal shrieked, and a geyser of white shot into his face. Bits of curdled milk and other refuse he'd discarded down the garbage disposal stung his eyes, worked their way into his mouth. Mike gagged, holding his hands in front of his face to fend off the assault, but the rotten spray was too powerful.

Mike's scream was reduced to an incomprehensible garble. He stumbled and blinked repeatedly, grabbing blindly for the roll of paper towels he knew was somewhere on the granite countertop. Once he found them, , he wiped at his face, frantic to get the acidic, spoiled milk out of his burning eyes, and the rotten taste out of his mouth. The geyser continued to explode like a miniature Vesuvius. Mike, now braced against the far cabinets next to the dishwasher, watched as the final remnants of curdled milk, pureed banana peels, and who knew what else splattered on the floor and counter, coating everything in reeking nastiness. He stood frozen, scared out of his wits, not knowing what do to next.

Could it get any worse?

The refrigerator opened on its own, answering his silent question.

A mewl escaped his lips. "Oh Christ."

A cabinet opened up and hit him on the ass with such force that it sent him lurching forward. He tried grabbing the countertop, but the goo from the garbage disposal made a firm grip impossible. His feet fared no better when they came in contact with the gunk-slick tile. Momentum, coupled with the slippery floor, sent him shooting forward like an out-of-control ice skater. Mike's feet slipped out from underneath him. He went airborne then landed on his ass with an impact that sent waves of pain up his tailbone. Screaming, he cannonballed toward the Sub-Zero, fingernails clawing at the floor, legs spread open. His inertia shot him straight into the refrigerator door's edge, balls first.

Searing pain coursed through his every nerve ending. His sack felt as if it had been cleaved in two. Too shocked to even scream, he rolled on the floor, writhing in pain, his hands firmly cupping his family jewels. Through the fog of pain, he managed to grab hold of the door handle and pull himself up.

"What…the hell…is…happening to me…" he cried when his breath returned and his legs stopped quivering.

Once he was able to walk, he slid his feet across the floor, bracing himself on the countertops, and made his way out of the kitchen. He wiped his feet on a thick oriental rug, saying a silent thanks to the interior decorator for talking him into buying it, and staggered to the front door. Mike needed help. He didn't care what he looked like or how people would interpret his story. Let them lock him up in a padded cell. Better that than allow his own house to kill him.

The doorknob fought his slick hand. Mike wiped the goo on the wall and tried again. The damn thing wouldn't turn. With a foot against the wall for leverage he pulled with what little strength he had left. "Come on, you whore. Come on!"

He thought he'd pass out from the strain when the doorknob came free of the housing. The sudden lack of resistance sent him sprawling down on his ass. Dazed and on his back, Mike looked at the knob's stem; sheared clean off.

With a hysterical cry, he tossed the doorknob at the door, situated himself on his hands and knees, and crawled until he was able to use the wall to prop himself up and use the security panel. He found his vertical base and punched in an emergency code that had been programmed to contact not only security, but the local police as well. Nothing. No beeps, no keys lit up. He tried the code again. *Nothing.* He punched the panel.

A spark of electricity from the assaulted panel stung his fist and sent him into a mini-seizure. His teeth chattered and he smelled his own hair burning until the wave of blinding pain stopped and, almost at his physical limit, dropped to the ground like a wet sack.

Mike whimpered, his body one huge, never-ending hurt, and crawled to the couch. He maneuvered his way around the edge of the sectional, wanting nothing more than to let the doughy leather recliner wrap him up and allow him to fall into unconsciousness where the pain couldn't get to him.

He was halfway over the armrest when he heard the sound of a metal spring giving way.

The footrest exploded, catching Mike weak and unaware, and hit him with a loud smack. The force sent him flying through the air, ass over head over ass until he landed not more than a foot from the entertainment center. He heard and felt a sickening crack when his back slammed against the unforgiving hardwood. His lower body went numb.

Oh, fuck. Back. Back's broke. "Hellllp." His voice was a ragged gasp. "Somebody," he coughed up blood, "some...body....hellllp me..."

A shrill creaking noise, like metal being stretched beyond its limits, caught his attention. Despite his broken back he could still move his head. Painful as it was, Mike looked up.

He saw that the massive LED TV had begun to teeter. It now canted at a thirty degree angle. It rocked gently, then, with another sound of fatigued metal, it moved down several more degrees and came to a jerky halt.

His breathing quickened. The mounts that kept the thing from toppling forward were failing.

Another creak, another few degrees closer to falling.

Without the use of his legs, and with his strength quickly betraying him, Mike had no way of moving.

Creeeeeak. The TV was now parallel to the ground.

His voice came out as a wet, muted garble.

Crreeeeeeeeeeeeeeeeeak.

Through his blurry vision, Mike caught a fuzzy image on the large screen, even though it hadn't been on.

Creeeeeak...

The image became clearer. Mike had always thought Hi-Def was one of the greater inventions of the 20th century. As the image on the wobbly TV sharpened, he changed his mind.

A loud snap blasted through the house like a gunshot. The TV seemed to hover five feet over Mike's swollen body, suspended in time, a pair of mismatched eyes staring down on him.

Gravity reasserted its control, and the TV came down with frightening speed. In the split second before Mike's lights went out permanently, he thought he heard a laugh. Whether it was his own or not, he'd never find out.

* * *

"OK, boys. The real cops are here now." The homicide detective stepped underneath yellow crime scene tape and into the apartment. His nose caught a multitude of smells, none of them pleasant. Crime scene techs and first responders buzzed around the space like a well-orchestrated colony of bees. The technician closest to the huge entertainment center raised his hand.

"Over here, Ron."

Detective Ron Limerick popped a Swedish Fish into his mouth and made his way over, careful to avoid trampling on physical evidence.

"What in the name of shit happened in here, Smitty?" CDs imbedded everywhere in creation, some type of primordial slop covering most of the kitchen, busted piece of charred something or other caught in an air duct…what had he walked into? "Why do I always get the weird ones?"

Smitty looked up. "How the hell can you eat those things around all of this shit?"

Limerick popped another Swedish Fish into his mouth and shrugged. "They bring me to my childhood happy place so I can better deal with the malfeasance and atrocities of man. What've we got?" He pointed to the naked body on the floor, entire head hidden behind the largest flat panel TV he'd ever seen.

The tech shook his head. "I have no clue, Limerick. I've never seen anything like this. Without moving the TV, best I can tell is that he somehow landed here, and the mother of all televisions came swooping down and pushed his nose into his brain."

"That's different."

"Every day on the job is a brave new adventure."

"Truer words were never spoken."

"Funny you should get this case, now that I think of it."

"I wouldn't call anything about this 'funny'."

"You will when I tell you who the stiff is."

"Enlighten me."

"Driver's license IDs him as Mike Higgins." Smitty's eyebrows wiggled.

Limerick was shocked. "*My* Mike Higgins?"

"One and the same."

"Talk about poetic justice. Couldn't have happened to a bigger jerkoff." Limerick had worked the Anthony Fortunato murder case. Bad chain of evidence his ass. The case was squeaky clean. Everybody knew

Higgins was a dirty lawyer and rumors of jury tampering flew around the precinct like paper planes. He popped another chewy candy into his mouth and pointed to two plainclothes officers. "You and you. Get this TV off the guy's face."

They put on gloves and hefted the enormous TV, setting it aside. Mike's eyes were open in fright, and his lips were frozen in a permanent, soundless scream.

"Died screaming," Smitty said.

Limerick grunted. "Ya think?"

"What the hell is that?" one of the cops asked, pointing to the television.

Limerick and Smitty peered at the screen.

"What do you make of that, Ron?"

Mike brought his face to within a foot of the television. "They're eyes."

"You're shitting me."

"I'm not kidding. Look." Limerick pulled out a pen from his coat pocket and indicated the two residual images. "This one on the left is half-squinted. The other is clouded over, but it's definitely an eye."

"Jesus, you're right. Must have been watching some movie, huh?"

"Mmmmm. This is an LED, right? I didn't think you could burn an image into these."

"You can't."

"Weird." Limerick squatted down and noticed something clenched in Mike's right hand. He used his pen to pry it open. "What's this? Don't tell me you missed this, Smitty. You're getting sloppy in your old age."

"I swear that wasn't there when we got here."

"Uh huh." Limerick pulled a bloody piece of crumpled paper from the rigid fist. "I'll be damned."

"What is it?"

"This is a winning lottery ticket. Our lawyer friend here hit it big not long after the Fortunato trial. Used it to pull himself out of the financial gutter."

"Wish I had that kind of luck. All it takes is a dollar and a dream, right?"

Limerick's knees cracked as he stood up. "In the case of Mike Higgins, more like a dollar and a scream."

Smitty shook his head. "You're a dark bastard, Ron."

Limerick shrugged and popped another Swedish Fish in his mouth.

The Dance
Sarah A. Hoyt

"**E**tta," John said, as he walked into her cube, without knocking, something that always annoyed her. "I have something I want you to look into."

Etta looked up, feeling herself hold her breath, and waiting. Ever since John had become her captain, directly over her, she'd found herself doing more support work, and less—considerably less—real police work. She'd been pulled off the streets, for no other reason than her "excellent organizational skills." But she hadn't joined the force to be a secretary.

Oh, she knew why John was doing it. At least, she thought she did. They'd been partnered early on, when she'd joined the force, and they'd fallen into a relationship. She supposed, back then, in John's mind it had all been clear. He was going to marry her, and she'd quit the force and stay home to raise babies.

In fact, he'd finally told her just that, which had led to the end of their relationship. She hadn't joined the force to catch herself a husband.

He'd asked for a transfer, and had been working at a different precinct for ten years. Rumors had filtered back, and sometimes they'd found themselves at the same events—educational conferences, training events.

John had got married, a year or so after the transfer, but it hadn't worked out—long hours and danger had taken their toll. And now he was back, ten years older and somehow hardened.

He must have been thirty or so when they'd dated, so he wouldn't be all that old, but his face was all hard angles, emphasized by the straight eyebrows, the horizontal wrinkles of thought on his forehead.

Every time he looked at her, she could feel him wishing he could scold her. *He thinks I'm still the clueless rookie I was ten years ago.*

And now, perhaps John caught her expression of weariness. Something much like a smile curled at his lips. "I was wondering if you could do something…in the field. Not quite undercover, but not beat, either. They told me around here that you're the person who knows Capitol Hill best, that when it comes to tracking down a meth lab or finding a kid who's gone missing, you're the person to come to."

"Is there a meth lab?" she asked, and immediately wanted to kick herself for it. Of course there was a meth lab. There always were meth labs.

"Hundreds, I expect," John said. His voice had got deeper with time too, pleasantly gravelly. He gave her the smile again, a sop to stop her offense. "But I imagine you meant to ask if there was one we were trying to track down. That's different... and not quite what I wanted to see you about."

He perched on the corner of her desk, half-sitting half-leaning on it, one of his long legs bracing him on the floor. She worried that the cheap metal desk would fold, but she didn't say anything. Surely he knew? And maybe it was good for him to take a pratfall.

But the desk bore up bravely, and John said, "It might be drugs. We don't know." His smile turned into an expression of ironical disapproval. "Here's the thing, we don't know anything except that a lot of... ah... what you could call the Capitol Hill fauna, has been turning up in emergency rooms... dead tired. I mean, literally dead tired. A few of them have died of fatigue. And we can't figure out what's doing it. The hospital can't, either. They say it looks like these people have been... dancing themselves to death, which seems odd. Unless it's the effect of some new drug."

Etta moaned before she could stop herself. "The new designer drugs. Naked zombie cannibals, and now dancers!"

It surprised a cackle out of John, and he stood up, and slapped a manila folder on her desk. "That's the stuff we got from the hospital," he said. "The cases they've had. If it's a new drug, we should get hold of it before it goes out of control, right?"

"Right," she said. And then thought that of course he was sending her out on what could be called a *neighborhood gossip* tour. Nothing he considered dangerous.

It couldn't be just that he wanted to protect her. Not ten years after the end of their relationship. Besides, he hadn't shown in any way that he still cared for her. So it must be—had to be—that he still remembered her as a very incompetent rookie, and didn't really think she had changed.

She stared at the manila folder. Well, then. There was a remedy for that. She must go out and ... and prove to him that she could be entrusted with bigger and more interesting cases. Or ask for a transfer.

And it might come to the transfer. But for now she would take a chance at changing his mind.

She opened the folder and read the reports. The cases of extreme fatigue had started coming into the area hospitals two months ago, and they were all the same.

The people involved spanned a large variety of humanity, though they were all what could be called those who fell through the cracks of society: young and jobless, manual laborers of no exact abode, ex-cons, people who lived at the edge of the law, and a large number of the addled-and-drugged who made up the transient population of the city.

And all of them spent considerable time in Capitol Hill.

Capitol Hill, centered on Colfax Avenue, used to be the seedy heart of Denver. Even ten years ago, when Etta had joined the force, it was still—at best—a doubtful place, home to flop houses and low-income apartments, its streets populated by a mix of the working poor and the poor who had never worked at all. And the establishments along Colfax had been what you'd expect of the area: diners and bars catering to the low income patrons, pawn shops, tattoo parlors, and the occasional head shop or sex shop.

Now...

Over the last years Capitol Hill had gone a long way towards gentrification. Gone were the ex-police-officers and ex-military men who used to patrol the street at night to stop crime before it happened. Etta remembered them from her rookie days: big muscular men wearing T-shirts that read "Angels on Colfax" and acting like a female police officer needed protection, as much as anyone else.

They'd gone now, because the area wasn't nearly as dangerous anymore. And Etta had worked that part of town for the last five years straight.

Now she read the documents the hospital had given the police and frowned a little at recognizing some of the names of the regulars—and realizing some had vanished without her realizing. Well, in the last two months, she'd been busy with John coming here and...

Still she couldn't help but feel guilty that Joe-no-chin, or Deb-the-Stutterer had forever vanished from Colfax without her paying the slightest attention. They'd been homeless-and-doped with a bit of begging for Joe, and a bit of casual prostitution for Deb, on the side. Neither had been dangerous or prominent. Just people for whom Etta had bought a cup of coffee, now and then, people she'd cultivated to get information on the dangerous members of the community.

But—

But that they'd died and she'd never heard, and that they'd died in a bizarre way without her finding out till a month later, seemed subtly wrong.

The symptoms that had taken them to the hospital, and eventually killed them, seemed to be extreme fatigue, the kind of dehydration that you can get in certain marathon runners at the end of a run if they don't take care to hydrate, and also torn ligaments, and—Etta winced—skinned soles of feet, abraded from too much movement, too much friction.

Some of the younger people coming to the hospital with those symptoms hadn't died, though they'd taken days and days to recover. These, while recovering, often expressed a great wish to get away from the city, and spoke, confusedly, of dancing, or of some dance.

At first the doctors thought they were referring to some event, but since—

Since they'd come to think it was a praxis, some form of reaction to a drug. But even the most careful interrogation hadn't discovered anything about a new drug.

In the last page, almost casually, the doctors said that all of the patients showed the same tattoo of a vine on their right shoulder.

Etta chewed on her lip, while she thought. Night had fallen outside, or at least she judged it must have from the fact that lights had come on in the large room partitioned by grey cube partitions. Not that there was ever much light at her cube, which was located on the interior row, away from the windows.

She heard voices, smelled coffee brewing, and realized the night shift must have come in. They had their own cubes, over in another vast room of the nineteenth century building. That meant that John too would have left. And he probably wouldn't expect her to do anything about this case till tomorrow morning.

But Etta had other ideas. She'd go ahead and see if she could figure out anything. At any rate, Pete's Kitchen, the last of the old style greasy spoons on Colfax, served souvlaki, and she realized she was quite hungry.

She tucked the folder into her purse, which was a matter of jokes around the department, since it more closely resembled an old-fashioned doctor's black bag, and left, nodding at people on her way out.

She parked in Pete's Kitchen's parking lot, and walked around Race, to Colfax.

Pete's Kitchen, with the pig flipping pancakes on its neon sign, could have been found by a blind man by the smell of hot grease and Greek spices.

It was full, its glass-walled annex as crowded as the vinyl booths inside.

As Etta walked around the glassed part, she looked inside for someone she might know, who might give her some information on what was going on. But instead, she almost tripped on her potential informant, on the outside of the restaurant, sitting against the wall near the door.

He was a skinny kid who'd first shown up in Denver at the end of winter, and who'd quickly become a regular on Colfax. They called him Stringy Mike, and he had the sort of tick and nervous head movements that spoke of someone addicted to cocaine. But he was harmless, or nearly so. She wasn't sure how he lived, except by selling very small amounts of pot, and the recent legalization might have taken the floor out of that.

All the same, she was surprised to find him sitting there, with a baseball cap next to him, and a badly scrawled cardboard sign reading "Please Help." Well, to be honest, what the sign said was "Pleez Help" but she couldn't tell if that was ignorance or text-speak.

The second thing she noticed was that Stringy Mike looked tired.

Exhausted. *I wonder if he has a vine tattoo.* Aloud she said, "Hi, Mike. Come on inside. I'll get you a burger."

He looked up, and she got the impression he'd have jumped in surprise, if he had the strength to jump. He did look tired. Exhausted.

After a while, as though he were trying to hold an internal debate with himself, he said, "All right." And got up. As he walked into the diner, ahead of her, she noticed that he limped.

A middle-aged waitress led them to a small booth at the back, near the kitchen, and on the way to the bathroom, Mike sagged into the seat. His eyes were half closed by the time the waitress came around to take their order, and all he did was make a gesture to signify that Etta could order him whatever she wanted.

Etta noted that his clothes seemed more ragged than at any time she'd seen him in the past, and she wished she could check his shoes.

Over coffee and after eating a triple burger, he revived, at least to the point of no longer looking like he would fall asleep between fries. But her gentle prodding to find what he might know brought no information, and she decided to risk it all, "So, what about the dance?"

This time he did jump. Also, he half rose, and made as if to leave the booth. But she reached out and grabbed him by the wrist. "Stay," she said. "Tell me about it."

He shook his head. "There is nothing to tell."

"No? What is it? Where does it take place?"

He opened his mouth. He seemed to be trying, to the best of his ability, to speak, but no sound came. At last he said, "I can't. I can't. We can't. If we speak—to speak is to die."

And that was that. She couldn't get any other word out of him, and his struggle and inability to speak made her feel so guilty she'd bought him rice pudding and ice cream.

After he'd left she'd stayed at the table, trying to think over what she hadn't, in fact, found out. It seemed to her there was more than a drug at stake. Perhaps a cult?

She'd walked up and down Colfax, looking for other extremely tired beggars or transients, but she found none. In fact, the really weird thing was that there were no derelicts out, at all.

Granted, Capitol Hill and Colfax had changed and any given summer night, just after nightfall, it looked like a respectable, if artsy area. Most of the traffic out these days was not the prostitutes and drug addicts of, say, ten years ago. Instead, there were couples strolling around to the fashionable bookstores, the cool bars just opening up. There were even young families with kids in strollers.

But the thing about gentrification, Etta thought, was that you didn't quite clean up what was there before. You never did. Or not until the people who'd known the area as something else utterly moved on or passed away.

Instead, what you got was a glitzy, clean cover put over the edge of what was there before, and those who'd been in the area before, were often worse off than before.

She knew the places where bad things used to happen: the abandoned warehouse, the empty apartment buildings, the back alleys, the space behind the always-overfull dumpsters. Now the warehouses hosted a multitude of small shops on the ground floor, but the upstairs remained vacant and uncared for, with plywood over the windows. And the apartment buildings were cleaned up and renovated, but that meant the people who used to live in them could no longer afford them. And the alleys and the dumpsters... well, those would always be with them.

It was like seeing a beautiful scene painted on a crumbling wall. And you could still find derelicts if you looked carefully. Only she couldn't. And that absence disturbed her more than she could say.

Oh, sure, the restaurants and bars around here were now more expensive, and the apartments were out of the reach of most of the poor— but they still hung out around the familiar places. There were still soup kitchens and thrift stores and homeless shelters. So, where did all the needy go?

She walked up to the church where they gave out food this time of night, and there was no one outside it. The urban mission building looked similarly deserted.

Something was very wrong.

* * *

It got worse next morning.

She'd barely gulped down a cup of the station coffee—really, what did they make it with? Battery acid—when John came into her cube. She barely had time to look up, and he'd taken up a position, half-sitting at the corner of her desk. He looked exhausted. "What have you found?" he asked.

"How do you know I even looked?"

He shrugged his shoulders, minimally, as if to say he knew. She sighed. "Nothing much," and related what she'd discovered. "The thing is," she said. "I swear Stringy Mike would have told me if he could. He clearly couldn't. Then there are the vanishing homeless."

He gave her an almost-smile, which t somehow managed to make him look even more tired. "You know, many people would say that's something good. I mean, perhaps we finally managed to ship them all to the Springs."

She shook her head. "You don't understand," she said. "They have nowhere to go. And yet… they all vanished."

"Okay," he said. "Were they there when you first got to Colfax?"

She frowned up at him, trying to remember. The vagrants and derelicts were so much a part of Colfax she didn't notice them until they weren't there. But thinking, she could remember two guys talking by the alley when she parked, and a woman pushing a shopping cart along Race. "Yeah," she said. "But an hour later they were all gone. It was as though a pickup truck had come along, getting them all, you know. That couldn't have happened, right?"

"No, I doubt—" His cell phone rang, and he picked it up. His features grew grave as he listened. "Yeah," he said. "Got it. We might want to send someone…we might want to send someone." He slipped his phone in his pocket, frowning, looking like he was debating something with himself, then sighed. "I might as well tell you. Stringy Mike was found in front of East High School this morning. He was taken to emergency in an extreme state of exhaustion. Died a couple of minutes ago. I had asked them to call me—"

* * *

It was a desperate gamble, the sort of thing that a police investigator does when he or she runs out of all logical alternatives. Etta had run out of logical alternatives. She went to the morgue. She looked at Stringy Mike. He looked much younger and more innocent and much like he'd simply fallen asleep. While the young intern was rattling off about lesions and abrasions and horrible physiological effects, Etta could only think of the tattoo that had been found on all the victims. So she asked, "Does he have a tattoo?"

The intern stopped middle rattle, and looked at her, openmouthed, as though she'd asked him if the man had a nose. Then he said, in a tired voice, "They all have tattoos. I mean, everyone who is…all the ones who come in have tattoos. And usually are missing teeth." His look seemed to say that she must be very new to the police force, if she didn't know that.

She shrugged. "No, I mean a specific tattoo. Something in the reports I got said almost all the victims had a vine tattoo on their right shoulder."

"Oh? No one told me that. We didn't look. But we can."

He'd half-turned Stringy Mike over with one hand, and there on his shoulder, coiling delicately was what appeared to be a morning-glory vine, so perfectly delineated it might be alive.

"Say," the intern said. "That's a gorgeous tattoo. They normally don't have anything that fancy. My girlfriend has been talking about—"

But Etta interrupted him, "Can you hold him like that? I want to take a picture of that tattoo."

* * *

Colfax looked more cheerful during the day, and the homeless and transients were back, hanging out in the shadows, looking through dumpsters, begging from passerby.

It seemed to Etta only two things were different—they were moving as little as possible, and they all looked exhausted.

She started her own enquiry about the vine with them, but all of them acted just like Stringy Mike when she had asked him about the dance: like they wanted to speak, but couldn't. Like something was physically preventing them from speaking.

So she started looking at tattoo parlors on Capitol Hill. Like the diners that had become cleaner and more upscale—though she still had trouble accepting the fact that now Pete's Kitchen had marble-tiled bathrooms— the tattoo parlors had made the transition to a more upscale clientele. She went from one to the other, pushing past middle class couples come to make their love permanent in ink, and showed them the picture of Stringy Mike's shoulder.

After three of them had told her they'd never seen anything like it, she started wondering if perhaps she was wrong and this was not local work.

And then there was the fourth. They also hadn't done the work, but they talked: "It looks like the work of the creepy guy down the street."

"Creepy guy?" Considering she was facing a tall blond with abundant moustaches and a broken nose, who could have passed for a retired boxer and who wore full sleeve tattoos of dragons, she wondered who he'd consider creepy. He didn't look like the kind to be easily intimidated.

But he shook his head and said, "He has weird teeth. That serrated stuff."

"Serrated?"

"You know, they have them filed to points. And he looks skinnier than he should be... I don't know how to explain. Like he doesn't have the normal complement of flesh and bones. And all the women with him look the same, like they're too tall and stretchy, like the old Barbie dolls, you know, not quite real. And they're all blonde, and have this glazed look. But man, he sure can lay on the ink. Not that he does it... I mean, he hasn't stolen any business from us. He just seems to put this on all the homeless and the addicts. It's weird, man." He'd given Etta an odd look. "If I were you, I'd stay away from him. The place has the feel of a cult or something."

"Yeah," she said. "But I can't stay away. You see, I'm a police officer."

* * *

Creepy didn't even half-begin to describe it. The tattoo parlor was in the bottom floor of a building with boarded windows above. Unlike the other tattoo parlors, it had no sign proclaiming its name, nothing to identify it by.

Etta went in past a very dirty glass door, into a little room that ended in a grimy curtain. She cleared her throat, and after a while, a man came from inside. He was exactly like the last tattoo artist had described him. It didn't seem possible for his slender body to hide a full complement of viscera and bones.

As a police officer, Etta had seen her share of cocaine-slim derelicts, but this was skinniness that would require plastic surgery.

She showed him the picture on the cover and he nodded and smiled, and she got a look at his teeth. She took an involuntary step back. They didn't look like teeth that had been filed to a point. More like shark teeth, growing row on row.

But he said, "Yeah, I did that. Who? The skinny kid? Well, that's too bad. Come on in and I'll show you—"

Etta was trained. She should have been aware of someone coming up behind her. She would have been aware of someone coming up behind her, except that—of course—there was a wall there, and people didn't walk through walls. She had the sense of movement there – behind and over her left shoulder. And then something cool had touched her neck. And she'd collapsed.

* * *

She blinked, trying to clear grit from her eyes. And realized she was leaning against a wall, and tied up. And the guy with shark teeth was staring at her. "There," he told her. He came around and untied her. She was in the little room, past the curtain. Her shoulder hurt. She felt like she was coming up out of a drugged-out sleep, half-awake, and still dreaming. She remembered being…drugged? But what had they done to her?

"It's not a good idea," she said, hearing her own voice sound distant and robotic. "To drug police officers."

The man laughed and she had a glimpse of row upon row of sharp teeth. Just like a shark. He couldn't be human. "No," he said. "But you aren't drugged. It was just a little thing to make you sleep, so we could give you a beautiful tattoo like the one you asked about." He went and got a mirror, and brought it around to allow her to look at her shoulder.

They'd removed her T-shirt, but she still had her bra on. And there, next to the bra strap was a beautiful coiling vine, like the one poor Mike had worn.

A cold shiver went up Etta's spine, and she would probably be panicking, save for the remnants of the drug in her system. But what could a tattoo do to her?

She still felt woozy from the soporific, but she'd be damned if she let them see it. She'd been looking after herself for a long time.

"So you've marked me as if I belonged to your cult. What do you think that does?"

He laughed, a strange laughter that sounded like nothing so much as metal on metal. "You'll see."

* * *

Why was Etta dancing? She knew where she was. She even remembered coming there. Sometime between nightfall and 9:00p.m., she'd found herself walking back to Colfax, and up the fire escape to the room upstairs from the unmarked tattoo parlor.

Everyone was there, all the derelicts she'd missed from the street. Young and old, grey and thin or menacing and muscular, they were all there, dancing around and around, in a dance to an inaudible tune.

It's magic, Etta thought, and before her mind could shut out the thought, she thought that the tattoo artist looked like an elf on the cover of all those fantasy books. She'd never heard about shark teeth, but elves weren't all Tolkien had cracked them up to be. Not if you read the really old legends. And then there was—

The vine. It clearly had dragged her here. Magical tattoos, magical marks of any kind weren't that rare. Nor were stories of people kidnapped to work for elves all night long. Or to dance, for that matter. Wasn't there a story of some princesses?

She looked past the milling, hopping, dancing crowd of derelicts, and found the elf—she'd call him that, at least—with a woman who looked like him, standing side by side and surveying the crowd.

And from behind her came a whisper, in a familiar voice, "What possessed you to get the damn tattoo."

Without stopping the dance—she couldn't—she turned around and faced John, who was also dancing, dancing round and round, next to her.

"John," she said.

"Shhh," he said. "If I hadn't gone to your place, to ask you if you wanted to grab something to eat. If I hadn't followed you. You see, I started to suspect it was that tattoo too, and I asked around, but I didn't get one. I wasn't that stupid."

"I wasn't either," she said. "I wasn't either." She lowered her voice to a whisper. "They knocked me out and gave it to me."

His eyes widened. "I saw it in a book, you know. The vine. And I had sort of figured it out, so when I saw you walking here …I could shake you. You should have told me about the tattoo parlor, not gone in."

"I'm a police officer," she said. "You can't protect me from my job."

"I will protect you, if I can," he said. "Don't you know tonight is midsummer's night?"

She looked at him, in puzzlement, still dancing, round and round. He danced along with her.

"Midsummer's night is when the elves pay the price of their immortality," he said. "The newest one to join their circle gets taken— they used to think the devil took him or her. And that allows them to live longer. All of this, this dance, all of it gives more power to their magic. And I'd guess they move from city to city, before anyone can notice them too much, and use up the derelict population in the run up to midsummer, when they capture someone they can use for the exchange of their own life. It has to be someone young and healthy enough, see. It had to be you."

Out of nowhere, so it seemed, the clap of midnight sounded. The derelicts stopped dancing and the elf laughed. "The hour is upon us," he said. "Now comes time for the sacrifice to be paid to the Ever-Living one."

It seemed to Etta that the room filled with dark grey fog, that the fog formed into claws, and reached for her.

She felt as one touched her, as though ice were injected in her arm. And then John's arms came around her.

The entire room screamed. Derelicts came for them, clawing and fighting. Skinny hands dug at John's arms. Nails like claws tore at his flesh.

"I won't let you go," he said. "Hold on to me and don't let go. As soon as midnight is done sounding, the elves will have lost. There is nothing they can do, if I won't let you go. You see, I don't have the tattoo. I don't belong to them. And I won't let you go."

It seemed to take forever, the twelve resounding claps of midnight. But as long as they took, they passed, the last one echoing through the huge, dilapidated building.

Etta smelled sweat and blood, and heard a loud moan. The derelicts seemed to be waking up, confused about why they were there.

There were cleared throats, mutters, as they drifted out of the room.

It seemed like in no time at all the room was empty and very cold. She looked at John's arms. "You're all scratched," she said.

"It will heal," he said.

In the corner of the room there were two dead people. No. People was perhaps too much of an overstatement. They were the man with shark teeth and the beautiful blonde woman who'd been with him. In death they looked even less human. Waxen, like discarded dolls.

"They didn't pay the fee, you see, and whatever power kept them alive, collected."

Of common accord, they left the corpses behind and navigated down the fire escape, on shaky, tired legs. "I thought it was better to come in and pretend to be charmed than to come in guns blazing," he said. "I didn't want to believe it was enchantment, but I didn't see what else it could be. So I figured I'd pretend, because if it was enchantment there was a way to get you out. Tons of stories and ballads about it."

"I'm glad you figured it out," she said. "But you know, I really am not that incompetent a rookie. You don't need to guard me."

"I wasn't guarding a rookie," he said. "And I know you're not one. You're a competent officer. I know your record. But you're still Henrietta, and Etta, I've never loved anyone else. I was a young idiot. If I don't insist you leave the force, could we give it another try?"

Her mouth felt dry, which was odd because her eyes felt very moist. "We could take it a day at a time and try," she said. "If you're agreeable. Sometimes even I need someone I can trust."

Take One at a Rolling Donut
Brady Allen

> O rose, who dares to name thee?
> No longer roseate now, nor soft, nor sweet,
> But pale, and hard, and dry, as
> stubblewheat,—
> Kept seven years in a drawer, thy titles
> shame thee.
> --Elizabeth Barrett Browning, "A Dead
> Rose"

Rose Holmes liked to drive fast, and she liked to have the windows down. She had an old gray Buick Skylark—a '72—with a big-but-quiet engine, and she liked to feel it thrum, liked to feel the car buck forward in sex-machine ferocity when she pressed the accelerator.

She hummed along the interstate, doing eighty-five, passing cars right and left, never once using her turn signal for a lane change. She wore jean cut-offs and a Willie Nelson T-shirt. Her reddish-black hair swirled around her, medusa-like, and threatened to catch fire on the tip of the cigarette that was protruding from her lips like a cancerous white worm.

An Alice in Chains song fought its way through the factory-installed speakers: "Rooster." Rose drumbeat her hand lazily on the top of the steering wheel. She was not entirely sure of the words but sang along anyhow, the cigarette bobbing up and down between her lips. This song made her think of a giant crowing cock, his red comb glistening like blood on top of his head, his feathers bristling, and he had fangs snaggled throughout his beak.

Rose could make *anything* morbid or perverted.

In her mind, all of those Seussian creatures in *There's a Wocket in My Pocket* should have a big, holy-humping monster orgy. A wocket in my pocket? If that wasn't a sexual euphemism, what was? She envisioned a dong-shaped creature—there's a gassol in my asshole!

Rose giggled, smiled. Felt good.

She wasn't sure exactly where she was going yet.

Away.

She knew *that* for sure—she was going *away*, leaving her hometown behind. Family. Boyfriend of seven years, on and off.

She wanted to do something amazing. Wanted to make a name for herself on the road. Leave a trail behind her so long and so incredible that it'd end up preceding her soon enough.

But beyond that, it was up in the air.

There was a cooler behind the passenger seat, and it was filled with ice and Coors. A brown paper sack was nestled next to it, and it contained two bottles of Kilbeggan Irish whiskey. The booze would help her get through the shit-ass Chicago or St. Louis drive, or through whatever big city was along the route she chose to take.

She *had* to have the liquor for that. Big city traffic scared the holy fuck out of her. She liked it wide open like it was here in Ohio on I-70. Cars spaced out, three lanes at her disposal. Using every lane like she'd use an eager, horn-dog boy.

Besides airing out her car in the wide-open, there were other things that got Rose going. Alcohol was one. Sex was another. But these things, though necessary she guessed, were not as fulfilling as manipulating the accelerator and the steering wheel, while smelling the motor oil and freshly-mown grass outside her windows.

And she liked poetry and fiction. Especially poetry. *That* was another thing. Fragments, bits and pieces, some entire poems—it all rattled around in her skull, day after day, night after night. Classic poems, contemporary, famous poets, people whose names she couldn't remember, it was all up there somewhere, an entire world of words inside the colorful dust jacket of her mind.

A huge barn off to her left had bright red letters on it: *Happy 4th! The Lewis Family*. A combine was parked alongside it, and a few cows milled around the field.

Well, a big fucking happy Fourth right back atcha, Lewis family, Rose thought, giggling. She was a frequent giggler, usually as the result of her own screwy wit.

A farm smell, manure, was now mingling—rudely—with the motor oil and cut grass. Rose wrinkled her nose. It smelled worse than her father's morning constitution. He'd always dropped the bomb right before she had to go in there to get ready for school each morning. Certainly not the only reason she'd moved out and moved in with Dickie, her kind-of-sort-of boyfriend, but one of them. Dickie (his real name was Richard) preferred mornings for the porcelain plopper, too, just like her father, but he wasn't so shithole ripe.

But now she was leaving them both behind. And her stepmom and grandmother and little sister, too.

It would be a lie to say there wasn't a twinge of loneliness. Loneliness, sure, a natural reaction. That was human. But, if someone were to ask her if there was *regret* for just packing up and skipping out, she'd have to say nope-sir-eeee. None. It was her life. And the road—a road leading anywhere—was calling her.

And if she had stopped to tell any of them she was going—Dickie, her dad, her grandmother, her sister—they'd have tried to talk her out of it, and she might have let them. She was twenty-four, and the longer she stayed in Stairway Falls—it was a town with magnetic repellence (she liked that play on words)—the less chance she'd have of ever getting out. There were things to do, places to go. She'd never seen the Rocky Mountains, never been on the West Coast, never been to the bayous, and never driven down one of those long, straight lonely desert roads she'd seen in so many movies. She wanted to do all of this, and in her mind she was turning the car in every direction at once, the four wheels eventually flying off, one rolling north, each of the others east, south and west.

She looked around her. Everything looked so clean and so new. This was a road she'd traveled before, but never had she looked at it from such a perspective. All the shapes and colors seemed edged—pastels and dark hues, soft and harsh, pale and bright melting together in a surreal sort of happiness.

She felt alive now.

The horizon was full of sudden clusters of green where you couldn't tell where one tree ended and the next began, and random smatterings of buildings popped up here and there like tiny and sudden settlements. Such was Ohio.

She saw a bright green and yellow BP sign. Rose's last cigarette was flaming to its end, and she took the next exit to get some more smokes. "Might as well get a goddamn carton," she whispered.

Goddamn—she didn't even like thinking that word, much less saying it out loud. She wasn't a Christian, not really, not at all, she guessed, but there was still some fundamental spirituality in her that made her think of God or *a* god and be leery of him... or her. She had no worry for her *actions*—which many people would find problem with—but some hesitancy with the use of God's name. Her actions, she felt *no* guilt for them, *none*: the sex, the drinking, the occasional weed... the general hardcore-hard-ass attitude. But shit, she was going to have a hard time sleeping tonight because of what she'd just said.

She looked through the windshield, across the exit ramp and into the sky. *I'm sorry. And thank you for the road.*

* * *

Rose watched other people as she leaned against her Buick and pumped the gas. An old man, seventy or so, plaid shirt buttoned up to his neck, tried several times without success to swipe his card for "pay at the pump" off to her right. She was just about to help him when he turned tail toward the mini-mart. Judging by the scowl on his face, she didn't guess whatever greasy-faced kid was in there was going to get an earful of politeness. The man had left the radio on in his station wagon, and she could hear the Reds baseball announcers and periodic crowd noise.

A woman in a navy blue, power business suit was fueling her Mazda Miata. What a silly-looking little car, Rose thought. It looked like a toy. The woman's hair was pulled up in a harsh bun, her lips pursed, her eyes covered by sunglasses. Rose took her for a lesbian, or at least a woman who might consider it. She was probably married with no kids, though. Probably had her tubes tied from the start because kids would just fill her life with more unwanted hassle. She was a definite bitch—and her husband probably did all of the housework and licked her feet when she demanded it.

On the other side of Rose's pump, a young man, solid and rugged looking, certainly in his twenties, filled his pickup truck, while his girlfriend or wife waited in the car. Rose eyed him, obvious and flirtatious. She held her lips in a smirk. The muscles in his forearms bunched as he worked the pump. He had a day or two's growth of beard, and his shirt, some sort of red polo shirt for a job, it seemed, was unbuttoned at the neck to reveal a soft smattering of hair. He had bright blue eyes, and he glanced at her intermittently, nervous but interested, hesitant because of the cutesy bleached-blonde appendage in the truck's cab.

Rose wanted to have a little fun with him.

She stepped across the hose, straddling it, her ass pressed against the trunk of the car. She held the hose with one hand, sliding her fingers loosely back and forth, grinding her backside against the car. She winked at him and then rolled her eyes up in her head in a mock orgasmic flutter. She heard the Reds crowd cheer through the speakers of the plaid-shirted old man's station wagon.

This boy couldn't hide *anything*. He was trying to pretend he wasn't looking, but his face was flushed red. The girl in the truck had her nose in a magazine. She was wearing a matching red polo shirt.

"Is that your girlfriend?" Rose asked, almost whispering. The girl's window was cracked slightly, but she didn't appear to be paying attention. Rose squeezed the hose between her legs.

The Buick was full, and the pump clicked off. "Oh," she said, "that was fast. Too fast." She glanced directly, obviously, at his crotch. He adjusted the pleat of his khakis. "I didn't even, you know, I didn't... yet."

Rose stepped back over the hose, slid the nozzle into place on the pump. She put a little extra shake in her steps when she moved around the pump and by him, angling toward the mini-mart.

It was cool inside, and goose pimples broke out on Rose's flesh. The cooler thrummed and jingle-jangled in the back of the store. It wasn't a greasy-faced kid behind the counter; it was a big, round, smiley-faced woman in her fifties. Rose brushed by the old-timer in the plaid shirt, and he went out the door behind her. Two other people were in line. She milled around and looked at the Pringles and Combos for a moment, waiting for the rugged boy to come in and pay. She moved around to the candy bar rack and looked outside. He was walking toward the store now, and she grabbed a Snickers, timing her move to the counter just right, stepping up behind him in the line.

She unwrapped the Snickers, took a bite and breathed heavily, purposely, against his back, admiring the muscles in his shoulders. "Oh," she said. "Oh, Jesus, this is gooooood. Mmmm."

The boy shifted his weight, digging into his pants pocket for some money. Rose leaned in even closer and got up on her tiptoes. "Do you want a blow job?" she asked, and she took another bite of her Snickers.

The boy turned to her halfway. "What?" he said out of the corner of his mouth. He was terribly flushed.

Rose put her tongue in her cheek and rolled it around in exaggeration. "Do you?" she asked. "Want one?"

"One what? A Snickers? I didn't hear you."

"A blow job," she grinned.

"Are you kidding?" His eyes sparkled. Excitement. Worry. A wonderful combination, Rose thought.

The line moved ahead of them. The boy stared at her, his face growing redder by the millisecond.

"Sir?" the jolly woman at the counter said. "You ready?" The boy didn't budge; he just stared at Rose. She liked that.

"Meet me by the restrooms," Rose whispered. "I'll be there after I pay."

"Sir? You get gas?" the woman said again, still smiley.

The boy paid and went outside, eyeing Rose as he stepped through the glass door. Rose got a two-pack of Winstons, paid for those, her Snickers and her gas. She tossed the Snickers in the trash as she stepped outside.

* * *

The restrooms were built into the side of the car wash. The boy was leaning into his truck, saying something to the girl in there. She wasn't even looking up from her magazine, really, and he shut the door and headed around to the restrooms, maybe in the truck's sight line, maybe not. Rose wasn't sure. And didn't care.

Rose tossed the cigarettes in the window of her Buick as she passed it and walked directly to the women's restroom. It was unlocked and she stepped inside, leaning against the door. The boy was hanging around the entrance to the men's room. Rose curled her finger and motioned him toward her. He hesitated, glanced toward his truck—the girl *still* had her nose in the magazine—and made a beeline toward her.

Rose grabbed him by the shirt and pulled him inside, shutting the door behind them and pretending to turn the lock. That made it more exciting.

The room held one sink, one stall and a paper towel dispenser.

He was breathing heavily. "Are you serious?" he asked. "You're going to—"

"Is that your wife?" Rose asked. "You're what? Twenty-five?"

"Twenty-six. No, it ain't my wife."

"Girlfriend?"

"Okay."

"Okay what?"

"We work together. Okay, she is. Kind of."

"Yeah, I've got a 'kind-of-sort-of,' too."

"Yeah?"

"Take down your pants."

"Just like that?"

Rose reached for his fly, pulled the zipper down, pushed the boy gently against the sink basin.

"Goddamnit. You're just gonna suck—"

"Don't say that."

"I'm sorry, but you're just going to do it right here. Now?"

"Don't say 'GD.'"

"Sorry. I'm sorry." He unfastened the button, pulled down his khakis and boxer briefs.

A box cutter fell from his pocket. Rose picked it up and slipped it in the back pocket of her cut-offs.

"It's for my job," he said. She noticed the stitching on his shirt: *Reardon Imports and Packaging.*

Rose watched his dick rise right in front of her. It was short and pudgy, pretty thick. He wagged it at her.

Jesus, Rose *hated* "the wag." It was the most fucking annoying thing a boy could do. "Listen," she said, "Don't wag—"

The restroom door swung open, and the blonde appendage walked in, at first oblivious, and then furious when she did a triple glance at Rose's face, his face, and his penis. "Louie? What—Louie?! What the goddamn is—why?" The blonde stood there, leaning against the open door, and a ray of sunlight fell across Rose's face.

Louie (Rose thought that named reeked of a man who would beat his wife and kids one day) just stood there, his pants and underwear around his thighs, his penis falling, defeated—there was no sense in pulling his pants up, that's what Rose guessed must've been going through his mind. He stuttered: "She was—Tonya, I didn't—we didn't—"

"Gawd-*damn*!" Tonya said.

"Don't say that," Rose said, not moving an inch, holding her ground comfortably.

"Who in *hell* are you?!" Tonya asked.

"Betty," Rose said, and she wasn't sure why.

"Louie, who is she?!"

"She said her name was Betty, I guess." Louie finally became conscious of his pants again and pulled them and his boxer briefs up, not even zipping up or fastening the button but just pulling his shirt over them.

Tonya looked back toward Rose. "Betty? *Betty.* Why are you in here with my man's penis?"

"His penis came with him," Rose said.

"You *bitch*," Tonya said, and she reared back to hit Rose.

Rose ducked low, dodging the blow, and she threw her shoulder into Tonya's stomach, driving her against the door, knocking the wind out of her. Rose ran for the Buick, jumped onto the hood and slid across, opened the driver's door and gunned the engine.

She was about to lay some rubber in the lot, but she looked over and saw Tonya on her ass, slumped against the open door. Louie was standing over her, no longer red, but white as a triple-bleached sheet. She could tell by the heave of Tonya's shoulders that she was either crying or still trying to get her breath.

Rose put the Skylark into drive and idled over toward them. The blonde woman slowly stood up, and Louie didn't look like he was ever going to be able to move again. He was terrified.

Rose reached over and rolled the passenger side window all the way down. "I'm sorry," she said. "I wasn't going to suck him. Probably not, anyhow." She looked at Louie while she said this, and she saw some kind of hurt come across his features. It was true, though (and she felt a little bad for him, for them); she mostly just wanted to see if she could get him to do it. She definitely wasn't going to do it after "the wag."

"Gawd-*damnit*!" Tonya yelled, and she pulled a box cutter from her own pocket.

This time Rose did lay some rubber.

* * *

God would not have liked the phase of life she was beginning that day. It was possible that he wanted to give her a chance to set upon the right path, but Rose didn't reckon she was arrogant enough to think that of her and God's relationship. Theirs was more one of leaving each other alone: she didn't follow all his bossy rules, and he didn't take the time to answer prayers.

The word that escaped her lips just as she was taking a bite of a donut in a quaint café not far from the small city where Louie had given her "the wag," though, *was* "Goddamn."

It was expelled due to the complete shock and surprise at what she was seeing on the television mounted in the corner, up near the ceiling. It seemed that someone had cut off a young man's genitals at a gas station and hung them from the antennae on his truck, after having slit his throat, leaving him to bleed in a gas station restroom. His girlfriend had given the police the first name of the girl who'd done it and explained that she'd left in an old Buick, maybe from the 1970's. The media was calling her "Box Cutter Betty."

Rose wondered at this. There were no photos so far, no license place given that she knew of.

That bitch killed her own boyfriend?

Rose tossed some money on the counter and wrapped her three donuts in some napkins, heading out to her car. She got in and pulled around to the side of the building, away from the road and the windows. She swapped the black Willie Nelson T-shirt for a pink one that said "Pussy Surprise," and she put her hair up high in a bun.

She sat there for a moment, pulling small pieces from a glazed donut and nibbling on them. For some reason, she found herself thinking back to high school. There had been a few suspensions. One of the most memorable was when their science teacher, Mrs. Goodbottom (yes, that was really her name), had asked if anyone could explain the reproductive habits of the porcupine, and Rose had stood up, squeezed her tits, and said, "I'll do it for the sexual revolution! The answer is, with their pricks!"

They do it with their pricks. Clever girl.

Rose had been so horny through most of high school that she could barely sit still. Nobody thought it was weird for the guys, but girls like her were proclaimed sluts who had "unhealthy sex drives." The safe sex poster in the high school health classrooms in the early 90's had been a big tease, just daring adventure.

But now she wondered if she should be scared. Was there any way she could actually be blamed for—Jesus, Jesus God—for cutting off the guy's nuts and all? She became conscious of the box cutter in her back pocket then, and she removed it and laid it on the seat next to the donuts.

She felt a brief pang of emotion in her chest for Louie, naïve and rugged man-child, despite the "wag." He deserved better than nuts-on-a-truck for a way to exit the wide, wacky world. She even felt a brief loyalty to him and considered going after that Tonya cunt and kicking the crap out of her. She envisioned cutting the gal's tits off and gagged.

Rose reached behind the seat and grabbed a bottle of Kilbeggan. She twisted off the cap and took a long, hard pull from the bottle. Her eyes watered, and she felt better instantly.

She cranked both the driver and passenger-side windows down to let some semblance of a breeze flow, and after another swig from the bottle, she didn't want the donuts anymore. She chucked them out her window toward a copse of trees beyond the parking lot. They landed next to a trash container just short of them.

A police car pulled into the café parking lot. Rose screwed the lid on the Kilbeggan bottle and slid it under the front seat. It was a highway patrol car she saw now. The driver started to park in the front but then made a quick adjustment and pulled around to the side where Rose was parked. Rose loved her Buick, but old cars like this always drew attention.

The patrolman stopped with a space between them, shut off his engine, and then climbed out of the car. Rose pretended to be fixing her hair in the rearview mirror. She could see him looking toward her in her peripheral vision. He stood there for too long. She finally looked his way and waved. He tipped his wide-brimmed hat and waved back and then walked around front of the café.

Her urge was to tear ass out of there, but something caught her eye.

It was a squirrel.

And it was interested in her donuts.

It was moving in that paranoid and twitchy way that squirrels do, like he was tweaked out a bit, and he wanted to grab the one whole donut that was left.

He lifted the sucker onto its side, did a dramatic hyper-twitch, and then sent the donut rolling along the parking lot. A person couldn't have done it better with practice.

But it did not appear that Mr. Squirrel had wanted this to happen. He chased the donut down and lunged at it like he was trying to molest it on the fly, missed (weren't squirrels blessed with fine motor skills?), collected himself, and then jumped on it and knocked it down, pressing it up tightly against his body, wrapped up between his little limbs, all the while still twitching like he was getting his nuts off with it. Finally, he managed to run off into the copse of trees, donut secured.

Now Rose would leave. She was just fixing to start the engine, when a thick-fingered hand grabbed the window frame of her car, and the patrolman said, "Everything okay with you, ma'am?"

He was friendly-looking, tall with a big ol' round head, clean-shaven, and he was holding a sack of something from the café and a coffee in his other hand.

"Yeah," Rose said.

"Coming from somewhere or heading?" he said. He nodded toward the cooler and her big duffel bag in the back.

"Oh," Rose said. She paused very briefly, thinking. "I'm heading back home. Had a get-together with old friends."

"Where's home?"

Was she being questioned?

"Stairway Falls," she said. "Ohio." She suddenly couldn't remember if she'd crossed over into Indiana.

He leaned over and smiled in at her. "I know it's here in Ohio," he said.

He drummed his fingertips on the open window for a second. And then he said, "Uh oh!"

Rose avoided acting startled, though she was, and she said, "What?"

"Box Cutter Betty!" he said and then pointed to the box cutter lying on the passenger seat. He laughed, then, a deep, soulful laugh.

Rose measured her words and spoke calmly. "I saw about that on the TV inside," she said. "That's crazy. I hope they find her."

The patrolman laughed again. "It didn't last long," he said. "They called it off a few minutes ago. The girlfriend confessed to... the, uh... castration."

Rose spoke slowly and calmly again. "Oh, that's good."

"Well, listen," he said. "Be careful on your trip back, alone and all. Especially wearing a shirt like that. A lot of men out there with no responsibility."

"Okay, thank you."

He walked over, got into his car, and drove away after a moment of fiddling around.

It was strange. Rather than feel a sense of relief, Rose felt a little bit disappointed, unfulfilled. She waited until the patrolman must've been a good ways away, and then she lit a Winston, started her car, and pulled away toward the westbound ramp.

She drove until she reached it and hit the interstate doing over seventy. She'd driven a few miles and had been sipping from the Kilbeggan a bit when a big truck threw a hubcap, and it went spinning off along the side of the road. Rose pictured the driver leaping from the truck cab and chasing it down, all jittery and twitchy like the squirrel back at the café, before finally gathering it in and wrapping his legs around it and humping it to hell and back.

She'd never fucked a trucker. There had to be some good-looking ones that didn't employ "the wag." She'd hang onto the box cutter for a funny threat, just in case.

The Devil's Own Luck
Danielle Ackley-McPhail

I left the knives behind. Everything I had left in life has been ripped away because I left the knives behind. Pain born of more than exile tore at Paolo's chest worse than the frantic clawing of lungs in vacuum. He was sixteen and all alone in the universe. Too drained to resist such despair, he huddled in the little pocket of space he'd carved out in the center of the stacked cargo. Storage containers shielded him top, bottom, and sides as he gave in to the silent tears burning their way past his frozen soul. He leaned against the molded plastic crates, not even caring if they shifted with his weight, halfheartedly wishing they would tumble, crushing his body as life had done his spirit. His sister would have scolded him.

How he wished by everything he'd once held sacred that she still could.

Terlinda's compressed ashes rested heavy against his heart. He tempted fate by keeping them close, but could not bring himself to let her go. The remnants of her physical self would surely draw her *mulò*—her ghost—to him. Would that be a blessing, or a curse? He could not say. All he knew was the black velvet pouch containing the cube of her remains wrapped in her favorite scarf served as the sole touchstone left to Paolo's life before he'd killed a man, sliced him from neck to nut sac with antique knives passed down in his family for generations. Knives as distinctly Romani as the nanite-infused tattoos scrolling every inch of Paolo's skin. Knives he had left buried deep in the corpse.

Might as well have signed his name.

None among the Kalderăs Clan held blame against him, but the Rom had a saying: *family before all others.* When a friendly dockmaster warned them that the military base on Xerxes had deployed forces in pursuit of the Caravan, Paolo slipped away at the next refueling station, determined to protect his remaining loved ones. He'd made it as far as the outpost orbiting Io before the grunts caught up with him. After that it had been one near miss after another.

Until now. This encounter could not yet be called a miss.

His bitter heart resisted anything even vaguely resembling prayer to any faith. Instead his thoughts maintained a silent litany: *I'm not here. I'm not here. I'm not here.* Though there seemed little reason to cling to life, of one thing he was certain...no one would claim justice on him for the righteous vengeance he had wrought. Tran did not deserve to be mourned. He did not deserve to be remembered, save as a warning to others.

Barely realized at first, Paolo's breathing increased, growing louder and more aggressive as he thought of the man who had brutalized and killed his sister. The sound filled the small space where Paolo hid until he worried it would filter out to the storage compartment beyond.

He buried his rage before it betrayed him. Slowing his heartbeat and muffling his breath, he curled his body into a compact ball as only a trained contortionist could, head nestled in the pocket formed of arms and tucked knees. *I'm not here. I'm not here. I'm not here.* Weary beyond bearing, Paolo lost himself in sleep's oblivion as the phrase repeated in his head.

* * *

The subtle sound of engines cycling down to dock woke him.

Crap! He couldn't believe he'd overslept. Instinct ordered him to scramble for his post before Terlinda gave him more grief about penalty fees for missing their scheduled docking window. It was her favorite gripe. Swearing beneath his breath lest she hear him, Paolo jerked, snapping out of the knot he'd huddled in. Or tried to, anyway.

A nova erupted in his head as the back of his skull thudded against something hard, and his foot—likewise striking an unyielding surface—stung with the impact. Immediately he curled back into a tight ball. *What the hell?* Where was he? Why wasn't he in his bunk? Drawing nearly spent air through clenched teeth, he resisted the urge to groan as he tried to fight past the pain. His lungs strained and more than sleep fogged his brain. It took him several long moments to realize what had happened. The reality he'd retreated from.

As he became more alert, Paolo examined the signs his subconscious had already interpreted. At some point during his ill-advised nap the crates he'd hidden among had been loaded on a ship going God-knew-where.

"*Mama dracului!*" Paolo hissed the curse in his native Romani, *the devil's mother.*

Tears stung his eyes and he found himself close to his limit. Ready to give up...to embrace his fate. The Clans had a word: *Prikàza.* It meant retribution visited on one who upset the spiritual balance. In other words, the Devil's own luck. With each misfortune that befell him, Paolo found it harder to believe he was not such a one, though he could not believe Terlinda's *mulò* responsible, as legends claimed.

Locking his jaw, he banished thoughts of ill luck, lest they invite more, and with tight, controlled motions, maneuvered in his hiding space until he crouched by the end he had staged as his exit. Had the placement shifted during loading? Was he even now trapped with no room to move the loose container out of his way? He had to try as his cocoon of air swiftly soured, each breath ending in a low, harsh cough. Taking care not to press against any other surface but the one that should be safe, Paolo cautiously pushed outward. A faint scrape froze him.

Slower. He must not draw attention if any were around to hear. That bright and shiny thought set off another wave of worry. Sound or silence, it wouldn't matter if his exit opened in plain sight. Gritting his teeth, he forced the concern away, not ready to allow fear to literally suffocate him. Again he set his shoulder to the crate. Fraction of an inch by fraction of an inch, he edged it out from under the burden of its brothers. Even were he willing to shove his way out, it would not have been possible. It took all of his strength just to shift the container in these careful measures.

And suddenly, even his strength was not enough.

Paolo clenched his eyes tight and swallowed his panic. He forced himself to run his hand slowly along the surface of the crate in search of any detail that might reveal the issue. As his fingers reached the bottom edge he had the answer. He'd pushed the obstacle far enough that it had tilted infinitesimally, wedging the crate between the pallet it rested on and the container above. Paolo settled back on his heels and considered the matter.

If he pressed upward enough to free the edge he could destabilize the tower of crates, bringing them down on top of him. Shoving with more force until the one stuck came free could cause the same fate. If he waited, surely he'd expend the last of the air before anyone would chance to find him (such would be a typical *Prikàza*). But…if he shifted his pressure… like so…and nudged down and out on the tilted edge…*like so…*

The crate landed with a soft thud onto what he presumed was a cargo bay floor. Paolo braced for what seemed the inevitable, but the remaining stack did not, in fact, topple down on him. He drew several deep, shuddering breaths of fresher air into his lungs and grimly resisted the urge to drop prostrate in the space now sufficient to accommodate the length of him. He was not free of his unexpected prison yet, and even if he were, it courted danger to remain in the open. After resting a few moments he put his shoulder to the crate. Though both his lungs and his muscles burned, he once more pushed, this time in an effort to clear enough of a gap to crawl past the barrier. For a moment he feared himself trapped after all, but finally, with much straining, he created a gap just barely wide enough. Paolo silently thanked both his ancestors and carnival training equally as he contorted his muscles and turned his head, flattening sufficiently that he cleared the crates, losing no more than a layer or two of skin on either ear.

He slid his back along the top of the displaced crate and carefully drew out his legs until he moved free of the confinement. As he lay a moment in the near-dark, soundlessly catching his breath before he attempted to shove the crate back into place, he heard a noise; a hard *thunk* as of a hatch opening, followed by the sound of someone slowly clapping. An LED mega-cluster above his head came to instant life. Paolo tensed, his eyes squeezed closed against the sudden light. Spent, he wasn't quick enough to roll off of the crate. Before he could drop out of sight or reach, a firm grip pinned him in place.

"Consider me impressed," a man's gruff voice said from just above him. "For that matter, consider yourself impressed as well." A thick, calloused fist slammed into Paolo's jaw.

* * *

Paolo woke to jags of pain burning across various points of his body, but predominantly his jaw and his shoulders. The jaw was obvious. Being knocked senseless hadn't left him unable to remember how he'd gotten that way. But the shoulders…it took him a moment to figure that out. By the spread of his arms, it felt like someone had slid a roughly three-foot length of thick conduit across the base of his back and lashed his wrists around the ends, like a makeshift stock. Primitive, but damned effective.

There was little doubt, at this point, that the Fates had judged against him. Despair saturated his soul. He lay in the heap he'd been left in, head hanging, legs twisted, and back bowed. He didn't bother to look up at the sound of the hatch opening. In fact, he willed his body lax. Let them believe him still insensible. Nothing about his situation led him to expect this ship, or its crew, were upstanding or legal. Better to use this moment to observe and perhaps learn something he could turn to his favor.

By the distinctly different footsteps, Paolo knew three people had entered the chamber. Three men, he would guess by the heavy sound of each tread. Two moved to either side of him. Before he realized their intent they had each gripped an end of his stock and hauled him up high until his feet dangled like a puppet. And still he forced his body to remain slack. The men just laughed and shook him until his arms screamed as he himself would not. Paolo resisted the urge to lash out with the legs they'd foolishly left unbound. He did send a silent command to the nanites beneath his skin to project the illusion of continued unconsciousness, though, before opening his eyes to study his captors.

Rough and prosperous were the first words he'd use to describe them. They appeared like standard space tramps, lean and hungry with banged-up gear, but each of them wore quality compression suits that gave lie to their overall impression. Their suits were void of any markings for rank or identification. Each of them had a utility pouch slung around their hips.

"Enough," the third man said with firm authority as he sauntered up to stand before them. He ran his hands over Paolo like a customer assessing goods in the market. "Bloody hell...a Gyp."

Paolo gritted his teeth at the racial slur, but continued pretending unconsciousness.

The leader's hand locked on Paolo's chin, gripping it hard. He forced Paolo's head back until they stared eye to eye, though only Paolo was aware of that. He catalogued the man's face: square, with a cleft chin and too-full lips, hard eyes and heavy brow. A thin, straight scar marred the left cheek, and another, more jagged example bisected his right eyebrow. His teeth were decent enough, but his breath foul. Paolo barely bothered noting the dark brown hair. It was too easily changed. But that face. Paolo would remember it. The Rom believed in vengeance nearly as much as luck, be it good or bad.

Oblivious to Paolo's true state, the leader went on. "No. Not worth keeping. Too big to crawl the conduits...too small to be of use for anything else that needs doing." Then the man tracked a finger over Paolo's tattooed face. "Besides, he's a Gypsy...definitely not worth the amount of trouble he'd be.

"We'll leave him with the rest of the marks," the leader continued. "Strip him of anything worth having and then get your asses back to the cargo bay. We have less than an hour to shift the goods over to the *Barbary* and disengage before this heap dives in to the asteroid belt."

The man pivoted abruptly and headed for the hatch.

Something in his words triggered a memory. Faint, but insistent. Aside from the luxuries they offered, the Rom made great trade in information. A while back the Kalderăs Clan had learned of a band of pirates operating in fringe space, the areas past the edges of the more active trade routes. One of the known pirate vessels was the *Barbary*.

Paolo bared his teeth at the departing man's back, only to hiss in pain as his holders dropped him abruptly to the ground. Ingrained training had him remain relaxed as he fell. He didn't tense until the first booted foot took him beneath the ribs. Something cracked and he could not help but cry out. Pride cut the cry off and experience prompted Paolo to tense his muscles against the rest of the men's blows, but not to fight back. Understandably his illusion of unconsciousness fell away as his focus turned toward minimizing the beating. He did not let it go on for long, just enough to satisfy the thugs, before begging mercy. They laughed and aimed a few more kicks, until their leader's voice sounded over the wall comm.

"Get your asses to the bay! Anything we're forced to leave behind comes out of your cut."

Paolo, struggling to breath and startled by the sudden sound, lost focus on his tormentors. An unexpected kick connected forcefully with his already abused jaw. What color existed in the hold bled off leaving Paolo's vision briefly awash in shades of grey. He closed his eyes and fought not to be sick as his head bobbed uncontrollably. When rough hands began to paw among his clothing he attempted to kick out at them. The men laughed, the sound oddly muffled, as they slapped his feet away. He bucked and thrashed as they stripped him of the little he had left in the world, all but his clothes. But when one of them snatched the velvet pouch containing Terlinda's remains from around his neck Paolo raged and tried to ram him with the end of the conduit.

"Give her back! That's worth nothing to you!"

He knew he should have kept his mouth shut even as he spoke, but by then it was too late. With a smug sneer the pirate slid the pouch over his bald head in a blatant taunt. Paolo imprinted the man's face on his memory and lunged at him, but the other man yanked him back. Again, they laughed and one of them landed a punch in his gut. A shove sent him backward to the deck where the impact of his weight against the length of conduit felt as if it all but crushed his forearms. Before they could start beating him again, the wall comm squawked once more. Paolo recognized the leader's voice, though he could not make out the words past the agony buzzing through his brain. He lay in a haze as his assailants delivered parting blows, then left the chamber, harsh laughter trailing behind them.

It would be so easy to give in to his misery and fate, were it not so contrary to the Rom nature. Paolo instead focused on his pain. On compressing it. On shoving it deep into a mental hole where he could not feel it.

A lifetime of training returned his breath to slow, steady measures and his will forced each abused muscle to relax as he assessed his situation. Whatever the reason for his assailants' primitive measures, they worked to Paolo's favor. First he tested the bond around his wrists. He gritted his teeth as he flexed his hands and attempted to roll his wrists. It did not feel as though they'd bound him with rope or cord. It took effort, but he dropped his gaze and bent his body until he could just see the dull grey strips of duct tape that held him secure.

Paolo cursed. He did not have time to strip the tape, presuming there was even a surface to scrape it against. The leader had said they'd not quite an hour before the unpiloted craft entered the asteroid belt...and almost certain destruction.

About ten minutes had already passed. Paolo would have to work fast to free himself. Vengeance demanded it, as did the sheer cussedness of the Rom, which drove Paolo to preserve what life he had whether it seemed worth the living or not. At the end of everything, the Romani people were survivors. And even if Paolo were not confident of his own will to live, the leader of these rogues mentioned marks…victims. He would not stand by as more innocents like his sister were lost. The pirates were known for attacking colonizers, mostly automated ships sent out beyond settled space in search of inhabitable planets. That meant somewhere on this vessel as many as 160 people were ensconced in preservation tanks. The cargo the pirates stripped from the ship were the colonists' settlement supplies and what little personal goods they had paid to bring along. In other words, goods that meant the world to them. The Rom themselves had a history of picking pockets or fleecing the unwary, but seldom of robbing marks of their livelihood or *lives*.

Anger sent tension through Paolo's body. Tension was counterproductive to the task at hand. Closing his eyes and emptying his thoughts, Paolo instead focused on the muscles in his shoulders, arms, back, abdomen, and buttocks. With fine adjustments he worked them, stretching and contorting respectively, until slowly his hips and ass rested on the conduit, then slid backward over it. For a few moments, he allowed himself to rest, jaw clenched against the pain the familiar actions caused his abused flesh before he buried it deep once more. He sat with the conduit wedged beneath his thighs, arms stretched taut and head pounding. In his mind he heard Terlinda's voice muttering and kvetching: *No…no… No stopping in the middle. There will be time for resting when you've stopped the bastards.* Paolo could almost picture the outrage snapping in her dark, doe-like eyes and chuckled before he remembered. Outside of his thoughts, he would never hear her bossing him again. But she was right, figment or not. Those men had taken her from him all over again, stealing the last thing that mattered to Paolo, just as they threatened to do to the unsuspecting colonists.

He was not ashamed to admit that Terlinda mattered to him more, though he would gladly thwart the pirates in all the evil they planned. Taking his time in freeing himself would not get her back. With the memory of his sister driving him, Paolo manipulated his body, moving and contorting, stretching his back until there was room enough between himself and the conduit to allow his knees to pass. He then bent and tucked them against his chest and flattened his toes until they also pushed their way past the length of pipe, which along with his arms, now curled in front of him. For a brief instant Paolo laid there trembling, breath sawing past lungs that would not fill fully as damaged ribs painfully reminded him of their presence. Even so, triumph sang the length of his nerves at this small success. But he was not yet free.

Fighting to ignore the muscle aches and pain pricks in his arms, Paolo drew them up toward his face, shifting his shoulders until his right wrist came within reach of his mouth. The skin was puffy and red and the fingers tingled. He tried not to think of the passing minutes as he gnawed at the tape, desperate to find or create an edge that he could then strip away. All the while his experienced ears strained for the subtle changes in the engine noises. Had the men fled to the other vessel yet? He did not believe so, as the ship's engine worked hard, as if burdened beyond standard specifications.

He could not let the thought distract him from his task. Biting and tearing, biting and tearing. With a deep-felt urgency, he tore his way through the tape, stopping only to spit as the fragments clung to his tongue, leaving a chemical residue that caused his mouth to water in protest, which interfered with his efforts. Finally, the last strands snapped. He nearly screamed as every nerve ending flared and pulsed with restored blood flow.

"Căcat!" Shit! Paolo bit off the curse as he shook the hand to restore sensation enough to free his other wrist. He lost some skin in his haste as he ripped the last of the tape away. Weary and aching, he wanted nothing more than to sink to the deck and let his body recover, but time would not allow it. He had thirty minutes left to save his ass and the ship with it.

And all he could think of was getting his sister back.

Paolo scrambled to his feet and staggered to the hatch, his body throbbing with the wasted effort. No matter how he worked the bolt, the way remained barred. The pirates had locked the compartment, showing an annoying bit of foresight. Gritting his teeth, Paolo turned to the wall comm. A standard-issue unit, it had basic system access: emergency alerts, ship-wide communications, climate controls for the compartment, and a bare-bones ship's schematic, enough to show someone where they were and how to get around through the corridors. Not enough to show Paolo the maintenance infrastructure, but it did identify the ship's class, which served just as well. A nomadic race dependent on spacecraft for their existence, the Rom made sure all in the Clan had a basic knowledge of existing ship design; how to identify them, fly them, and—if need be—disable them. Paolo himself had excelled beyond basic in all three regards. He easily recognized the ship as a Portmann-class colonizer. The Portmanns were an economical design, compact and frugal with space. According to the schematic he was not far from the engine room. If he could get there he could sabotage the engines before the ship nosedived among the asteroids.

Paolo searched the walls for a maintenance hatch. He discovered it in the corner of the room and nearly broke his vow to never again lift prayer to any god as he dropped to his knees, hands running frantically around the edge of the removable panel. A shuddering, relieved sigh sent sharp jags of pain through his abused torso as he found the pressure points that popped the panel away from the wall. Perhaps he wasn't quite as cursed as he feared… Paolo cut the thought off and made a sign against evil.

Such careless hope tempted the Fates to prove a man wrong.

He was about to duck through the hatch into the infrastructure of the ship when instinct drew his shoulders tight and made his belly burn. Memory of the strength and cruelty of his captors stopped him mid-crouch. Paolo turned and snatched up the conduit to which he'd been secured. It would make a serviceable club, if just a bit unwieldy.

At least nominally armed, he exited the compartment. He set the pipe down and pulled the hatch back into place behind him before picking up his makeshift weapon once more. Then he oriented himself, calling to mind the memory of the schematic and marrying it to his knowledge of the Portmann design. Paolo crouched and slipped in among the conduits and wires, contorting himself to pass among the infrastructure. He kept an eye to his left, watching for the reinforced bulkheads visible at regular intervals to mark the proper distance past the intervening compartments. When he judged he had gone far enough he turned left, and made his way through another tangle, before stopping by a full-sized maintenance hatch. If memory were correct, this brought him to a corridor that led to the engine room. Unfortunately, this was as far as the maintenance area extended. The heavily armored engine room was self-contained in case of catastrophic failure. From here he must venture into the open.

Not for the first time in his short life Paolo wished the holographic properties in his tattoos could be used to appear invisible. Such an illusion was beyond the capability of the nanites imbedded beneath his skin, however. Instead, he used his skills as a sneak—something all among the Rom learned almost before they walked—to keep to the shadows created by the support struts that ran the length of the corridor at intervals.

Ten minutes had passed since he'd escaped when the corridor he traveled intersected with another. The sound of boots thudding on the deck came from his right. Paolo pressed himself into the shadow of the nearest strut. He stilled his breathing and visualized the nanites mimicking the wall behind him. Not the same as being invisible, but close, as long as he did not move. The footsteps came closer and Paolo could not completely silence the growl that rumbled in his throat as a familiar, bald-headed man entered the intersection. Terlinda's velvet pouch still hung around the pirate's neck.

Paolo struggled to remain motionless. Every nerve prickled with the need to snatch her away. His grip tightened on the length of conduit and he slowly eased his foot forward only to draw back as another voice called out from down the corridor at Paolo's back.

"Yo, Bock. What the hell are ya doin'? Cap's lookin' for ya. He's pissed."

Paolo squeezed his eyes closed and pressed tighter into his corner niche, his ears straining for any indication the man drew closer.

Bock stopped, casting an annoyed look over his shoulder. "Forgot somethin'. I'll be right there."

The slightest bit of tension eased from Paolo's shoulders. He could hear the footsteps fading as the other pirate walked away.

Bock grimaced. A hard light glimmered in his eye as he turned and continued the way he'd been heading. Paolo fought back the urge to cry out in frustration. The pirate moved in the opposite direction of the engine room. Paolo could follow the man. He could stalk in Bock's wake, waiting for a chance to reclaim the pouch containing his sister's remains, but would there still be time to stop the vessel from its ill-fated rendezvous with the asteroid belt?

Paolo sighed in frustration. His gut burned with the decision he knew had to be made. There were lives at stake and Terlinda would not have thanked him for putting the dead before the living. He couldn't go anywhere, however, until the way was clear. Creeping to the end of the corridor, he willed the nanites to mimic the floor, then dropped low to peer around the corner.

Bock had stopped in front of a compartment with *Cryo-Storage* stenciled beside the hatch. His manner and the way his gaze kept darting down the corridor spoke of the man's desire not to be caught. Paolo tensed as Bock opened the hatch and slid inside. Something in his expression echoed Paolo's memories of Tran.

Instinct sent Paolo to his feet and halfway to the cryo-storage compartment before the conscious decision had been made. As he walked he called to mind every detail of the pirate captain's face…his clothes…the timber of his voice. Every nasty expression and unconscious mannerism. With each step, Paolo transformed a little more until he stood before the compartment as the perfect image of the man who'd condemned him. He slowly opened the hatch to the sight of Bock running his fingers over the surface of a preservation tank he prepared to extract. If not for the trans-alum glass the man's hand would have fondled the young girl encased inside. Fury lunged up from Paolo's belly in reaction, drawing his muscles taut and rolling his lips back in a snarl. The girl looked nothing like his sister, but wore Terlinda's face all the same, in Paolo's mind. His breathing sped up and his fingers tightened on the conduit he still carried. He must have made a noise because Bock pivoted around. Judging from the way the man's face paled the nanites must have translated Paolo's rage onto the pirate captain's expression.

"Aw, come on, Cap…can't we bring along just one? We could all use a soft berth to sink anchor in…"

Paolo growled and fought the violent impulses bombarding him. In the back of his thoughts a clock frantically ticked away the doomsday hour. There was no time for beating the bastard to a pulp. The desire must have translated to his expression, though.

Bock fell silent but did not move away from the preservation tank. He looked sullen, the set of his jaw rebellious as he shifted his stance into something more dangerous.

"She's mine, then," he insisted as he pivoted full around, body tense and aggressive. "My cut of the spoils ...you can't argue against that, yeah?"

Paolo's gaze fixed on the pouch hung around the man's neck. His fingers ached to snatch it from the man's dead carcass. All it would take was a solid swing of the conduit to the side of Bock's bald head. It was an effort to resist, but Paolo had to if he and the unsuspecting colonists were to come out of this alive. He focused on channeling the pirate captain. Voices were trickier than physical appearance, but Paolo was a fair mimic.

"Get back to the *Barbary*, now," he ordered in Cap's voice. "Or I'll kill you myself and you'll have no share! We're running out of time."

Bock's features hardened and his eyes took on a hard gleam that did not bode well for Paolo. The pirate started forward, his hands fisting, when the comm engaged and the captain's voice crackled across the line.

"Bock, you have two minutes to get your ass on the *Barbary* or we're leaving you behind. We've got a military cruiser headed this way."

The captain's words triggered a violent pounding in Paolo's chest. A military cruiser? What were the chances it was tracking him? He couldn't figure out how, but clearly they had some way. Farfetched as it sounded, it began to look like his name had changed to *Prikàza*. On the bright and shiny side, his bad luck likely improved the colonists' and his own chances of survival. Of course, that last might have proved a bit too optimistic, judging from the way Bock looked at him.

The pirate's expression cycled from stunned to disbelieving and settled on enraged. As the man lunged forward, Paolo raised the length of conduit and swung it with all his might. The blow connected with Bock's shoulder and sent him careening into the bulkhead. The pirate caught himself and pushed back until he aimed at Paolo once more.

"I don't know how you did it, but you're dead, Gyp," Bock growled, making the only assumption he could.

Paolo laughed, his borrowed face set in grim lines. "I'm not that lucky," he said as he swung again, only to have the pirate grab the conduit. Before he could remove it from Paolo's grasp the ship jerked beneath their feet, likely jarred by the *Barbary's* ion wake as the pirate ship departed with haste. Or maybe they'd already entered the edges of the asteroid belt. Either way, the disruption sent both combatants to the deck in a heap, Paolo on top, smiling with satisfaction.

If there was anything the Rom knew it was how to fight dirty.

As the two of them tumbled, Paolo released his grip on the conduit and instead grabbed for the pouch hanging around Bock's neck. He then yanked the man's head toward him as he sent his own slamming forward.

Blood erupted from Bock's nose and his eyes rolled into his head. Paolo got his feet beneath him and fought the urge to twist the lanyard in his hands until Bock's face went blue. Breathing hard with the effort to resist, Paolo instead spat on the pirate.

"Well you're certainly not good enough for *my* sister!" he growled as he slipped Terlinda's remains over the unconscious man's head, before kicking him back to the deck. Paolo hung the pouch once more around his own neck and quickly secured Bock with duct tape from the pirate's utility pouch.

Biting back a groan of pain from his earlier beating, Paolo struggled to control his breath. He lost himself a moment as his eyes locked on the young girl in her preservation tank. So like his sister…and yet so not like her. Something healed within his heart at knowing he had kept this one safe.

The jarring, raucous sound of a proximity alarm broke Paolo from his musing. He lunged for the wall comm by the compartment hatch and called up the ship's alert system. He cursed at what he saw.

There wasn't time to stop the vessel from entering the asteroid belt. Fortunately, the Portmann class had decent hull shielding—more than capable of absorbing blows from the dust, pebbles, and head-sized rocks that mostly made up an asteroid belt—and it was equipped with auto cannons that could take care of the bigger bits, as long as someone was at the helm to steer around anything the size of a shuttle craft or larger. Paolo swallowed hard as acid scored his throat. Their only hope now lay in *him* navigating a path through that relentlessly tumbling obstacle course. He was better than good as a pilot, but navigating an asteroid belt alone was a tricky proposition.

As he ran for the command deck, Paolo gripped Terlinda's remains and prayed for all he was worth.

Rolling the Bones
Patrick Thomas

Buster Hardy stopped in front of the mirror to straighten his hat and give himself a wink. Humming, he opened his bedroom before heading down the boardinghouse stairs.

At the bottom of the steps, he paused to grab the hands of a little girl in a homemade dress that had seen better days and several previous owners. He spun her around and grinned as Emily giggled.

"Somebody's in a fine mood this morning," said the matronly woman in a housecoat as she prepared breakfast. "You cut quite the dashing figure in that hat."

"Thank you, Mrs. McGillicuddy," Buster said.

"He should. It's my hat," Jimmy the Schnoz said.

"Listen, Schnoz, my three fives beat your pair of aces. You know the rules – you don't bet nothing you don't want to lose," Buster said.

"So you're in a good mood because you won Schnoz's hat?" Emily asked.

"Nah, that's just the icing on the cake. My darling Pamie agreed last night to be my wife," Buster said, with a grin so large the smile threatened to push his cheeks off his face.

Mrs. McGillicuddy squealed, threw both arms up and gave Buster a hug followed by a kiss on both cheeks. "That's wonderful. Have you told your mother yet?"

"I'll put it in my weekly letter to her when I write it this evening."

Jimmy held his hand out and Buster shook it. "Don't know why you'd ruin a perfectly good life by getting married, but you got a great girl. She, on the other, must be a little touched in the head."

Buster's eyes narrowed and his hands became fists. "Why would you say that about my girl?"

Jimmy smiled. "Simple. She agreed to marry you. Something's got to be wrong with her."

"Does this mean you got the job too?" Mrs. McGillicuddy said.

"Heading over there this afternoon for an interview after our weekly game with the riveters."

"I hope you get it," Emily said. "I'd hate for you not to be able to pay the rent and for us to have to kick you out on your keisters."

"Emily! Such language," Mrs. McGillicuddy said.

The girl looked down, but Buster could see her trying to hide a smile. "Sorry Ma."

"And you know we won't be throwing out our two favorite boarders. Especially since Buster's own mother would be having my hide. We grew up together up in Parker's Glen. Not to mention we're only having eggs this morning due to Buster's good graces."

"It was nothing. The dice were smiling. And ever since Black Tuesday, beggars can't be choosers."

Jimmy sat and took a bite of eggs. "I feel naked without my hat."

"I know what you mean. I feel so fully dressed with it," Buster said.

"That may be so, but there are no hats at my table."

Buster took it off and hung it on the back of his chair. "Sorry Mrs. McGillicuddy."

Jimmy reached over to try and grab the headgear. Without turning away from his food, Buster slapped his hand with his fork.

"Ow!"

Once breakfast was done, the boys said their farewells and headed out into Hell's Kitchen. Like many others in New York, the Great Depression had taken its toll on the neighborhood. Hell's Kitchen had fallen on rougher times. It wasn't the safest of places, but Buster and Jimmy were well-liked and were usually left to go about their business.

"You really going to keep my hat?"

"You mean my hat. And yes, I am."

Buster stopped beside a gorgeous woman with bleach blonde hair, wearing pink clothes far more expensive than most of the Hell's Kitchen neighborhood could afford. The beauty was unloading sacks of potatoes in front of a building that a hand-painted sign proclaimed *The Dashiell Chandler Soup Kitchen.*

The woman looked up and smiled at the young men. Buster tipped his hat. "Good morning, Miss Chandler."

"Good morning, Buster. Good morning, Jimmy. Nice hat, Buster. It looks good on you."

"It's my hat, Miss Chandler," Jimmy said.

"Hmm, looks better on him."

Buster turned and smirked at Jimmy. "Thank you, Miss Chandler."

"So Schnoz, was it cards or craps?" Kaye asked.

"Cards."

"You've got to watch that tell," Kaye said.

"What tell?"

"You scratch your nose when you lie."

"I do not." Kaye laughed and Schnoz realized his finger was scratching right above his nostrils.

"Can we give you a hand bringing in the potatoes and apples?" Buster said.

Buster was impressed by the woman's strength. She was carrying two sacks of potatoes that would be heavy for a big man.

"That would be lovely, thank you."

The men went over to the back of the truck. Not be outdone by a woman, Buster grabbed two sacks of potatoes and regretted it. Jimmy went for a box of apples, stopping to pull one from the box and stick it in his pocket. Buster glared at him.

"You've done it. What do you always say – *It ain't stealing if you're starving,*" Jimmy said.

"We ain't starving this week. When we were starving, Miss Chandler made sure we ate. Put it back."

Jimmy sighed and put the apple back in the box. The men helped Kaye Chandler finish unloading the truck.

Inside there were families eating breakfast.

"You boys available to help me out with lunch? Arturo's got a job interview," Kaye said.

"I thought Arturo worked for you?" Jimmy said.

"He does, but he's an architect. He'd rather be working in the field he loves. Pays two bits plus lunch."

"Gee thanks, Miss Chandler, but you see, we've got us a previous engagement," Jimmy said, already heading for the door.

Buster put his hand on Jimmy's shoulder. "Which ain't till two o'clock. So long as you don't mind is leaving at one thirty, we'd be happy to help you out."

"Thanks, Buster. You know where everything is."

"Miss Chandler, before we get to work… I actually came to ask you a favor."

"What is it?"

"I have a job interview at a construction site. I got no experience, but some of the boys I play cards with helped me get my foot in the door, but there's going to be a hundred other guys in line. The guy who owns the company travels in some of the same high society circles that you do, so I thought it might help my chances if I could name-drop."

Kaye Chandler smiled. "I'd be happy to give you a reference. You're hard-working and honest, unlike some others." She turned toward Schnoz.

"Why you giving me the eye? I'm honest."

"Really? Then why are you scratching your nose? And what's that bulge in your pocket?"

"Maybe I'm just real happy to see…"

Buster slapped his friend in the back of the head. "Give her back the apple. And don't talk like that to Miss Chandler. She's a lady."

Jimmy bowed his head and pulled out the apple. "Sorry."

"Keep it. Who else is going to want it after it's been in your pants? Now you boys head into the kitchen and get to work."

* * *

At 1:30, the two men left the soup kitchen and headed toward Midtown.

"That wasn't so bad was it?" Buster said.

"No, it wasn't. Gotta admit, Miss Chandler has the best eats of any soup kitchen in the city," Jimmy said, patting his stomach.

Buster smiled. "Is that why you had triples helpings?"

"Hey, she said we could eat. She never said how much. So you find lucky for our weekly game with the riveters?"

"After my baby saying yes to me last night, I know I'm the luckiest guy in the world."

Jobs were scarce in New York, but there was still construction work. Iron workers who put the frameworks of new skyscrapers together worked regularly and for good wages. And they liked to have their fun too. On Wednesdays, one group took an extra-long lunch which they liked to spend playing cards. The boys had heard about it but didn't know how to get in. Then, by chance, they met one of the men in a different card game. Buster lost big to him, which Jimmy suspected he did on purpose. Buster would never say one way or the other. The man was so happy he invited the pair to join the game. While they didn't always win, there were weeks where the only reason they made rent or ate was because of that game.

They gave the traditional shave and a haircut, two bits knock on a wooden shed on the construction site on 34th Street. The door opened a crack. "It's about time you to get here. You're late. We were worried we weren't going to be able take your money home."

"No such luck, Sam. Although who takes whose money home has not yet been decided," Buster said.

The newcomers took their seats with six other men.

"I'll deal," Jimmy said.

The man who had invited them into the game, Tom, pulled the deck of cards out of his hands. "No way, Schnoz. You cheat."

"I'm shocked and dismayed that you would make these heinous allegations," Jimmy said. Buster smiled and touched his nose. Schnoz quickly pulled his finger from his face.

"You still ain't dealing," Tom said. He handed the deck to Buster. "You do it."

"Why Buster and not me?" Jimmy said.

"Because, unlike some others, Buster don't cheat."

Buster shrugged as he shuffled the cards. "My mama told me it was wrong."

"Just can't figure out how you win so much. Somebody as lucky as you are in cards must be unlucky in love," Tom said.

Jimmy snorted. "Nope, Buster's got all the luck. His gal said yes last night when he popped the question to her."

"You're engaged?" Tom said.

"Yep."

"Congratulations. Now run away in the dead of night, get out of town and never look back," Tom said.

Buster dealt the cards. "I thought you were happily married."

"I am, at least as happy as married can be. And do not listen to what people tell you about marriage. I work harder at home sometimes than I do here," Tom said, looking at his cards. "I'll take two."

Jimmy rolled his eyes after seeing the cards he was dealt. "I'll take three."

There is a knocking at the shed door, but just three raps. Lunch pails and hats were quickly put over the cards on the table as Sam got up and opened the door.

"Emily, what are you doing here? Does your mama know?" Buster said to the little girl.

"She sent me. You got a telegram," Emily said handing him an envelope.

"Who'd send you a telegram?" Jimmy said.

"Probably, FDR congratulating me on my engagement."

Tom laughed. "The next time you talk to him, tell him most of us aren't too impressed by his New Deal yet."

Buster read the telegram and the blood drained from his face. "Oh no."

"What?" Jimmy said.

"My Pop died. Gotta get home to Parker's Glen by tomorrow for the funeral."

"This some sort of scam to play on our sympathy?" said Lester, another one of the riveters.

"If it was Jimmy that got that telegram, I'd be half-inclined to agree with you, but not Buster. You have enough money to get there, son?" Tom said.

"I spent pretty much everything I had on the ring. Don't worry, I've hopped a few trains in my time. I'll get there."

Tom held up a couple bucks in his hand. "This ought to see that you don't have to risk hurting yourself to pay your respects to your pa."

Buster shook his head. "Appreciated Tom, but I can't take it from you. A man's got his pride."

Tom nodded, then tossed the money into the pot on the table. "I understand about that. I bet and I fold."

Sam threw through some bills in the pot. "I'll see that and I fold too."

The rest of the riveters followed suit, then it came around to Jimmy "I'll see that money and I'll call."

"I thought Buster was your friend," Tom said.

"My best friend, but he is also wearing my hat. I want a chance to get it back and I've got a damn good hand. There's no way I'm gonna fold."

"That's fine and dandy, but it ain't right. You don't do the right thing or you ain't invited back to this card game again."

"Tom, come on. You gotta be kidding me," Jimmy said.

"Do I look like I'm kidding?"

"Fine, despite the fact that I got me four ladies in my hand, I'm folding."

"Fellas, I don't know what to say. Thanks." Buster stood and picked up the pot. "Oh, boy. Tom, I'm sorry, but I'm going to miss the interview."

"Buster, there will be other jobs. You only get one pa. Go take care of your mama."

Buster nodded got up and walked out of the shed.

Jimmy got up to follow, but couldn't help himself. He lifted up Buster's cards to look. "A pair of sixes. I knew it."

* * *

The Erie Railroad train got Buster to Parker's Glen, Pennsylvania after ten o'clock at night. There weren't any cars on the road. In fact there weren't many roads, so it took him the better part of an hour to walk to his parent's' home. When it was in finally in sight, Buster sped up the pace. Lights were still on despite the late hour. Perhaps friends were visiting and comforting his mother.

The screen door was closed, but the front door was open. Someone was talking, so Buster stopped outside to listen and peak through a gap in the curtain.

"As we both know there's no way you're going to come up with the money that you owe me for this house," said a fat man in an expensive suit and hat. The suit was tailored to cover the expanse of his belly.

Mildred Hardy's mother's face was red, a mixture of anger and embarrassment. "I owe the bank, not you."

"That's what you don't seem to understand, Mildred. I *bought* your mortgage from the bank. That means I can call the money due at any time and I'm calling it in now. You're still a good-looking woman. I've liked you ever since we were kids. We can come to an arrangement for you to still live here, free of charge."

"And exactly what kind of arrangement do you have in mind? You want me to do your laundry or sewing?" Buster's mother said with bitter sarcasm.

Herman Boggs laughed. "I already have a maid. I bet you are regretting turning down my offer to marry you and choosing John instead."

"John was a good man."

"Maybe, but he was also a poor man. I bet he didn't leave you anything other than his debts. Things are bad out there. You don't want to be out on the streets. Best you and I come to an arrangement." Herman lifted the back of his hand and stroked the side of Mildred's face. She pulled back like the touch had burned her skin.

"So you want me to be your whore."

Boggs laughed again. "I prefer the term mistress, but whatever makes you happy, my dear."

"What does your wife think of this arrangement?"

The fat man shrugged. "I don't know and don't really care. She knows where her bread is buttered. She won't make any waves. You know I'm making a fair offer. What do you say?" Boggs asked, his hand reaching out and cupping Mildred's buttocks. The woman answered him with a hard slap across the face. Boggs grabbed hold of her and threw her against the wall. Buster stepped inside, hauled back and slugged Boggs in the jaw. The fat man hit the floor like a sack of potatoes.

Unfortunately for Buster, he had only listened to what was going on the room and didn't actually look more than through the crack before he leaped and swung. A meaty hand grabbed Buster's shoulder and spun him around. Buster found himself looking up into the face of a giant of a man whose other large hand knocked him across the face. Buster hit the floor like a somewhat smaller sack of potatoes. The giant held onto his suit jacket and it torn across the seam as Buster fell.

"Boss, you want I should take care of this guy?" the giant said. Buster noted his suit was every bit as expensive as his boss's.

The big man helped Boggs to his feet. Boggs walked over and kicked Buster a few times in the side, then got a look of his face. "Buster, is that you? Sorry you had to hear what was said, son."

Buster stood. "I ain't your son. Get out!"

The big man shut his mouth with another kick, this one to his left eye.

"Boggs, you need to leave," Buster's mother said, bending down to help her son. "And if you touch my son again, Harold, I'll make sure you limp out of here."

Boggs and the giant Harold laughed. "Mildred, I'll leave you to consider my offer. Again, I'm sorry for your loss. Have a lovely night."

* * *

The funeral was well attended and a lot of folks came back to the Hardy household afterward. Lots of people had brought food, although neither of the Hardys felt much like eating.

Buster accepted the condolences from the friends and neighbors he had grown up with, almost all of them asking how he was making out in the big city.

Just a couple of hours into the gathering, Boggs and his muscle darkened their door yet again.

Before his mother could stop him, Buster leapt up to meet the two men at the door.

"You're here to try and kick my mother out of her house on the day she buried her husband?" Buster said.

"Herman, what's he talking about?" said James Donovan, who lived next door, although in Parker's Glen that was still a ways down the road.

"I bought the note on this house from the bank a while back. Now I'm having some cash flow issues, so I'm asking for what I'm owed. Nothing more," Boggs said.

"Oh, you're asking for a hell of a lot more than you're owed," Buster said.

Boggs smirked. "Want to tell everyone what that is?"

Buster started to open his mouth, but stopped when his mother burst into tears and ran into the kitchen.

"There's got to be some law. You can't just come in and do this," Buster said.

"I can do anything I want to," Boggs said.

"Buster, I didn't want to ask before, but how'd you get that black eye?" Mr. Donovan said, standing up and with him most of the other men in the room. As big as Harold was, there were a lot of people in the room and Buster smiled when he realized Harold was looking nervous.

"Boggs, why don't you tell him how I got that?" Buster said. "And why Ma had to spend part of this morning sewing up my jacket."

"How am I supposed to know? Probably bumped into a door. This is my property and I want you all out of here."

Another man in a suit, just as expensive as Boggs's, stood up. "Actually, you can't do that. You have to give proper notice of eviction."

"Who the hell are you?" Boggs said.

Mr. Donovan went over and put his hand on the man's shoulder. "This is my brother Bobby. He's a lawyer."

"So what? You want to sue me?"

"I work in the Lackawanna County DA's office in Scranton. I won't sue you, but if I find you've done something wrong, I'll sure as hell bring you up on charges."

Boggs looked worried for the first time. "There's no need for any of that. What say we let this visit serve as my eviction notice and we'll have everyone out by morning."

"Afraid not. There are procedures to be followed, including good faith effort to allow the money to be paid," Bobby Donovan said.

Boggs smirked. "Okay. Mrs. Hardy…" Buster's mother came out of the kitchen. "Do you have the money that is owed on the mortgage?"

"You know I don't Herman."

"I'll make payments," Buster said.

"I'm afraid a couple dollars a month ain't going to cut it here," Boggs said.

Buster pulled a wad of bills out of his pocket. "I've ninety-four dollars."

"Well, that certainly is a lot of money, but I'm owed eight hundred seventy dollars on the mortgage. Ninety-four just isn't enough."

"Give me a chance to pay it off. Take this as a down payment and I'll get the rest to you in six months."

"I'm just not looking to wait that long. I'll give you three days. You don't have the money by then, I will start eviction proceedings. All official like," Boggs said with a nod to Bobby Donovan.

Buster's mother narrowed her eyes and stared Boggs down. "That means for at least the next three days this is still my home and I can tell you and your goon get the hell out."

Harold stepped forward, but Boggs put a hand on his shoulder. "I assume that means you've turned down my other generous offer?"

"Damn right it is. Get out of here."

The two men left and the folks in the room passed a hat around and came up with another seventy-three dollars to add to the pot, but it still wasn't enough. Everybody went home, leaving mother and son alone.

"Buster, do you think I should have taken his offer?" she said.

"Absolutely not. Mrs. McGillicuddy has a room that's not rented. You can always come home with me, Ma. The money I send home every month would more than cover the room and board."

"It may come to that, but I just don't want to leave my home. I raised you and your sister here, before she moved down to Florida."

"She always liked the warm weather. Don't worry Ma, I'll get the money."

"Exactly how you planning to do that? Rob a bank?"

"Probably best if I didn't tell you," Buster said.

"Gambling? How many times have I told you about the evils of gambling?"

Buster smiled. "At least a couple."

"That's right. You know your father almost lost this house years ago gambling. I practically left him over it. But he stopped and he never went back."

"With any luck I can use the money we have and grow it to enough to pay Boggs off."

"Do you really think ninety-four dollars is enough?" she said.

"I count one hundred sixty-seven," Buster said.

"Oh no. Your father didn't leave me anything but that mortgage. I need something to start over with so you're not getting this money. You got ninety-four to try with."

"You mean you're giving me your blessing to gamble?"

"Desperate times call for desperate measures. And just this one time. And I don't care what the cause is, you still don't cheat. If I've told you once, I've told you a thousand times…"

"I think it's probably closer to two thousand."

She smiled though her sadness and went over to her sewing box and opened up a small panel. Ma Hardy pulled out a pair of red dice with white dots and put them in her son's hand. "Your father always said these were his lucky dice. I took them from him and never told him what I did with them. Gamblers are superstitious, so I figured if he didn't have his lucky dice it would lessen the temptation to gamble. You on the other hand need all the luck you can get."

"Thanks, Ma. I'll head back to the city in the morning. I'll be home in plenty time to save the house."

* * *

"You sure about this, Buster? These ain't the kind of guys you can unmeet," Schnoz said. "I mean you had to borrow six bucks from Emily to make the hundred buck buy-in.

"I'm sure Schnoz. I'll pay Emily back. This is the only way to keep my Ma from ending up in a Hooverville." Buster reached his hand in his pocket and held his father's lucky dice. He sent out a silent prayer for his father to watch out for him and help him in this game.

Snake Eye Smith was a big man. One look in his eye was enough to tell someone he was also a mean one. And there was just the single eye. The other was covered by a black patch that wasn't big enough to hide the scar that went from forehead to cheek.

"Mr. Smith, my name is…"

"Don't care, so long as you got a hundred bucks. You do have a hundred bucks and are not wasting my time, right?"

"Yes sir." Buster fumbled in his pockets and took out his money and waved it in the air.

"Put it away. I don't need to count it."

"Because you trust me?" Buster said.

"Hell no. I don't need to count it because for every dollar you're short, I'll break a finger or toe," Snake Eye said.

"But what if someone is more than a double sawbuck short? There's only twenty digits to break," Jimmy said.

Snake Eye smiled, but it wasn't a pleasant or happy thing. It was more the look of a lunatic drowning kittens down a well for fun. "Then that person will never have to worry about playing craps or anything else ever again. New meat, meet the boys, boys, this is the new meat."

They were three other men in the alley, all the dressed in suits and ties. A tall skinny guy stood near Snake Eye. The other two tough looking men stood across the alley. The four men eyed each other warily. If rumors were to be believed, Snake Eye worked for Rhino Johnson and the other two worked for Wolf Hopkins. Rhino and Wolf weren't at odds with each other, but they weren't exactly friends either.

Snake Eye picked up the dice. Buster bet against him which earned him a look.

"Don't think I'm going to roll a winner?"

"Well, your nickname is Snake Eye," Buster said.

The mobster laughed and rolled a pair of ones, making the pair from the Hopkins mob chuckle.

"Beginner's luck," Snake Eye said.

This time Buster bet on Snake Eye and he rolled a one and three.

"Little Joe from Kokomo," said the skinny man.

The next roll was a pair of twos, so Buster won again. Out of the next dozen rolls, he won nine.

Again he bet against Snake Eye and the mobster rolled a Jimmy Hicks or a six. His next roll was a seven.

"A Skinny Dugan. Sorry boss," the skinny guy said.

Snake Eye shrugged.

"Hey, how about letting someone else roll?" asked one of Wolf's men.

Snake Eye shrugged and handed the dice to Buster. "Think you can handle it, meat?"

"You betcha," Buster said, putting down his original hundred, along with all of his winnings.

"All in, meat? Gutsy. I like that. You've been having a good run of luck tonight. Let's see if it keeps," Snake Eye said.

Wolf Hopkins's men bet against Buster. Snake Eye and the skinny guy bet on him.

"If I win this I'm out," Buster said.

"If you lose too," Snake Eye said, looking at the money the other men with much deeper pockets put down. "Let's hope you go out with a smile."

Snake Eye handed him the dice. Buster reached in his pocket and pulled out his red dice.

"Would you mind if I used my father's bones?" Buster said.

Snake Eye took the dice, held them up to the street light. "Sure, I don't see no problem with that."

Buster shook them in his fist, then held up his hand to Jimmy. "Blow on the bones."

The four mobsters laughed.

"I ain't no dame. Blow on 'em yourself," Jimmy said.

Buster rolled his eyes and blew into his fist, then rolled.

"Seven!" Snake Eye said, picking up the dice and handing them back to Buster.

With a silent plea to his father, Buster rolled again and got another seven.

"And the new meat wins!" Snake Eye said, picking up all the money on the floor of the alley. He took a hundred out of the money he owed Buster.

"For the house," Snake Eye said.

Buster did a quick count and realized he had over two thousand dollars. "With my compliments. Thank you."

Buster reached down to pick up his dice, but one of Wolf Hopkins's men beat him to it. The mobster rolled them and they came up seven. He did it again. Another seven.

"These dice are loaded."

"No, they can't be. They were my dad's. He'd never cheat," Buster said.

"I don't care if they're La Guardia's, they's loaded." The two men pulled guns. Snake Eyes and his skinny partner did the same. "What kind of crooked game you running here?"

The accusation made Snake Eye snarl. "You calling me a cheat?"

"Did I stutter?"

"I don't take that from nobody." Snake Eye lifted up his gun and it seemed like all four men were racing to see who could pull their triggers first. From where Buster was standing, they all seemed to win.

Jimmy was close to the mouth of the alley and made a run for it. Buster wasn't so lucky and dove for the pavement.

Seconds later it was all over. Buster lifted up his head and could have sworn he saw the four men walking away, but he blinked and now they were all lying on the alley, blood pouring out of them. Nobody was moving. Buster reached down to pick up the money he'd dropped and his hand went right through the bills. He did it again and this time his hand went below the pavement. He looked down to see his own body as bloody and lifeless as Snake Eye and the others.

"What the heck?" Buster said and looked up to see a man in black robes and a hood that hid his face. Buster looked closer to see a skull staring back at him.

"Oh my God! Am I dead?" Buster said. Initially, it wasn't directed at anyone in particular, but then he turned toward the Grim Reaper for an answer. Buster could've sworn that the skull had just rolled its eyes, even though it had none.

"YES," said a voice as cold as the grave that sounded like it was coming from all sides at once.

"But I can't be dead. I have more than enough money to pay off my ma's mortgage and even set me and Pamie up in our own place. You can't take me. I'm not ready to go."

It sounded as if Death chuckled and put its bony hand in front of his face to cover it.

"MORTALS ARE NOT EXACTLY IN A POSITION TO TELL ME WHAT I CAN AND CANNOT DO. WHY IS IT SO IMPORTANT FOR YOU TO GO ON LIVING?"

Buster explained, first about his mother's situation and then about his own engagement.

Death shook his head. "DO YOU THINK YOU'RE THE FIRST MORTAL TO LEAVE UNFINISHED BUSINESS BEHIND? YOU CAN MOVE ON TO THE AFTERLIFE. YOU CAN STAY BEHIND AS A GHOST. NEITHER REALLY MATTERS TO ME."

"Okay, I'll go if you promise to deliver the money to my mother. And a hundred skins to Emily McGillicuddy."

"I AM NOT SOME ERRAND BOY. I CAN UNDERSTAND ABOUT THE MONEY TO YOUR MOTHER, BUT WHY TO THIS OTHER WOMAN?"

"She's a kid and I needed more money to get into this game, so she loaned me her savings, which consists of six bucks. I promised I'd pay her back with interest."

"THE CHILD WILL HAVE TO GET USED TO DISAPPOINTMENT."

"This isn't right. I said I'd go, but not before the people I care about are taken care of," Buster said, then puffed up his spirit's chest. "I'll make you do it."

Deaths laughter would have made Buster's blood run cold if it hadn't been spilled all over the alley.

"YOU ARE A GREAT FIGHTER, THEN?"

"Not particularly. I don't know if I can beat you, but what do I got to lose by trying? I'm already dead."

"AND YOU'LL BE DEAD A LOT LONGER THAN YOU WERE ALIVE. I CAN HAVE SOME INFLUENCE ABOUT WHERE YOU MIGHT GO AFTERWARD. TRUST ME, THERE MANY AFTERLIVES YOU DO NOT WANT TO GO NEAR." Suddenly a large scythe appeared in Death's boney hands. "OR I COULD JUST CHOP YOU INTO PIECES AND LEAVE YOUR SPIRIT HERE ALONE, UNHEARD AND UNABLE TO MOVE FOR ALL ETERNITY."

Buster put up his hands like he'd seen them do in the movies. "I don't care. I've gotta take care of my mom. So go on. Put your blade down and fight like a man. I'm not afraid of you."

Death's skull moved as if the bony ridges above his eyes were eyebrows. "YOU'RE NOT?"

"Actually, I'm more terrified than I've ever been in my life." The Grim

Reaper gave him a look. "You know what I mean. Being afraid doesn't change what I gotta do."

Death nodded and looked down at the corpse that had once been Buster. "YOUR BODY IS BEYOND SAVING, BUT THERE IS A WAY YOU COULD GO BACK AND INTERACT WITH THE WORLD. AND I DO ENJOY THE OCCASIONAL GAME. I'D BE WILLING TO PLAY YOU FOR A CHANCE FOR TO RETURN TO THE MORTAL WORLD FOR A TIME.

"What are the stakes?"

"IF YOU WIN, I'LL ALLOW YOU TO RETURN TO THE WORLD AS A GHAST."

"Is that like a ghost?"

"NO. YOU WOULD HAVE A BODY OF SORTS. PEOPLE WOULD BE ABLE TO SEE AND HEAR YOU, BUT YOU WOULD NOT HAVE FLESH OR BONE."

"I'd be able to take care of what I need to?" Death nodded. "What if I lose?"

"THEN YOU ARE MY SERVANT FOR THE NEXT CENTURY."

"So if I win, I live for a century as this ghast thing?"

"LIVE MAY NOT BE THE CORRECT TERM, BUT YOU COULD RETURN FOR A CENTURY."

Buster spit in his palm and stuck out his hand. "Deal."

Death spit on his bony palm and shook Buster's hand. Then he waved and a chessboard appeared with two chairs.

"SHALL WE BEGIN?"

"You said a game, but you never mentioned chess. First off, I don't know how to play."

"THEN IT WILL BE A VERY SHORT CONTEST."

"How about something I know the rules for to make it fair. Cards, poker, or even rolling the bones."

Death's brow bones rose again. "ROLLING THE BONES?"

"Another word for craps. Are you familiar with it?"

"WITH THE BASICS, BUT IT IS SO SIMPLE. A GAME OF CHANCE, WHEREAS CHESS IS A GAME OF SKILL."

"There's skill involved in craps. So are we going to play or are you chicken?"

Death laughed again. "VERY WELL. WOULD YOU LIKE TO ROLL OR SHALL I?"

"I'll roll," Buster said.

"VERY WELL THEN, ALL THAT'S LEFT IS TO DECIDE WHICH DICE TO USE. THERE APPEAR TO BE TWO SETS. CHOOSE."

Buster bent down and started to reach for the red dice, but even in death his mother's voice telling him not to cheat echoed in his head. The first time was different because he didn't know the dice were loaded. He did now. Should he tell the Grim Reaper or try to pull one over on Death himself?

"No. This is like one of those duels I've heard about. I issued the challenge and named the game. You should be the one allowed to choose the weapons."

"FAIR ENOUGH. ANYTHING ELSE I SHOULD KNOW?"

Death stared and Buster turned away and tried to take a deep breath. His spirit form mimicked the living one, but no air moved. "Dice can be altered to give the person rolling an unfair advantage."

"I SEE." Buster swore the Grim Reaper smiled. "GOOD TO KNOW." Death bent over and picked up the red dice that had once been Buster's father's and dropped them in his hand.

Buster stood staring at the dice, his mother's words still reverberating in his mind. "Are you sure these are the ones you want to use?"

The Grim Reaper nodded. "GET ON WITH IT. ROLL THE BONES."

Buster shook his hand and went through the motions of blowing on the dice, all the while wondering why he could now touch something solid, but couldn't moments before. Buster's hand went down and the dice flew out.

"SEVEN. AS I UNDERSTAND IT, YOU NOW HAVE TO ROLL A SEVEN BEFORE YOU ROLL ANYTHING ELSE IN ORDER TO WIN. A VERY DIFFICULT THING."

Buster reached down and his hand went through the dice. The skull under the hood again seemed to grin as its bony hand picked up the dice and placed them again in Buster's palm.

Buster shook his hand and again rolled the bones, wanting desperately to close his eyes, but unable to not watch.

Two sixes.

"I BELIEVE THAT'S CALLED BOX CARS. YOU ROLL AGAIN."

Buster and Death repeated the process and he rolled a three and a four.

"SEVEN. WELL PLAYED BUSTER HARDY. AS PER THE TERMS OF OUR WAGER, STEP FORWARD."

His spirit legs trembling, Buster did as instructed. The Grim Reaper placed a bony hand on each side of his head. There was a flash of light that made Buster twitch. His non-body felt like it was burning and melting. He fell to all fours, all of him aching as if he'd done a week's worth of hard work in an hour.

First thing he saw were his hands. They were different. For one thing, he could almost see through them. The rest was translucent and tinged with an eerie blue glow. He rose slowly to his feet and looked himself over, suddenly embarrassed.

"Why am I naked? A moment ago I had clothes on."

"THEN YOU WERE A SPIRIT WITH CONTROL OVER HOW YOU AP-

PEARED. YOU BELIEVED YOU WERE WEARING CLOTHES, SO YOU WERE. WITH A GHAST IT IS SOMETHING ENTIRELY DIFFERENT. IF YOU WANT TO WEAR CLOTHES, YOU'LL HAVE TO FIND THEM ON YOUR OWN."

Buster looked down at his own corpse. "What about my body?"

"THE MORTAL AUTHORITIES WILL HAVE TO TAKE CARE OF IT AS THEY WOULD ANY CORPSE."

"That just seems wrong, but thank you," Buster said, bending down to pick up his winnings.

"WHY ARE YOU ONLY TAKING SOME OF THE MONEY?" the Grim Reaper asked.

"It's the part that's mine," Buster said.

"THESE MEN HAVE NO FURTHER USE FOR IT AND FROM WHAT I KNOW OF THE POLICE IN THIS CITY, THEY WILL TAKE THE MONEY, CLAIMING IT AS EVIDENCE, BUT VERY LITTLE OF IT WILL MAKE IT THERE. NONE OF THESE MEN'S HEIRS WILL SEE IT. YOU WILL BE MORE LIKELY TO MAKE GOOD USE OF IT."

"I guess so." Buster watched as he glowed, brightening up the alley. "How will I be able to work looking like this?"

"YOU WILL GLOW AT NIGHT OR IN THE DARK. IN THE LIGHT OF DAY YOU WILL BE ABLE TO APPEAR HUMAN WITH EFFORT. NOW I SUGGEST YOU LEAVE. YOUR FRIEND RAN AWAY NOT ONLY TO SAVE HIMSELF, BUT TO SEEK ASSISTANCE. HE'S APPROACHING NOW WITH A POLICE OFFICER AND TWO BUSTER HARDYS WOULD UNDOUBTEDLY COMPLICATE MATTERS."

Buster nodded. "So, do we have to pick a place to meet in a century?"

Death laughed. "DON'T WORRY, BUSTER HARDY. I WILL FIND YOU WHEN YOUR TIME IS UP."

The Grim Reaper walked to the mouth of the alley and faded away.

"Wait. How do I get out of here?" Buster said. He put his hand up against the alley wall and felt the brick. "Supposedly ghosts can walk through walls. Maybe if I focus I can too."

Buster's fingers eased through the brick as easily as pushing into mud. He continued to walk, but when he got to the hand that held the money it wouldn't go through.

Shrill whistles let him know the police were getting close. Buster rolled all of the money up tightly and covered it between both hands so none stuck out and tried again. This time it worked and passed through.

It was odd moving though the wall. There is no light, yet he was able to see. He could hear and sense the cop in the alley. Carefully and slowly, he stuck his head back out in time to see the cop examining all the corpses. Schnoz was weeping over his corpse. Neither seemed to notice his head so Buster waited and watched some more. The cop went through the dead men's pockets, putting what he found in his own.

"You said this was a crap game. Where's the money?" asked the cop, a sergeant.

"I don't know," said Jimmy.

"I don't believe you. You want to know what I think happened? You came across what happened here, picked up the money for yourself and then came to report it to cover your tracks. And your pockets," the sergeant said.

"But I'm not lying. I didn't do anything wrong," Jimmy said.

"Bad idea to lie to an officer of the law, sonny. Real bad," the sergeant said. The crooked cop lifted up his Billy club and swung it toward Schnoz's head.

Buster came out of the wall, faster than he had ever been able to move when he was alive. He caught the wooden club in the palm of his hand before it could hit his friend's head.

"What in blazes?" the sergeant said.

Buster pulled the Billy club out of the cop's hand and smashed it down over his knee, breaking it in half. He then reached over with the money in his hand and reached into Schnoz's jacket pocket, putting the bills inside.

He turned and pointed at the cop. "You don't touch my friend."

The sergeant stepped back and pulled his gun. "If you think I'm going to be listening to a naked man without the sense to come out of the cold before he turned blue, you've got another thing coming. Put your hands above your head."

Buster surged forward and yanked away the cop's gun. He was stronger too. Making sure it was covered by his fingers and hands, Buster stuck it barrel-first into the brick wall and let go with the handle sticking out. The gun had become a part of the brick.

The cop tried to shove Buster aside, but his hand went through him. Frightened, the flatfoot reached up to pull his gun out of the wall, but it was stuck fast.

"If you don't want your head sitting in there next to your gat you'd better step aside and let us vacate," Buster said, then turned and winked at his friend.

"Buster? Is that you?" Jimmy whispered.

Buster grabbed Schnoz by the shoulder and moved him toward the street, then stopped by his own body which seemed to be staring up at him. Buster stopped, then bent down and touched the side of his own face. With his fingers, he closed the eyelids on his corpse, then closed his own for a moment. When he opened them, he took the hat off the head of the dead body and put it on his own. He grabbed Jimmy and hustled him out of the alley before the cop grew a backbone and tried to stop them.

"Buster, how can this be you? I saw your dead body. And you're blue,"

Jimmy said. "Are you a ghost?"

"Apparently I'm a ghast."

"A gassed? What the heck is that?"

"I'm still figuring that out," Buster said.

"How'd that happen?"

"I challenged Death to a game of craps and won."

"Which dice did you use?"

"My dad's."

Schnoz laughed. "So you literally cheated death."

"I guess so, but I let him choose the bones. Even warned him that they might be loaded."

"You are one lucky son of a gun. I assume you got the money?"

"Actually, put it in your pocket. I don't seem to have any of my own."

"I noticed that. Why didn't you grab any of your clothes? Except my hat."

"There was quite a bit of blood on them. And it's my hat."

"Not if you're dead. When you died, it should have reverted back to its previous owner, which is me."

"Still not happening, Schnoz."

"What you gonna do now?"

"Head back to my room, put on my old suit and head up to Mom's to pay off the mortgage."

A lady of the evening was walking toward them on the street and gave Buster a slow up and down stare, then let out a whistle. Buster smiled and tipped his hat to her.

"Nice…" The woman looked right below his waist, then back up to his face. "…hat."

"Thank you, miss."

"You boys looking for some company?"

"No, thank you," Buster said.

"Pity. I'd have given you a great price."

The boys made an attempt to sneak back into Mrs. Mcgillicuddy's boardinghouse without waking her up. Turned out there was no need as she was waiting up in the kitchen and she heard them come in. "Buster, Schnoz, how did it go? Did you get the money to save your mother's house?" she said, stepping into the foyer. When she noticed the naked glowing man she took a step back.

Emily had also been having trouble sleeping and came out when she heard the boys and walked in front of her mother. "Buster, why are you blue? And naked?"

Mrs. McGillicuddy pulled her daughter close and covered her little one's eyes with her hand, but Emily pulled a finger down so she could still look.

Embarrassed, Buster took off his hat to hold it in front of his groin. "I can explain…"

"So can I," Jimmy said. "Buster was killed, but he got better. Kinda," Jimmy said. "And he still won't give me my hat back."

"So you're a ghost?" Mrs. McGillicuddy said.

"Actually he's aghast," Jimmy said.

"What's that?" Emily said.

"Buster don't know exactly but he's working on it. He rolled the bones against the Grim Reaper himself and won, so he gets to come back like this," Jimmy said. "And he's naked because his clothes got shot up and are all covered in blood."

"Let me go get some clothes on," Buster said, quickly rushing up the stairs, making sure he kept the hat in front of him.

He was halfway up when Mrs. McGillicuddy said, "Oh, Buster."

The ghast stopped and looked back. "Yes, Mrs. McGillicuddy?"

"Nice bum."

Emily giggled as she peered out from between her mother's fingers.

Buster's cheeks became a darker shade of blue and he switched his hat so it covered his posterior as he ran the rest of the way up to his room.

Buster came down and they sat down at the table and he expanded on what Jimmy had already told them as best he could.

"It's all sounds so farfetched, but still I'm glad you're still with us in the land of the living, even if you are a bit on the turquoise side," Mrs. McGillicuddy said.

"That's a raggedy suit," Emily said.

"I only owned the two. I can get a new one with the money."

Jimmy smirked. "What money?"

"Very funny," Buster said, reaching in and through Schnoz's coat pocket. He closed his hand around the money and pulled the cash back out.

"You could be the world's greatest pickpocket," Jimmy said.

Buster opened his hand and put the money on the table.

"Ain't seen so much cabbage before in all my life," Emily said.

"That reminds me, I have to give you back six dollars plus interest," Buster said.

"And why would Buster be having to give you back money?" Mrs. McGillicuddy said, glaring at her daughter.

"I needed it for the buy-in and Emily was kind enough to help out. Here's your money with interest," Buster said, counting off some bills and putting them in the girl's hand.

Emily counted them. "There's a hundred dollars here."

"That's too much," Mrs. McGillicuddy said.

"Nope. She helped me when I needed it, so it seems fair to me,"

Buster said.

"Hey, what about your best buddy?"

"Schnoz, we both know whatever money I gave you would just flow through your fingers like water. Mrs. McGillicuddy, I'd like to pay Schnoz's and my rent for the next six months if you'd let me," Buster said.

"That would be fine," Mrs. McGillicuddy said. Buster handed her a stack of her own.

"There's a lot more than six months' worth here," she said.

"Think of it as a thank you for all those times you let us slide until we had the money to pay you in."

Mrs. McGillicuddy stood and kissed Buster on the head. "I'd hug you, but then you might have to become engaged to me instead of Pamie. Now go take care of your mother."

"If I leave now, I should make the next train to Parker's Glen."

"I'm going with youse," Schnoz said.

"Jimmy, you don't have to."

"I insists. I ain't never been there and you might need my help with the tough guy," Schnoz said.

"You mean if I need somebody to run and get the cops?"

"Why sure… hey, wait a second. That ain't fair. I ain't bulletproof or like one of those masked types who take out bad guys."

"I know Jimmy. I'm just teasing."

They got to Parker's Glen early in the morning and made the walk to the Hardy home.

"It's amazing. Ever since the sun came up, you almost look like a person," Schnoz said.

"I am a person," Buster said.

"No, I mean like a human. A living one. Your color is still a bit off, but from a distance most folks wouldn't even notice."

"Good, I don't want to scare Mom if I don't have to."

When they arrived, Buster turned the knob, but the door didn't move. "That's odd. Usually the door is unlocked during the day."

"So, can you stick your hand through the door and unlock it from the inside?" Schnoz said.

"Maybe," Buster said, lifting up the doormat, picking up what was underneath it. "Although I think using the key would be simpler."

"Mom, I'm home!" Buster shouted as he opened the door.

"I ain't your mom and I oughta shoot you for trespassing," Boggs said, stepping out of the kitchen with his goon Harold behind him.

"What are you doing here? We said three days. It's only been two," Buster said.

"I changed my mind. I really didn't feel like waiting, especially after your mom hurt my feelings and turned down my generous offer. Besides, we all know that riffraff like you was never going to get that kind of money."

"You're wrong. I got your money," Buster said.

"Who'd you have to kill?"

"You don't want to know. Now get out of my mom's house."

"It ain't your mom's house anymore. It's mine."

"I'll tell Bobby Donovan."

"Go ahead. He went back to Scranton. He ain't a DA for our county. You really think he's going come back here and make trouble? He ain't got the time."

"That ain't right," Buster said.

"Welcome to the real world, junior. The only thing left to figure out here is whether or not you leave under your own power or whether somebody's going to have to carry you out."

"Don't worry, Buster. There's two of us and two of them. Them's even odds in my book," Schnoz said. Bogg's goon pulled a gun. "Why do you gotta cheat like that?"

"Time to go, boys," Harold said.

"I don't think so," Buster said, reaching out for the gun. His hand closed around the barrel. When he pulled away, part of the weapon came with him, leaving the goon with just the butt of the gun. Buster reached out to shove the giant Harold back, but instead his hand slipped inside the man's rib cage.

The goon convulsed. "My chest! So cold. What are you doing to me?"

Buster really didn't know, but wasn't about to admit it. "I'll do a lot worse unless you go sit on the floor in the corner and don't move."

"Okay," Harold said, his body trembling like he had been out in frigid temperature for days.

"Okay, what?" Jimmy said, stepping right up behind his friend.

"Okay, sir?"

"That's better," Jimmy said. "Now go sit and don't make trouble if you know what's good for you."

Buster slowly slid his hand outside out to the man's body and turned toward Boggs, opening his other hand to the show the gun pieces before he tossed them on the floor.

"I'll give you your money and then you are going to sign over the house to my mother," Buster said.

Boggs took a step back, but then stopped. "Go to hell!"

"Not for at least a hundred years. Welcome to my world, Boggs." Buster grabbed hold of the fat man's shirt and jacket, meaning to lift him off the ground. He managed it and a whole lot more.

"Buster?" Jimmy said.

"What Jimmy? I'm a little busy."

"How you doing that?"

"Doing what?"

"Flying," Jimmy said.

Buster and Boggs both looked up, then down. They were off the floor and only a few inches away from the ceiling. Boggs gave up any pretense of being a tough guy and started to whimper.

"Jimmy, would you be so kind as to open the back door?"

"Why certainly," Jimmy said, strutting over to the exit.

Buster leaned forward, flew out the door and up into the sky, far above the houses and tree until the pair were over the Delaware River.

"Don't drop me," Boggs said.

"Then give my mother back her house. "

"No."

"Okay, but we're staying up here until that happens. I'm a little warm and I think my hands are getting sweaty." Buster floated up another fifty feet over the mountain the town sat on. Buster looked down and Boggs moved his head in the same direction and whimpered again. "I hope my palms don't get too slippery and make me accidentally drop you before you decide to do the right thing."

"You wouldn't dare."

Buster smiled and floated back over the river, then opened his hands. "Oops."

The fat man plummeted, screaming. Buster dove down and caught Boggs by the collar.

"You're getting awful heavy, Boggs. And my hands are feeling real slippery. Last chance."

Buster started loosening his grip one finger at a time. Boggs broke by the third one. "Fine, I'll do it."

Buster lowered him to the ground in front of the house.

"Sign the mortgage now."

Boggs quickly took the papers out of his pocket, signed it, and handed it over.

"Thank you. That wasn't so hard, was it?" Buster said. Boggs glared but kept his trap shut. "Jimmy, bring out Harold."

Acting like he was a tough guy, Jimmy shoved the goon out the door. The men turned to leave.

"Wait," Buster said and slapped the money into the fat man's palm. Then he turned to the goon. "You tore my other jacket when you hit me the other night. Gimme yours."

"No."

Buster smiled, shrugged, and lifted his hand toward the man's chest. "Have it your way."

The goon stepped back, quickly stripping off his jacket and throwing it at Buster. "Fine, you can have it."

"If I hear about either of you bothering my mom or any of our friends again, I'll be back. Next time, I won't be this nice. Now get lost."

The two men walked quickly, the illusion of pride forcing them not to run.

"Buster, you're like one of those heroes in the pulps like Detective Mydnight or The Pink Reaper."

"Not really. I'm just protecting my mom. How do you think she'll react to seeing what I've become?"

"You mean the whole dead and blue and glowing in the dark thing? She probably won't even notice."

Buster sighed. "Schnoz, you're scratching your nose. Let's go find my mother and bring her home."

What Happens in Vegas
Robert E. Waters

> *But as for you who forsake the Lord*
> *And forget my holy mountain,*
> *Who spread the table of fortune*
> *And fill bowls of mixed wine for Destiny,*
> *I will destine you for the sword,*
> *And you will bend down for the slaughter.*
> --Isaiah 65:11-12

I never enjoy going to Vegas, especially with my boss Joe Littlecloud. Whenever we visit, something bad happens. And this trip was no different, as we stood outside the Royal Gold Casino looking down at the mangled corpse of an unfortunate young lady. The tour bus that had hit her lay stalled on the sidewalk, its victim's blood smeared across its dented bumper and broken headlight. As I looked at her I had to admit that I was quite taken by the sight of her dishevelment. I tried licking my lips with cupped hands and coughing to mask my growling stomach. The boss noticed anyway.

"Don't even think about it," he said, kneeling down to study her impact wound more closely. "This one's not for consumption."

My name is Horus Ruth. I'm a ghoul. Don't ask why. Joe Littlecloud is an Apache *Diyin,* a shaman possessed with bear spirit and an inhuman ability to observe subtlety. We work for the FBI-VPA, the Federal Bureau of Investigation of Violent Paranormal Activity. We had come to Vegas for a little R and R, take in the sights, hopefully play a little poker, and to attend a conference. And here we were, standing in the middle of the street, staring at a murder victim. Well, we hadn't established that yet.

"How'd she die?" I asked.

Littlecloud chuckled. "She was hit by a bus."

"No shit," I said. "But why? From the looks of her, she seems capable, well-dressed, fairly clean and educated I suspect. Why would she step out into traffic?"

I'd actually witnessed the tail end of the event. I'd been standing at our hotel window, enjoying the evening lights, the muffled sounds of Sin City through the window, wondering where I was going to get my dinner. I heard screeching tires. I looked down and saw this woman being struck by a bus and tossed about thirty feet. Dead on impact.

"Suicide, perhaps," Littlecloud said. "Or maybe just bad luck."

I shook my head. "Bad luck, maybe. But not suicide. It just doesn't feel that way."

He looked at me in that inquisitive way he does with eyebrows raised and mouth tight. "What do you suspect?"

I couldn't say. But when you've been in the business as long as I have, you pick up on things. Littlecloud had great connections to the spirit world, great empathy and perception. But he lacked strong ties to the paranormal. That's why he hired me. I have more contacts in the seedy undead underworld than any assistant in the Bureau.

From the waning heat of her corpse, I was picking up a strange vibe. A different, non-suicidal kind of vibe. I just couldn't place it yet.

"Let's speak to the bus driver," Joe said.

He was sitting inside the door of his bus, rubbing his forehead like he had a headache. A uniformed officer was giving him the third degree. We shooed the officer away and asked our questions. "Your name?" Littlecloud said, leaning on his snake head cane.

The old man cleared this throat, said, "Sampson Kale, sir."

"From your perspective," I said, "can you tell us what happened?"

He nodded, though leaning away from me, clearly unnerved by my stooped demeanor, grey sallow flesh, and dark wrappings. "Sure. I was driving down the street here, on my microphone, giving my passengers the dime tour, pointing out casinos, theaters, bars, what have you. Like I've done a million times before. Then suddenly this woman was in front of me, right in the street. I tried stopping. I hit the brakes, but I struck her anyway. Or, rather, she struck me."

"You?" Littlecloud said, dragging his ample brows upward again. "Explain."

"Just like I said. I wasn't going very fast. I can't see how she would have been struck so hard and flown so far. She must have struck me."

I huffed. "What, like a bird or something?"

He nodded. "Yeah, just like a bird strike."

"But we heard your tires screeching," Joe said nodding to me. "You were hitting those brakes pretty hard."

"Well, sure. It's a big bus, fella. It takes a while to get it to stop, even if it's moving slow. But look at that damage." He pointed to the front of his bus. "Ain't no woman that thin can do that kind of damage just by stepping off the curb."

The old man had a point. The dent on that bumper looked like it had been made by a Louisville Slugger. It certainly didn't add up, although the young lady's wounds did confirm the man's conjecture. Her face, skull, neck and shoulders had been pretty much reduced to mush.

We thanked him for his questions and went off to canvas the area more thoroughly. Littlecloud pulled a feather fetish and rattle from his pocket and bounced around the bus, hoping to scare up vagrant spirits that might give him clues. I returned to the body.

I admit I did so because I was still hungry. The sight of her was painful, but I was one to always face my fears (or hungers, in this case) head on. I knelt beside her and studied her wounds once more.

There was no doubt about it: She had struck the bus very hard. I estimated that the differences in speeds had not been that much apart. Meaning, she had struck the bus roughly at the same speed the bus was going. I put on a glove, unfolded a flap of torn green blouse from her shoulder, and studied the wound there.

Very odd, I thought. This particular part of her body had burn marks, and the flesh did not show signs of impact. Rather, the lacerated skin had markings consistent with something blowing out of her, erupting outward as soon as the impact occurred, as if it had pulled her into the oncoming bus. And one other thing that was equally interesting: she held dice in her hand, large red semi-opaque ones like they use in casinos. She gripped them hard.

I looked around to make sure no one was watching. I dipped the middle finger of my right hand into her shoulder wound. I pulled it out and massaged the blood with my thumb. I smelled it.

I was wracked with nausea. The grey skin on my right arm rippled with goose bumps. My stomach heaved, my mind whirled. I tried keeping my balance as I looked deeply into the blood.

Terrible dark-red eyes stared back at me.

I blacked out.

* * *

Normally, when something like this happens to us, we screw our courage to the sticking pate (as Shakespeare might have said), and keep on the case until it's solved. However, like I mentioned, we were in town for a convention. The National Paranormal Investigators Conclave, or N-PIC as it is more commonly called in the government. Littlecloud had already begged off the East Coast Regional to deal with a dragon issue. We weren't about to miss this one.

I awoke quickly after passing out, wiped the blood away from my finger, and told the boss some harebrained excuse as to why it happened (starving, dry desert air, etc.). I didn't want to tell him the truth; not yet anyway. He would have insisted that we skip the con and keep working. But he couldn't afford to do that. He had to attend. His career was in jeopardy.

So I cleaned up quickly, and we went to the convention center for the first night of the Conclave, with strict instructions to local law enforcement to keep us informed on the investigation of the dead girl. We were out of our jurisdiction, in a way, although since I had seen the accident in part, we were effectively involved whether we liked it or not. But there was an unspoken rule among paranormal investigators which required out-of-towners to report any official business in which they were involved. Littlecloud followed bureau rules and did so. He got an earful. Nobody likes Joe Littlecloud butting in on their turf.

"I see no reason for you to be involved any further, Joe," ex-vampire-cum-investigator Casper Dean said as we hovered around a punch bowl. I was scarfing down fish appetizers that lay by the dozens on tiny wheat crackers nearby. "We'll take it from here. I have my people on it already. I'm sure it'll amount to nothing more than a suicide."

"Casper," Littlecloud said in his best condescending voice, shaking his head as if he were scolding a child. "Surely you will not fall into the old trap of Confirmation Bias. Are your men seeking evidence to confirm what you already suspect?"

That got the fang-man's goat. "Nonsense," Dean said, slamming down his empty cup. "We're professionals, Joe, and I thank you to remember it. We seek both confirming and disconfirming evidence, and we do not need your assistance."

"I'm sure that is true. But since Horus witnessed the event himself, we'll keep in touch with your officials, per Bureau procedure, and of course share with you and yours anything that we might find."

Dean snarled, and for a moment, I thought he was going to flash his fangs. Then I remembered that he had had them removed during his extensive cosmetic surgery to fix the blight of his vampirism. Once it had been discovered that a virus, much like Herpes but of course, more deadly, was the cause of vampiric bloodlust, then it was easy enough to medicate and keep under wraps. Casper Dean had done just that. Many more, however, refused to do so. That's why vampires are still prominent and very, very deadly.

Dean walked away angry, but Joe didn't care. "He'll botch the case like he always does," he said to me as he ladled out another cup of spiked mango juice. I nodded agreement.

"Don't be so sure."

The voice was feminine and familiar. We turned together to face a dark-haired woman who had come up behind us at the table.

In the days prior to my turning, when I had a workable penis and balls worthy of the name, I would have considered her very attractive. But Trina Newcastle was just another human to me now. An exceptionally intelligent one, I'll grant you, and one nearly as competent as my boss. Littlecloud certainly would agree to that assessment.

He stumbled a bit with his punch, wiping his left hand on his tan half-coat and offering it to her. She took it with a slender hand that gave away nothing in its subtle pressure. She smiled and said, "Dean is not as bad as you think, Joe. He earns his pay here in the desert."

"He's a glorified gumshoe with a penchant for blood," Littlecloud said, holding her hand longer than acquaintances usually do, letting his thumb run across her pale skin. She let him linger.

"He's not a vampire anymore."

Joe shook his head. "A person cannot hide from their nature, Trina. You know that better than most."

She stiffened and tried to pull her hand away. Joe held it tightly, not letting her go. She curled a deep red lip, flashed a spot of tongue through veneered teeth. I thought she was about to cast a nasty curse spell, but instead she smiled, squeezed back, and said, "How's the weather in Baltimore?"

Littlecloud let her go. "Same as in Portland, I suspect. Wet and muggy."

"And you thought you'd come west to teach us all proper investigative practices." She could not hide her smirk.

"I'm not here voluntarily," Littlecloud said, setting his cup down carefully, never taking his eyes off of her. "The council wishes to have a few words with me."

She huffed. "Yes, we do."

That she was on the council, sitting in judgment against my boss, did not sit well with me.

"Joe has done nothing wrong," I said, standing as straight as possible, staring into her dark blue eyes. "He saved the fucking city, for Christ's sake."

Newcastle stared right back, gave a little chuckle. "We will determine for ourselves what Joe Littlecloud did and did not do pertaining to the dragon Hydrastigor. We will find out what he chose to divulge in his report... and what he chose to keep secret." She bent low. "Keeping secrets, Horus, can be quite damning."

Did she just wink at me? I pulled back several inches. I could have sworn the flesh beneath her right eye twitched, as if she knew I was keeping information from Littlecloud about what I had seen in the dead woman's blood. I did not know much about Trina Newcastle, and the boss had not spoken much of her, but I gathered that they had had intimacies in the past. But what I did know of her was that she was one of the best spiritualists in the world, with an insight into the corporeal realms like no other investigator in the Bureau, and she was a damn fine spell-caster. Perhaps extra-sensory perception was part of her gift as well.

Joe didn't let her accusation stand. "If you have something to accuse me of, Trina, do it in the council chamber. Not here over a bowl of punch."

She giggled, sincerely I believe, and laid her hand gently on Littlecloud's chest. He seemed to melt beneath her touch. "You're a very funny guy, Joe. I miss that about you. Good luck tomorrow."

She left a kiss on his cheek and dashed away. Littlecloud stood there, watching her disappear into a throng of colleagues. He cleared his throat. "She's quite lovely, isn't she?"

I blanched. "She just accused you of lying in your official report, and you stand there checking out her ass. I swear, Joe, you live people are—"

"Life is more complicated than you think, Horus," he said, straightening himself, fixing his collar, and moving toward the ballroom. "Relationships are… layered."

As if a ghoul's life isn't complicated? One day, I was as alive as Littlecloud, a college student enjoying my youth. The next, I was kidnapped by an Egyptian priest with designs to rule the world and turned into the monster you see before you today. He thinks I can't understand complex relationships? I shook my head. Sometimes, I know why people find my boss annoying.

I said nothing, however, and we proceeded into the ballroom where opening ceremonies were about to begin.

The phone in my pocket began to vibrate.

I fished it out, flicked it open and read the new text message. I read it carefully, twice.

"Damn!"

"What is it?" Littlecloud asked.

I pushed the phone back into my pocket. "There's been another accident."

* * *

I convinced Littlecloud to stay at the Conclave. He needed to glad-hand and politic anyway before tomorrow's council meeting. It wasn't anything he liked doing, but it was necessary. Besides, I could canvas and interview by myself, and I could sneak away with no one knowing or, honestly, caring.

This time it was a man, mid-twenties. Alone in Sin City, come to town just a couple days prior from Tennessee, to catch the sights and to do a little gambling. In his broken left hand he held a red poker chip decorated with the name and insignia of the place he was staying: Belmont Hotel and Casino. He'd just left a third floor tournament of Texas hold'em when he stepped into a dark elevator shaft and plunged to his death. His body got tangled in the cables on the way down. They nearly tore him in two. *Unlucky bastard!*

I was hoisted down by harness into the shaft to check it out. Two officers were waiting, one plain-clothes. I recognized him.

"Felix Renfield," I said, offering my cold gray hand. He declined it, still sore, I supposed, from my teasing of his name at last year's Conclave in New York. "What do you make of it?"

He shrugged. "The man fell to his death." He pointed at the bloody cables. "Got snagged around there, ripped his stomach wide open."

"How it is possible that he fell? How was the door of the elevator open? What's the protocol in this place for such a thing?"

"It's a mystery," Renfield said, kneeling down beside the corpse. "Inoperable elevator doors are kept shut so as to keep something like this from happening. But just a few seconds before our victim fell, the door opened."

I shook my head. "Was he distracted? Was he talking to someone, not paying attention, and thought the elevator was working?"

Renfield shook his head. "No, we got it on video. He was alone. He walked right up to the door, it opened, and he fell in. Looks like a possible suicide."

Just like the female victim in the street not twelve hours ago. This young man had thrown himself at death just like she had. "Suicide? Was he responsible for opening the door?"

"No."

"Then it was a homicide."

"There's no proof of that, Ruth. There was no one else in the video. No one pushed him. He fell on his own volition."

I huffed. Big word for such a small man. No, Renfield was a fine officer, but these pure humans... they fight tooth and nail to try to deny what's right in front of them. They live in a world of faeries, vampires, werewolves, witches, dragons, and ghouls, and yet they keep trying to fit rational causes to unusual events. I suppose from Renfield's perspective, it's best to apply Ockham's razor whenever possible; makes his life much simpler. But Littlecloud and I come at it from a different angle. We've seen things, fought against things that would literally make Renfield's head explode with the blink of an eye. No, what happened to this boy was not coincidence. There's no way that a man could have walked out alone in a crowded casino and into the waiting mouth of a dark elevator without being compelled to do so, without someone there near the elevators in witness to the event. No. This boy had been set up and murdered.

"Have you informed Special Agent Dean about this?" I asked.

"Yes," Renfield said. "We've been instructed to secure the site, collect evidence, and await further instructions."

I nodded. Joe was right. Dean was going to botch this. He'd wait too long, let evidence languish, fail to question suspects. I wondered how a guy like that could continue to be a field agent while a brilliant man like

Littlecloud had to fight for his job? Politics, politics, politics...

While Renfield and the other officer fiddled around with useless evidence near the cables, I took a quick peek at the mangled stomach. Nasty, bloody, quite delicious-looking I had to admit, but the thing that caught my attention was right below the right rib cage. A big hole blasted out, as if something had ripped through the flesh. And around it, black burn marks. Just like the girl.

When they weren't looking, I took out a handkerchief, pushed it into the hole to get a good sample of blood, then tucked it into my boot. I then tugged on my harness cable and was pulled out of the elevator shaft.

* * *

For protocol's sake, I spent a little time after the elevator shaft asking questions of the people in the casino. Did you see anything? Was the victim acting in an unusual manner? I got no useful answers. Some of them weren't even aware that a death had occurred, so caught up in their own lives, their own problems. Or perhaps they had been mesmerized not to remember. I tried divining such a spell: nothing. I wasn't qualified to detect ethereal energies. That's more of Joe's department.

Afterward, I was literally starving. So I combined dinner with work and went to the Clark County morgue, where an old acquaintance of mine, Dr. Gunter Faber, provided forensic and clinical autopsies on paranormal entities. He was also a skilled phlebotomist. Few in the country know blood as well as Dr. Faber.

He passed me a lightly frost-bitten hand from a murdered gang member and took my messy handkerchief. He sniffed it. He grunted in that American-German accent of his. "Potent."

"Indeed," I said, nibbling the ring finger. The actual ring, fortunately, had been removed.

He motioned for me to follow him into a back room. I did so, sniffing loudly against the pungent methanol and formaldehyde stink that hung in the air like a cloud. I would have vomited had I been alive.

"Whenever I see you, Horus," Faber said, flicking on a light to reveal his personal office, "I know my evening is going to be shot."

"Lucky it was me and not my boss," I said, finishing off the pinky. "He'd have regaled you for hours with ancient stories of ritual dancing and vision quests."

He nodded, spread the handkerchief out on a clear glass table, and studied it carefully with a magnifier he popped onto his right eye like a monocle. "From a murder victim?"

I nodded. "Almost certainly. Don't know the true cause yet, but..." And then I told him everything I knew, including the fainting spell after seeing those terrible red eyes in the blood of the girl. He listened carefully, nodded on occasion, then went to his desk and produced a small mason jar filled with a clear liquid. Inside the liquid were leeches.

"*Hirudo medicinalis*," he said proudly, grinning from ear to ear as he held the jar up into the light. "Europe's medical leeches. Used for centuries. Fascinating little monsters."

"But the blood is all dry," I said, finishing the hand and tossing the knuckle bones into the waste basket beneath the table.

"It is, but there's a lot of it, and these little fellows should be able to eat enough to give me a good reading."

I shook my head. "I don't follow."

He seemed annoyed at my lack of blood knowledge. He opened the jar and fished out three leeches with long tweezers. He dropped them on the middle of the handkerchief where the dried blood was thickest. "They will be drawn by the powerful smell of this blood," he said, "and regardless of its composition, will hit it strongly with their anticoagulants, anesthetics, and other juices, making it a gooey liquid. Then they'll feed. Once they get nice and ripe, we'll see what we've got. Grab a magazine and relax. This will take some time."

I was in no mood to read or relax. I was frankly in no mood to be here in a cool morgue, despite Faber graciously giving me dinner. My mind was on Littlecloud, wondering what he was doing, whom he was speaking to. His interrogation would begin tomorrow, but I wanted to be with him now, helping him prepare. At some point, I too would be called before the council to answer questions. Not tomorrow, though. Still, we did not need these murders, this distraction from the true issues at hand. We had not come to Vegas to get involved in another mess; we had messes of our own. But when does anyone come to Vegas without getting involved in something nefarious?

I watched the leeches feed. There was one who seemed to have found a font of salty goodness, sucking and growing, sucking and growing until it was the size of a spring carrot. I was amazed at how quickly it had grown, while the other two seemed to flounder around the edges, barely making a dent. Faber seemed surprised too.

He put on goggles and a surgical mask, motioned for me to step back. He took a scalpel and placed the blade against the warm, meaty flesh of the leech. From his pocket he produced a circular box, like a snuff container, and set it aside. "Okay, let's see what we got."

He cut a perfect line down the length of the engorged leech, letting the newly consumed blood flow out of the wound. He set the scalpel aside, opened the snuff box, and pinched out a spot of green dust. He held his thumb and index finger above the cut and slowly massaged them back and forth, letting the dust fall into the cut.

Nothing happened for a full minute. Then an image, dark and conical, shot out of the leech. It was like a little funnel cloud, a mini-tornado of black smoke and red, radiant eyes. It swirled through the air like a dervish, looked at me, screamed, and then flew toward my face. I dropped instinctively, and the evil little imp flew past me and dissipated against the office door.

"Holy shit!" I said, collecting myself. "Just like the image I saw in the girl's blood. What the hell is it?"

Faber, clearly in shock, waved his hand. "An invasive spirit, for sure, but I've never seen anything like it."

"Explain."

"Well, invasive spirits travel through the blood, using the pumping motion of the heart to enter the arms, legs, and brain to take control of their hosts. This is typical. But most of them aren't strong enough to last very long after they have done what they are going to do. Thus, they leave very little residual trace behind. This one... that was no spirit we saw. That was its afterimage, its footprint, if you will. A creature strong enough to leave an image like that after the blood has already dried... well, I've never seen anything like it. Whatever spirit resided in that man's blood, it was not placed there in the normal manner. There's serious voodoo involved here, Horus."

Great! Just what I wanted to hear. "Do you know what kind of spirit it was?"

Faber shook his head. "That's above my pay scale. You need a real master of the spirit world to give you that answer."

I sighed deeply. *Damn it all!* I knew of only one person in town with that expertise, and I was not looking forward to speaking with her again.

* * *

Near midnight, I found Littlecloud in the bar of our hotel, finishing off what I assumed to be his third gin and tonic. He was calm, relaxed, huddled quietly beneath his bear-fur cloak, fiddling with his cane and keeping his eyes focused on the rows of liquor bottles behind the bar. I took the stool beside him and brought him up to speed on everything, including what I had seen in the dead woman's blood. He listened and said nothing.

It's hard sometimes to read him. He's an Apache shaman possessed of bear spirit. He believes that he is the reincarnation of a murderer and wife beater, sent back to Earth to atone for his sins. The bear spirit possessed *him*, he claims, as punishment; for you see, while a bear spirit gives its host courage and strength, a sense of place, an earthliness not present in other totem sprits, like the coyote or the bat, it also saturates its host with violence, unpredictability, and thus one must always work to control the rage therein, and to push against the base instinct of the bear which is to lash out and kill to protect itself. And that is why Littlecloud has bear spirit: the bear forces him to tame his rage.

He took a sip from his glass and said, "Tomorrow at one, my first interview begins. I will spend the morning preparing my opening statement. You may attend the interview, but you may not speak unless asked a direct question."

"I'll be there."

Littlecloud set his glass down. "I don't want you there. Wednesday morning, you must attend. They will ask you questions at that time. Tomorrow, I want you to review surveillance video of the casinos that the victims were at. Find these people and study their movements on the floor, see what games they played, where they sat, who was around them, who they talked to, what they ate, drank. Learn everything you can. Don't you find it odd that they both had game items in their hands when they died?"

I did find it strange for the lady to have dice. That is not an item one usually walks out of a casino with; they can be pretty protective of those things. But the poker chip hadn't registered. It was quite common for people to buy souvenir chips at casinos, and if this guy was an outsider, it made perfect sense. "The thought had occurred to me," I said.

"And don't you find it even stranger that the impact of their violent deaths did not sling those objects from their grasp?"

Now, I felt like an idiot. I had been so focused on the victims' wounds and the possible reasons for them that I had overlooked that oddity. I lied. "That thought had occurred to me as well."

"Then let it possess your entire thinking tomorrow," he said, begging off a fourth drink offered by the bartender. "Pay close attention to their hands. And keep your Bible in mind as well. In particular, the Book of Isaiah."

"Pardon?"

He rattled off a quote from that chapter, from rote memory, which was surprising coming from an Apache with little interest in a Christian god. I was quite familiar with the Bible myself; or, rather, I used to be before my turning, but it had been decades since I had cracked the leather binding of my copy. I did not recognize the passage that he was speaking of.

"What does it mean?" I asked.

"It means that good fortune – or *luck* as some people call it – is a blessing bestowed by God and He alone, and if you forget that, then He shall destine you for the sword. Luck, Horus, is not something that comes from the wind. If it exists at all, it is a divine gift from God. People come to Vegas to gamble, to throw dice, to lay chance to the wind in hopes of finding a bit of luck. Looks to me like our victims came to Vegas and found a whole heap of luck and were then bent to the slaughter because of it. But how, exactly? And why?"

He stopped, and I guess expected me to answer. I had no answers. I had learned over the years that his questions were hunches. He had a hunch, but he wasn't prepared to say what it was or to act upon it. I, on the other hand, sat in the dark. I didn't understand what he was driving at, but perhaps in the surveillance footage I'd find the answers. Now only one issue remained before us.

"Don't worry about Trina," he said, climbing from his stool and straightening his cloak. "I'll speak to her tomorrow."

"But she's a bitch, Joe, sitting in judgment of you. Why would she condescend to speak to you again?"

Littlecloud paid his tab and snickered. He tapped his cane upon my shoulder, his eyes bright with energy. "Oh, my recalcitrant little undead friend. There are many, many ways to communicate with someone without speaking. Haven't I taught you anything?"

Too much if you ask me, but I kept that statement to myself and followed him to the elevator and on up to our room where we needed to grab a few hours' sleep.

We both had a busy Tuesday ahead of us.

* * *

I sat in front of three flat LCD screens in the Royal Gold Casino's security office, flipping back and forth between video clips, focusing specifically on the few hours leading up to the first victim's death. It took me a while to find her in the morass of casino patrons, but I finally spotted her leaving the slots and making her way to a craps table, where she spent the better part of the day throwing dice.

She'd been a pretty woman in life, soft dark hair, gentle features, someone that I might have admired before my change. A downhome personality, and although I could not hear what she was saying, she had greeted everyone with a generous smile and a pleasant demeanor. And she knew her craps too, no doubt about that. She flung those dice down the table with consummate skill, and won more than she lost.

She took a break at noon for a bite to eat. Nothing strange there; she ate alone at the bar, nursed a Fuzzy Navel until about 1:00 p.m., talked to a few people and the bartender, but nothing stood out as unusual about any of it. She certainly didn't have anything in her hand, and certainly not the dice that she had held in her death. At around 1:30, she returned to the floor.

She went back to the slots for a little while, making some decent coin there, cashing it all in for chips. She left the floor for a couple hours after that. Where she went I do not know. But she returned around 5:00 and went back to the same craps table she had been at in the morning. A different group of people were around her; I checked that very carefully, seeing if anyone was the same. Sure, they could have had on different clothing, but it was an entirely different composition of people. More men now than women, and multiple ethnicities as well.

She started off really well, very well in fact, winning a huge stack of chips. Looking at the pile in front of her, I estimated she had won nearly fifty grand. Why she didn't stop there I couldn't tell you; some people are stupid. Anyway, shortly after that, something happened to the dice that the table was using. They disappeared. People started looking around the table, the stick man, the box man, and even the other two dealers. They couldn't be found. The box man replaced the missing dice with new ones, and the game proceeded.

But her fortune had changed. She started to lose, placing her bets wrong, letting things ride when she should have reconsidered. Her dice began to fail her. She got frustrated more and more, illegally switched her dice from hand to hand, tried to hand chips to a dealer, was warned several times to follow proper table procedure and etiquette. By the time she had lost forty-five grand, she stalked away, leaving her remaining chips on the table.

Ten minutes later, she lay dead in the street.

The videos played out in similar fashion at the Belmont Casino.

The guy was an average sort, seemed to me. His identification and hotel records put his residence in Memphis, Tennessee, and why he had come all the way out west when he could have easily boarded a gambling boat on the Mississippi is anyone's guess, but there he was, the fifth player at a table of Texas hold'em.

He'd joined the tournament officially at its start, and had several excellent hands right away, winning a large sum and looking to sweep the table. However, at around the forty-five minute mark, he seemed to lose a ten dollar chip. He paused the game, looked around the table, had the dealer at hand look as well. It was nowhere to be found. He got upset about it, wanted it replaced, but the dealer would not do so. From that point on, he began to lose, and badly. Everything went cold, and he grew more frustrated until at one point he slammed down his hand and stumbled away, seemingly drunk although I can attest that I never saw him drink anything harder than water.

Five minutes later, he stepped into a dark elevator shaft and plunged to his death.

In both cases, the missing poker chip and dice were found in their respective hands after death, somehow missing scrutiny when the items were searched around the table. Clearly, those items were not in their hands when they disappeared, or they would have been spotted; one cannot palm a set of dice in a casino and keep them hidden from highly skilled personnel trained to spot cheats and thieves. Those items were in their hands, disappeared, and then reappeared. How and by what source?

I reviewed the videos over and over, concentrating each time on a different part, zooming in on areas that would seem vacant and uninteresting. My undead eyes began to blur, grow fuzzy. I stopped for an hour, took a breather, checked them again.

Then things started to fall into place. Where there seemed not to be patterns, there were. When it seemed that the other gamblers around our victims were different, they weren't... at least not one patron. It was a subtle similarity, one that would have missed even my scrutiny had the gentleman not rolled up his sleeve during the poker game. I had to run the video frame by frame, but I found it.

In each game, there was one patron that had a Star of David tattoo on his wrist. The person with that tattoo began to win regularly at the same time that our victims began to lose. And casino records clearly indicated that the person who ultimately won at each table was the person with the tattoo. They cashed in their chips and left the casino shortly thereafter. It was a different person with a tattoo in each game, but the tattoo was the same, with the same red color, located on the exact same location of the right wrist. Coincidence? Perhaps, but given the nature of our victims' deaths, something more was afoot here. I had no clue what it was.

I left the casinos near 1:00 a.m. and went to the Conclave to tell Littlecloud of my findings. They had adjourned for the day, and from the look on his face, it had not gone well. I told him what I had discovered. He seemed to be listening, but part of his mind was in some far-off place, preoccupied on what I could only guess. It was hard sometimes to tell with him. He was either thinking about his hearing or he was deep into contemplation about our case.

"Did you hear what I said?" I asked him as he hailed a cab.

He nodded.

"And did you get a chance to talk to Trina?"

A cab pulled up and he opened the door, waited for me to step in. "No," he said. "There wasn't an opportunity. But we can wait a bit on that. Your discovery is the first step to enlightenment on this matter. It's time for us to do what we have come here to do, Horus."

I climbed in. "And what's that?"

He shut the door behind us, turned to me and smiled. "Gamble."

* * *

There are no hard and fast rules that prevent paranormals, wizards, sorcerers, etcetera from gambling. The casinos in Las Vegas will take anyone's money. But there are restrictions, coupled with company mages in plain clothes that roam around the floors trying to detect cheating (and they're damn good at it too). A telekinetic spell applied to a pair of dice, for example, could guarantee the correct number every time. Casinos frown on that sort of thing. So there are rules to be followed.

Littlecloud was not allowed to carry in his cane, his bear cloak, or any fetishes whatsoever. It was practically a strip search. I wasn't allowed on the floor at all, although I can assure you that ghouls do not carry any additional luck or tricks up their sleeves when it comes to chance. Our luck runs out when we become undead.

So I watched from the video surveillance room. Littlecloud chose roulette and set himself up handsomely with a nice pile of chips. There were six players on his wheel and none of them struck me as out of place. None of them had tattoos save for one lady who had a cat's paw near her left ear. Initial bets were placed, the croupier spun the wheel in one direction, the ball in the other direction. Around and around it went, and while both were spinning, Littlecloud placed a few more bets, opting for a range of pockets based on the proximity of the wheel's layout. It was a common move for roulette players, and a safe one to employ to begin the game. Picking the exact color and pocket the ball was going to drop in was tricky at best. But he'd get there. Around and around the wheel went, and sometimes Littlecloud won, sometimes he lost.

Then he began to win, a lot, moving from range betting to picking the exact color and pocket. His chip pile grew, and grew, and grew. People left the wheel, came to the wheel. This went on for over an hour. By that time, Littlecloud had racked up about a hundred grand.

Then a black-haired woman showed up, petite, nondescript, nothing you'd write home to mama about. She conducted some range betting for a bit, hit a pocket here and there, then went on a winning streak at nearly the exact same time my boss began to overload his colors, make wild bets, show apprehension in his selections, even once being reprimanded by the croupier for trying to bet after the lady had declared *rien ne va plus.*

And then it happened, just like with our victims. Littlecloud lost a chip. It simply disappeared. Everyone looked for it. Littlecloud even allowed them to search his body to ensure he hadn't pocketed it by mistake. It was simply gone. It wasn't even in his hand.

The game went on for a little while after that, and then Littlecloud placed his last bet. He lost, and with that, every single chip he had earned. He staggered away from the table, drunk-like, disoriented.

I let him do so, trying frantically to zoom in on the lady to find that tattoo I had discovered on the other gamblers. Nothing. She was clever, keeping her body angled away from the camera to block her wrists. From that, I knew that she *knew* someone was watching, and I knew then that this was not some random spiritualist trying to scam a few extra bucks on a junket to Vegas. She knew she was being watched, and that meant there was a larger conspiracy at play.

She left the table and I wanted to follow her, but Littlecloud had left first, and he was out there somewhere. I went to the coatroom where his belongings had been stored. He had gotten them already and had wandered out of the casino.

"Shit!" I said, and went after him.

I went out into the hot afternoon Nevada sun, looked left, right, and couldn't find him. I took a chance and searched right, trotting down three blocks, looking everywhere as I went. Don't let people tell you lies: Ghouls can be in sunlight; we just don't like it much. I cupped my hands over my eyes as I searched, and finally, I found him.

He was in a brawl with three street thugs halfway down an alley. They were actually trying to get away from him, but he had employed some magic, and they were lined up against the wall, and he was beating one of them with his cane. The other two struggled to break free from his spell. I sped down the alley, fearful of what might happen.

Then it did. Littlecloud's bear spirit awoke. His body changed, his cloak became his body, thick fur spread from the cloak to his arms, shoulders, face. He was turning into a bear, and if I didn't stop him soon…

I leapt and hit him square in the side. One of the thugs, abject terror on his face, pulled a pistol and fired off a round. It was meant for Littlecloud's head. It found my side, ripping through the hollow flesh of my chest as I pushed my boss down. The spell was broken, and the three goons ran off.

Littlecloud shivered beneath me as he transformed back into his human shape. His eyes rolled back into his skull, his mouth opened, and out came a black mist, a swirl of heated dust and red violent eyes. Just like the beast I had seen in both victims' blood. I took a swing at it. It ignored me and instead opened its ethereal maw, flashed long white teeth, then snapped at me as it shot across the alley to dissipate against red brick.

It was gone, but luckily, Littlecloud was alive. What had happened to the spirit's first two victims had not happened to my boss. I had taken the bullet that would have killed him.

I took a moment to reach in and pull the bullet out. I don't have blood in the traditional sense anymore. It's more of a gooey black oily substance, and so it was like working through syrup to pull the little piece of metal out of my side. It had broken three ribs on impact but already they were healing.

Littlecloud was fine too, now fully back to normal, but sitting upright, naked save for the bear fur cloak that hugged his shoulders. In his hand, he held the poker chip that had gone missing.

"Are you okay?" I asked.

He nodded, his eyes fixed on the chip. "Yes, and thank you. That bullet would have killed me."

"All in a day's work. What happened? You were winning like mad... then you stopped. Why?"

He did not speak at first, content instead to contemplate the question by rotating the chip over and over between thumb, middle and index fingers. He cleared his throat, then said, "Something possessed me, and I know now what it is. I know what we seek."

"What?"

He wouldn't answer. It's uncommon to see fear in Littlecloud's eyes, but it was there, in full bloom. He was afraid. He swallowed. "We need to speak to Trina... and quickly."

* * *

She refused to see us at first. She was on the committee sitting in judgment against my boss; it was unprofessional and frankly, against the rules to meet with interviewees during Conclave. But she relented, and came to us shortly after midnight, wearing a fake face and loose-fitting clothing. We met in the hotel bar.

Trina sat down across from us in a booth. She was blonde and pudgy, in stark contrast to her quite lovely and feminine dark hair and shapely features. She almost looked normal under her disguise.

"I don't have long," she said, accepting a glass of red wine from our waiter. She swirled it around, took a sip, set the glass down. "What is it you want?"

Littlecloud had left his bear cloak in the room. He sat in a tie-dye T-shirt and ball cap, his grey flowing hair rather ridiculously shoved beneath the brim. He looked like a middle-aged man trying to hide a bald spot. "We have a serious problem on our hands, Trina. Those accidental deaths, those *murders*, that we have been investigating... they're being committed by Babylonian gods."

Whoah! But that was my boss for you: One moment forcing you to read the Bible to pick up a subtle clue; the next, hitting you with a hammer. He had not bothered to mention this to me before Trina had arrived.

"What are you talking about, Joe?" she asked.

"Isaiah, chapter sixty-five, verses eleven and twelve. Gad and Meni, Babylonian pagan gods, representing good and bad luck. Some also call them good fortune and destiny. Believed to have been worshipped by Israelites in Babylon, and featured as ill-begotten spirits in The Bible. One cannot exist without the other, and they stand in direct conflict to the notion of an all-powerful, all-seeing God. There can be no good luck or bad luck in a monotheistic system. God rewards you with whatever fortune you are worthy of and chooses your destiny. There's no such thing as luck, and to believe so, to pay homage to such blasphemies, calls upon God to smite you where you stand."

Trina listened to all this with mild interest, sipping her drink and trying to hold off a smirk. "You don't believe in all that, do you?" she finally asked.

Littlecloud shook his head. "Of course not. There is not just one God. That has been proven over and over again throughout history. But believers have a nasty habit of ignoring the truth, relying instead on faith to inform their judgment. Christian mages have for centuries been able to keep this notion of one God alive by tempering the astral plane, holding off the spirits by diluting the corporeal realm with shields, incantations, mana and prayer. You know this better than anyone. But someone has broken through it all. Someone has called Gad and Meni through the gap, and they are being used to steal good luck from one person and give it to another.

"I experienced it as I played roulette today," he said, finishing his whiskey and setting the shot glass aside. "I felt a wave of good tidings, good luck, I guess you could say. And this was no trick, no incantation of my own to give myself an edge. I was going to. I have *diyin* magic that I can call upon that few security mages know about. But I didn't need to. Once I started playing, I started winning, and the rush of joy and happiness during my streak was powerful. I knew something had invaded my body. But I could do nothing about it. I was trapped by it.

"And then it changed. My good luck was suddenly gone, and I felt a deep melancholy, a sadness, a frustration. My mind grew cloudy, and I began to make mistakes. Nothing I did was right. And that's when I knew that something was working against me, something else had invaded my body, and had kicked Gad out. I knew then that is was Meni, for there could be no other spirit powerful enough to expel Gad. And someone standing beside that table was the cause of it all. They had put Gad in me first to rouse my natural good fortune. Then when it was at a fever pitch, they expelled Gad by throwing Meni inside, forcing Gad out and into another host body at the table. They stole my good luck, Trina, and left inside me an evil god, with no way out, desperate to escape.

"That's what happened to our victims. Imbued with an evil pagan spirit, they wandered away, under Meni's control, and when it found a way to escape, it threw the woman at a bus, and forced the man to fall to his death. Because only through death, through truly bad fortune, can Meni escape."

Trina looked like she was about to laugh, obviously unconvinced at what she was being told. She cleared her throat, said, "Ridiculous. God-spirits can only enter the body through a portal, an object, or in your experience, a fetish, that must touch the host. And I don't see how something like that could be allowed to enter the casino with all their security measures and—"

Littlecloud interrupted her by placing the poker chip on the table. He pointed to it. "That is their portal. For me and the man, it was a poker chip. For the woman, dice. You know what this means, don't you?"

"No."

"It means that employees at the casinos are working with whatever group is using these gods to fix the games. These portals are already placed within the chip and dice populations, distributed to the tables, and when the right person, with a heightened aura of good luck, touches the portal, in flows Gad... chased by Meni in time. These pagan gods have been doing this forever, Trina. And each time they chase, they get stronger, and stronger, and stronger, until even their masters will not survive them. They will break free and encircle the globe. Thousand, maybe tens of thousands, will die from aggressive swings of good and bad luck before they are brought back under control."

Trina sat back, a growing balminess to her skin. I could tell that the edges of the spell that kept her false face in check were beginning to erode. She didn't have much time left, but what Littlecloud had said troubled her.

She sighed deeply, then said, "Okay. If what you say is true, what do you want me to do about it?"

Littlecloud rubbed his face. He did this when he was frustrated. "Do I have to spell it out for you, Trina? You need to do two things. First, you need to convince them to cancel the hearings and the Conclave. This is a grave matter that must be dealt with now before it gets out of hand. Bullshit politics can wait, and if the committee wants to find me guilty, then I'll accept my penalty afterwards. But now we must unite and end this threat.

"Second, no one in town knows spirits better than you. I need you to help us track down the source of this conspiracy."

"Yes," I said, finding a chance to break in. "We know some things about them. It's a Jewish group, perhaps from Israel, who are the ones reaping the benefits of the Gad-Meni chase. I've spotted them at the tables. That's all I know. I do not know if they are willing conspirators, or being coerced, but they are involved."

Trina shook her head, sat up straight. "Can't do it. I can't call off the Conclave just on your speculation, Joe."

"Dammit, Trina," he said, his eyes glaring anger. "I'm not some fucking noob agent without a clue. I'm Joe Littlecloud. Twenty years experience. I know what I know, and I know this is right. You *know* I'm right."

"I know nothing of the sort," she said. "All I know is that you have a theory. It's a decent one, but you have no evidence. Not yet. And they aren't going to call it off on your hunch. They will assume you are asking to do it in order to get out of sentencing."

And they'd be right, I thought. This whole thing with Hydrastigor was a fucking circus, a waste of money, and a waste of time. And I intended on telling them that tomorrow at my interview. And judging from the look on Trina's face, I wasn't going to get out of that either.

We sat there in silence for a long while. The palpable friction between them was obvious. When people attuned to the spirit world, the paranormal, are angry with each other, it's felt by all those around them. I'm undead, but even I could sense the anger, the rage, the love, the disappointment, between them.

Trina finally stood, shook her head. "I'm sorry, Joe. I cannot ask them to call off the Conclave. I love you, but I cannot do it. You have no evidence. Get evidence, and then, perhaps…"

Joe was about to say something, but he was interrupted by screeching tires, a loud crash, and screaming coming from the street in front of the hotel.

We rushed out. Across the street, a cab and a truck had struck head-on, and in the center of the truck's hood lay the mangled body of a woman, holding a child in her tightly closed arms. Littlecloud drew his badge from his pocket, flashed it around to force the pedestrians out of the way.

Trina could not speak. She just stood there, mouth open, her fake thick fingers across her quivering lips. Littlecloud leaned over the victims, and I stood beside him as he fished underneath the woman's body.

He pulled out her bloody hand and opened it to reveal a playing card. A jack of diamonds. In its center lay a black, smoldering hole.

He yanked her arm up, not caring for discretion, humility, common decency. He pulled the arm straight and flashed the card it held in front of Trina's face. "Here's your fucking evidence!"

Trina said nothing. She changed right then, back to her dark hair and slim figure. She began to cry. She fell back three steps, turned, and disappeared into the crowd.

Littlecloud laid the woman's arm down gently, then fell to the street, crossed his legs and sat there, silently, his head down, rocking back and forth, whispering an Apache prayer in hopes of helping the woman and her child into the Hereafter.

I sat beside him in silence until the Las Vegas police arrived.

* * *

Trina tried to cancel the Conclave, but she failed. At noon on the third and final day of the conference, Joe Littlecloud was suspended from active duty for six months, Grade One pay, effective immediately. I had my interview, and they refused to listen to my answers. Politics and professional jealousy won the day. The Hydrastigor event in Baltimore was a rough ride, and people did get killed. But people always get killed when paranormals are at large. My boss had saved the day and destroyed possibly the last dragon to ever terrorize the world. Mistakes were made, but he prevailed. That stands for nothing?

He was low, lower than I had seen him in a long while. His bear spirit gives him great strength usually, but like all living, breathing things, even bears sometimes get the blues. He was ordered to suspend his investigation of the recent deaths, and booked a plane back to Baltimore, where officially his suspension would take place. The LVPD would finish the investigation.

We went back to our hotel room to gather his things. He packed his suitcases full. We hailed a cab, and I took him to the airport. He asked me to stay behind for a few days, keep an eye on the investigation. I was not suspended, so the Conclave had no authority to order me back to the east coast.

We stopped for coffee, and I took care of a little business, per Littlecloud's direction. Then we proceeded to the airport, and I kept the meter running in the cab while I put him on the proper flight. From the gate window, I watched as the plane disappeared through a bank of clouds.

I returned to the cab and went back to the hotel. When we got there, I asked the cabbie to pop the trunk.

The real Joe Littlecloud unraveled himself and stepped out.

"Who the hell did you actually put on the plane?"

I shrugged. "The guy working at the coffee shop."

I gave him back the coin he had slipped to me after the Conclave, the one Trina had given him which, when pressed into the palm, changes a person's visage, just like she had done last night. That's what I had used to pay for the coffee. "He'll return to normal somewhere over Kentucky. Newcastle came through."

He nodded, stretching for his cane in the trunk. "Trina's heartless sometimes, too by-the-book in my opinion, but she loves children."

He grew pallid again, the image of the dead child still weighing on his mind. He shook his head and said, "Let's go to work."

I smiled. That's exactly what I wanted to hear.

* * *

Since the LVPD assumed Littlecloud had left the state, we did another setup. This time, we picked a more obscure casino, a small one near the end of the strip: Brinkman's Bar and Lounge. Primarily a slots place, they held nightly craps tables and poker tournaments. We wanted to see just how expansive this conspiracy was, and Littlelcoud was up for some dice throwing. I didn't care for craps myself. Just wasn't my kind of game. I decided long ago that putting your fate into pips was as bad as throwing it behind Egyptian madmen. Live and learn.

Trina sat beside me as we watched through the security cameras while Littlecloud started his game. Her job was to monitor the astral plane, to detect the appearance of any spirits – in particular Gad and Meni – as soon as they appeared. My job was to spot the new gambler who would arrive at the table roughly at the same time. If we played our cards right (no pun intended), we would be able to detect and capture the perpetrators of this scam soon.

It took thirty minutes for Littlecloud to get into a groove before he started hitting the numbers. He was dipping deeply into his own pockets to keep going. For a moment there, we thought it was going to be a bust, and then he got hot, started hitting his stride. He couldn't lose. He threw his dice solidly, always striking the far wall of the table correctly. The pips rang true. Even the box man seemed impressed with his rolls.

Then I spotted him, an elderly gentleman somewhere in his sixties. Thin, tall, a little stooped at the shoulders, but otherwise no worse for wear. He wore a grey business suit with no tie. But he had on a watch which he tried to keep in place so that the band covered the tattoo on his left wrist. Yet there it was: the Star of David. But this time, it was twisted, contorted, stretched and angular, almost unrecognizable, and I wouldn't have given it a second thought myself if Trina hadn't begun to convulse beside me. She was picking up some serious spirit activity, and this occurred at the exact same time that the old man appeared at the table and began placing bets.

Then just like the others, he began to strike gold, and Littlecloud began to fail. We watched this play out for about ten minutes, and then I shook Trina hard, trying to free her from her trance. Her eyes had rolled back into her head, and there was a little drool down her chin.

"Trina!" I shouted at her, grabbing her shoulders tightly. "Wake up! Joe has left the table."

She came to, and I could sense immediately her fear. She shook away the cobwebs, said, "We have to get him."

"We have to do both," I said, "get him and that man."

This time, both my boss and the old man had left the table at approximately the same time. That troubled me. We left the security room immediately and went down to the floor.

We didn't even clear the steps before two ugly thugs produced pimp sticks and started wailing on us.

Trina hit the first with an immobility spell, which made the goon drop hard to his knees. But that didn't hold him for long; he was protected by defensive spirits that gave him great strength against her best punch. He was on her again in a few minutes, overpowering her with a headlock. I tried helping her, but the other guy put his stick into my gut. I slashed his face pretty good with my nails and jumped on his back and started biting his neck. I was just about to partake of his jugular when additional muscle flew through the revolving door of the lobby and pointed riot guns at us. Now, I'm undead, and it takes a lot to kill me. But six carefully placed rounds in my head *will* kill me… dead as a duck. So, we relented. Trina dropped her arms. I crawled off the man's back, and we gave up peacefully.

We were taken outside where a dark van awaited. Joe was already inside, hands tied tightly behind his back, his fetishes, cane and bear cloak nowhere to be seen.

"How the mighty have fallen!"

The words came from behind me, from back inside the casino. I turned to see the pale, smug face of an ex-vampire.

Then a black hood went over my head, and I was tossed into the van.

* * *

Somewhere along the route that the van was taking, I was knocked cold. When I awoke, I was sitting alongside Littlecloud and Trina, who were themselves tied up tightly in chairs, our hoods removed to reveal that we were in a vacant warehouse, the kind of place you might find in a rundown distribution district back in the day when America and its economy was in far better shape than it was today. It was an old building with rotting crates and sacks, discarded pallets and rusty girders that served no purpose but to give the place a muggy, oxidized smell. The mixing aromas made my stomach growl, I'm sad to say, reminding me that I hadn't eaten in a long, long time. For a ghoul, that's bad news.

A few minutes later, a metal sliding door squealed open and in walked the old, grey man that had played at Littlecloud's table. Closer, he was not as meek and broken as he had seemed on camera. Instead, he walked straight and upright, no stoop in his shoulders. He wore a very nice dark blue suit, an Ivy League tie, and smiled a line of freshly polished teeth. He was rich, clearly, and didn't mind showing it. He came to us in confidence, a burly thug on either side of him for protection.

"You have disrupted my plans, Littlecloud," the man said, his thick Israeli accent making it difficult for my ears to discern his words clearly. He smelled nice, though.

"Oh, I think you did that on your own," my boss said, "Mr. whoever you are. Playing chance with pagan gods can get you killed."

"You may call me Ze'ev if you like."

"Dr. Abraham Ze'ev?" Littlecloud said.

The man nodded. "In the flesh."

I had to pick through a swell of irrelevant information in my mind to remember the man. I had never met him personally, but his name was certainly known well enough among intellectuals.

Dr. Abraham Ze'ev had been one of the leading mathematicians in the country, best known for the Numerical Predictability Theory, which postulated that a person attuned to the beats and measures of time and space could predict with perfect accuracy, a chain of numbers rolled in sequence with any given randomizing device, such as a pair of dice, or a thoroughly shuffled deck of cards. And therein lay his downfall. He ceased theorizing as many academics do, and instead put his theories to practice. His love for numbers and gambling took him into casinos undercover, where he racked up enormous sums of money, literally beating the casinos at their own game. But as most masterminds are wont to do, he got too cocky, too greedy. He was eventually caught, tried, convicted, and served ten years in a New Jersey penitentiary. Afterwards, he presumably returned to Israel. And now, I guess, he had decided to come back. Lucky us!

"I'm surprised that a man of numbers," Littlecloud said, "of statistics and logic, would condescend to summon spirits to do his dirty work."

Ze'ev chuckled. "I'm an old man now, Littlecloud, and an old man learns a thing or two over the years. It is our reward for good service and duty to life." He pulled up a chair and sat down beside us, as if he were just one of the guys. "What I learned is that it is impossible to predict with absolute certainty an infinite chain of numbers. I can predict a hundred numbers in a row... only to miss the hundredths and one. And thus my theory is shattered. Without absolute predictability, chaos reigns.

"The problem resides in nature itself, Littlecloud. Nature has an inherent flaw that goes back as far as the primordial soup: unpredictability. It resides in the cytoplasm of every cell in our body, and it prevents order in our universe. This asteroid hits earth, this one does not. This egg is crushed in the jaws of an alligator, this one survives. Billions of years of random choices, born out of luck for some things, misfortune for others. Gad and Meni... they have been spirits in our world since the dawn of time, Littlecloud, and they have helped me see the light."

"And what light is that, you sicko murderer?" I couldn't help myself. The words came out of my mouth before I realized I'd said them. My blood sugar was low.

Ze'ev rose and walked over to me, a petulant little smile on his thin lips. He raised his hand as if to strike me. I braced, but the blow did not come. Instead, he raised his hands higher above his head as if he were an evangelist, and said, "The light, Mr. Ruth, is that it does not matter. If nature is inherently unpredictable, then all we can do is soften the blow and be the best person for our family, our friends, and our country, for as long as we tread this imperfect world.

"And so before I die, I've decided to give back to Israel what this world has so sorely taken from it. It's dignity, its freedom, its strength. Millions of dollars have been transferred from my students to banks there, and that money will be used to better their lives. It's the least I can do."

"You are killing people, doctor," Littlecloud said, straining at his bindings. "Your ends do not justify the means."

Ze'ev shook his head. "I'm killing no one. I'm merely allowing Gad and Meni to do what they have been doing forever. And they have not yet finished the chase. There is one more game to play, one more bet to place, before it is all over."

He walked to an electrical box attached to the wall. He placed his hand on a lever. He turned to us, smiled, and pulled it.

The floor beneath our chairs collapsed, and we slid down chutes. Between us, Trina screamed at the abruptness of our fall. Littlecloud and I ended the slide hard against iron bars. Trina slid out into the middle of an arena, face first onto a hard floor. Her chair shattered, and her bindings gave way. But her face and neck carried the bloody marks of the skid. And all around us, like we were in a pit bull arena, crowds cheered.

Through the roar of the crowd, I could hear Ze'ev speak. "A billion dollars rides on this game, ladies and gentleman. A billion dollars. Place your bets now!"

I dared to look around. Businessmen, moguls, gangsters, oil barons, you name it, were there, fists full of money, plastic, gold coins and chains, and everything else waving in the air as bets on the fight. For a fight would surely come, for what other reason would he throw Trina into a pit if not to fight? But fight what?

A door slammed open across the pit. In walked a beast seven feet tall, long, muscular legs, claws an inch long, mouth and face contorted into a devilish grin of sharp, messy teeth. I strained to see who, what it was. Its teeth were sharp, but there were some missing. My undead heart leapt in my chest. It was the unbridled, unrestrained feral form of a vampire.

Jesus Christ!

* * *

I knew that Casper Dean was involved. I knew it even before I had caught a glimpse of him at the van. But I didn't realize he was involved this way. He was supposed to have been cured of vampirism, but apparently it didn't take. He lacked canines, I could tell, but his other teeth – in this wild, unhindered form – didn't need them. They were sharp and deadly. I feared for Trina.

She was no slouch. She gave off the visage of a normal, untouched human woman. But she had powers of her own. I just didn't know how long she could last against this monster that Casper Dean had allowed himself to become.

They circled the pit, eyeing each other, the rich audience whooping and hollering as if they were witnessing a cockfight. In a way they were; only one would emerge from this fight. I could hear Littlecloud screaming, giving Trina desperate advice through his iron bars, but they could do little good. This was her fight, and I couldn't see a way out of it… yet.

Dean struck first, leaping at Trina with arms extended, claws rigid and determined. She ducked the strike; not a bad move in her torn power suit, with blood coming down her face and clouding her right eye. She scrambled across the pit, mouthing some inaudible incantation and waving her hands around. Her motions drew smoke from thin air, and she tossed it at Dean like a spear. It struck him and pushed him back against the pit wall, holding him there like a wrestler pinning a foe. Dean struggled to break free. This gave Trina a chance to right herself, breathe deeply and plan her next attack.

The crowd, meanwhile, was not stopping at all. Money exchanged hands aggressively, whole wads of it, diamonds, gold chains, everything you could imagine. Anything of value that these patrons possessed were passed to three young people near the lip of the pit, who took the bets and scribbled numbers onto pads of papers. I squinted. Each had a Star of David tattoo on their wrists.

I looked around the pit again. Ze'ev's goons were strategically placed at ten-foot intervals around the pit, the barrels of assault rifles peeking out from beneath black corduroy jackets. It hit me: no one was coming out of this place alive. The pit, the betting, the fight, all staged by Ze'ev to lure them here to steal their money. So my only question was how would Gad and Meni factor into this?

The answer came quickly. Two roping spirits, long tendrils of grey smoke, snaked through the crowd and filtered into the pit. Trina and Dean were trading blows in the center. One of the grey spirits struck Dean, the other struck Trina. They both shivered as if chilled. Gad must have chosen Trina, for she stood rigid quickly, and struck out with her newfound fortune against Dean, slinging him across the pit with a rope of blue smoke. She jerked him around like a ragdoll, using his face to wipe up his own vampire blood that had leaked all over the pit floor. Littlecloud was egging her on through his iron bars. I had to admit I was feeling a bit excited and confident myself. Perhaps Trina would prevail, and we'd get out of this nasty affair.

Then things changed, as I knew deep down that they would. Meni hurled itself out of Dean like black vomit, swirling out of his bloody and bruised mouth like sewage water. Gad pulled out of Trina's throat. They passed each other in the space between the combatants, and reentered new hosts.

Now it was Dean's turn to be lucky. He lashed out against Trina who had stumbled back, dazed and confused. He struck her three times across the face. A tooth sprang from her mouth, blood followed. Dean picked her up and flung her into the crowd, who then mercilessly flung her back. She was not moving. I thought she was dead. And then Gad and Meni traded places again, and she got up with newfound strength, and began to wail on Dean's skull.

Over and over, the two Babylonian gods chased each other through their hosts. Each time I thought the end was near, one of them sprang back up, and it started all over again. But I could see the end coming. Trina's face was almost nothing now, and Dean's looked no better, but he had the advantage. He was undead, and feral, and stood two feet taller than her, and weighed at least 200 pounds more. He could take that punishment; she could not.

Then it happened. Gad sprang back into Dean, and with his last ounce of strength, drove his clawed hand into Trina's throat, and she fell. This time, she did not get back up.

The crowd silenced. You could hear the proverbial pin drop, but I knew that things were not over. I could smell Littlecloud. He was changing.

I wasn't sure how his bear spirit would react without his fetishes, without his cane and bear fur cloak which gave him great power. But then, these were unusual circumstances. And he loved Trina. Perhaps not as much as he had done in the past, but seeing her there, on the floor, mangled and near death, I could not imagine the kind of emotions going through him. I didn't want to know. In bear form, my boss had taken down a dragon. Heaven help a lowly vampire.

Littlecloud's iron bars shook, rattling the entire structure that we were in. His voice changed to guttural wails, moans deep and deliberate. I could smell him, a strong musky odor that permeated the air. He was changing, and no amount of chains and chairs would keep him down.

He burst through the bars, in full bear form, a grizzly this time, ten feet tall easily, broad as an oak, with barrels of muscle for arms and legs. Dean fell back, shocked at the size of his new foe. The crowd went wild, and money once again changed hands.

But it didn't last long. Gad and Meni tried cycling through their hosts again, tried to find penetration in the bear and vampire, but they could not find access. Whether it was Littlecloud's lycanthropy that was different and they could not handle it, or whether it was his rage, neither Gad or Meni could penetrate his thick fur, and they flew around the pit like wisps of smoke, chasing each other in a funnel cloud.

Dean tried chasing them himself, hoping to gain purchase of Gad, throwing himself through the god-spirits, hoping it would enter his body and give him strength. Littlecloud refused to let him go, chasing him around the pit, slashing with his powerful paws, leaving deep cuts across the vampire's legs and arms. By the third cycle around, Dean was faltering, falling, crawling to get away. Littlecloud leaped upon him, putting his full weight on the beast's rib cage. He stared Dean deep into his eyes, and then stomped.

Dean popped like a bloated tick. But he was still alive, being undead and all. He wiggled his head around violently, trying to bite the bear's feet. Littlecloud roared and drove his snout into Dean's neck. The bite was so strong that the vampire's head fell off and rolled across the pit floor.

It was over. Well, not entirely.

Gad and Meni had found new flesh in the crowd. A brawl broke out as they chased each other through the bleachers. Littlecloud, still in bear form, jumped into the crowd. "No!" I screamed, fearing that he would, in his current state, tear everyone to shreds. But he did not.

Showing marvelous restraint, he pushed through the crowd and went after Ze'ev's thugs, who had pulled their guns and were taking potshots into the crowd, downing people with each trigger pull. He severed the spine of one thug with a slap of his paw, and crushed another's skull. The rest turned and ran.

Then the crowd panicked and began running themselves, looking for exits, ignoring their money and gold and diamonds being left behind. Littlecloud obliged them by tearing a hole into the warehouse wall. Sunlight streamed in, and the crowd went to it.

All the while I had been working on my restraints and finally, I was free. I crawled back up the way we had fallen and found Ze'ev there, taking aim at Littlecloud through a high-powered scope. I jumped him immediately. His rifle misfired and tumbled from his hands.

He went down, and I took the time to eat slowly. I didn't care for his pleas, his apologies, his cries for mercy. What was the point in all that? We were in the midst of a bloodbath, and I was a ghoul. My boss was out there somewhere, chasing bad guys. Gad and Meni were free to do as they wished. I was famished.

So I ate, heartily, completely, until I could eat no more.

* * *

I found Littlecloud in the pit with Trina's head on his lap. He was naked, but human again. He was exhausted. He had been crying.

I went to them and checked her out. I pressed my cold fingers against her throat. No pulse. I put my hand next to her mouth and nose. No air. She was dead.

"I'm sorry," I said, placing my hand on Littlecloud's knee. "She was a good woman. I wish we could have known each other better."

Littlecloud nodded. "She had qualities. She put up a good fight. I wish I could have saved her."

"Indeed, but you saved a lot of people today, Joe. It seems odd saying that, I know, with so many corpses around us. But it is the truth. A lot of people are alive because of you. Ze'ev was going to kill everyone."

"I know. But Gad and Meni are out now, and many more will die before they are brought under control."

"But they will be brought under control, and you will be responsible for that."

"I'm suspended, remember?"

I couldn't help but smile. "True, but when has that ever stopped you?"

He smiled back, brushed a strand of hair from Trina's brow, then leaned over and kisser her softly. "Let's get out of here."

Together, we carried Trina's body out of the pit and walked into the hot light of the sun.

The matter was over. Ze'ev was dead and his terrible schemes were concluded. Casper Dean was dead as well, and the NVPD would have a lot of explaining to do. But our part in this terrible ordeal was finished... for now at least.

As we walked away from the warehouse, I had a rush of confidence. A surge of good fortune overtook me, and I wondered... perhaps Gad and Meni were not gone after all. I paused in panic, looked at myself as if I were seeking a mosquito's bite. And then I realized how foolish that was. I was already dead. Neither Gad nor Meni could harm me the way they could harm living flesh, and even if they were still with us, it did not change the facts on the ground. Our time in Vegas was over, and I promised myself then and there that we would never, ever return.

I've kept that promise to this day.

This Is Only Going To Hurt
g. Elmer Munson

Frank cracked an eye open and stared at the clock. It was too blurry to read, but the darkness outside told him all he needed to know—it was too damn early. When the phone rang again, he reached for it. He knocked over a bottle of something, and it dropped to the floor.

Fuck. He slapped his hand around the cluttered nightstand until he found the phone. *Should have turned this thing off.* He fumbled with the keypad and sighed when he found the answer button.

"Yeah, who's this?"

"It's Barron," a voice said.

"You're not my brother," Frank said. "You're a girl."

"I know," the voice said. "It's *about* your brother. He's missing."

"Who is this?"

"Xiuying," she said.

Frank sat up and reached for the lamp. As soon as he clicked it on, he squeezed his eyes shut and dropped back down to the bed. The light was not helping his head. "What do you want?"

"I need your help," she said. "Barron needs your help."

"He wouldn't even call me if he was dying," Frank said.

"I know. That's why *I'm* calling." Frank opened his eyes and looked across the room at his desk. Amid the scattered paper and empty bottles, a framed photo of him and Barron remained upright. It had been taken years earlier, back when Frank was an honest cop and Barron still lived in New York. They looked like friends, but things had changed.

"Where is he?"

"I last saw him yesterday," Xiuying said. "He had a meeting. He never came back."

"What do you want from me?"

"Come to Guangzhou, help me find your brother."

"I can't fly to China," Frank said. "I'm not even supposed to leave the country."

"I know. Your brother told me."

"Oh yeah?" Frank said. He sat up again and looked at the stack of documents on his desk collecting bourbon stains. "What else did he tell you?"

"He told me you have no love for Internal Affairs. He told me you would leave the first real chance you got."

"That sounds like bullshit," Frank said, even though he knew better.

Barron knew better. Frank's investigation was not going well. *Maybe it is time to go.* "A ticket to Guangzhou is damn expensive."

"It's already paid for," Xiuying said. "You leave in four hours."

"That's not a lot of time," he said.

"Then you'd better get dressed."

* * *

The plane landed in the middle of a storm. Thunder crashed overhead and rain pelted the windows, but Frank couldn't care less. He'd ordered so many single-size bottles of bourbon he couldn't finish them all. He had half a dozen stashed in his jacket. He had to stash the empties in the seatbacks of the surrounding passengers. One of his neighbors opened her mouth to protest, but Frank gave her a look that he hoped would shut her up. He couldn't tell if it worked or if she just gave up, but she *did* stop talking. That was all that mattered.

As the plane taxied to the terminal, Frank closed his eyes and wished for sleep. He knew there was no rush. He could barely see the lights in the distance, and once he got there customs would keep him for another hour or so. It was better to let the locals off first. At least they knew where they were going.

Something hit his arm and he opened an eye. Across his lap sat a pile of little plastic bottles. On either side, his seatmates were staring out the window. There was just the hint of a smile escaping one woman's otherwise straight face. Frank laughed and closed his eyes. *I deserve that,* he thought.

He sat that way until the plane came to an eventual stop. All around, passengers were gathering their things and chatting on their cell phones. Frank waited until the plane had gone silent before opening his eyes and standing up. The cabin was deserted. He had no bags, so he headed up the empty aisle toward the front. There stood a petite stewardess carrying a bag of trash. She looked up at Frank and dropped the bag.

"Oh," she said. "Are you lost?"

"No, just taking a nap," he said. "Thanks."

She tilted her head, put on a strained smile, and stepped to the side as he passed. "Thank you for flying Air China," she said.

"Yeah, thanks," he muttered as he stepped into the tunnel and walked towards the terminal.

* * *

Xiuying was waiting for him at the far end of customs. Although they'd never met, she stood up and waved as soon as they made eye contact. She wore too much makeup, and it had run slightly down her cheeks.

Makeup and tears never mix, he thought before glancing out a window. *Or rain, either.* He walked up to her and she smiled.

"Welcome to Guangzhou," she said.

"Thanks. You must be Xiuying?"

"Yes, pleased to meet you," she said before dropping her eyes. "Barron spoke highly of you."

"I doubt that," Frank said. "And what do you mean *spoke*?"

"I—I'm sorry," she said before reaching up to give Frank an awkward hug. "This must be very hard for you."

"I stopped hurting years ago," he said. His arms hung limp at his sides.

"Oh." Xiuying dropped her arms and stepped back. "We should go. I have a car waiting for us."

"Lead on then," he said.

"Don't you have any luggage?"

"I travel light."

"Oh." Xiuying started walking toward the exit and Frank followed. The airport was huge but at close to midnight it was mostly empty. People glanced at him as he passed, but no one said a word. Xiuying kept silent as well. Her eyes stayed on the ground until they reached the pickup area. She looked up and waved to a small white van idling in a no parking zone. Frank could barely see it in the rain.

"This is for us," she said as the van crossed through the line of taxis and hopped up on the curb. The driver wore the largest pair of sunglasses Frank had ever seen. He also wore the ugliest polyester shirt Frank had seen since the 1970s.

"Well I feel totally safe," Frank said. He reached forward and tried to pull open the side door but slipped and fell into the side of the van. He laughed to himself and reached for the handle.

"Are you drunk?" Xiuying asked.

"Me? Not possible." Frank unconsciously tapped the spot in his coat where the bourbon bottles were hid and smiled. He opened the door and looked inside. Although there was room for at least six people, there were boxes filling all but one spot in the far back. "It's so cozy."

"It's all I could get on short notice," she said.

"How long is the trip?"

"About forty-five minutes. You can sit up front if you prefer?"

"No thanks," he said. He climbed in the far back and reached for a seatbelt. There was none. He looked at Xiuying but she was already closing the door. As soon as she hopped in the passenger's seat, she said something in Cantonese and they were off. Frank slipped a bottle out, downed the contents, and stashed the empty under the seat. No one spoke.

Forty-five minutes of nothing but streaming lights, passing cars, and pouring rain. The silence in the van and the pattering of the rain made it hard for Frank to stay awake. He was still buzzing from the flight and just wanted another drink. Or a bed. Or both, he wasn't picky. He only had four bottles left, and if he could, he wanted to save them for later. He tried not to look out the window because it made him feel sick. Most of the trip was through empty countryside. He kept his eyes closed and zoned out.

He wasn't sure when the country turned to city; he figured he must have blacked out. He opened his eyes and wished he didn't. They were headed down what Frank hoped was a one-way road. The van weaved between dumpsters and parked cars, past mopeds and farm animals. He reached for another drink when the van stopped at the opening to a small brick alley. Xiuying handed the driver a stack of Yuan before jumping out and opening the side door.

This must be our stop. He grabbed the door and pulled himself up and out. "Thanks for the ride," he said but the driver only stared at him through his huge sunglasses. *Yeah, fuck you too,* Frank thought as he slammed the door shut. The van took off, leaving Frank and Xiuying alone. The alley was dark, but not completely. There was a streetlight near the entrance that cast just enough of a glow for Frank to see. The rain had slowed to a drizzle.

At the far end, Frank could see the reflection of the moon on the Pearl River. He heard an engine echo through the streets and glanced behind. There was only Xiuying, lighting a cigarette while staring down the alley. She tucked the lighter in her pocket and blew smoke at Frank.

"What's down there?" he asked.

"There's a building," she said.

There are lots of buildings. He stepped toward the entrance and looked up. There were windows and balconies along the alley, all at least two or three stories up. Most were empty, but on one an older woman carried a bucket of something in her arms. She glanced down at Frank and dumped the liquid contents into the alley before disappearing from view. *Nice.*

"What building?" he asked.

"At the end, by the docks."

"And?"

"Barron had a meeting down there," she said. "He went but never came back."

"Did you look for him?" he asked. She continued to stare, ignoring his question. "Did you call the police?" She blinked and looked at Frank.

"You're not from around here," she said.

"And neither was Barron," he said.

"Exactly."

Frank looked around but they appeared to be completely alone. He shrugged and walked toward the alley. "You know which one, right?"

"Oh yes," she said. "I know." She followed close behind as Frank worked his way through the dark alley. He splashed in puddles and stepped past the sticky mess the woman had dropped from above; it smelled like rotting fish. He heard something moving around them but could see nothing but brick. There were no doors along the sides, but Frank could hear the sound of floating docks scraping together. They had nearly made it to the river. He reached in his jacket but found an empty space where his holster had once been.

I should have brought a gun. He glanced behind him. Xiuying was still there, crouched down over the soft glow of a cell phone, blocking it from the rain.

"Everything okay?" he asked.

She looked up and nodded as she jammed the phone back in her pocket.

"What kind of place is this?"

"A shipping company," Xiuying said. Frank froze.

"Wait, *what* shipping company?" Xiuying didn't say anything. Up ahead, a door scraped open and Frank crept forward, again reaching for his missing gun.

"Something's wrong," he said.

"You've got that right," Xiuying said. Frank turned back and saw her swing an expandable baton toward his face. He had just enough time to wonder where she had hidden it before everything turned white.

* * *

Frank woke to pain. He couldn't move his hands. His face felt like it had grown twice its size. He could move his jaw but it hurt like hell. He couldn't open his left eye. His right eye cracked open enough to see that he had something over his head. It smelled like dirt and itched something terrible.

Burlap, he thought. *How nice.* There were people nearby. Frank could hear their voices but had no idea what they were saying. He recognized Xiuying's voice, but it sounded like all the others were men. He had a hard time separating them; it sounded like there were at least five. They spoke for a while until a door crashed open and a new voice shouted over all the others. Everyone fell silent.

Frank tried to stay perfectly still. There was movement around him but no one spoke. He tried to slow down his breathing but was having a hard time sucking air through the dirty burlap. Someone whispered right behind Frank and the group laughed. Frank flew forward and crashed on a concrete floor. The sack was ripped from his head and fresh pain screamed through his skull. Warmth spread across his cheeks as fresh blood ran down his face.

Frank bit down on his cheek to keep the room from spinning. He opened his eye and looked up at the group of people surrounding him. One was Xiuying but four of them were men he'd never seen. The last man was standing off to the side; *he* was different. He wasn't Chinese; he was from New York. The sight of him standing there made Frank wish the sack had never come off.

"Harris," Frank whispered. He hated that his voice sounded so meek but he couldn't speak any louder. "I never told." Frank felt himself starting to beg. He did his best not to. It wouldn't work. "I never gave you up," he said. "I didn't even *work* narcotics."

"Narcotics?" Harris yelled. "Shows what *you* know." He stepped forward and kicked Frank in the face. The pain was excruciating, but it wasn't over. Harris raised his boot and stomped it down on Frank's stomach. Frank threw up but lacked the strength to roll to the side. He lay on his back, choking on his own blood and vomit as the people around him all stood and laughed.

Harris reached in his pant leg and pulled out a boot knife larger than any Frank had ever seen. Harris smiled as he leaned in close, the blade pointed at Frank's throat. Frank tried to roll to the side but two of Harris's men moved in to keep him still. His feet and hands were bound so he could barely move. Frank was still nauseous and having a hard time drawing air. When the tip of Harris's knife touched Frank's neck, he once again threw up.

Harris's men jumped back with sounds of disgust. Harris stood and cursed, shaking his hand where a bit of vomit had splashed. He kicked Frank in the side. Frank rolled over and his mouth drained. He drew in a great gasp of air before one of the men grabbed him from behind.

"Hold him still," Harris said. He came around to face Frank. He was no longer smiling. "This suit costs more than you," he said. "Now you're gonna pay for it."

There was a banging on the warehouse door. Harris lowered his knife and looked at Xiuying. She shrugged and headed to the door. Harris stashed the knife and twirled the air with his finger. His men moved in and grabbed Frank from all sides. They dragged him behind a stack of shipping crates and put the burlap back on his head.

Frank heard the door open and someone starting speaking in very excited Cantonese. Harris spoke with him for a couple seconds before yelling to the men in the warehouse. Frank heard boots on concrete, all headed for the door before it slammed shut. He kept still, listening for even the slightest sound. The warehouse was silent.

He struggled against the ropes, but the more he moved the tighter they became. He kicked at the floor and tried to boost himself to a sitting position but that didn't work either. He took a deep breath but began to choke on the filthy air, so he shook his head back and forth like a dog. He felt like he might throw up again but had to get the stinking sack off his head. He kept shaking, doing his best not to pass out. He stopped when someone spoke.

"Stop moving," a woman's voice said.

Frank froze in place. It didn't sound like Xiuying. He had thought he was alone.

"Hold still." The sack was removed from his head and he looked up. There was a beautiful young woman staring at him. Her eyes lit up when she saw him. "Frank," she said.

"Who are you?"

"Xiuying," she said, "I live with Barron."

"Xiuying just left."

"No, that was Meifing. She works with Harris. I called you, but she got to you first."

"Why?" he asked.

"I don't know, but I followed from the airport."

"Well can you help me with these ropes?"

Xiuying stepped behind Frank and tried to loosen his ropes, but she had no more success than he'd had.

"Maybe try the workbench," he said. "There might be a knife."

"Right." Xiuying checked through drawers and found an old box cutter. She came back and said, "Hold still."

Frank eyed the rusty blade and tried not to move. "You don't have to tell me twice." He closed his eyes and waited to be freed. He felt the ropes fall away from his ankles and stretched his legs. *Ahh, that's nice*, he thought. Then he felt the pain.

"I said hold *still*," Xiuying said. She stood and stepped back as the rope fell from around his wrists.

Frank rolled over and looked at his hands. Blood flowed down one arm and dripped on the concrete. "Shit," he said. "That *hurts*." He grabbed at the cut and tried to stop the flow. Xiuying grabbed her shirt and tore a strip from around the waist. She handed it to Frank.

"This will help." She tore off a larger strip and tried to wipe the blood from the floor while Frank covered his wrist. He wrapped the torn shirt and tied it as best he could before reaching in his coat and grabbing a bottle of bourbon.

"This will help too," he said before downing the contents. He stashed the empty in his pocket and looked around. "We need to get out of here."

"There's just one exit." Xiuying pointed to the door. "And they just used it."

"How'd you get in?"

"While you were asleep, they left you alone. I snuck in to find you, but they came back. I hid behind the crates."

"That's not helping us," Frank said. He looked around the warehouse but there was nothing except for the workbench and multiple stacks of shipping crates. He glanced at the closest pile and saw they were labeled for shipment to New York. *Well what do we have here?* He picked up a small hammer and pried off the top of a box. As soon as he cleared the packing material from the top, he dropped the hammer.

"It's not drugs," he said.

"What?" Xiuying asked.

"Harris was right. It was *never* drugs." Frank reached in the crate and pulled out a .45 caliber pistol. He handed it to Xiuying and grabbed another for himself.

"Is it loaded?" she asked.

"Not yet." Frank searched through the crate and pulled out a box of ammunition. "I do believe this is our lucky day." He loaded the magazine and tossed the box to Xiuying. As she started loading her weapon, Frank heard voices from outside the door. "Shit," he whispered. "Where did you hide?"

"Back here," she said. They headed for the back of the warehouse and ducked behind a stack of crates. From his hiding spot, Frank could see the door open.

Harris's men walked in and closed the door behind them. They gathered around the workbench and started talking while one of them grabbed a clipboard to write something down.

Frank looked at Xiuying; she had finished loading her weapon and was staring at the group of men. *I hope she knows how to use that thing,* he thought before they all stopped talking. Frank looked over and saw them pulling guns from their waistbands and looking around. One of them pointed to the smeared spot of Frank's blood on the floor and whispered to the others. They fanned out and headed for the back of the warehouse, their guns pointed at the stacks of crates. Frank tapped Xiuying on the shoulder but she didn't look up. Instead, she stood and started firing.

Frank stepped out and shot the nearest of Harris's men. The others opened fire and bullets sprayed all around them. Splintered wood flew through the air as the crates were destroyed. Frank felt something burn across his thigh. He dove toward another stack of crates but Xiuying stood her ground. She shot two of the other men before Frank even hit the ground. He rolled over and aimed at the nearest man, but with a click, the slide of his pistol locked to the rear. It was a sound he heard repeated throughout the warehouse as everyone fired their last round almost simultaneously.

Of the four men, only two were still standing. One was holding his stomach where Xiuying had shot him. Blood poured from his wound, streaming between his fingers and dripping on the concrete floor. He looked like he might fall over at any moment. The only one who wasn't shot threw his empty pistol at Frank before running for the door. The other two men were on the ground. Neither moved.

Frank wiped at his cheek and came back with a trickle of blood. *Lucky.* He looked over at Xiuying; her arm was bleeding but it didn't look bad. No more than a scratch, like he'd gotten on his leg. The guy who had been shot in the stomach finally fell over into a puddle of his own blood. *Very lucky*, Frank thought, at least until Harris walked in the door.

He looked at the three dead men scattered on the floor, then stared up at Frank. It was the first time Frank had ever seen Harris look surprised, and it only lasted a second. When Harris glanced down at Frank's gun, he smiled.

"You're empty," Harris said.

"I might be," Frank said. "Or I might have a full magazine just for you. Where's my brother?"

"Your brother was a putz," Harris said.

"Was?"

"I only worked with him because of his contacts here in Guangzhou."

"My brother wasn't crooked," Frank said. He stepped toward a stack of crates that had been shot to pieces and glanced inside. There were a few loose bullets sitting in the bottom of the crate.

"No, not really," Harris said. "He didn't know what I was shipping, but he didn't *not* know either. The important part was he knew his way around customs."

"Then why get rid of him?"

"Because of you. When you got busted, Barron wanted me to squeeze the cops to let you off. He even threatened to go to the feds if I didn't."

"So you killed him?"

"Wouldn't you?"

"I think I'll kill *you* instead."

"With what? An empty weapon?" Harris asked. He reached down, pulled the knife from his boot, and stepped forward.

Frank looked at the bullets in the crate. They looked dirty at best. He saw movement out of the corner of his eye as Harris pounced. Frank reached in, grabbed a round, and threw himself backward. Harris's blade sliced the air in front of his face as Frank dropped the round into the chamber and released the slide.

Harris was on him before he even landed on the floor. His teeth were clenched tight, his face burning red. He pushed forward and drove his blade deep into Frank's stomach.

Frank pressed the trigger and the gun fired, but something inside jammed and the barrel exploded. Frank felt hot metal shred his hand and burn into his chest. His ears rang, but in the background he heard Xiuying scream. As he hit the floor, he saw Harris's face go slack. It was over in less than a second, but to Frank it felt like a lifetime.

Frank's vision grew fuzzy as the pain took over. Xiuying was there. She pushed Harris to the side and looked at Frank's wounds. He had a ragged hole in his chest, and Harris's knife was sticking out of his stomach. Blood flowed everywhere.

Xiuying grabbed the handle but Frank screamed before she could pull it out. Across the warehouse, the door flew open and Meifeng ran in with two other men. They stopped and stared at the mess on the floor. One of them pointed at Harris and screamed out something in Cantonese. Both men ran from the warehouse. Meifeng stood for a moment longer before pulling out a cellphone. She started typing on the screen as she turned and walked out the door.

Frank heard shouting in the distance. He felt his strength pouring through his chest as Xiuying held his hand.

"Hang on, Frank," she said. "They'll be here soon."

Frank wasn't sure he believed her, but he hung on anyway.

* * *

Frank woke to the sound of BBC International. He opened his eyes but everything was dark and fuzzy. He recognized the glow of the television set and enough of the surrounding room to know he was in a hospital. There was someone sitting in a chair by the bed. By the hair he guessed it to be a woman.

"Xiuying?" he asked. The woman shifted in her chair and let out a light chuckle. He tried to sit up but nausea kept him down.

"Well, well," she said. "Welcome back." She turned on the light and moved closer so that Frank could recognize her. It was Meifeng. She was smiling.

"Where is she?"

"Oh, don't worry about your little girlfriend," she said. "I took good care of her, but I believe we have unfinished business, you and I."

"But, Harris is dead," Frank said.

"*Harris?*" she asked. She stood and closed the door. "You didn't think *Harris* was in charge, did you?" She held up a bottle of clear liquid and reached for Frank's nearly empty I.V. bag. She ripped a hole in the top, spilled out whatever was in there, and replaced it with the bottle's contents. She reached down and released the clamps.

"What's in there?" he asked.

"A little something to help you relax," she said. "I know you prefer bourbon, but this is a local shaojiu that I'm *sure* you'll love." She pulled out a cigarette and lit it, puffing smoke in Frank's face. She set the lighter on a rolling cart next to the bed.

Frank watched the solution run down the tube toward his arm and thought, *This can't be good*. He flexed his arms and shook his head to clear the nausea. The I.V. bag was within reach. So was the lighter.

Meifeng moved closer and pulled Harris's blade from her waistband. Frank closed his eyes and took a deep breath.

"Oh, don't worry about a thing," she said. "This is only going to hurt." She leaned in close and brought the blade to his throat.

"This is only going to hurt *a lot*."

Frank threw his arm out, knocking the blade to the side and slicing his throat in the process. He had enough painkillers in his system to deal with the pain, but he was aware enough to know it was deep. He ripped down the I.V. bag and splashed it in Meifeng's face.

She screamed and brought up the knife, blade aimed for Frank's chest. He reached over and grabbed the lighter. As the blade came down, he struck the flint and threw the lighter at Meifeng.

The alcohol burned quick, lighting her face and catching her hair. She followed through with the knife, but Frank knocked her arm to the side. She dropped the blade and slapped at her face, screaming all the while. Frank pulled a pillow to his neck and held it tight, trying to stop the spray of blood. As Meifeng set the room on fire, the world around him began to fade.

"Oh, don't worry," Frank choked through a mouthful of blood. "It's only going to hurt." He laughed a bit as the inferno around him faded to black. "It's only going to hurt *a lot*."

Missing: Apple of Discord
Diane Raetz

She was a Dish. A Babe. A Doll with the greatest gams in the history of legs, pins that went on for days. A body that put hourglasses to shame. A picture perfect puss with a rack to die for. Literally. Men by the thousands had died in her name—egged on by her beauty, her vanity, and jealousy. I'd despised for her thousands of years and still I whistled as she slithered into my office. She was Aphrodite, Goddess of Love and Beauty, and the most beautiful creature on earth. She was the ideal that every artist, actress, model and poet aspired to. They didn't know how selfish, self-centered and egotistical she was. They hadn't watched thousands of men die in wars started by her incessant need to be admired, loved, and worshiped. They hadn't watched Ajax, Hector, and Achilles die in a useless war caused her inability to think into the future and her refusal to consider the consequences of her actions. They hadn't had their wife stolen from them during one of her fits of jealousy and then tortured into insanity by her setting a series of 'reasonable tasks' such as sorting random grains into piles or a trip to underworld to collect an iron box full of 'beauty enhancement' products. And they hadn't turned their backs on their heritage, their home, their calling and most of their family for eons just to avoid her. But there she was.

"Hello Eros."

Her voice rung with the happiness of a million loves but I heard the whisper of a million losses in the lower register of her voice. After all, my beloved Psyche was one of those losses. I stood and hands clenched tightly on the edge of my desk and just barely brushed my cheek against hers. "Hello Mother," I replied tonelessly.

I expected, and was geared up, for a fight similar to the million other fights we'd had. The one where she yelled at me for wasting my talents working in a detective agency and I told her to jump in the River Styx but she surprised me, "Is Hermes in?" In the hundred years I'd worked for Hermes she hadn't asked for him once. She liked to stop by and order me to make certain people fall in lust. I liked to tell her to go fuck herself. After what she did to Psyche she had no claim on me—no right to command my power. I must not have answered fast enough. She tapped her foot as though she was annoyed and said again, "Hermes?" but I heard something other than annoyance in the mystical beauty of her voice. I heard something that sounded suspiciously like fear.

Surprised, I studied her closely. In 5000 years Aphrodite hadn't lost her perfect figure, her charm or her luminescent beauty. She had matured from a gorgeous ingénue to a femme fatale in full command of her power, but for the first time I saw tightness around her eyes and a hint of lines around her mouth. Either Aphrodite was aging or something was seriously disturbing her. I hadn't noticed any change in my annoyingly boyish looks so I assumed the latter—but assumptions were foolish when powers were in play, and Aphrodite's power put my small abilities to shame. "No Mother, he's out."

"And he's expected to return…" She let the sentence dangle dangerously. Nearly every other god in the world would have jumped in fear at the tone of her voice. I waited patiently. My Psyche was lost in a world of my mother's making—alive in body, dead in spirit. I'd already seen the worst she could do and she'd lost her power over me. You can only lose the love of your life once.

I shrugged, "Beats me. I'll let him know you were looking for him though, when he returns." I fought to appear casually insolent, knowing it would hurt her, but even in my head I'd fallen into the more formal cadences that the Twelve required.

Her eyebrows clenched, and daggers literally formed in her eyes. I'd angered her; not a big surprise. In the last 3000 years I'm not sure we'd had a longer conversation without her screaming and me snarling. "I. Need. To. Speak. With. Him. Now!"

"Have you tried his cell phone?" I put every ounce of disrespect I could muster into that question.

And there was the eruption, "Of course I have you arrogant child. You fool. You…" I quirked an eyebrow and the word "…brat" disappeared into a howl. Score one for me. Yes I was being petty but my mother had once given my wife over to her assistants for whipping. She deserved every ounce of pain I could mete out to her.

I waited the howling out, oddly satisfied to have upset my mother again. Sadly, seeing her incoherent with rage was one of the high points of my month—and I don't want to think about what that means about me. Satisfied, I was willing to get down to business. I used my best professional 'assistant's' voice, "Can I help you with anything?"

Her eyes narrowed. She knew the offer was insincere and yet… I was employed by Hermes so there were things she could get me to do. Not a lot, of course, but, for example I'd always make sure to leave a message for him. My own personal ethics required that I run *Hermes' Knows* as professionally as possible and that included providing top quality service to everyone. Even the woman I hated.

She stormed out, throwing her problem into my lap as she left, "The Apple is missing!"

There was only one apple that would upset my mother that way. I sat down shaking. "The Apple of Discord?"

The look she threw me said it all as she stormed out of the room. War—major nasty world changing war—was on its way if the wrong person found the Apple. And with my boss MIA it was up to me to find the artifact from Hades.

* * *

There was a note from Hermes indicating he'd gone to play poker with Loki, Eshu and Dionysus. Even though I dutifully tried to find my boss I knew I was going to strike out. With endless booze those tricksters were likely to be at the table for days. And even though Hermes could hear his name whispered in the wind during an elephant stampede, he had an extraordinary ability to go deaf when he was off having a good time.

Sitting at my desk, I tried to come up with a plan on how to detect the missing Apple. The Apple of Discord is an apple made of gold—and a very powerful artifact of war. Eris, my Super Bitch Goddess of a cousin—and I use that phrase in the non dog way—had the Apple inscribed with the phrase "To the Fairest" and tossed it onto the floor at a wedding guested mainly by Greek gods. Needless to say every goddess there claimed the Apple. Through threats, intimidation, and bribery the claimants were whittled down to three—Hera, Athena, and Aphrodite. All three were, to be honest, gorgeous. And all three were powerful enough not to concede to the others, so they decided they needed a judge who would be impartial, unbribable, and honest. Somehow, and I still haven't figured out the logic, they wound up with a twenty-year-old sheep-herding prince (don't ask) named Paris judging which one of them was the fairest. Needless to say they all ignored the rules—none of them were content to just be judged on their beauty—and tried bribery. Hera offered to make Paris a powerful king. Athena offered to make him a brilliant general and my mother offered the love of the "Most Beautiful Woman in the World," forgetting or not caring that the "Most Beautiful Woman in the World" was the much married Queen Helen. In a move I'd yet to forgive her for she stole my arrows, made the unhappily married Helen fall for Paris and the two ran away to his father's palace in Troy. A ten year war broke out, tens of thousands died and in the end I think the only one who was happy was Cousin Eris. She feeds on chaos, strife, and discord.

Four Goddesses, including my mother, had an interest in the Apple. They were all, in my mind, viable suspects. I almost eliminated my mother, but in the end I left her on the list. I'd watched too many film noirs where the bad guy (or gal) was the person who'd opened the case.

I began to form a plan. I'd visit the Eris first. My reason for choosing her was simple. As terrifying as the Goddess of Discord could be, she was still the least scary of the bunch. If I struck out with her I would go to Aphrodite's home and check out the lay of the land. If nothing else it behooved me to check out her security system and see where the Apple had been displayed. I had no doubt the Apple of Discord was prominently displaced. Mother was always ridiculously proud she'd won the damn thing—although I had no idea why. Paris liked her bribe the best—not necessarily her looks. Any plan that involved Athena or Hera was going to wait to be formed until I'd tried the other two. The Twelve, although my relatives, were scary gods. Mother wasn't likely to kill me. The same couldn't be said for Athena or Hera in a bad mood.

I stood up and shook the kinks out of my body. I took off the too-big suit jacket I wore to hide my wings and carefully stretched out them to their six foot length. They were a shiny gorgeous white. Everyone gasped at their beauty when they saw them and I hated them with a passion. If I hadn't been trying to hide my wings from Psyche, hadn't been trying to pass myself off as normal, she never would have fallen into mother's trap, and I'd have my wife with me; safe, sound and normal today. Instead…

I shuddered in depression and forced my mind away from the past, walked out onto the balcony and thrust myself into the sky, losing my cares for one moment in the joy of flight. As much as I hated my wings I couldn't bring myself to hate flying. It was—and will always be—the most exhilarating thing in the world, except making love to the woman I love. And that hadn't happened in over a thousand years.

I flew home reluctantly. When Psyche had first been restored to me, I'd spent years trying to lure her back to sanity. Now, hope long since gone, I found excuses to be away.

The marble I'd constructed the palace out of glittered in the sun, but the inside was dark—all shutters drawn and only a candle every fifty feet marking the dark passageway. We'd found that Psyche screamed less in the dark. Cloaked by my home's darkness I crept to Psyche's room. Tethys, her nurse, silently opened the door and slipped outside.

"How is she?" I couldn't help myself from asking.

"Quiet." A welcome word—the quiet days weren't good but they were a hell of a lot better than the other ones.

"Can I?" I asked the Titan nurse. I always deferred to her judgment. Zeus would kill me if he knew I housed a Titan in my home, but I'd stopped worrying about it a long time ago. She was the best nurse I'd ever found for Psyche. We'd gotten away with it for nearly 900 years and I couldn't see any reason why that would change.

Her smile was as sad as I felt. "I think so. Yes."

With that I slipped into the room and went as quietly as I could to my fragile wife's bedside. "Spiders, oats, Easy Breezy Beautiful…" She tossed and turned muttering what sounded like nonsense to anyone who didn't know her. Unfortunately I knew what each word meant and as always they were daggers in my heart. "Talk to Hades …Pandora. L'Oreal."

"Hush, love," I tried to comfort my wife. "You're safe. With me."

"Ants. Ants will sort the wheat."

"Yes they will," I agreed, knowing that in her mind she was trying to complete one of the cruel, impossible-to-complete tasks my mother had set for her. She'd failed and been whipped by my mother's assistant, Sorrow, for the failure. Even though we'd tried every salve on the market, her skin still bore the scars from that day. The scars on her soul were far more damaging than the ones on her back and legs.

I sat by her side for a long time trying to think of some way to pull her out of the mists. Nothing came to mind. We'd tried human drugs but they didn't work on her immortal body. The river Lethe had failed to erase memories engraved not just on her mind, but also on her soul. Apollo had labored for years in vain to cure her. She was gone, lost in an agony of my mother's creation. I wanted my wife back, and the gods help me, I would have done anything to achieve it. Unfortunately nothing came to mind.

Finally I stood to leave. Unable to resist, I brushed a kiss across her forehead and turned to go, tears in my eyes. Idly I wondered if I'd ever stop crying for my lost love. Distracted, I bumped into a nightstand that had stood by her bed for a thousand years. I flailed and my wing brushed against her arm and she began yelling "Wings! Flight! Eros! Wings!" before her words were swallowed by endless screams. Some part of her remembered that my wings started the fight that led to this disastrous outcome. Some part of her still blamed me. She couldn't bear them near her and I'd caused her to fall into a fit that would last days, weeks, maybe months.

Tears in my eyes, I bolted from the room as Tethys ran back in, the two of us nearly colliding in our haste. "Is there anything…"

"Just go." She pointed to the door, more weary than anything else.

I'd have cut off my own wings if it would have helped Psyche—I'd tried that nearly 2000 years ago. Several times. The last time I'd tried to do penance that way Apollo healed me and Hermes gave me a job to distract me. They'd threatened to have Zeus shove a lightning bolt up my butt if I tried it again. I ran from my wife's wordless screams in order to keep myself from ripping them out again. Even I wasn't masochistic enough to want to have 50,000 volts of electricity rattling around my innards.

At long last I pulled myself out of that corridor and walked to my own room—the only room in the whole palace that was bathed in light. I'd hidden myself in the dark when I first courted Psyche. If she ever came back from the Hell she lived in I wanted her to see me in the light—I would not make the same mistake twice. I would not hide my differences from her again. And even as I made that vow again I knew I was doing too little too late.

Refusing to dwell any longer on my doomed love, I changed from my jeans and tee-shirt into a toga—Eris would only speak to gods when they dressed 'appropriately' and took my bow and arrows out of the safe. I rarely wore them. In my opinion people should find their own loves and lusts but Eris would be insulted if I didn't come in full uniform as it were. Even though she wasn't one of The Twelve it did me no good to fight her when throwing a toga over my head was so easy.

My cousin loved war. Most war gods and goddesses enjoyed their power, being brilliant generals and gaining land, tribute and power. Not Eris—no she enjoyed the fighting, the injuries, and the dead, so I had no problem figuring out where to find her. I thrust myself into the air—and after Psyche's screams there was no joy in this flight—and hovered over the Middle East looking for where the worst fighting was taking place. Sure enough, there was Eris, disguised as a human, egging a Syrian commander into dropping a chemical bomb onto his own people.

I whipped out an arrow and with the practice of 3000 years, shot the commander in the heart. The bloodthirsty gent went from planning a horrifying attack on his own people to, "Ah my dearest Eris, my beloved one, come away with me from this sordid affair and walk in the gardens with me." He leaned over and whispered in her ear, "Shall I compare thee to a summer's day?" The man with the job of a jackal had a hint of style. I'd expected the wham bam thank you ma'am approach.

"What are you talking about?" my cousin demanded angrily. "Order the damn bomb already."

"How can I think of death when you stand there cloaked in beauty?" For the record, my cousin had the worst complexion in Olympus—bugs regularly crawled in and out of her zits. Beauty might be in the eye of the beholder, but even then Eris was no beauty.

"What in Hades is wrong with you!" she hollered at the love-besotted fool.

"You smell of springtime," the man declared rapturously. I rolled my eyes—springtime and decay, I added silently. My arrow had worked almost too well. The fool would do anything for Eris and she was smart enough to figure out that anything meant included deploying weapons of mass destruction. It was time for me to act.

I plunged down in between the two figures. "Eros, why in Hades did you do that," my cousin growled. For her it was almost a pleasant greeting. Maybe she liked her hapless suitor.

I rolled my eyes. "Eris, you know that we've all agreed not to use chemical weapons. Why do you insist on cheating?"

"Cause it's stupid," she said flatly. "We can use bombs, guns, magic, and whatever the hell Hephaestus comes up with but we're supposed to hold back on chemicals? What's the dif?"

I gave her the party line: "You can't control chemicals. They'll spread wherever." But in my heart of hearts I didn't believe a word I was saying. Bombs weren't controlled.

"Yeah, and Ares' meltdown last year killed how many people? That was totally under control wasn't it?" The winning point for Eris; I stopped fighting. Ares killed millions in his breakdown over Mommy Dearest. We'd had to dump him in the River Lethe, nearly drown him and thank Heaven that his memory had been wiped out, to keep the entire planet from exploding into war. Now Ares had the mind of a three-year-old— and we were trying to raise him as fast as godly possible. A three-year-old God of War could wreak a lot of damage fast. I was babysitting on Friday. Yet another line on my "Why I hate my mother" list. It was a long list.

I shrugged rather than let her see that she'd won that game of one-upmanship, "Whatever." I nodded at the fool who was trying to braid Eris a headband out of daisies. If he knew her at all he'd make her a necklace out of grenades instead. "I thought you'd be playing with your new toy, not this clown. Or would it be an old toy?" I debated aloud, hoping to pique her interest. "Either way I figure…"

"What in Hades are you talking about?" Eris interrupted me as I'd hoped she would.

"The Apple. I heard you got it back. That artifact has got to be 100 times stronger than sarin gas—I mean the last time you used it you caused a legendary war. What will dropping sarin do besides make you look like the biggest loser ever?"

"What fucking apple?"

I rolled my eyes theatrically. "The Apple of Discord, duh. Heard around the blogosphere that Aphrodite gave it back to you. Word is that she found it." I pitched my voice higher in an imitation of the soft breathy baby voice my mother liked to use to manipulate people. "Too much work to take care of. So many people wanted to take it and use it and sometimes it even seemed like it had a mind of its own."

She got a pinched bitter look. "I wish I had the Apple back. Dumbest thing I ever did was tossing it away like that."

"Tossing it away?" I didn't have to feign incredulity. "The Trojan War is legendary, babe. People have remembered that war for three thousand years. Almost no event, except maybe the birth of that messiah God over in Israel has ever been as immortalized. You couldn't have come up with a better use."

"Really?" I'd never seen Eris happier. "You think? I always thought that if I'd kept the Apple I'd have been able to create so many more conflicts— so much more trouble."

I shuddered inside—Eris with the Apple of Discord for the last 3000 years might have caused the entire planet to erupt into an endless war, but I kept my tone light and casual on the outside. "For my money a war that had gods and men engaged for ten years and has been sung about and studied for thirty-five hundred years is a crap-load better than a bunch of smaller wars, but to each his own." I looked at the map on the besotted general's desk. "Besides you seem to be doing okay without the Apple, what with Syria, Iran, Iraq, Russia, Afghanistan, and the United States all in play."

Again she looked pleased; Eris didn't get a lot of compliments so they went a long way with her. "I do okay." The bitter look came back. "But I could get this whole region in one giant war if I had the Apple."

I was convinced that Eris was telling the truth. If she had the Apple she wouldn't be able to resist using it, and the Middle East would have erupted into an all-out nuclear war. I didn't want that—Earth was way more interesting than Olympus, but I couldn't say that to her. It'd just make Eris mad. So I made small talk as I stretched out my wings prior to flight and then, "Now I'm curious. I'm going to go check with Aphrodite and see if she's still got the Apple, and then track down where the rumors came from."

Eris gazed at the infatuated general. "I've got business of my own to attend to." I suspected that business including launching the sarin gas I'd interrupted minutes before. Part of me hated the idea, but it wasn't my job to keep the Syrian humans safe. I had bigger fish to fry. Just as I was about to take off she said, with a hunger in her eyes that couldn't be hidden, "Tell Aphro that if she wants to get rid of the Apple I'd be happy to take it off of her hands."

"I will," I promised her. It was an easy promise to make given that Aphrodite (allegedly) no longer had the Apple and, knowing her, if she ever got it back it was going into her home under a secure lockup, not back into circulation.

I stopped off quickly at work to grab a new suit—and to check and see if Hermes had surfaced. No on Hermes—he was still off gambling. Oh well, at least I was able to change. There was no way in Hades I was willing to let my Mother Dearest see me in uniform. It would give her too much pleasure—and the illusion she had some kind of control over me. It was bad enough that she was going to see me working the case.

When I got to the Aphrodite's palace I got a bit of a shock. Charis, the Goddess of Grace answered the door and was, apparently, running the staff. For well over a thousand years Charis had been my mother's private secretary. What in Olympus' name was she doing acting as a butler? And where was Adonis?

After the proper greetings—Charis insisted on getting me settled in the library with a tea tray I had very little interest in—she sat down to gossip with me. "What happened to Adonis," I asked, knowing she'd be dying to tell me the latest and greatest. "Did she get rid of her boy toy?"

"I'd say Hephaestus is more to blame," she said softly while sinking gracefully into a chair. "Aphrodite was perfectly content to keep Adonis…"

"I'll bet she was," I muttered under my breath. He was a weak immortal—insanely pretty, jealous, petty, and pretty much powerless. For the last eon or so he'd been Aphrodite's butler/chauffeur/pool boy/boy toy. He was totally besotted with her—would do anything she wanted, sink to any low, seduce anyone she asked and commit any crime she wanted.

I got a half-raised eyebrow in response to my comment as she continued undisturbed, "… but Hephaestus said that they needed a new beginning and he must be gone before the wedding."

"She said yes?" I was shocked. Mother didn't like to see her prizes slip away.

Charis radiated happiness. "I think she's changed. She really seems to be in love with him this time. His deformities—that she couldn't stand when Zeus forced them together ages ago—don't seem to bother her anymore, and she's thrilled by his new inventions. She thinks they're…" Charis made air quotes. "Cool. She's shows anyone who'll hold still the Venus 1000 he designed for her. "

I was afraid to ask what a Venus 1000 was. Mother had no concept of boundaries. None. "I hope you're right," I muttered under my breath. I wish I believed her. But the cynic in me was convinced that mother played lip service to Hep while plotting to keep her plaything on the side. Where would she hide him that the God of Manufacturing wouldn't be able to see him? That was the question.

After a few more minutes of chatting about this and that I asked to see where the Apple of Discord had been displayed. I expected it to be in her trophy room. It wasn't. It had been stored in her very decadent bedroom, and let me tell you, no son—even an estranged son whose powers were dedicated to causing people to fall in lust with each other—should see that bedroom. I don't want to know what she did with the various plastic, flesh and robotic things that protruded from the bottom of the clear glass bathtub she had on full display in her bedroom. Looking at a particularly disturbing robotic tentacle that seemed to be computer operated, I began to grasp why Aphrodite had fallen for Hephaestus. He would be able to turn her weirdest, kinkiest fetishes into reality. None of her other lovers—Ares, Adonis, Anchis, etcetera—were able to do that. I wondered what Hera had done to Hephaestus' sanity. Being literally thrown away and then later banished from Mount Olympus had to have had some impact. Based on the toys he provided for Aphrodite, I had to assume it was nothing good.

The Apple had been displayed on a shelf above the bathtub in a small display case. I could feel the magic from one of my arrows permeating the area. Mother, damn her, had stolen a piece of my power to create one of the traps. I could sense other magic although not well enough to determine the exact trap—one had something to do with light and another magical beasts. I also felt a magical containment field of some kind. In addition, there were the non-magical traps for the unwary—a laser system that surpassed anything at the Louvre and a nifty device that would cause a deafening sonic boom to anyone foolish enough to touch the (missing) Apple. It didn't take me five minutes to announce, "This was clearly an inside job."

Charis gasped. "Adonis? Do you think he took the Apple?"

"He's the obvious choice. But not the only one."

"Then who else?"

I ticked the names off on my fingers, "Hephaestus could have taken it. He might not like Aphrodite to have a trophy of her previous conquest around. That's one of my thoughts. Or it could be Athena—the Apple is a powerful artifact of war and with Ares out of play she's the most powerful war goddess we have, and we all know she's always lusted after it. She could have planted someone in the household to steal the Apple for her. Then there's Hera. She's never liked Aphrodite and her relationship with Hephaestus is complicated to say the least. Or Mother might have taken it just to make me dance to her tune. The list is almost endless. Heck, even you could have taken it."

"Me?" Charis seemed more amused than disturbed at being put on my list.

"Eris, for one, would pay a lot for the Apple. You could have cut a deal with her." I didn't believe Charis committed the crime, but it was worth floating the idea.

Looking at me through eyes that seemed suddenly flirtatious, Charis smiled secretively to herself. I suddenly found myself mildly aroused intrigued in a way I haven't felt for a thousand years. A moment later she was smiling openly, back to her normal self and so was I. "Trust me, Eros. I have ways of getting anything I want. I certainly don't need to be making deals with that witch."

I let out a shaky breath. "Yes," I agreed, "you do."

"And, for the record, boy, I didn't take the damn Apple," a male voice boomed into the room. I turned to see Hephaestus, cleaner and handsomer than I'd ever seen him, with his black hair curled, wearing a suit that was tailored for his body, and frowning down on me. His deformed leg was hidden by the pinstripes and he carried a jewel-inlaid cane. Mother had definitely begun a makeover of our former blacksmith. "Truth is, boy, that while I despise the Apple of Discord, I would never have removed it.

It's too dangerous to be out in the world and I happen to know that the best protection in the world is right here in this room." He frowned. "I designed it myself."

The boys comment rankled, as it was meant to, but I let it go. There was absolutely no point in fighting with one of The Twelve over a subtle insult. Granted, I regularly ignored my own advice when dealing with my mother, but she was a special case. Instead I kept my gaze on the display case and as politely as I could and said, "Not good enough, I guess."

"Not against someone who knew the keys to all seven defenses," he said somberly. "You were right when you said it was an inside job, but the insider wasn't me."

"Seven defenses," I said, tacitly accepting the God of Manufacturing's declaration of innocence. "I only counted six."

"Then I haven't completely lost my touch." He gazed on the empty cabinet and said with absolutely no change in the tone of his voice at all, "It has to be that son-of-a-bitch of a pretty boy. He's been with her forever. If Aphro told her secrets to anyone it would have been that useless piece of shite. Find the turned worm and you find the Apple."

I agreed with him and left the palace all the while thinking to myself, yeah, Hep has no issues at all. And I'm a monkey's uncle. I needed to make sure security around Ares was tight until he grew into his power. I was about half convinced that Haephestus had gotten rid of Adonis—permanently—and he was just Aphrodite's boy toy. She lived, loved, laughed with and fought with Ares for millennia. I shuddered at the thought of what a jealous god could do to a hapless opponent.

I had to confess that seventy-five percent of the reason why I was pursuing Adonis had to do with the fact that I had no interest at all in confronting Athena or Hera. Hera, in particular, had developed a fondness for stringing up her enemies and burning them. I had no desire to spend the next hundred years being tortured by my grandfather's wife.

My best guess on where to find "that son-of-a-bitch pretty boy" was with his foster parents, Hades and Persephone. Persephone doted on her 'little boy' and would do anything for him. I asked my little cousin Thanatos, Goddess of Death, to give me escort so I could politely question both the gods of the underworld. They swore they hadn't seen their little boy and I awkwardly left as Persephone was crying on Hades' shoulder claiming that "she always knew that slut would bring her baby to no good." I couldn't argue with the goddess—in fact, I completely agreed with her. Adonis had been completely corrupted by Aphrodite.

After that little adventure we were kicking back, taking a break from the great Apple hunt and watching an old Bogie and Bacall movie-eating popcorn and babysitting Ares when I sighed heavily. "Man, Bogie had it so easy."

"He was gasping for air when I took him," she told me somberly. "I wanted him to live, but I could hardly let him suffer that way." She sighed and looked back at the screen. "He was so smart, sexy, suave…"

I leaned over and tweaked a curl in her short pixie cut. That and the fact that her body was stuck in a prepubescent form had confused the ancients into thinking she was a boy. 3000 plus years later and everyone still thought she was a dude. "If I'd known you were crushing on him I would have shot him for you. With the love arrow of course."

"He loved Lauren." She grabbed another popped kernel and chowed down. "I wouldn't have wanted to break up true love."

I dropped a brotherly kiss on Thany's hair and kept to myself Bogie's numerous infidelities and addictions. Better she keep her illusions, right? Besides, there was no point in speaking ill of the dead. Thanatos was sweet, but oddly protective of the souls she brought to Hades.

The movie continued but she was clearly thinking about something else. She paused the movie and made what I considered to be a terrible suggestion: "You could ask the Oracle for help."

I made a face. "I hate dealing with Delphine."

"Why?"

"She's full of incoherent poetry that doesn't rhyme and inevitably sends people, namely me, off in the wrong direction just for shits and giggles. She once sent me off to chase Pandora's Box in Nilfheim. She claimed the dragon had it."

Thanatos shrugged. "The Oracle is never wrong. If she clearly said that it is in Nilfheim then that's where it is. I can ask Hel for you if you want. We're friends." I didn't have to ask—there weren't too many female death gods, and Hel looked about the same age as her father Ares …well the half that looked human anyway. The half that looked like a skeleton was ageless. I found the smell of rotting flesh that surrounded her at all times disgusting, but it didn't seem to bother Thany. She was a death goddess who had been looking for a mom for a long time. Hel was an obvious choice of a substitute.

"It isn't there. I must have misunderstood Delphine's psycho babble about the dead, dragons, and frozen mists." Then I thought about what my cousin had said. "Damn it, I had to give Hel three freaking arrows just to be able to enter Nilfheim. And I had to find the dragon a date, just for a chance to look through his treasure pile."

My cousin was in the middle of a giggle fit. "I can't wait to see who Hel uses the arrows on." Still laughing, she told me, "Next time call me. I know everyone who deals in death. Okay?"

"Okay," I agreed fighting my own smile. I could let down my burdens around Thany in a way I couldn't around almost anyone else. If the Grim Reaper could find humor in the world, so could I.

Thany was still giggling. "I took an emo poet who committed suicide last week. Think I should retrieve him from Hades and give her to Hel?" Death had a weird sense of humor sometimes. She grabbed another handful of popcorn and changed the topic. "So why'd you want Pandora's Box anyway?"

"It's full of hope," I said gruffly, no longer smiling. "I thought it might help Psyche."

Laughter done, Thanatos nodded sadly. "I get that." She hit play on the movie again.

Ten minutes later Bogie had said goodbye to Bacall—for the first time—and caught a cab. The cab driver identified him, reminding me of a grief I had with *Dark Passage* and movies in general. "See how every time Bogie is really stuck he gets exactly what he needs? Lauren Bacall just happens to be painting in the hills at exactly the same time as he breaks out of jail. The taxicab driver identifies him, but rather than calling the police he helps Bogie get plastic surgery. With all our power we can't find Adonis, but Bogie's got Lady Luck on his side, that's for sure."

Thany paused the movie, suddenly serious. "Why don't you ask Lady Luck for help?"

I rolled my eyes. "Adonis is able to hide from me even when I've got an arrow in my hand and I'm totally planning on shooting him. And he's able to hide from you, even when you're calling him to the afterlife and he's going to be susceptible to Fortuna and her stupid wheel?"

"Well why not?" She made a face. "He's spent forever with your mother. If anyone has learned how to hide from either of your powers it would be him."

I made a face at her. I so did not appreciate my powers being compared to my mother's. Was she right? Yup. Did I have to like it? Nope. She continued on uninterrupted. "And he was raised by Persephone. I'll bet you anything that she dumped him in the River Styx—and was smart enough not to hold his heel. So I've got very little power over him. But luck? Good or bad, everyone is subject to that."

Yeah, and that's what worried me. I feared Fortuna. Even dealing with the Oracle might be a better option. Ages ago, when I was visiting Rome, I'd spun her wheel and wound up trapped in the form of a fat flying baby for over a century. Ugh. Once I got switched back to my real form I left Italy as fast as I could.

What scared me the most was that Fortuna didn't seem to have much control over luck. Instead she seemed to be a conduit for it. She had a huge wheel of fortune, and unlike the TV show, it wasn't primarily made up of chances to win money. Instead it was full of random acts of fate. Some options were pretty normal like 'win the lottery' which was canceled out by 'lose job'. But Fortuna's wheel also was filled with weirdness. For example there's a story that Zeus asked Fortuna to spin the wheel for him. The wheel stopped on 'major god forms out of sea foam.' And hence my mother was born. Another time, more recently she spun the wheel and Earth was invaded by vicious basketball playing aliens—and defeated by cartoon characters. I could not make this stuff up. Honest.

"I don't see how Fortuna is going to help me. I mean she might find Adonis for me—I'd have a one in about a hundred chance. But I'd have the same one in a hundred chance that she'll make a pig governor of New Mexico. Not that a farm animal couldn't do a better job than some of the politicians I've seen out there... but I digress."

"So how do we make Lady Luck work for us?"

We both thought on it for a moment and then Thanatos smiled broadly. "I know! We load the dice. Weight the wheel? That doesn't sound as smooth."

"Are you freaking nuts! Do you know what she'll do to me if she catches me?"

"Fine. Spin her real wheel instead, which will do anything from cast you into a fiery volcano to grant you your heart's desire."

My years as a chubby baby with wings came back to me and I shuddered. "I'm not doing that again." People don't talk to babies. They tickle your toes and make weird goo goo gaga noises. The worst part of my years in Rome was being treated like an infant with wings.

I seriously began to wonder if I could just let the Apple surface. I was a god of love. My job wasn't to stop wars from breaking out everywhere. Heck I wasn't even a very good detective. I probably had ten cousins with more aptitude from sneaking around than me.

I thought about what life would be like if the Apple of Discord surfaced in the wrong hands—and it was weird to think about the fact that Aphrodite was the right hands. She'd kept it safe, put a containment field around it, and displayed it in her bedroom. Hera or Athena would have started wars with it. Paris had chosen better than I'd ever realized.

World War III would be a nuclear war. Of that I had little doubt. The gods would survive—probably—but mankind as we knew it would be gone, as would animals and most plant life. Very little, besides cockroaches and Twinkies, could survive a 150 kiloton bomb. Somehow saving the world had become my responsibility, and my little cousin's suggestion was the best idea I had. I was really going to deal with Fortuna.

"What's your plan, short stuff?"

"Ooooh I ought to." She raised her fists, laughing.

I rumpled her hair and said, "Spill."

She smiled wickedly. "We'll create an app for her. And weight it so that it gives you, and only you, a good chance of getting your question answered. Maybe twenty-five of the opportunities would have something to do with Adonis. We'll set up the other seventy-five to be fairly harmless. And we'll create the app to be legitimate randomness for everyone else. That way if she tests it on someone else it works properly."

"Can you do that?" My programming skills were limited at best. I couldn't even imagine trying to create an app that would fool a goddess.

"I'm not that good at programing," she admitted. "But I know someone who is."

"If it's Hermes, he's AOL," I warned her.

"Hephaestus."

"If you can get the God of Manufacturing onboard we're golden," I agreed. "He hates Adonis so he'll probably say yes but…"

"Oh, he'll say yes," Thanatos said, looking at her father—Hep's former rival for mom's attention—who was busy stacking bricks and knocking them over with small explosions, laughing hysterically the whole time. "He owes me. Big time."

* * *

Fortuna lived in a carnival about forty miles west of Rome. Most of the gods like to live away from mortals—Fortuna chose not only to make her home in a human suburb, but opened it to man, god and monster 360 days a year. Weird. Most days she wore a gypsy turban and told fortunes with her spinning wheel, but they weren't fortunes the way that say Delphine told fortunes. They were just a collection of awesome to weird to horrible things that could happen pasted to her wheel. People would step right up, pay two dollars, and SPIN THAT WHEEL. Little did they know whatever they spun would happen. It disturbed me that she was playing with people's futures that way, but I said nothing. I guess we all did worse on a regular basis.

We arrived after midnight so the carnival was closed. I was hesitant to disturb Fortuna so late, but Thany had no such concerns. She marched over the goddess' trailer and pounded on the door. "Toony, I've got a present for you!"

"Toony?" I whispered, hoping the television blasting *Wheel of Fortune* would cover the chortle in my voice. Toony was such an innocent nickname. It brought to mind cartoons, not power. Maybe I'd be less concerned that I was to Spin the Wheel (or at least activate the app) if I thought of Fortuna as Toony. Kind of the same trick mortals used when thinking of people they feared as being naked.

My third cousin stepped out, a tall dark-haired woman with a penetrating voice. "Thany!"

"Toony!" They embraced happily as I quietly leaned against the rickety stair railing and wondered if my cousin was friends with every immortal in the world.

"Eros." Fortuna's gaze and voice gave nothing away as she stared at me. I nodded my head to mask my feelings. *I can do this,* I told myself. I could survive another century as a fat flying baby if need be. She looked as if she was about to say something, but Thany, in her bubbliest of moods, dragged the goddess away and onto her own faded plaid couch. A few moments later the goddesses were on the couch giggling away about people they both knew. Since I had no desire to hear about Hera's latest planned revenge, I tuned them out until Thanatos handed over a smartphone we'd picked up especially for the goddess to Fortuna. "I have an app you might be interested in Toon."

"Ah, Bah. I do not want your phone and this 'app' that you talk about. I do not like these smart phones and computers and such. They've only made things worse. Separated us from our roots. Made us live in a sterile environment. Me? I live in contact with the real world. " Fortuna's trailer had been decorated in about 1952 and I didn't think it had been updated since. If the real world consisted of chipped Flintstone glasses and faded flower tablecloths then Fortuna lived in the real world. In my opinion Fortuna was wrong. Maybe Artemis, living in the woods with her bow, nymphs and endless hunt was living in the real world. Maybe Hep, with his towers of glass and worldwide manufacturing facilities was living in the real world. But a trailer and a carnival that was stuck in 1950 was not living in the real world.

I had another concern. Our plan to get her to use an app was doomed. I mean, this was not a goddess interested in the twenty—first century. That was for sure. That meant I was going to have to give up Fortuna as a possible source of information or spin the real wheel, and I wasn't sure I had the guts to look at my unadorned future. Fate hadn't been terribly kind to me recently.

But I underestimated Thanatos. She marched over to the stove and picked up a hotplate. "WTF is this anyway Toony? An asbestos hot plate? They haven't made one of those since Vesta was a virgin." She pointed to the black and white television. "And that? You know you can watch your shows in color now. We've been able to for *fifty* years." Her fingers swept across the cracked linoleum countertops. "You know what's nicer than linoleum? Granite. Or quartz. Or if you want to go old-school marble. We use it all in kitchens now." Her little temper tantrum seemed to drain away. "Come on Toony, live a little."

Fortuna smiled, "Ah, little one. If it is so important to you I will take a look at this 'app' of yours. Thantos squealed in something approximating glee and the two of them huddled over the phone. I found myself thinking that it was possible Death was quite the actor. She was doing a much better job than I was of portraying a friendly visit. All I was doing was holding up the wall and praying everything worked out ok. "The phone is already on, so all you need to do is touch this screen to turn the screen on. And then see this wheel? That's the app that Hep designed for you."

"Interesting, but why do I want such a thing?"

Thantos rolled her eyes as only a teenage girl could. "Cause you can take it with you silly! Now give it a try."

Lady Luck, in the tone of a woman indulging a favored child asked, "And who should I try it on? You?"

"Yuck, no! I don't need you to spin your wheel to know my fortune. I've got another eon of carting the dead off to Hades ahead of me." Thantos pointed at me. "Eros has had a run of bad luck for a while now." Thany was apparently the master of the understatement. I had an insane wife and a mother I hated. That was more than a run of bad luck. "She continued, "Let's see if better fortune is coming his way."

A small smile played around Fortuna's lips, "Is this what you want too, Eros?"

The moment upon us, I hoped I was hiding my trepidation and said with something approximating unconcern, "Sure. Why not? Things could hardly get worse for me," I lied while hoping that "Why not" didn't mean that I'd find myself serving in Hades or some other less-than-enjoyable future. We'd only weighted the app. We hadn't guaranteed an answer for me.

She stared at me and I hoped my nonchalant attitude was holding and my inner fingers crossed weren't showing. A moment later she said, "As you will." She pointed the phone at me and pressed the app. I closed my eyes and prayed I hadn't made an enormous mistake.

"Ah, what do we have here? The answer you seek is in Hell." She read the statement with just a hint too much of satisfaction.

Oh cripes. What had I done? The only Hell I knew was the Christian version—and they were busy denying the presence of any other god. I doubted even Thanatos had friends there? My fingers were clenched so tight they were bloodless.

Thanatos' brow was wrinkled and she mouthed at me, behind Fortuna's back, "I don't remember adding that one." Wonderful, I thought as I grabbed the back of the couch very tightly to keep from demanding answers—and possibly screaming loudly. The Fortuna's powers probably unweighted the app and exposed me to any number of futures. What I knew of the Christian Hell was that it was a particularly vicious one— nine rings of Hell with sinners being forced to endure tortures that ranged from endless vicious storms without shelter to being boiled in oil and heated blood. Without an escort I could wander there in observing and be stuck forever. Thanatos on the other hand jumped up off of the couch, looked around Fortuna at the phone and squealed happily. "Thanks,

Toony. You're the best!"

I was still standing there stunned as Thany grabbed my arm and dragged me out of the trailer. Fortuna stood at the top of the stairs. "I am the best," she said with a smile. "And next time you want to know something, just ask. Don't play foolish games with me, Little One."

"We will," Thanatos called back. As we walked away she shook her head. "I never get anything over on her. I don't know why I keep trying."

I pulled us both to a halt, "What?!"

"Oh Toony and me, we go way back. This human, Stylianos Spyridakis, was tormenting the crap out of her, following her around, begging for good luck and generally being a pest. Normally she'd just put up with that crap, but the asshole got sexually aggressive with her so I took him to Hades. Since then we've been friends."

"Then what was the app about? The weighted fortune? The whole let's try to trick Fortuna?"

She sighed. "Fortuna's powers don't work the way most of us do. She's just a conduit for them. You had to spin the wheel to find out anything of import. I tried to make it as safe as possible, but honestly I failed. I didn't think her powers would change the electronic answers. I didn't think things out very well, did I?"

No you didn't," I said bitterly. "Now you've got me going to Hell where I've got no power and no allies..."

Thanatos smiled. "What do you mean no allies? If need be I can escort you around the Inferno silly—but I don't have to. Fortuna's accent confused you. She didn't say H.E.L.L. She said H.E.L. As in the Norse Goddess. You've already met her."

Breath I didn't even know I was holding rushed back into my body. I could deal with Hel. I'd done it before. Just as I was about to head North she grabbed my hand. I'll take you. No way am I missing the end of this story. Thanatos was about to shift us through space and dimensions when she stopped and giggled, saying, "I hope you've got a couple of extra arrows. In case the first ones didn't do the trick."

"Yeah, I do." I didn't bother mentioning it, but I also had a couple of lead arrows in my quiver. I could pull anyone out of an unwilling enchantment. The gold arrow's effects wouldn't last forever but if she'd found a weak minded fool she could have sway over them for some time. I'd given her the arrows but nothing in our agreement said that I couldn't reverse the effects. Hel was a grim girlfriend for most.

* * *

We arrived in the Norse underworld Helheim and before I knew what was happening my arm was being bit by a huge gray dog. "Ouch!" I screamed and I kicked out and got Garm directly in the nose. He growled and launched himself straight at my neck. Oh shit, was my only thought. When Garm killed even the gods couldn't leave Helheim. I didn't want to be condemned to an eternity in the endless gray haze. I did wonder for a moment though if my Psyche's quiet days were spent wandering a world like this one. She often muttered about fog and not being able to see beyond the mists.

I was curled in a ball expecting to be ripped apart when I was saved by Thanatos. She'd instantly grown a foot and was in full Grim Reaper attire. She growled back at the dog and it landed on the floor whimpering at her feet. Suddenly she was a prepubescent teenage girl again, down on her knees, rubbing Garm's head and singing, "Whose a good doggy. You're a good doggy, aren't you?"

I dropped down next to her and, as Garm growled warningly at me, said, "That's weird."

She had her head buried in the dog's neck so her next words were pretty garbled. "What's weird?"

"Last time I was here Garm was very friendly. Now he's ready to bite my arm off."

"We just scared him, popping in like that. Didn't we boy? Huh?" She was making raspberries at the dog and laughing as he licked her buzzing lips.

"Maybe," I conceded. "But well… where's Ganglatia and Ganglot, Hel's servants? One of them is always with Garm." Garm had nearly condemned Thor to an eternity in Helheim and when he'd escaped he'd insisted Garm be constantly supervised. The other gods agreed and Odin decreed it.

She stood up, one hand still on the dog's head. "You're right. That is weird. Let's go find them."

I squinted through the endless mists of Helheim—why oh why do underworlds have to be so dreary—and and could just make out Eljudnir; Hel's home, all of ten feet way. It sounded like a bar fight. . As we climbed the rotting concrete steps, a body went flying through the window. I had a funny feeling we'd found the Apple of Discord.

Thanatos muttered, "Uh oh," and flashed back into her Grim Reaper guise, told the dog to stay and pushed me behind her. "This doesn't sound good. You'll be safer if I guard you."

"Safer from what?" I muttered, but stayed where she put me. It was quite possible I didn't want to know what Hel could do to me.

Inside it appeared as though a full-scale bar fight had broken out … without the bar. Instead, couches, chairs, a TV, laptop, dishes, pots, pans, and etcetera were used as weapons of destruction. And since the dead weren't going to die again, this fight could go on for a very long time. In the midst of this insanity Hel was screaming loudly for the fight to end, and alone in one corner Adonis—dressed all in black—was plucking at guitar strings, tears flowing and staring at the Goddess of Death with a look of adoration on his face.

"I'll take Adonis," I shouted over the noise.

"I've got Hel."

We split up and I made a beeline for Adonis. "She's such a sweet seductress," he sighed gazing at Hel.

It was pretty obvious that Hel had shot Adonis with my arrow but I was still kind of surprised that he had fallen. I thought his love for my mother protected him. So instead of asking what in Hades was going on in Helheim, I found myself blurting out, "But what about Aphrodite?"

He plucked a few sad chords in the guitar. "I don't want to be mean about your mother, Eros, but she's not a good woman." Yeah, like he needed to tell me that. "I was with her for eons. Thousands of years. And she betrayed me with an oaf." Tears welled up again and he burst into a rendition of "Lying Eyes." It was a little trite, but I got his point. Although if you thought about it, Adonis was more of the boy across town and less of the rich old man, and I'd really given his song choice way too much thought.

"Well he is her ex-husband and you two were never faithful and…" Wait. Why was I defending her? I needed to focus on the problem at hand. Where was the Apple? And how was I going to get it out of Helheim and to safety without starting wars everywhere?

He interrupted my introspection. "Death is the great equalizer," he told me somberly. "I don't know why I didn't see it before. She'd never betray me because she's sees all and truly knows what's in my heart."

And her bottom half was a skeleton who smelled like rotting flesh I added silently. Hel wouldn't betray him because she couldn't do any better. Even the dead didn't want to lie with her.

I had no idea what to do. Did I free him with the lead arrow? Or did I allow Hel her fun and assume that sooner or later the effects of the golden arrow would wear off? It was a dilemma. He switched into something that sounded frighteningly like American country music:

"There's pictures of you and I on the walls around me
The way that it was and coulda been surrounds me
I'll never get over you walkin' away"

I shuddered and fingered the lead arrow. Maybe I'd free him from love just to avoid the bad chording.

"That's what your mother was to me," Adonis said sorrowfully.

* * *

Thanatos gestured urgently to us and I grabbed the depressed singer who was screaming out an out of tune version of "Love Stinks" by the wrist and hustled over to the two death goddesses. Thanatos was considerably less concerned about the ethical dilemma of Adonis being in love with Hel then I was. There was something frantic in her eyes as she shook the poor musician. "Did you give her the Apple of Discord?"

His eyes got dreamy. "My fairest treasure to the fairest of them all. She who brings a dreamless sleep to us all."

Instead of rolling her eyes at the bad poetic utterances, she held him up over her head. "Did you tell Hel what it was?"

"I told her it was a gift from the heart," he stated indignantly.

"Oh Zeus!" She dropped Adonis and he landed hard on the ground. I looked around wondering what the problem was. Surely Hel wasn't happy with her land being turned into a never-ending war zone and would give us the Apple of Discord. Hopefully Thanatos could bring us directly to Aphrodite's palace and we'd get it into its containment field.

"I thought it was one of Iaunn's Apples. One of the Apples of Immortality," Hel disclosed, heartbreak in her voice. My stomach cramped as I suspected I knew exactly what was coming. "They're supposed to make you look young and beautiful." She gazed for a moment on her new lover. "I wanted to be gorgeous for you. I wanted you to have someone better than..." She waved at her skeletal lower half wordlessly.

Adonis gripped her hand. "You are young and beautiful, dearest. You're all that I could ever hope for. How can you be Hel when you are in my heart?" As chaos reigned amongst them, the two gazed into each other's eyes and I hoped that the infatuation the arrows brought would mature into true love. I motioned to Thany. It was time for us to get out of there. They could both keep their delusions about each other for a little while longer.

* * *

Back at Ares abode, while the ancient war god read *Green Eggs and Ham,* I shrugged. "I guess that ends the case of the missing Apple of Discord." I'd let my mother and Hep know what happened to the Apple. My mother would be upset. I had a feeling that Hephaestus would be perfectly happy that it was destroyed.

"So what do you think will happen?" Thanatos' eyes on me were not the eyes of the teenager she appeared to be but rather the ancient she was.

I shrugged. "The arrow will wear off, infatuation will wane and they'll both wonder what they saw in each other." That was the most likely outcome. I'd keep my wish that they'd both find happiness to myself.

"Not that," she said while muttering quietly, "Love gods—they never see the big picture." Then to clarify since I was clearly an idiot, "The Apple?"

I didn't see what the big deal was "She'll digest the Apple and chaos will lessen in Helheim?"

Thanatos chuckled a little grimly. "I don't think so. Not to be too graphic but she hasn't got a digestive system."

I looked at her with dawning horror. "Discord will reign in Hel forever?"

"Yup." She looked glum. "I wish there was something we could do. I mean I always thought the dead deserved their rest but the Norse dead will be condemned to fight endlessly."

I thought of what I could say to comfort her. "Some people think the ultimate punishment for undeserving souls isn't fire and brimstone. They think that it's boredom, having nothing to do for an eternity."

She grinned suddenly. "Well time in Hel will never be boring!"

I flipped on the television and settled in to watch *Excalibur* when Thanatos jumped up in glee. "The Holy Grail. That'd cure Psyche. Let's go find it."

I settled deeper into the couch and reached for the popcorn. "I've been searching for it for a millennium. Even rode with Lancelot looking for it."

She rolled her eyes. "Stupid. You needed to ride with Galahad."

"That's easy for you to say in hindsight."

For a moment I thought she was going to argue with me, and then she said, "I know people. I can help you find it."

I looked at Ares wrapped around his book, covered in chocolate, asleep on the floor and then to Thanatos' cheerful eyes and I felt hope enter my heart. "I'm sure you can." I grabbed a handful of popcorn. I had a family who cared about me and for one night I was going to enjoy it. The quest could start tomorrow.

TAMAM SHUD
Georgina Morales

*T*he shadows in the one-bedroom apartment closed in, suffocating Alfred while the sun outside shone with the promise of freedom, a promise that failed to touch him. Through the window in the living/dining area, a yellow beam of light touched the skin of his arm.

Alfred stared at the dog tag hanging from his neck, so similar to the ones he had worn during the war. For soldiers, the tags were a means to identify their bodies. In the case of sixty- seven-year-old Alfred, his tag would tell a stranger who to call on the day that he finally lost his mind. His daughter's idea, and the only thing standing between him and a retirement home.

The small metallic plaque grew heavy; a weight of lead that threatened to crush him.

His daughter was wrong; Alfred wasn't senile. He recognized the optimistic odor of fresh paint hiding the humidity that threatened to bring down the thirty-year-old kitchen walls. He heard her whisper into her phone, pondering if the old man was too far gone to live on his own. Alfred hadn't been a good father, and he knew Gwyneth didn't want him in her home. No, reality in all its messed up glory did not escape him.

Through the open window, a gust of wind caressed his white hair. At least the years had faded some of the bad memories too, like the years of raising her daughter after Teresa had died. That he had spent most of those years in a drunken haze hadn't hurt, either. She was a good woman, though, visited every week, brought him food; sometimes she even kept him company.

Alfred evoked his wife's face, searching for peace in her sweet, cobalt gaze. An ethereal mist without edges or features formed in his mind. He held his breath; his heart sprinted. A pearl of sweat materialized on his forehead. Alfred concentrated harder. The mist dissolved into nothing.

Light hurt his dark brown eyes when he opened them.

He strode across the apartment to his bedroom. From the top shelf of the closet, he got a twenty-two inches square cardboard box that Gwyneth had brought for him after Teresa was gone.

For hours Alfred pieced his past together again, assigning names to faces he hadn't seen outside of pictures in ages. From under one of the albums peeked a piece of green cotton. He grabbed it with shaking hands. Teresa's favorite blouse. The color remained vibrant from being sealed inside the box, and when he put it to his nose, it held the flowery essence of his wife. A burning sensation spread through his chest. Trapped in the cloth, a manila envelope had flown out of the box and landed next to him. He didn't need to open it, inside was Teresa's death certificate.

Alfred embraced the blouse and wept. The cotton turned darker with his tears, and he thought of the times his wife's shoulder had filled that space. When cancer had extinguished her light, it had left him in a darkness that surrounded him to this day. An immeasurable hole of despair grew inside his ribcage. Alfred wished God would let him die.

By 4:30, the painful grumbling of his stomach told him he couldn't put off eating any longer. With slow, tender motions Alfred rearranged the treasures remaining inside the box, making space for the ones he'd taken out. At the bottom of the container, a dusty hardback tome lay at an angle. His heart skipped a beat as he grasped the bound leather cover.

The corners of his mouth curled up. Teresa had given him the book for his birthday the year she had gone back to college pursuing a teaching degree. A poetry book. What does an ironworker know of poetry? But Teresa's voice had opened him to a world of soft words and deep meaning far away from the nightmares that had tormented most of his adult life.

His wife's warm voice echoed in his mind, bathing him like a balsam to soothe his aching heart.

That night Alfred slept with the book by his pillow. He hoped for good dreams where his wife still breathed next to him.

* * *

Electricity crackled in the air as the gray sky filled with clouds. The blue sea in front of him danced peacefully even though thunder split the sky. Near the surface a silhouette circled in the murky water, preparing to attack.

A pit opened where Alfred's entrails should have been and a layer of sweat covered his palms. Fog masked the horizon; from the void inside, a sailing ship came forth. Shadows cloaked the deck. The cold hand of fear squeezed his dry throat.

In the dock where Alfred stood, an unnatural calm prevailed. The wind stopped blowing, seagulls flew by in silence, the ocean didn't swoosh as it cradled the ship. Goosebumps covered his skin.

Standing on the vessel's deck, a black shape came clear against the burgundy landscape as evening turned to night. It was a young man with tan skin and bulgy arms. Alfred couldn't distinguish the face. The acrid taste of bile filled Alfred's mouth. He had to run away from the sailor but his legs didn't respond. He tripped and fell. There were two suitcases at his feet. Children's clothes lay scattered. A broken doll with a white sweater and lifeless sapphire eyes stared at the sky.

Alfred averted his eyes from the doll. The shadowy man was now inches from his face. The man's eyes burned like tempered steel dissecting Alfred's tired soul; the pupils swirled in a maddening river. They reminded Alfred of open sea, a place in the middle of nowhere, a scream no one hears, a suffocating body buried deep...

* * *

Alfred woke up with a start. The chirping birds announced the arrival of morning even though the apartment remained dark. A big lump nestled in his throat. He was out of breath and wetness covered his pillow. Making sense of his dream was like searching for the correct word and not quite remembering it.

To hell with it, he thought.

He got up and went about his chores, more because he needed to fill his time rather than out of interest in a clean bathroom or freshly washed clothes.

Soon Gwyny will be here.

* * *

"Did you stop by the bank?"

"Like every Monday, Dad. I still think it's a bad idea for you to go out, though," answered Gwyneth while unpacking grocery bags.

"I won't go far, just a couple of blocks to one of the cafes on Ashton Park. I'm going insane here!"

Pregnant silence filled the room.

"I'll read my book and eat lunch; be back by three. I promise; you can call." Alfred's voiced turned higher in tone and lower in volume, making him a pleading child.

Gwyneth opened her mouth but before she could say a word Alfred added, "Doctor said I needed the exercise, remember?"

"Fine," she conceded with a roll of her eyes. "I'll call you every afternoon at 3:30 to check on you. Now, I need to go. Dan and the kids will be home early and I want to have dinner ready. Will you be fine?"

"Sure! If that stupid wall doesn't crumble and bury me." He pointed to the new crack running across the wall between the kitchen and the dining room.

"Not again! I expected the paint to buy us more time to gather the money." She grimaced, "I know thirty years is a lot, but if you'd brought in a contractor, this wouldn't be happening."

He shrugged and gave her his sideways, half-smile.

She sighed and grabbed the car keys from her purse. "I have to go now. There's fresh food in the fridge, enough to cook a decent meal every night. No more hot dogs, got it?"

Gwyneth sounded like Teresa all those years ago when she reprimanded the kids. She had the same piercing blue eyes.

"Do you want me to cook something? I could—"

"Oh, stop it Gwyny. I'll be fine. I can fix my own dinner; been doing it for a long time."

Alfred put one wrinkled hand on her arm; it quivered with age. When his daughter looked at it, her brows pulled together in worry, he hid both hands behind his back.

"Enjoy yourself, Dad," Gwyneth whispered when they reached the building door. She kissed him goodbye and stood there, watching him walk away.

Alfred glanced back several times and waved goodbye, smiling. On his other hand, he held his book. Gwyneth answered the gesture but the light mood never touched her eyes. Then she walked left, toward her car. Alfred's cheeks hurt from smiling so much.

Fifteen minutes later, Alfred sat on the first available chair on a terrace without looking for a specific cafeteria. No wonder his doctor wanted him to exercise; three blocks and his lungs were about to implode. While he waited for the waiter to come, and for his pulse to regulate, Alfred thumbed through his precious book. A delicate musky aroma rose from the yellowy pages.

Cold wind blew on his neck, like someone breathing on him. The hair on the back of his head stood on end, and his limbs tensed as they'd done during his war years when danger was close. He allowed his eyes to wander. Nothing stood out. People walked their dogs, jogged, chatted, used their phones. Then he saw her. In a direct line from him, a lady on the other side of the park stared at him. She wore a plum peasant blouse paired with a white skirt and sweater. She had dead-pale skin and thin lips twisted in disgust. A chill ran down Alfred's spine.

"Excuse me, sir? These tables are for customers."

Alfred whipped his head to the voice, glad to break away from the woman's bewitchment.

"I'm, uh—I'm a costumer. Just waiting for a waiter," said Alfred, making a conscious effort to keep his sight on the young server.

"We don't have waiters. You have to get in line at the register, see?" The kid had a squalid complexion and cheeks full of pimples. His condescending tone made Alfred want to smack him, but most of all Alfred wanted to read his book in peace.

"But this is the last free table. If I stand in the line, somebody else'll take it!"

"Maybe you could leave your book?" said the kid looking into the store.

Behind the cash register another young man mouthed undecipherable words between clenched teeth. Kid number one hurried to his side without paying more attention to Alfred.

I'm not leaving it here for someone to—

"I'll tell you what, I'll go order both of our drinks and we share the table. That a deal?"

Alfred faced the gentle voice coming from behind him. It was the creepy lady in the peasant, plum blouse, except the anger had vanished from her features.

"I'm Jestyn, by the way." She extended her right hand and her thin lips parted in a smile that revealed two lines of perfect, white teeth.

"I, um …How did you get here so fast?" Alfred met Jestyn's hand with his while tipping his head to the side, looking back more closely. It was impossible to have crossed the park so fast. She wasn't even panting.

"Sorry? I was just walking home from work." She squinted and pointed in the opposite direction with her thumb. "I…" The thirty-something woman averted her eyes and fixed her skirt before going on. "I realize you must think I'm a stalker or a crazy lady and if you don't want to talk to me I get it, really. It's just that—is that the Tamam Shud?"

"Wha—how did you know?" Alfred's forearms hurt where the edges of the tome sank into his skin as he pressed the book between his arms.

"I teach poetry at the community college and that is a famous and rare book. The school where I studied had a copy, but I'd never met someone who owned one." She blushed.

"I had no idea it was that rare, or famous. My-my wife gave it to me a long time ago." Alfred felt overwhelmed but there was an odd familiarity in Jestyn's presence, a sense of belonging. "Why don't you sit down and tell me about the book."

Her face lit up. "But first we must order. We don't want Mr. Pimples back."

"Black coffee and a grilled cheese, please?" Alfred gave her a twenty and sat again. He would not let the book out of his sight, good feeling or not.

When he saw Jestyn get in line, Alfred ran his fingers through his hair. "What's wrong with me?" he whispered. "I know nothing of this woman!"

A couple sitting at the table to his left shot a furtive look his way.

"What? Don't you talk to yourselves sometimes?"

The couple turned away from Alfred, afraid and outraged at the same time.

"This is why Gwyny doesn't want me to go out. Next thing you know, I'm spilling my guts." *Why, yes! I live alone, why don't you come and visit?* "When she's back I'm outta here," he continued, ignoring the dirty looks coming from his left.

"Well, here's your order, sir," Jestyn joked. Her voice floated in the air like a birdsong. "So, did you know the original manuscript is Persian and had a different name?" Jestyn took the seat in front of him. "When it was first translated to English in 1859, the translator retained the final line of the original manuscript: Tamam Shud. It means—"

"Finished." Alfred opened the book on the final page and ran his fingers through the adorned typography.

* * *

"Yes, yes. I'm eating well and taking my medications, but I think these walks to the park are really helping." Alfred switched the phone to his other ear.

"I'm sure!" said Gwyneth with a chuckle. "And talking to people is a great way to keep your mind active, too. Just be careful, Dad." Concern permeated her voice. "I know you like this new lady but don't give her your information, 'kay?"

"I'm not stupid, Gwyny; wasn't born yesterday."

"I know, just saying. She could be a scam artist, for all we know."

"I've witnessed many things in my years. I think I'd recognize a scumbag when I meet one and a thirty-something college teacher ain't it." Why did this kid underestimate Alfred's ability to navigate the world! He had done it for over sixty-freaking-years.

"Yeah well, maybe one day I'll tag along and you can introduce us. But in the meantime, tell me more about her. What do you guys talk about?"

What can we possibly have in common, you mean? Alfred thought.

It was a valid question; one that Alfred kept asking even after three weeks of daily rendezvous. It wasn't easy for a man his age to open up, especially because he carried so much baggage on his shoulders, but Jestyn made it simple. She was sociable, funny, and a teacher through and through. Not only was she intelligent and cultivated, but her patience knew no bounds.

They talked about the book, about poetry, about life and death, and Jestyn listened to him. With her, he was a man again, not a sixty-year-old on the brink of senility; and when she laughed, the world shone. Jestyn was the woman Teresa could've been. And for the first time in decades, Alfred wasn't having nightmares.

But not one of Alfred's arguments convinced Gwyneth of Jestyn's worth.

"Maybe she really should join us one afternoon," Alfred said to himself after setting the earpiece on the receiver.

The clock hanging from the living room wall marked 11:50.

"I better get on my way."

Alfred grabbed the book and hurried down two flights of stairs to the street level. A block later, a fire had kindled in his lungs. His arthritic limbs didn't appreciate the uphill walk, either.

When will it get easier!

He leaned against a tree in the corner of the park as he scanned the cafeteria for Jestyn.

Thank God she's late.

In front of him, Ashton Park extended for two more blocks. Artificial trails demarcated by shrubberies encouraged children to find different ways to get to Summertown Sprinkler, where a water sprout lured them with the promise of wet fun. Today however, the black rubber tarp designed to cushion little feet remained empty, as it had been since Labor Day.

Alfred saw water vapor rise from the wet surface, but instead of mixing with the fresh air and disappearing, it accumulated near the ground effectively turning into fog.

"What the hell..." Sweat covered Alfred's forehead.

The fog became thick, concealing the rest of the park from view. The sun hid behind foreboding clouds and a shadow darker than night floated where the spurt of water should have been.

Alfred's heart thumped against his ribs like a trapped animal fighting for freedom. A wave of nausea forced him to cling to the tree trunk. Dizziness blurred his vision. Heat rose to his head. The silhouette from his nightmares stared at him from behind the haze.

I've finally lost it. Dear God, Teresa, I'm crazy!

Alfred dropped to the grass and puked into the tree bed.

"Are you okay?" Jestyn's voice drifted to him.

When the tingling sensation in his fingers subsided, Alfred opened his eyes. Jestyn frowned under the warm sunbeam. The droning in his ears lessened, replaced by the relaxing sounds coming from the fountain. Ashford Park greenery stretched out as far as he could see.

"C'mon, you need to sit." Jestyn guided him to their usual table, then got a latte for each one of them.

The slight sour taste of coffee inundated Alfred's mouth, his buttocks conformed to the uncaring metallic chair, Jestyn's rosy perfume penetrated his nostrils. Alfred held to his senses like an anchor to the world.

"Thanks. I guess I'm more out of shape than I thought," said Alfred, trying to make light of the situation." Or maybe it's the crazy weather. Freaking Indian summer," he muttered.

"Nothing to be ashamed of. You should take it easy and tell your doctor, though. Prevent something serious." Jestyn's voice trailed off with the caw of a black raven. Her electric sapphire eyes peeked over her bronze shades, along with an ugly black and blue blotch under her left eye.

Alfred's mouth fell ajar.

Jestyn pushed the frame up the bridge of her nose and squirmed under his alarmed gaze.

"So." Alfred cleared his throat. "How was your weekend?" He took another gulp of coffee.

"Okay, I guess." Jestyn's shoulders fell, her frame relaxed. "Grading college essays can hardly be called thrilling," she joked without humor.

Alfred pretended to be engrossed in his cup of coffee, unsure if their friendship granted him enough grounds to ask her about the mark. Jestyn kept looking behind her as if expecting someone to be there. She toyed with strands of her auburn hair, pulled up the long sleeves of her knitted top, then pulled them down.

Wait; are those bruises on her arms?

"I'm sorry Alfred." Jestyn bit her lip and straightened nonexistent wrinkles on her skirt. "I'm afraid I'm not good company today. I have a lot on my mind."

"Is everything all right?" But Alfred knew the answer; the clues were right in front of him.

"Oh, yes. Yes, just tired. I'll be fine tomorrow." Jestyn hesitated before going on. "Alfred, what did you see in the park earlier today? Was it a man?"

"A man?" Alfred was astonished, "No, why? Did you?"

"No, of course not. It doesn't matter. Will see you tomorrow, 'kay?" She kissed him on the cheek and walked away with slouched shoulders.

* * *

Alfred was back on the dock watching the blackened sky swirl like a witch's cauldron brewing toxic potions. Disconnected from the looming storm, the sea danced gently into the horizon, except for the area underneath his feet. There it had the green tint of a poisoned swamp where things went to die. The obscure silhouette swam in that water, so close to the surface that Alfred could distinguish its twisted, twig-like spine.

A pressure built in Alfred's throat. He choked. His hands flew to his throat, searching for the culprit. Nothing. He opened his mouth, tried to gasp, but no oxygen relieved him of his agony. His heart broke, like crystal that burst into shards. A million needles stabbed him in the chest. He fell into darkness.

A face jumped at him; a twenty-something young man with suntanned skin and maddening pits for pupils. Alfred had seen him before; he was a sailor and with him Death and Misery traveled. The man screeched. Viscous threads of saliva landed on Alfred's skin.

Desperate, Alfred fought the darkness. He couldn't tell up from down, but a wet surface chilled his back. Alfred turned on his stomach and crawled, but his sweaty palms slipped against the wooden floor. Children's clothes tangled his legs.

The sailor pulled Alfred's hair backward, stretching his neck in an unnatural, painful angle. The weight of the man's brawny body fell on him. He showed Alfred a broken porcelain doll. "Remember her?"

Alfred stared at the toy, soiled and with a spider-crack that ran through its cheek. The crack expanded, pieces sank, holes riddled the once pretty face. The remaining porcelain features elongated, causing the eyes to droop. Its colors melted together.

From the sailor's fingers hung Jestyn's screaming head.

Jestyn's cry for help echoed in Alfred's bedroom, awaking him. Except it hadn't come from her. He didn't remember yelling, but his sore throat said that much.

Alfred sighed and turned on the light. *No more sleep for tonight.*

* * *

On Tuesday, Alfred sat at his usual table for two hours without a sign of Jestyn. When a light drizzle began, Alfred gave up. He didn't want to miss Gwyny's call and it was close to 3:30.

"Maybe tomorrow," he said to himself.

A block before getting home, a downpour struck. Alfred's checkered shirt and khakis stuck to his body like a second, restrictive skin. Rivers ran down the side of the street, sometimes making whirlpools in front of sewer openings. In one such whirlpool, a small toy boat circled; its two white sails hoisted despite the storm. Alfred looked up and down the street for a child.

Not a soul.

"*Help!*" Jestyn's voice roared louder than thunder.

Electricity traversed his body. "Jestyn?" Alfred asked in a broken voice.

Alfred perceived movement on his peripheral vision and whipped his head in that direction but missed it. He got the impression of a shadow man, though, darting from building to building in hiding.

"Murderer," whispered in his ear the voice from his nightmares.

Alfred recoiled so hard, his spine made a cracking noise. The street remained deserted. Acute pain lodged in Alfred's chest. His fingers became numb, and the surreal sensation of being in a dream flooded his mind. He rushed toward his apartment complex, not caring about his arthritic knees, twisted back, or tired feet.

"Remember her?" the voice asked neither far nor close.

"Aaaaagh!" Alfred put his hands to his ears and ran the rest of the way.

He flew up the stairs to the second floor where he froze at the sight of his doorstep.

Looking at him with dull sapphire eyes lay the ceramic doll.

Alfred kicked it hard, unleashing years of pain and hate, destroying the symbol of his fear until there was nothing but marred shreds of clothing. Then he kicked it once more down the stairs. Inside his apartment, the phone rang.

"Hello?" Alfred picked it after the fourth ring.

"Oh, hi Dad. Thought you weren't home. How's your day going?" Gwyny sounded tired.

* * *

It had taken all of Alfred's strength to leave the apartment on the days following that rainy afternoon, but he wanted to see Jestyn. For a week he walked to Ashton Park praying for sunny days, avoiding shadows, jerking at the most insignificant breeze blowing in his ear. And he did it for nothing; Jestyn never came.

On Friday, Alfred decided to look for her at the college if she didn't show up that day.

The sun warmed up the otherwise chilly afternoon. Alfred walked into the street with the book under his arm and a sense of purpose in his soul.

A few feet away a burly man with sun-kissed skin erected as an obstacle in Alfred's way.

Not you again.

Alfred wanted to run back to his apartment and hide under his bed; yet a nagging voice in his head encouraged him to confront his fears. This was no man but a vision conjured by his sick mind. And he needed to make sure Jestyn was fine.

The world twirled around him, but Alfred marched on in a straight line that should put him directly in front of the man that terrified him so much. Alfred didn't lift his gaze from the sidewalk but when he reached that spot, no one was there.

A light breeze stroked his white hair; it seemed to whisper but the words escaped him.

Alfred refused to yield to his anxiety. He ignored the palpitations of his heart and didn't turn to check who might walk at his back.

After getting his coffee and a small sandwich, he sat on the same spot he had sat for a month and prepared to read his book.

"She won't come anymore," said the man slapping his big hand on the iron wrought tabletop.

Alfred stared at him. A piece of undigested turkey breast came up his throat; he swallowed it for the second time. It was the man he had seen just minutes before. His resemblance to the figure from his nightmares was uncanny; the same muscular complexion and skin color, the same maddening eyes. But this one was flesh and bones.

A chill ran down Alfred's spine.

The man opened his calloused hand and liberated a bejeweled talisman of about two and a half inches. A silver boat with zirconia-encrusted sails that rocked atop topaz waves hung from a broken silver necklace.

Alarm inundated Alfred. He had seen Jestyn wear the piece.

"Are you Jestyn's husband?" Alfred tried to remember if she had ever mentioned his name. "Prestige?"

The man gritted his teeth. "Murderer," he spat, and with one swipe of his hand, Alfred's coffee and half-eaten sandwich crashed into the pavement.

Every person within earshot turned to the noise; outrage, fear, confusion, and disapproval painted in their faces.

"It's not my fault! He's the crazy one picking a fight!" said Alfred pointing to the empty space next to him. The man was gone.

Murmurs filled the air. The faces turned away. Some people left.

"Sir, I'm sorry but I have to ask you to leave," said Mr. Pimples, keeping a few steps away from Alfred.

Behind him, the other kid stood by Mr. Pimples in meek support.

"I—I'm sorry kid; it wasn't my fault. You saw the other guy did it, don't you?"

"It—" Mr. Pimples changed his mind when the other elbowed him. "Yeah, I'm really sorry but customers have complained with my manager. I'm afraid you can't come back here anymore, man."

"That's okay. Sorry about the mess," said Alfred begrudgingly as he grabbed the necklace from the table and his book from the floor, thankfully far from the spoiled food.

Once back in the safety of his home, Alfred set the locket on the kitchen counter. His fingers released their grip and he could almost hear them screech like rusted gears. On his palm, small wine-red flakes remained.

Alfred's heartbeat accelerated. He gasped.

In between the stones, the same flaky, red substance marred the otherwise perfect beauty of the piece.

Blood.

Turkey pesto ciabatta soared out of Alfred's stomach and into the sink.

* * *

Alfred woke up from another nightmare and sprang to a sitting position. The dark swallowed the details, but he recognized the familiar contours in the bedroom, such as the kids' pictures on the walls and the small table by his bed. Alfred willed the pounding in his thorax to synchronize to the constant tick tock of the clock on the nightstand.

Another night spent in the company of terror, one more day without a clue of Jestyn's fate.

Prestige's dramatic present had pushed Alfred to stay away from the mystery of Jestyn's whereabouts. He worried a persistent search for his friend or answers might bring trouble to both Jestyn and him. But his dreams refused to understand. The message in them rang louder each time: Jestyn was dead, by her husband's hands.

He covered his face. Sobs racked his body. If only he could exorcize his fears.

When the last tear dried Alfred realized the only way he'd find freedom was to bring justice for Jestyn. But he would need his daughter's help.

Without getting out of bed, Alfred reached for the phone next to the clock and dialed.

"Hello?" answered a sleepy Gwyny.

"Oh, it's you! Good. I didn't want to wake the whole house. Listen, I need your help." A rush of energy coursed through Alfred's veins.

"Dad, what's the matter? It's five o'clock on a Sunday morning!"

"Yeah, I'm sorry," said Alfred biting his lower lip. "I couldn't wait."

"What could be so urgent?"

"Remember that lady I met a month ago? She's disappeared; I think her husband killed her." Alfred held his breath.

"What? How can you say something like that!"

Alfred's hopes sank a bit. "You don't have to believe me. Just come with me to the cafeteria on Ashton Park. We'll ask a few questions there, and maybe later we can go to the college where she worked."

"You're out of your mind, Dad."

"Look, I'd do it by myself but the husband's a piece of work and I'm, you know, not at my prime." Alfred let her digest the information.

"Okay. I'll be there at noon," Gwyny huffed. "But if we don't find anything, you'll drop the shtick without complaint. That a deal?"

"You got it!" Alfred squeaked in delight.

He toiled around the house and whistled, daydreaming that this would be the storm to bring him closer to his kid. Alfred could not erase the years of negligence, but maybe helping Jestyn would show Gwyny how much Alfred had changed.

Close to 1:50, Alfred went to the window expecting to see Gwyneth get out of her car and walk into the building at any moment.

Why is she late? This is important!

The joyful cries of children running in the street drifted in the otherwise still afternoon. A mother called their names, "Anthony, Lucia, wait for Mommy!"

As the woman passed the street light in front of his building, Alfred saw a man leaning against the pole. A shock of electricity tightened his muscles.

Jestyn's husband smirked at him. On the opposite sidewalk from the man, a green '97 Honda Accord parked. A woman with curly chestnut hair got out and walked to the passenger side.

"Gwyny!" yelled Alfred.

Prestige pointed to Gwyneth with his index finger, but his eyes remained fixed on Alfred. He arched his brows and blew her a kiss. Then he walked toward her.

"No! Gwyneth!"

Gwyneth faced the apartment window. "I'm getting the groceries out, be there in a minute."

"Leave it! Get up here *now*!"

Something in Alfred's appearance must have convinced her because she ran upstairs.

"Dad, Dad, what's going on?" said Gwyny as she jumped the last flight of steps two at a time.

Alfred waited for her with the door opened. "Get in before he catches up!"

"He?" she said looking behind her shoulder.

Alfred pulled her by the elbow into the tiny apartment and shut the door with a force that echoed through the staircase.

"I expected you hours ago."

"Yeah, I know. Who's 'he'?" Gwyneth's voice sounded like a whistle after running up two floors.

Alfred crossed the living/dining space to the window and hid behind the yellow curtains without saying a word. He ventured a glimpse outside; Jestyn's husband had vanished.

"Dad, you're freaking me out! Who did you see? Do you even know who I am?"

"Of course I do! What kind of question is that?" This wasn't the scene Alfred had conjured in his mind this morning. "We should eat lunch and let the cafeteria thing for later, I think."

"Whoa! First you call up at five in the morning because you can't wait a minute longer, and now you want to leave it for later?" Gwyneth's authoritative voice made it clear that she was the one in charge.

"I—I'm just hungry." Alfred rolled his eyes.

"Yeah, sure." Gwyneth raised one eyebrow and shook her head.

"Oh, great. I haven't done anything and you're already exasperated!"

"I was late because I went to the cafeteria, Dad."

"Oh really? Then what happened?"

"I spoke to the manager."

"Did he know us? I don't think I ever saw the manager." Alfred shrunk under his daughter's scrutiny.

"Oh, he knows you, all right; as does every other employee there. They call you 'The Crazy Old Man.' He says that for over a month you sat at the same table, talked to yourself, and annoyed the hell out of other patrons." Gwyneth paced in the space between the dining room table and the sofa.

"What? No! What about Jestyn? She was there!"

"There was never anyone else. He told me they asked you to stop going there a week ago, after you became violent and broke a few plates." Gwyneth clutched the back of a chair and studied Alfred's response.

"No, no! He's lying! The husband must've threatened him. Please, you have to listen to me!"

"They didn't ask you to stop going?"

"Well, yes. But it was him who broke the plates!"

"It doesn't make sense, Dad." There was no anger in Gwyny's voice, neither love nor caring. She had turned into a shrink trying to separate truth from figments of a sick mind.

"Outrage boiled inside him. "Prestige doesn't want anyone asking questions because—"

"Who?" Color drained out of Gwyneth's face.

"Prestige, Jestyn's husband."

Gwyneth pressed her temples with the palm of her hands and sighed. "What else do you know of this man?"

"Not much, we never talked about these things. She called him Pres, said he'd recently retired from the Marine Corps."

Gwyneth sat on a chair in the dining room, her body slumped in defeat.

Alfred understood he was losing the battle even though he didn't know why. He opened the top china cabinet drawer where he kept the ill-fated piece of jewelry. Between the red velvet designed for cutlery and the talisman was a folded letter he hadn't seen before.

"The last time I saw Jestyn, she had bruises all over. A week later, the husband paid me a visit and gave me this." Alfred set the necklace on the table. "It was hers, and it's caked in dry blood."

The air in the room thickened.

"How-why do you have it? She took it with her..." her voice quivered.

"And you say I'm the one who talks nonsense?"

"This has no blood anywhere," said Gwyneth, rotating the talisman to examine it from every angle. "And what's that paper you're holding?"

"Dunno. I haven't read it."

Gwyneth took the letter from Alfred.

"Sweet Jesus!" She said after a second. She doubled over herself and sobbed like a child. The paper in her hands looked yellow and brittle with age.

Wasn't it stark white just a minute ago? Alfred thought.

"You never said she left a letter," said Gwyneth to Alfred in a broken voice.

"You're not making any sense!"

Gwyneth eyes sparkled with fury. She proceeded to read the letter out loud. Her voice shook as much as her hands.

Dearest Pres,

It breaks my heart that we have come to this. For years, you have battled your demons and I know you've tried. Believe me, I do. But I can't do this anymore. It tears me apart to leave you behind but I have to think of Gwyny. She doesn't deserve this. Remember all the dreams we had? Raising our family? Watching our kids grow? I'll do my best to live by those dreams. Do not look for us and take care of yourself.

Please understand; we can't let the war wreck her life, too.

I'll always remember eighteen-year-old Pres, fighting for a better world.

Love, Teresa

Alfred's world tumbled down. Teresa? But she'd died of cancer thirty years ago!

Heaving, Alfred lurched to the kitchen sink where he spewed thick threads of saliva. A million pins prickled in his limbs and the ringing in his ears began anew.

"Oh, no. You won't get out of it. Sick or not, you better explain how it is that you have these things!" said Gwyneth following him into the kitchen.

The room swirled too fast for Alfred to keep on his feet. He leaned on the wall, its humid, wobbly surface doing little to improve his equilibrium.

"Dad!" yelled Gwyny. Her complexion had grown dreadfully pale, and she seemed to have aged ten years. Her sore eyes bore a hole on Alfred.

"I don't understand! All I want is to help Jest—"

"Enough with the bullshit!" cried Gwyneth, "Tell me what really happened!"

"I didn't do nothing!" he defended himself. "Prestige did, he killed her! Now he's pinning it on me!"

"Dear God, are you really that far gone? It is you, Dad. You *are* Prestige!"

"What?"

"Look at your fucking tags! Prestige's your middle name!" Gwyneth's face was red with rage.

Alfred read his tag, dumbfounded.

Alfred Prestige Boxal. 67 years old. Retired marine.
In case of an emergency contact Gwyneth Graham (203) 608 9939

"That's my mother's letter from the day she left." Gwyneth slapped the wall, making it vibrate at Alfred's back.

"No, Teresa died of cancer!" Alfred raked images in his mind.

"That's what your senile brain concocted so you could go on living?" Gwyneth was livid.

"*I'm not delusional!*" Tears ran down Alfred's cheeks like burning rivers.

"The fuck you are! She abandoned you."

"That's enough, Gwyny!" pleaded Alfred.

Gwyneth stepped away from him, pacing in front of the fridge. "Read the fucking letter, Alfred, c'mon. Read it and tell me that's not Mom's handwriting."

The mere sight of the crumpled paper made Alfred want to vomit again.

"Why is it fair for you to hide behind oblivion while I must live with the scars?" Gwyneth lowered her voice to a whisper. "For years I saw you come home drunk and abuse mom until you passed out on that vermin-infested couch out there. You called her names, hit her, and made our lives miserable. I spent my life wondering why she hadn't taken me with her."

"But—" blurted Alfred but he quieted.

Gwyny leaned against the metallic sink, her knuckles white with the pressure. "You let me believe she had abandoned us. I was angry at her for so long…"

"I hate you!" she said through clenched teeth.

Gwyneth snatched the first object she found on the dish holder and threw it at her father. Alfred ducked and the heavy metallic teapot crashed against the wall. The impact caused a section of the old plaster, weakened by years of humidity, to crumble to the floor, revealing the last secret.

There, between two studs, rested Teresa's mummified corpse. Her once white sweater, flirty skirt, and plum peasant top slung awkwardly on her consumed body. As they stared into infinity, an opaque film spoiled what in life had been striking cobalt eyes. Her mouth hung agape in a silent scream.

Chaos ensued in the small kitchen. Gwyneth screeched and her knees buckled under her. Out of instinct, she tore the wall with her bare hands between moans and sniffles, fighting for a last opportunity to embrace her mother.

The levee destroyed, memories overflowed Alfred. Every action, every spoken word resonated with crystal-clear definition in his mind.

The apartment morphed to its original open-floor concept. It was 1922 again, Gwyny was two, and he was an ironworker with marital troubles. By some ironic twist of destiny, Alfred had chosen that Friday to stop drinking and get home early. He'd found two suitcases by the door, a note on the dining room table, and the baby sleeping on the sofa. Teresa's perfect porcelain skin grew so pale.

Alfred cried and begged. Why wouldn't she give him another chance? He loved her so much. He couldn't live without her.

Teresa's lean body slumped out of his hands and into the shaggy carpet. The necklace he'd given her as a promise of love was tangled between his fingers, broken.

He turned to face his daughter. In the same spot where once the suitcases had stood, Gwyny's grown up figure rocked Teresa's corpse.

Oh, God. What did I do?

Knowledge suffocated him. Alfred stumbled to the window, grasping for air.

On the sidewalk, Teresa looked up at him. She smiled peacefully, no bruises on her skin.

"Tamam Shud," whispered Alfred.

The woman faded into the background.

He had no idea where he was or what the words meant. But there was a sense of freedom in them.

Cursed Luck
John L. French

First the ones in black broke in, vigilantes whose laughter and violence frightened the crowd, scattered the players, and killed a good number of her guards. She herself was disabled, a bullet to the head that was quicker than her magic. It did not kill her, could not kill her, she was not meant for Hades's realm, but it weakened her so that she lay longer than a day gathering her strength, drawing it from the casino that was her temple. And when she had recovered, after she had used most of her power so that she could walk and talk and get about the business of remodeling and reopening, then came the lightning.

Fire fell from the sky, thrown from the heavens by the hand of a vengeful god—her father, whom she had disappointed in far too many ways. He had come at her bidding to take a woman he wanted, only to be robbed and cheated of his prize by the ones in black. Angrily he had struck out, bringing storm and thunder to the coast town where she lived and worked, making sure that his bolts struck her temple to finish the destruction started by the gunplay.

So as she stood midway between the burnt rubble of what had been Coast City's finest casino and the charred remains of what was once one of its finest boarding houses, Tyche, Goddess of Chance, vowed that all involved would pay.

* * *

It was night in the city. The owner of an east end diner left his restaurant to make a late deposit. It was risky he knew, walking the streets with so much money, but it was even more risky to leave it in the safe—or worse, the register, for stickup men to come and take it away. Besides, it was only a two-block walk and he varied the hours he made the deposit.

When he left, a newly hired waiter took a break and made a phone call. A payphone up the street rang. "He's on the way," the waiter said. The man on the other end hung up and walked toward the diner, looking for the owner. As he did so a shadow detached itself from the wall behind him and followed.

Almost there, the owner thought just before he was pushed from behind. Stumbling forward, he fell into an alley. Cursing his luck, he hoped that the robber would take only the money and not his life.

The crook wanted both. He had decided long ago that "no witnesses" was the best way to stay out of prison. He drew his .38 and was about to fire when laughter came from deep within the alley.

The gunman knew that sound. It was the mocking laughter of one of the city's cloaked vigilantes. It was the sound many of his fellow crooks had heard just before they died. It was the sound of his own death.

Fight or flee? The gunman decided on both, firing two shots into the blackness and hoping to get lucky before running away. Laughter told him he had missed.

Maybe it was chance that caused one of his hastily fired shots to strike an outside circuit box. Maybe it was that bullet that caused the spark that sent current to a darkened street lamp near the alley's mouth. Maybe the long neglected lamp would have sputtered on anyway. Or maybe it was just bad luck that caused the alley to be flooded with light.

"Run!" shouted the man in black who was now a well-lit target, a target who could not shoot back for fear of hitting the diner's owner. The man dropped as a bullet whizzed over his head. He rolled as another shot hit the ground where he had just been.

"Run!" he shouted again then loosed a fusillade of bullets at the street lamp that had betrayed him. All his shots missed but at least this time the would-be victim listened to him. The diner's owner ran one way as he broke from the alley. The gunman, not interested in trading shots in a now fair fight, ran the other.

Alone in the alley, the man known to both foes and allies as the Nightmare looked up at the street lamp. *Damn the luck*, he thought. That the owner had gotten away was some consolation but he wished that he had been able to bring down the robber. *Another night*, he decided as sirens in the distance told him that he should make his own escape.

A week after he had dodged bullets in a not so dark alley, the Nightmare was sitting against a dirty wall in an even dirtier bar called The Jade Dragon. Despite its fancy name it was one of the city's sleaziest dives. He was, of course, not dressed in his usual black but in an oversized sweater and trousers from some church's charity bin. Nursing a watered drink, the Nightmare was listening to those around him.

A child named Toby Barnes was missing, believed to have been kidnapped. The Nightmare had been asked by his police contact to help find the boy. The Jade Dragon was the third bar the Nightmare had been in that evening hoping to overhear some word as to who had done the deed or where the boy might be stashed. He was about to give up and try a fourth place, maybe Dago Mike's, when…

"Heard there was a snatch."

It was a man on the Nightmare's right whose table companion replied. "Yeah, a D.A.'s kid. Supposedly by some new guy in town, goes by the name of…"

That's when the door to the Dragon burst open and a man rushed in. "The cops!" announced the newcomer. "They've called for the dragnet. Everybody's being snatched up." He looked over his shoulder to the outside. Behind him came the sounds of sirens and police whistles. "They're almost here. Clear out."

The Dragon rapidly emptied and while the Nightmare had no problem in evading the police sweep, he had missed his chance to discover the name of the kidnapper. With the underworld shut down for the night, he went home, hoping that someone else would have better luck in finding the missing boy.

Ten days later, in the early morning hours when no one but a paid-off watchman was about, a battered truck pulled up to a warehouse on a city dock. Inside the building were fine silks from the Orient, tapestries from the Middle East and carvings from Africa. The men in the truck had no interest in any of these. They were not there to steal but instead to teach a lesson to the importer who refused to pay extra docking fees, exorbitant labor costs and protection money to the mob boss who had claimed the docks as his personal fiefdom. Their unloading of cans of gasoline and kerosene was interrupted by "No fires tonight, boys!" spoken through a bullhorn.

The men looked to see that four patrol cars, a transport wagon and an unmarked police cruiser had followed them on to the dock and that ten policemen with drawn guns were facing them.

The men were not fools. They knew that while the use of flammable liquids was against the law, the simple possession of such liquids was not. They quietly surrendered. What they did not know was that one of the cans already unloaded had been damaged during their ride and was leaking its ignitable contents on the ground. They, and the police, found out when someone discarded a lit cigarette.

The fire spread quickly and was not extinguished until a good third of the warehouse and its contents had been consumed by the flames.

Stepping away from the fire scene, Police Lieutenant Jerome Easton spoke to the shadows where he was sure a certain man in black was waiting. "Thanks for the tip. Damn shame the way it worked out. Just bad luck I guess."

Bad luck indeed, the Nightmare thought. *There seems to be a lot of that going around.*

* * *

Following the conflagration at the docks and after several other close calls with bullets fired too close, inconvenient car lamps that exposed his position and miraculous escapes by criminals who once would have fallen prey to either his guns or his fists, Michael Shaw, the man who was the Nightmare, was sitting alone in a booth at Moran's, a mostly quiet little bar on the city's eastside that poured a good drink at a fair price. Shaw was sipping the finest Irish whiskey on either side of the Atlantic and thinking that maybe it was time to give up the masked life and find another way of serving society. *I'm losing my touch*, he thought, *with all that's gone wrong lately I should stop before I get myself or someone else killed.*

He had quit once before, had even declared the Nightmare dead, but had returned to save a family and end the reign of a gang boss. Raising his glass and staring into the golden liquid, he asked aloud, "And what good did it do?" True, the family, at least most of it, was safe, but the gangs went on. They were hydras, cut off one head and two others rise in its place.

"What was that you said, Michael?'

Shaw looked up to see Moran himself, the diminutive owner of the bar, standing at his table.

"Nothing, Seamus, just reliving the past and pondering the future."

"Not that you can affect either one. Taking care of oneself in the present is enough for a man to do." Seeing that Shaw's glass was nearly empty, he asked, "Now can I be getting you anything else?"

Shaw shook his head. "Nothing more, Seamus, unless you managed to bottle some of that 'luck of the Irish' I've heard so much about. I could use some, mine's gone all sour."

"Luck of the Irish," Moran snorted. "Five hundred years of English oppression, famine driving out our youngest and finest and now a civil war that pits county against county and brother against brother. Aye, we Irish have the luck all right and none of it's good. I often wonder what great power we offended in the past to be so cursed. But that's our problem and not yours, Michael. Unlike ours, your troubles will soon pass, unless of course you've gone and incurred the wrath of a god or two. But how likely is that in these days and times?"

* * *

Later that night, as Shaw watched the sun come up through the window of his study, his mind went back to a night of pain and fire, of laughter and gunplay in a seaside casino. He had saved the woman he loved, he had been pulled from death's embrace and he had defied beings who called themselves gods. There was the Thunderer. Shaw had mocked him to his face. And there was the Lady, the one who operated the casino. Tyche, the goddess of chance and fortune, and it was her temple he had raided. It was his mockery and her failure that had brought down the lightning that had destroyed it.

Had he incurred the wrath of a god or two? Shaw thought it very likely.

* * *

He went back to where it started, not as Shaw, not as the Nightmare but as just one of the many looking for work, any kind of work, honest or not, as long as it paid. He found where Tyche's place had been and watched as men and their machines built a new boarding house on the now vacant lot.

"They hiring?" he asked another onlooker.

The reply was a shake of a head. "They were, but you're about a week too late and there's about a dozen ahead of you."

Shaw nodded, as if he had expected the answer. "Isn't there a gambling joint around here? Hear it's run by a jane. Maybe she could use someone for, well, something. Anything really."

The man pointed to the construction and laughed. "In that case you're a couple of months too late. There was a fight, some masks shot up the place then burned it down. Damn masks, legal killers if you ask me."

"The dame, she reopen anywhere?"

Another shake of the head. "Not here. She's got a racket in the city, working a joint for a fella named Boyd." The man looked away to watch a wood frame being put in place. "But if it's work you're looking for and you're not choosy, I know a juice joint that needs a bouncer."

He turned and found himself alone. "Where'd the hell he go?" He shrugged and went back to watching other men work.

* * *

Finding a casino in the city was not difficult. Finding the right one took weeks. Each night Michael Shaw visited a different gambling den— playing every game, placing small bets and losing every time. If he stood at nineteen, the dealer would have twenty. If he had a ten and a queen, the dealer would turn up blackjack. At roulette he'd bet on odd and see even come up. He'd bet red only to see black. And if he bet both the ball would fall in the green.

Each night ended in frustration. It wasn't the losing; it was his not finding the source of his ill luck. Maybe he was not meant to, maybe it was part of his cursed fortune that he would fail at whatever he set out to do.

No, Shaw would not believe that. To do so meant that his life and the lives of all those around him were ruled by nothing more than chance and fate, that they lived only at the whim or design of higher powers. That he would not accept. Luck did play a part, but only that—a part. Reason, logic, determination—these too were part of the great whole. And it would be these that he used to find the one he sought.

Night after night of methodical searching paid off. The place that he sought was on the west side, in what appeared to be just an ordinary restaurant. Unofficially it was known as Fortune's Palace. Even as his limo pulled up to drop him off he felt—something, a frisson in the air, an enchantment maybe that drew one to it and promised fulfillment if only one would come inside and take a chance.

Knowing what his chances were, Shaw stepped inside. After giving the password, he was escorted past the diners and into a spacious rear room where he found slots, tables, wheels and, best of all…

Her.

Tyche.

The cause of his ill luck.

Though he had never seen her, Shaw knew her right away from the description of others. Dressed in a green gown that fell about her like a robe, Tyche moved among the gamblers like the goddess she was supposed to be—talking to some, listening to others, granting favors and maintaining order as needed. This was her temple, where worshippers placed offerings on her altars of chance in hopes of changing their lives. She drew her strength from this place and it showed in her face each time a wheel was spun or a card dealt.

But such could be said of any casino, every casino—anywhere men and women placed a bet and called on her to be their lady that night. Why then did she limit herself to just one place? And why, if the rumors were true, did a goddess deign to work for a common hood like Emmett Boyd?

Like many others in the room, Shaw watched her, but from a distance, not getting too close for fear that she would sense his other self. And when he was not watching her, Shaw examined the room, looking at entrances and exits, places to hide and avenues of escape. For as much as he did not want to admit it, he knew that soon the Nightmare would have to pay a visit and confront the goddess in her own house.

* * *

He watched for five nights—from the front and the back, at ground level and from rooftops. He did not see her leave. That might mean that she could blend with the darkness or that she had left in disguise. However, Lady Luck was not a creature of shadows and the Nightmare had been trained by the best to see through artifice and disguise. No, it was most likely that Tyche seldom left her temple—few deities did—and she lived somewhere on the second or third floor.

Probably the third floor. More natural light came in and it gave a better view of the city. Perhaps in the past few days, in the early morning hours, just before dawn chased men like him back to their quite ordinary and unexciting lives, she had looked out and seen him. Seen him lurking, watching for her, looking for a way in. If so, did she care? Would she try to stop him, or simple rely on the bad luck with which she had cursed him?

It did not matter. He had to make the attempt, had to confront her to find out what he must do to get her to lift the curse, and if he could, in good conscience, do it. It was that or give up his crusade to bring a measure of justice to the city.

There were several ways inside. He discounted the easiest. Scale the outside? One loose brick and there would be a quick fall and a sudden stop. The fire escape of the adjacent building? A rusted bolt breaking at the wrong time would lead to the same result, only much noisier with heavy metal falling on top of him. No, his approach would have to be carefully planned and well thought out to eliminate even the slightest possibility of chance.

Even as he planned the long circuitous route that would have him entering through the rooftop door, the Nightmare realized the extent of what Tyche had done to him. Three months ago he would have thought nothing of climbing a wall or fire escape and trusting to luck and skill to see him through any difficulties. Now he was second and third-guessing himself, and unless he shook off the resultant paralysis he was a beaten man.

To hell with it, he decided. Luck might be against him but his skill had yet to fail. *To hell with rooftops and fire escapes and rooftop doors.* Leaving the darkness of the alley, the Nightmare crossed the street and approached the front door.

He did not give luck the chance to work against him. Pressure in the right places followed by a push and the door gave way.

The restaurant was empty, the chairs turned up for the morning cleaning crew. Noises came from the rear, the casino staff finishing up for the night. He ignored them. He knew from his previous visit that there was no entrance to the upper floors from the rear room. There were, however, stairs to his right and these he took.

The second floor was used for storage and supplies. She had to be on the third.

The Nightmare cautiously climbed the stairs, looking for handholds and prepared to jump aside if a tread broke beneath him. Making it to the third floor without incident, he thought about drawing one or both of this .45s. *And what good would they be against a goddess, Michael*, he asked himself. Laughing quietly, he opened the first door he came to.

There she was—Tyche, Goddess of Luck. As before, she was in green, wearing a floor-length gown that was almost but not quite transparent under an open robe that was just as sheer.

Goddess or no, Shaw thought, taking in her beauty, *this is a woman a man could worship*. Another time, another place, different circumstances and Shaw might have been that man. But not then, not tonight, not when the game was being played for more than physical satisfaction.

"I knew you would come to me, Master Nightmare, to beg the lifting of your curse."

"I come, but not to beg. To request, to bargain, to warn perhaps; but not to beg."

Some women seem more beautiful when they grow angry, when they drop the façade society tells them they must maintain and let their true selves show. Tyche was not one of these. Her features darkened and perhaps some of her true face was revealed.

"You would bargain with me, mortal! You would threaten a god!"

"You would not be the first, Lady Tyche. And yet here I stand, asking but not begging you to lift the curse."

"Would you know why I cursed you, Master Nightmare?"

The man behind the mask smiled. "I can imagine."

"No, you cannot. You laid waste to my temple, my site of power, and your actions caused it to be burned to the ground. Despite that, and the gunshot that further weakened me, I might not have sought you out. It was fair combat and even one such as I must now and then be humbled. But it was afterward, once the fire was out and I was goddess of a smoking ruin, that a curse fell on me. The curse that was and is Reuben Sol.

"I owe this Reuben Sol. It was from him that I leased the buildings that housed the casino and hotel. It was he who provided the liquor and who paid off the authorities. And it was he who provided the men you fought and killed. And because of this, because of you, I was in debt to this ... mortal, a debt which I had no means to pay."

"You could have walked away."

"How little you understand my kind, Master Nightmare. There are few rules that bind us, but Obligation is one of them. So to pay what I owe I work here. Sol arranged it with an associate of his, one Emmett Boyle. Boyle gets a house cut of sixty percent. Sol gets half of the remainder to settle my debt. Much of that covers what is called 'vigorish,' interest on my debt that accrues faster than I can pay it off."

That doesn't leave you much to live on."

"If it did, would I be living in this...hovel?"

The Nightmare looked past Tyche at her apartment. It was neat and functional, nicer than what most people had those days, but nowhere near worthy of a goddess.

"Why don't you just use your power over Chance to affect the play in your casino? Have the dice roll and the cards come up your way. The more money you make the quicker your debt is paid off."

Tyche shook her head. "The players, whether they know it or not, are my worshipers. I cannot cheat them. There must be balance. The bad luck with which I cursed you comes from others' good fortune. No, I am bound to Sol and through him to Boyle. And as the cause of my misfortune, you shall suffer as long as I do."

"My Lady Tyche, my actions were the result of your own doing. You took the woman I loved. I saved her. It was as you said, 'fair combat.'"

The goddess laughed in disdain. "Of those rules that bind us, none say that my kind have to be fair to mortals. You may go, Master Nightmare. May this first visit be your last, or this city will become the luckiest in the world, for all of its ill fortune will fall upon you, and you will not be safe even in your own home."

The Nightmare bowed, exaggerating his movements so as to make a mockery of the courtesy and the person to whom it was directed. "Let it be as you wish, Lady Tyche," he said as he again stood straight, "my skills against your curse."

With that the Nightmare left. As he did, Tyche heard his laughter coming from the stairway, full of confidence and promising doom.

* * *

Even as he issued his parting challenge to the goddess of Chance, the Nightmare asked himself, *But can you deliver?*

Outside, he changed back to Michael Shaw and hailed a taxi. Given his current circumstances he thought it best to let someone else drive, figuring their luck would be better than his. In the back of the cab he reviewed his meeting with Tyche.

She had mentioned balance, telling him that his bad luck came from someone's good luck. Came—or caused? He would have to ask Easton if the police were catching more crooks than usual. Or maybe the ones that got away were the lucky ones. *Bad for me, good for them. I lose, someone else wins.*

Which brought his mind back to the casinos. In all of them, even Tyche's, he had lost every wager. That meant others had to win. An idea started forming. It grew when he remembered the goddess's warning:

"May this first visit be your last."

His true first visit had been as himself, as Michael Shaw. Tyche had not detected it, had not felt the curse at work. It was nice to know that infallibility was not one of her attributes.

A plan formed. And when he remembered what Tyche had said about obligation, he had to stifle a laugh that he unleashed only after the cabbie dropped him off in front of his stately manor.

Michael Shaw was no stranger to gambling. He owed his fortune to his great-grandfather, who was said to have won Shaw Manor and a great deal of money in a poker game. It was also said that his great-grandfather's winning was due more to his manipulation of a marked deck than any amount of luck. Shaw's grandfather took chances on gold mines and oil wells, most of which paid off. His son, Shaw's father, was the "white sheep" of the family—honest to a fault and loathe to take any kind of chance. It was left to Shaw to carry on the family tradition by playing the stock market, winning a game that had recently cost so many so much.

And now he played for higher stakes, risking not money but his reputation, his freedom and his life, wearing the mask of the Nightmare and standing between both sides in the eternal game of cops and robbers.

Michael Shaw knew gambling, it was in his blood, and he knew gamblers. If criminals were a superstitious lot, then gamblers were even more so. He was counting on this knowledge.

As Shaw, he became a regular at Fortune's Palace. Each visit he placed more than token bets, placing 100 dollar chips first on the dice tables and then on blackjack, wagering more in an hour than most men made in a year.

It did not take the other gamblers long to notice his play, both his betting and his losing. They latched on to him, watching where he placed his chips then betting against him. Every night he played. Though he could afford it, every night he lost a fair sum of money. Everyone else won, except the house.

Begging the ghost of his great-grandfather to be forgiven the sin of deliberately losing, Shaw played and lost for a week. No one noticed him. Pit bosses are trained to watch the winners and encourage the losers. Tyche walked the floor and ignored him.

It was on the fifth night that he began to feel a certain tension in the air and noticed added security around the tables. Someone, maybe Tyche, possibly Boyd, had begun to suspect that they were being cheated but could not figure out how. On the sixth night he saw the goddess talking to two men, cheap looking hoods in expensive suits, ones no doubt designed to give them sophisticated airs. Boyle, and probably Sol, Shaw thought. Behind the men, their eyes watching the crowd, were even cheaper hoods, gunmen whose ill-fitting clothing did nothing to disguise the bulges of their weapons.

Shaw watched the group from a distance. Tyche was shaking her head, the two men were nodding theirs. None of the three looked happy. *Do they know with who, or rather, with what they are dealing?* Shaw could not help imagining Tyche losing her temper and calling down godlike wrath on them. That just might solve her problem and his, and if not for the possibility that more or less innocent people would be injured, he might have looked for a way of causing it to happen.

Something was said. The argument ended with the goddess, Boyle and Sol—accompanied by the thugs—leaving the casino and going up to her apartment.

I am glad that I don't have my working clothes with me, Shaw thought. *The temptation to listen in might have been too much. I'd be caught and that would end the whole deal. Or else I'd try blasting my way in and thanks to the curse I'd be killed along with everyone but Tyche, leaving her the only winner._*

Instead he imagined what was happening. Boyle explaining to Tyche the need to increase revenues—or else. Sol outlining what the "or else" might entail. Shaw wondered if Tyche would try explaining things as simply a run of bad luck.

Smiling at the possible irony, Shaw left the casino. It was time for part two of his plan.

* * *

He was back in the Jade Dragon, again dressed in charity clothing, a mostly empty bottle in front of him. Apparently drunk, he talked loudly to anyone who would listen.

"I tell you it's a sure thing. I got it from one of her dealers. This dame Tyche is tired of turning most of her jack over to somebody else. She's fixing to bring Boyle down by busting her own joint. The fix is in for Friday night and there's heavy sugar to be had."

The Dragon was the Nightmare's fourth stop. There was just one more to go.

* * *

Shaw's last stop was Moran's. He arrived just before closing time and took his usual booth in the back. As he sat down he was greeted by the tavern's diminutive owner.

"Michael, it's been a while, for either of you. I thought perhaps you had retired your friend in black—again."

"No, Seamus, my other self is here to stay as long as he's needed."

"Then your luck has come back, has it?'

"No, Seamus, it's a bad as ever, but I've found a way to work around it. And I'd like your help in doing so."

* * *

The "fix" as the Nightmare had put it, was set for the following Friday. That Wednesday, a few men and women recruited by Moran got to the casino early.

"I'll stake them, Seamus," Shaw had explained to the bar owner, "and we'll split whatever they win."

"And if they lose?"

"Then the losses are all mine. And to be honest, I hope to lose a lot."

Shaw did. It was as he had hoped. Playing with his money, the men and women sent by Moran lost it all.

"What now?" Moran asked after Wednesday night had drifted into Thursday morning.

"They used my money and so my luck followed them. Same thing Friday night, Seamus. My money, my risk. I'll be there as well. And call everyone you know. Tell them to call everyone they know. I will as well. Tell them to be there and make sure that they know who our players are and to bet big against them. My bad luck is going to break the bank at Fortune's Palace."

* * *

That Friday, the Palace was crowded and there was anticipation in the air. The usual crowd was there—the bored, the compulsive, the reckless—all looking for the momentary thrill that gambling provided. Others, those who had heard the planted rumors and believed them, were there as well. Shaw and Moran's recruits were present as were dangerous-looking men brought in by Boyle and Sol in the event that the stories they had heard were true.

Shaw played recklessly, making wild bets that he had little chance of winning even without his curse. Other gamblers followed, playing against him and raking in the chips. Men and women at other tables, using Shaw's money, also lost while those in the know won big.

Looking around, Shaw did not see Tyche. The hostess of Fortune's Palace had yet to make an appearance. He did, however, see Boyle and Sol walking the floor, watching the play, checking out who was winning and losing and no doubt trying to figure out how they were being cheated and by whom.

Dice were changed, decks of cards were exchanged, dealers and croupiers were replaced. Nothing stopped the steady drain of the house funds. Finally, the hoods gave in. The word was given and one by one the gamblers were paid off and the tables closed. Fortune's Palace was closing several hours early.

Shaw was one of the first to leave. Going to his hired car, he removed a bag he had left in the back seat then released the driver. The car drove off. Shaw found a dark alley, opened the bag and examined its contents—black mask, black coat, black gloves, a brace of .45s—his working clothes. Donning them, he let Michael Shaw give way to the Nightmare.

"Time to play," he said. Taking a length of rope from the bag, he made his way back to Fortune's Palace.

It was not the night for the direct approach. It was the night to pit his skill against the curse. Entering the house next to the casino, the Nightmare cautiously made his way to the roof. There he tread carefully, feeling for weak areas and soft spots. Soon he was atop the Palace.

A new rope, the best and strongest he could find. The chimney looked firm, all the bricks in place and no loose mortar. Tying the rope tight, he lowered himself down.

The Nightmare had been prepared to slip or jimmy the rear third floor window. Instead he found it open. He nodded then, laughing to himself, slipped through it.

A quick flash of his torch showed him that he was in Tyche's bedroom. Memorizing the position of the furniture he made his way to the bedroom door. Turning the knob slowly, he eased it open.

Men were talking.

"...trying to pull," one was saying. "We heard the rumors, the talk on the street. You're running a game on us."

"I assure you, gentlemen, the only games I am running are downstairs."

"Well you ain't running them so good," said another man. "This last week you've lost more than all the other joints together. Explain that. No, don't bother, there's only one explanation and it's what we think it is."

There were scuffling sounds, then a slap, then a woman's cry. The Nightmare prepared himself for Tyche lashing out but nothing came. *Of course not*, he realized, *Tyche's still in debt to these hoods. Obligation may prevent her from harming them.* He listened, waiting for the just the right moment.

"This ain't working, sister. You did good on the shore but that's when you were making all the dough. So we're gonna try something else."

"What's that, Sol?"

Tyche's question drew lecherous chuckles from both men. "Emmett here's got other places, other—houses. A classy, good-looking broad like you, you could entertain a special client or two, maybe three, each night. A couple of months, maybe more, you'll be in the clear. You know, on your feet and off your back."

"How dare you!"

Here it comes, the Nightmare thought. But instead he heard a slap then the sound of a body hitting the floor.

Then the other man, Boyle, said, "There's a bedroom back there. Why don't we let her start tonight, just to make sure she's got the goods. Rubes, she owes you more than me. You go first. I don't mind seconds. You boys can hold her down then take your own turns. All three at once if you like. Let's break her in right."

Drawing his .45s, the Nightmare stepped back to allow the door to open. When it did he let loose a laugh, a laugh designed to reach into the souls of those who heard it and draw out their fear and terror, a laugh that told them that their sins had been found out, a laugh that warned them that this could be the last night of their lives.

The Nightmare stepped through the door, for the moment the master of the room, his cold voice announcing, "This lady is under my protection."

Sol and Boyle moved back. The guards stepped forward, their hands going beneath their coats.

"This is private business, Mask," said the shorter of the bosses. "Now get out of here before there's trouble."

"It's my business now, Sol. And there won't be any trouble if you and your friends leave now and promise not to bother the lady again."

"She owes us."

"Yes, she does, Boyle. But there's lots of money downstairs. Take it all. Leave her with nothing then leave her alone. Do this and we all walk away."

As he talked the Nightmare slowly lowered his guns, wondering if the guards were as stupid as they looked.

"And if we don't?"

Before answering, the Nightmare quickly looked down at Tyche, who was still on the floor. "My lady, about my previous request?"

"Granted."

"I thought it might be. To answer your question, Boyle, leave or be carried out. Your choice."

The three guards were as stupid as they looked, or maybe they too were under some type of obligation. At Boyle's "Take him" they moved to draw their weapons but not before the Nightmare could raise his automatics. He shot them each once, then shot them again to be sure.

Two more shots, neither from the Nightmare's gun. The doorframe behind him splintered. He turned to see Rueben Sol aiming his revolver. Two guns went off at the same time. Sol's bullet missed. The Nightmare's did not.

"What about you, Boyle?" the Nightmare asked, his voice raised so that the remaining gang boss could hear over any gunfire-induced deafness. "We're in a casino. Care to try your luck?"

Boyle shook his head. "I know when the game's gone against me. I'll take the deal. The money and she walks."

This time the Nightmare's laugh was one of mockery mixed with amusement. "That was before. Now you get half and she keeps half." Raising his .45, he pointed it at Boyle. "Or she can take it all."

Reluctantly Boyle agreed. "Done."

"Now go before we change our mind."

Boyle fled, leaving the Nightmare alone with the goddess.

"Your obligation to this one," he looked at the body of Rueben Sol, "is at an end. Just as you planned."

"What do you mean by that, Master Nightmare?"

"Goddess, I'm human but not stupid. Your curse was not all it could be, more inconvenience than mortally dangerous, nothing my skills could not overcome. And given the curse, I could not have found you had you not wished me to. Nor do I believe that you did not sense me playing and losing every night this week. You permitted it, perhaps tipped the scales just slightly out of balance. And my finding the window open was just too—lucky."

"And my plan was?"

"As you said, you could not move against Sol because of your obligation to him. So you set things up so that this"--he indicated the dead bodies on the floor--"would happen. You used me."

Tyche shrugged. "What of it? We gods have been using mortals for millennia. Your curse has been lifted. You may go."

"I am not so easily dismissed. I saved you. Or rather, by killing Sol I freed you. I now claim what was his, your obligation to him. You owe me."

The look on Tyche's face told the Nightmare that he had guessed right. Her nod confirmed it.

"I acknowledge the debt. What do you want?"

The Nightmare thought about this wide open offer. What did he want? Eternal good luck? No fun in that and it would only mean that his future bad luck would fall upon others. He looked at Tyche. She was one of the most beautiful women he had ever seen. But that would make him no better than Boyle and Sol. And he had briefly seen behind her human mask. Money? He had more than enough.

But these were just fancies. He had already decided what his demands would be.

"What I want is what I first offered Boyle and Sol. You leave this city, leave with almost nothing, with just enough to get started somewhere else. The rest of the money goes to the Police Widows and Orphans Fund."

"Is that all, Master Nightmare? Nothing for yourself?"

"I may take some of the money to cover recent gambling losses, but... no, wait, there is one other thing."

"And that is?"

"Should anyone approach you and say that the Nightmare sent them you will help them if you can do so without upsetting the balance."

"That I can and will do."

"Then we are quits, Lady Tyche. You should leave now. I'll contact the police about this mess. I would wish you good luck but that would be pointless. So I'll just say safe travels."

"Thank you, Master Nightmare, and may you be a little luckier than you were before we met. By the way, have you any suggestions as to where I might go?'

The Nightmare smiled. "There's a city in Nevada called Las Vegas. It sounds perfect for you and you for it."

Behind Closed Doors
Michael Laimo

"**W**hat happens behind closed doors, stays behind closed doors. It's no different than Vegas."

Grace Harrison flushed. It was a common sight for John, who considered himself lucky to have a spouse open to suggestion in the bedroom. *Promiscuity keeps the fuel burning.* That was her motto, fourteen years and counting.

Her glossed lips turned up. He liked it when she smiled this way. It meant she didn't care about the potential consequences. "Your career will go kaput if this gets out."

He placed a gentle finger against her lips. "Behind closed doors..."

She grinned, licked his finger, and led him into the bar.

* * *

It had been Grace's idea, long ago, to invite a third into their bedroom. They'd had a wide range of sexual adventures over the years. Pornographic movies, mutual masturbation, role-playing. They'd done it all...almost. Having been-there-and-done-that, Grace yearned to take things a step further. Her fantasy of being with another woman (with John's participation) was one of those steps.

No man in his right mind would snub a shot at every man's fantasy.

Not even a state senator who planned to run for governor.

"I'm only human," John had argued, the political collapses of McGreevy and Spitzer badgering his horned-up mind. "If the president could score a hummer from an intern in the Oval Office, then I should be fine."

Grace had responded, "As long as it stays behind closed doors, right?"

Right...

* * *

They entered the bar at the Ritz Hotel, a trendsetting spot for socialites in need of a little downtime. Grace considered it a safe milieu to put their plan into action. It was always sparsely populated, with Saturday nights rumored to draw only those attracted to an alternative lifestyle. Swingers.

Having come here before, they'd been approached twice by couples looking for a swap. But neither Grace nor John had wanted another man in the bedroom. Only another woman. *And one*, John had joked, *who didn't know a lick about politics.*

This part of their mission, the *hunt*, was intimidating for John. His campaign announcement was still six months away, and despite rarely being recognized in public, he and Grace both knew that would change. The woman they chose to share their bed with would have to be honest, trustworthy, particularly if she remembered John's face when it started popping up on the local news.

Nothing a few drinks won't take care of...

The bar was dark and inviting, structured with black marble columns and brass trim. Small tables filled the remainder of the spacious area, bearing flickering dinner candles and accompanying wine list.

John picked a table near the window. He noted only a few scattered couples, and one single woman at the bar with whom Grace had already made eye contact with.

"You have an admirer." He grinned and fished a twenty out of his wallet. "What do you want to drink?"

Grace plucked the bill from John's hand. "Let me do the honors." She smiled as John gave her a consenting nod.

She walked to the bar. John sat down, folded his arms across his chest and watched her lithe ass shake, perfect as the day they met.

In a moment such as this, John couldn't help but think of the past and the means by which they met—as scandalous as their endeavor tonight. John, ten years Grace's senior, once worked on the city council as a mayor's aide. During his tenure, Grace—fresh out of college--was hired as the mayor's secretary. This kept them in close quarters, from the day they met all throughout their relationship, which continued unabated for three years until they were caught having sex on the mayor's desk.

The mayor was outraged, of course, nearly traumatized by the event. But he chose to avoid public scrutiny and allowed John and Grace to continue working for him—despite his better judgment—until his term ended a year later. John knew quite well that if the mayor had decided at the time to release him from his duties, he never would have excelled through the political ranks from state representative to state senator.

Our sex life didn't stop me then, and it's not going to stop me now.

John watched Grace as she sidled up alongside the blonde at the bar. The blonde spoke first, prompting a smile from Grace. The bartender took a few minutes to prepare their drinks—just enough time for the woman to accept Grace's invitation to join them at their table.

John's heart did a mad dash as he watched the smiling women rise from their seats. They walked side by side toward him, shoulders touching, eyes glimmering with anticipation.

John took this moment to assess the blonde. He saw a polished woman pushing forty with the look and poise of someone in her early thirties, enhanced breasts pushing out against her white knit top. Cleavage, dark and smooth.

"John, this is Christine."

John smiled, nodded. "Christine."

Christine extended her hand and John took it. "Pleased to meet you," he said, their handshake lingering longer than one offered solely out of courtesy. Sometime afterward, John made a surreptitious pass beneath his nose, relishing in her flowery aroma like a teenaged boy might after pleasuring his first girl.

The next few hours were spent chatting, laughing, flirting. Over and over, John kept wondering how the evening would end. Would Christine move on with her life with just her memory lingering to aid them in their fantasy?

Or…would this all become a reality?

As the night grew late, and the Ritz Bar grew more crowded, John's question was answered.

* * *

They agreed to follow Christine to her house, only a few miles away in the hills. Tailing her Mercedes, John and Grace talked about how attractive and sexy Christine was, how they might use her for their own pleasure. By the time they arrived at her home—a striking five bedroom in an exclusive area reserved for lawyers and plastic surgeons--they were geared to make it all happen.

They entered through the front door. John noted all the home's finer details: ornate furniture and accessories, crystal chandeliers, marble floors. "Nice place. You win the lottery?"

"Let's just say I married and divorced the right man."

More laughter. More flirting. Christine poured them drinks from a well-stocked armoire in the foyer before they moved into the living room.

A few drinks later, they all went into Christine's lavish bedroom.

Like the rest of the house, the bedroom was furnished exquisitely, a four-posted canopy bed facing a grand closet, twin oak doors slightly ajar before a huge oriental rug.

That rug alone must cost twenty grand, John thought, his awe for all these finer things shattered as the women began to disrobe.

John sipped his drink, watching them kiss: lips searching, bodies writhing, hands running all over. His heart clapped forcefully, filling his ears with a rush of thunder that nearly drowned out their summons to join them on the bed.

Nearly.

* * *

Just before the sun rose—when the sky began to show fringes of pink against the bedroom's sheer curtains—John gazed to his left where a nude Grace began to stir. To his right was the stunning, sexy, insatiable Christine, naked body still glistening with her sweat, Grace's sweat, John's sweat. The night had gone on forever it seemed, an eventful pleasure beyond all pleasures embraced by three willing people quenching their lifelong desires.

John kissed both women on the forehead, each one nestling against him, heads upon his chest. "Thank you, both of you, for making my fantasy come true."

The experience seemed well worth risking his career for. But he knew: the afterglow would soon dissipate and leave a strange feeling in its wake. So, he felt it important to repeat what they all agreed upon at the onset of their tryst. "All this stays behind closed doors. Right?"

Christine laughed. "I'm not the shouting-from-the-rooftop type."

"That's good, because if this gets out, I'll have to kill you." He made a mocking sinister face—eyes wide, teeth clenched—then rolled on top of his wife for one more round.

* * *

John awoke on Sunday to a light meal, and a note from Grace: *Went running, be back later.*

He showered and shaved. An hour later, he emerged and found Grace in the bedroom. She was still in her running gear, breathing heavily and doused in sweat.

John's comment of "Looking good, babe" led to playful conversation of their experience with Christine. He watched Grace as she undressed, the unnerving questions of *What did we just do?* and *What if?* smoldering in his mind. But these thoughts were soon extinguished as a naked Grace pulled him onto the bed, her desires still in bloom, Christine's perfume still lingering on her skin.

Damn, I'm a lucky man, John thought over and over again.

Until the following day.

* * *

A polished white SUV stood at the foot of the driveway to John's home as he pulled up. Leaning against it was a man in his late thirties, mirrored Ray-Bans partially disguising his eyes. He wore jeans and a black golf shirt that accentuated his body-builder's physique.

John lowered his car window. "Can I help you?"

"Yes," the man said. "You can."

John stepped from the car, keeping his distance. The guy unnerved him: the cocky grin, the way his thumbs were tucked into his pockets, biceps bulging. Add in the fact he wasn't planning on letting John pull into the driveway.

"Who are you? What can I do for you?"

The man snickered. "Who am I? I'm Christine's husband. You know, the woman who joined you and your wife for a ménage e trois a couple nights ago?"

John fell silent, at a loss for words. He felt panic rise in him, a sudden tightening in his chest, his mind screaming *She said she was divorced!* nearly drowning out the sound of his careening heart. His hands went up, palms facing forward, eyes now looking toward the dark windows of his house, an immediate concern for Grace's safety opening up in him like a flower in stop-action bloom.

He looked back at the man, at his dark sunglasses, at his muscles. "She told us she was divorced…" His voice was little more than a whimper, his subconscious telling him all too late now that he should have vehemently denied the encounter.

"Well, she's not."

"Look, please…I don't want any trouble."

"I'm not here to give you any."

A moment's hesitation: John, allowing the man's words to soak in. A buzzing sensation rose in his head. "Why…why are you here, then?"

"I'm here to cut a deal with you, John. Or should I say, Mr. Senator."

"A deal…" John muttered. *McGreevy. Spitzer.*

"That's right, a deal." The man untucked his thumbs and held his huge hands out. "I think it's only fair, since you had a threesome with my wife, that I have one with yours. Me, Christine, and Grace, one night."

Jesus Christ… John's head shook back and forth, seemingly of its own accord. "No. No way. Sorry. That's just not going to happen."

The man laughed, and John had it in his right mind to punch him, right then, right there. But John's mind wasn't right at the moment. It had just been taken for a sudden, devastating loop, all its circuits shorting.

The man knows who I am. Getting into a fight with this guy would ultimately open up my tryst to the world. And get my ass kicked.

A gaping wound to kill his career.

"What do you want? Money? I could pay you." John's words were feeble and ineffective.

"You saw my house, John. I don't need any money. All I want is what you had. And then we'll be done."

"Grace will never agree to it."

"I don't think you—or Grace--have a choice, Mr. Senator."

John laughed uncomfortably. "What...you gonna go to the press? No one will believe you. Or Christine, for that matter." He stepped back to the car, doing his damndest to push the sudden turn of events out of his mind. As far as he was concerned, the matter was closed. He didn't care how many muscles the guy had.

He was about to slide into the driver's seat when the man turned around, reached into the open window of the SUV, and pulled out a videotape. He held it up for John to see. "Yes, they will."

He stopped, staring at the tape. Anger and frustration erupted in him. Had his tryst been videotaped? If so, the truth stung like a snake bite, as painful as the details of Christine's bedroom coming back to him now, the bed, the Oriental rug, the closet *that was slightly ajar*. He cursed himself—easy to do so, after the fact, Monday morning quarterback—for being too drunk, too distracted to not peek into the two-inch gap of the closet that faced the goddamned bed. Who would have, with two naked women begging for your services?

He clenched his fists and teeth. A dull pain gnawed at his temples. "I don't believe it."

"Go ask Grace. She's inside, watching it right now."

"You better not have hurt her—"

"Relax John. I had a copy of the tape delivered to your house. It was addressed to her, with a note inside. She doesn't even know who I am... yet." He looked at his watch and added, "But I'm sure she's anxious for you to get home and explain everything to her."

The anger, the frustration, was confounding. John bit his lower lip, corralling the urge to scream and rush the guy, inflict some pain, some retribution, *anything*. Instead, he unclipped his cell phone. "I'm calling the police."

"Do that, and the tape goes to the press...Mr. Senator. Or will it be Mr. Governor? You make the choice, John Harrison. You've got twenty-four hours." The man got back into the SUV, looked at John through the open window, Ray-Bans shimmering.

"What happens if I don't?"

The man held the tape up. "We'll just have to wait and see then, won't we?" He drove off, leaving John to ponder how he and Grace were going to deal with a situation that might not stay behind closed doors after all.

* * *

"I see no choice, John." Graced sipped her coffee, the morning sun casting dusty beams through the living room window, onto the television screen. Here they watched the three hour video for a second time, trying to ascertain if Christine might have been in on it.

As exciting the encounter had been, reliving it now proved utterly painful, from the moment they saw themselves entering the bedroom, to the moment John and Grace got dressed and left, leaving Christine sprawled naked on the bed.

"In no uncertain terms will my wife sleep with another man." His heart was racing, as if he'd just run a marathon.

"John...do you hear yourself?" Her frustration, the irrationality, was clear in her voice. "Do you see how hypocritical you sound? I let you sleep with another woman."

"That's different."

"Why John? Why is it different?"

"Damn it, Grace, you sound as if you *want* to do this."

She shook her head. Tears welled in her eyes. "I only want to save your career."

John had to consider what Grace claimed as a sacrifice for him. Could he live with the humiliation, the betrayal? And who knew if the muscle-bound husband of the woman they only knew as Christine would leave them alone afterwards? It was a risky, uncertain situation, one they had no control of. One they could not avoid.

Or could they?

"The answer is no, Grace. We're not giving in."

* * *

They sat in the living room, watching the clock as it passed the twenty-four hour mark. For the hundredth time John examined the yellow padded envelope the tape had come in, and the accompanying note, large bold letters typed on plain white paper:

Grace—here's a little something for you to relive your experience. John will explain why you received this tape. You have until 6:00 tomorrow to call this number with your answer: 555-3372.

There was no if, ands, or buts about it. He wasn't going to let his wife to sleep with another man. *This* man.

He considered reporting the guy, calling the police, the FBI, telling them that there was a threat on his life. But even then—even if the man didn't get a chance to send out the tape—word would still get around of what happened. Someone would eventually alert the media. There might even be a trial...

Of course, he could just let the man sleep with his wife.

But it was too late for that now.

* * *

They burned the tape, the note, and the envelope in the fireplace, destroying all their memories, both good and bad, of the event they spent years fantasizing about. Soon thereafter, they went to bed. But they didn't sleep. Didn't engage in intimacy. Sex felt *wrong* to John now.

Hours passed. He remained awake, thoughts filled with darkness, of things reaching out to choke him, to sever him from the world of the living. At some point he fell asleep and awoke in a cold sweat, trembling under the covers until the sun broke over the horizon, its rays seeping in through slits in the blinds.

He pulled the covers off his head.

Grace was not in the bed with him.

* * *

"Grace?"

She was seated at the kitchen table.

She looked up at him, eyes wide with worry.

"Grace...what is it?" Then he saw: a padded yellow envelope, just like the one the videotape came in, laying on the table before her. Once again, Grace's name was scrawled on the front.

"I found it on the stoop when I went out to get the paper."

Without hesitation, John picked it up. It was light. This time there was no videotape inside. He tore it open.

Inside, a note:

Grace—both Christine and I are waiting for you. 12:00 today.

Below the handwritten note, taped to the letter, was a key and a handwritten address.

The address to Christine's home.

* * *

Twenty minutes later, John pulled up in front of Christine's, and presumably now, muscle-guy's home. The large house appeared different in the daylight, less erotic, filled with threat and perhaps a promise of violence. John hoped that when he—instead of Grace—walked in on Christine and her husband, hopefully nude and prone in bed, that they would fear for their lives. He would demand the tape and then bolt the room, never to return.

He'd been holding the key in his hand the entire time. It was wet with sweat, palm red with its impression. He tried the doorknob first. Locked. Hand trembling, he slid the key into the deadbolt…and turned it.

The click of the lock was the loudest part of his entry as he tiptoed inside. He told himself that he was doing nothing wrong, that he'd had a key—had been invited into their home—and that breaking and entering would not be an option for pressing charges. He went quietly through the living room—as pristine as he remembered it—and then the kitchen, seeing on the counter a set of steak knives set into a pine butcher block.

Just in case, he thought. He grabbed the largest one, too afraid to look at it as he walked down the hallway toward the master bedroom.

Just the fact that I'm walking through a strange home with a knife in my hand to protect me from a scene that could end up out of control, is grounds to end my career.

The bedroom door was shut.

He thought about knocking, but then that would've spoiled his planned element of surprise. For a passing moment he wondered what in God's name he was doing here, what he *really* planned to do after he entered the bedroom. But no answers came to him. Only false hope.

They'll become unnerved, they'll give me the tape, and then I'll leave…

He pushed open the door…and saw Christine.

No…

She'd been murdered, her throat sliced open, a pool of black blood surrounding her naked body.

The next few seconds passed like hours…and in this terrible lapse where the wide-open truth of the matter impaled his heart and soul like a stake, he became painfully aware of the stench in the room, of death and the beginnings of rot, of rigor mortis and the thin, gray pallor of her body.

The knife fell from his hand, right into a puddle of blood dripping from the bed. Now there were bloodstains on it.

Now it had his fingerprints on it.

He staggered from the room, down the hall, through the living room, putting one and one together and knowing that Christine had been dead for a while now, was perhaps murdered mere moments after he and Grace left. And then he realized with dreadful conviction that his DNA was everywhere in that bed, that *crime scene*, his hair, his saliva, his semen.

The man with the muscles, Christine's husband, had set him up.

He charged though the living room, toward the front foyer. He glimpsed out the front window. Two cops were walking up the driveway toward the house. A third was looking through the windows of his parked car.

He backpedaled, spun, staggered back through the living room, holding back his gorge as the stench of dead human assaulted him from the open bedroom. He spun right instead of left and bolted through the kitchen, eyeing the butcher block and the empty slot from where he took the knife. He lost his balance. The tile floor rose up to meet his face, knocking the wind out of him. Short of breath, he reeled up and out the back door, jogging across the backyard into the woods behind the house, his entire career passing before his tormented eyes.

* * *

John's mind ran in loose circles, keeping pace with his legs as he fled through the woods all the way to the next neighborhood, at least a mile away. Once there, he called home.

Grace picked up. "Hello?"

"Oh my God," he panted, breaths deep and ragged. "Thank god you're okay."

"John? What is it? Where are you? Are *you* okay?"

"No...I'm not. Not at all."

His mind continued to race. Something didn't make sense. *Why did muscle-guy send a key to Grace's attention? Did he assume I would come in her place? He must've seen me enter the house. That's when he called the cops, alerted them of the murder scene. He figured they'd catch me there and arrest me...unless...unless he meant to set Grace up? WHICH ONE IS IT?*

"Grace...I need you to pick me up, take me back home. The cops are going to come, question me."

"The cops? John...where is your car? What's going on?"

"I'll tell you when you get here."

* * *

The ride had lasted only a few minutes, but that's all it took for him to tell Grace everything.

"Her body, her body..." he kept repeating as they entered their home. Oh my God, Grace. What am I going to do?"

"You have to tell them the truth, John. Everything."

"How can I?"

"If you don't, you'll end up in jail. What's more important now? Your career? Or your life?"

John paced back and forth, hands pinned to his face. "Are the cops here yet?"

Grace looked out the window. "No...not yet."

"Damn...my car, they have to know by now."

"John...sit down, try to relax."

"Jesus, Christine, how can I relax?"

"Here...I'll put the television on."

Before he could protest, Christine had the remote in her hand. Then the news was on. And then...

And then there was John's face, plastered all over it. Fear and uncertainty assaulted him, *murdered him*, right down to the marrow. It was impossible that it was already on the news. Impossible, just an hour after Christine's body was found. Impossible that he'd been pinned as a suspect. *Impossible.*

But then John saw what was *really* happening. The news was broadcasting a clip from the videotape, where it showed him awaking between Grace and Christine, both women waking up, and then their tinny-sounding conversation, spelled out with scrolling words across the bottom of the frame:

"Thank you, both of you, for making my fantasy come true." A pause, then "And all this stays here, behind closed doors. Right?"

Christine laughing, her playful voice, "I'm not the shouting-from-the-rooftop type."

All three of them laughing, John adding, "That's good because if this gets out, I'll have to kill you."

The video ended, the frame frozen on his make-believe sinister face, not at all looking make-believe: eyes wide, teeth clenched, like a madman. A murderer.

John was so stunned, so bowled over, that he never heard the cops knocking on the door.

* * *

Grace sat in her car, watching, waiting, thoughts going back to John's trial, its conclusion now three weeks in the past, the publicity and hoopla finally winding down. The evidence had been solid against him, just as he feared. State Senator John Harrison had been found guilty of murder.

John would be serving life in prison.

Grace blew out a long, anxious, breath.

A sudden knock upon her window.

She startled, looked up.

The man with the muscles, Christine's former husband, looked in at her.

She lowered the window.

"You ready?" he asked.

She nodded, got out of the car, shut the door...then looked at him. "Is it true? Did everything really go down as planned?"

He went to her and hugged her tightly, whispering in her ear, "Tell me again, Grace. How did it feel?"

It was such turn-on for him, hearing time and time again how his lover of years had derived such immense pleasure from murdering his wife.

His cheating wife.

"*Wonderful*," she replied, this time telling no lie. "Thank you for allowing me to fulfill my fantasy." She grabbed his hand and led him across the parking lot, toward the hotel.

Different city, same type of bar inside, catering to those seeking an alternative lifestyle. Swingers.

"Now that I've allowed you to fulfill your fantasy," Grace's lover said, "maybe tonight I'll fulfill mine. Maybe tonight I'll get that threesome I've always wanted."

"Maybe," she said smiling, deviously, flirtatiously. "As long as you promise to keep it behind closed doors."

About The Authors

Trent Zelazny is the award-winning author of *To Sleep Gently*, *Destination Unknown*, *Fractal Despondency*, *Shadowboxer*, *The Day the Leash Gave Way and Other Stories*, *A Crack in Melancholy Time*, *Butterfly Potion*, and *Too Late to Call Texas*. He is also an international playwright, as well as the editor of the anthologies *Mirages: Tales From Authors of the Macabre*, and *Dames, Booze, Guns & Gumshoes: Classic Tales From the Dawn of Crime*. He was born in Santa Fe, New Mexico, has lived in California, Oregon, Arizona, and Florida. He currently resides back in Santa Fe. He also loves NBA basketball.

Jessica McHugh is an author of speculative fiction spanning the genre from horror and alternate history to young adult. A member of the Horror Writers Association and a 2013 Pulp Ark nominee, she has devoted herself to novels, short stories, poetry, and playwriting. Jessica has had fourteen books published in five years, including her bestseller, *Rabbits in the Garden*, and the gritty coming-of-age thriller, *PINS*. 2014 will see the release of three more novels, including the start to her edgy YA series *The Darla Decker Diaries*. More info on her speculations and publications can be found at www.JessicaMcHughBooks.com.

Matt Schiariti is an Engineer by profession, guitar legend in his own mind, and would-be author, time permitting. When he's not writing, he's reading. When he's not reading, he's enjoying a beer sporting a fancy name on the label. When he's not enjoying a fancy-named beer, he's most likely reading some more. Sometimes he does all three at once, to disastrous effect. Matt lives in southern New Jersey, with his wife, two children, insane dog, two curious guinea pigs, and three reclusive hermit crabs. He is the author of *Ghosts of Demons Past* and *Words With Fiends: A Short Story*.

Sarah A. Hoyt was born in Portugal and lives in Colorado. In between she worked as a waitress, professional steam clothes ironer(totally a word) and translator. She shares her home with too many cats, a husband and two sons. She has published over a hundred short stories in professional venues, including *Analog* and *Asimov's*. Her novel *Darkship Thieves* was the winner of the 2011 Prometheus Award. The sequel, *A Few Good Men*, is nominated for the honor. Her latest novel is *Noah's Boy* number three in her popular Shifter series. In her copious spare time she also writes mystery as Sarah D'Almeida and Elise Hyatt.

Brady Allen is the author of the recent collection of 23 weird and dark tales, ***Back Roads & Frontal Lobes***. He has published numerous short stories in U.S. magazines, journals, and anthologies, and stories in England and Ireland, as well. Two of his tales have been selected as honorable mentions in St. Martin's Press's ***The Year's Best Fantasy and Horror***, and two more were on the long list for ***The Best Horror of the Year***. His short story "Slow Mary" was nominated for a Pushcart Prize, and Brady is also a past recipient of an Individual Artist Fellowship in Fiction from the Ohio Arts Council. He teaches writing at Wright State University in Dayton, Ohio, and lives in Dayton with his two daughters.

Award-winning author **Danielle Ackley-McPhail** has worked both sides of the publishing industry for longer than she cares to admit. Currently, she is a project editor and promotions manager for Dark Quest Books. Her published works include five urban fantasy novels, ***Yesterday's Dreams***, ***Tomorrow's Memories***, ***Today's Promise***, ***The Halfling's Court*** and ***The Redcaps' Queen: A Bad-Ass Faerie Tale***. She is a member of the Garden State Speculative Fiction Writers, the New Jersey Authors Network, and Broad Universe, a writer's organization focusing on promoting the works of women authors in the speculative genres. Danielle can be found on LiveJournal (damcphail, badassfaeries, darkquestbooks, lit_handyman), Facebook (Danielle Ackley-McPhail), and Twitter (DMcPhail). To learn more about her work, visit www.sidhenadaire.com, www.literaryhandyman. com, or www.badassfaeries.com.

Patrick Thomas writes the fantasy humor series Murphy's Lore, which includes ***Tales From Bulfinche's Pub***, ***Fools' Day***, ***Through The Drinking Glass***, ***Shadow Of The Wolf***, ***Redemption Road***, ***Bartender Of The Gods***, ***Nightcaps*** and ***Empty Graves*** — as well as the After Hours spin offs ***Startenders***, ***Fairy With A Gun***, ***Fairy Rides The Lightning***, ***Dead To Rites***, ***Rites of Passage***, and ***Lore & Dysorder***. His Mystic Investigators paranormal mystery series includes ***Bullets & Brimstone***, ***From The Shadows***, ***Once More Upon A Time***, and ***Partners In Crime***. ***Assassin's Ball*** is his first mystery, co-written with John French. He co-edited ***New Blood*** and ***Hear Them Roar*** and was an editor for ***Fantastic Stories of the Imagination*** and ***Pirate Writings***. Patrick's syndicated humorous advice column Dear Cthulhu includes Have A Dark Day, Good Advice For Bad People, and Cthulhu Knows Best. A number of his books are part of the props department of the CSI television show and have been spotted on the show. His urban fantasy ***Fairy With A Gun*** was optioned by Laurence Fishburne's Cinema Gypsy Productions. Drop by www.patthomas.net to learn more or find out about The Patrick Thomas Show mockumentary.

Robert E. Waters has been publishing fiction professionally since 2003, with his first sale to **Weird Tales**, "The Assassin's Retirement Party." Since then, he has sold over 25 stories to various online and print magazines and anthologies, including stories to **Padwolf Publishing**, **The Black Library**, **Dragon Moon Press**, **Marietta Publishing**, **Dark Quest Books**, **Mundania Press**, **Nth Degree/Nth Zine**, **Cloud Imperium Games**, and the online magazine **The Grantville Gazette**, which publishes stories set in Baen Book's best-selling alternate history series, 1632/Ring of Fire. From time to time, he also writes short fiction reviews for **Tangent Online**. He also served for seven years as an assistant editor for **Weird Tales**. Robert is currently living in Baltimore, Maryland with his wife Beth, their son Jason, their cat Buzz, and a plethora of tropical fish who like to play among the ruins of a sunken Spanish Galleon. His website is www.roberternestwaters.com.

g. Elmer Munson is a New England writer of all things strange and unusual as well as the horrors of everyday life. His first novel **Stripped** is available from Post Mortem Press. His short work can be found in various print anthologies and ezines, as well as the collection **Tales From The Underground**. He has more works in progress than can be counted, so follow his adventures at www.gElmerMunson.com.

When **Diane Raetz** isn't working to ensure skyscrapers are built correctly and safely, she dabbles in the art of fiction writing. Recently she has edited **Apocalypse 13**, and **New Blood** (with Patrick Thomas). Her current fiction efforts include **Once More Upon A Time** and **Flesh and Iron**. For more information about Diane check www.padwolf.com.

Georgina Morales writes horror, mystery, and everything else that might give you nightmares. 2011 saw the debut of her first novel **Perpetual Night**. Her short stories have appeared in magazines and anthologies such as **Dark Moon Digest**, **The Sirens Call**, and **Gothic Blue Book**. She lives in New England along with her husband, two daughters, their beagle, and their old, grumpy cat. https://www.amazon.com/author/georginamorales

John L. French has worked for over thirty years for the Baltimore Police Department as a crime scene investigator and has seen more than his share of murders, shootings and serious assaults. As a break from the realities of his job, he writes science fiction, pulp, horror, fantasy, and, of course, crime fiction. Since 1992 John has been writing stories partly based on his experiences on the streets of what some have called one of the most dangerous cities in the country. His books include **The Devil of Harbor City**, **Past Sins**, **Souls on Fire**, **Here There Be Monsters** and **Paradise Denied**. He's also written several books with co-conspirator

Patrick Thomas, the latest of which is ***The Assassins' Ball***. John is the editor of ***Bad Cop, No Donut***, ***Mermaids 13: Tales of the Sea***, and ***To Hell in a Fast Car: On the Road to Death and Disaster***. One of these days John will get a website and a Facebook page but in the meantime he can be contacted at jfrenchfam@.com.

Michael Laimo's novels include ***ATMOSPHERE***, (nominated for the Bram Stoker Award in the category of 'first novel'), ***DEEP IN THE DARKNESS*** (nominated for the Stoker in the 'novel' category), ***THE DEMONOLOGIST***, ***DEAD SOULS***, ***FIRES RISING***, ***SLEEPWALKER***, and ***RETURN TO DARKNESS***. His short fiction has been collected in the books ***DEMONS FREAKS AND OTHER ABNORMALITIES***, ***DREGS OF SOCIETY***, and ***DARK RIDE***. NBC's Chiller Network has produced both ***DEAD SOULS*** and ***DEEP IN THE DARKNESS*** as original feature films. Michael can be contacted at Michael@Laimo.com

Edward J. McFadden III juggles a full-time career as a university administrator and teacher, with his writing aspirations. His first novel, a mysterious-dark-thriller called ***The Black Death of Babylon***, is now available from Post Mortem Press, and his second novel, ***Our Dying Land***, was recently released by Padwolf Publishing, Inc., and his new novel, ***Hoaxers***, is due out from Crossroad Press June 6th, 2014. His steampunk fantasy novelette, Starwisps, was selected for the Tangent 2012 Recommended Reading list. He is the author/editor of: ***Anywhere But Here***, ***Epitaphs*** (w/ Tom Piccirilli), ***Jigsaw Nation***, ***Deconstructing Tolkien: A Fundamental Analysis of The Lord of the Rings*** (re-released in eBook format Fall 2012), ***Time Capsule***, ***The Second Coming***, ***Thoughts of Christmas***, and ***The Best of Pirate Writings***. He has had more than 50 short stories published in places like ***Encounters Magazine***, ***Gothic Blue Book: The Graveyard Edition***, ***Tales of the Talisman***, ***Fantastic Futures 13***, ***From Beyond the Grave***, ***Defending the Future: Dogs of War***, ***Apocalypse 13***, ***Hear Them Roar***, ***CrimeSpree Magazine***, ***Terminal Fright***, ***Cyber-Psycho's AOD***, ***The And***, and ***The Arizona Literary Review***. He lives on Long Island with his wife Dawn, their daughter Samantha, and their mutt Oli. See www.EdwardMcfadden.com for all things Ed.

EDWARD J. McFADDEN III

<u>OUR DYING LAND</u> There is a dead zone in Arizona the size of Rhode Island, and no one can figure out what caused it.

<u>ANYWHERE BUT HERE</u> What would you do if your son and his dog disappeared into a rip in space- time? You would follow.

<u>DECONSTRUCTING TOLKIEN</u> In this collection of essays, stories, discourses, and tributes, Ed McFadden has gathered together a wide range of topics, perspectives, and outlooks on some of the most intriguing factors concerning THE LORD OF THE RINGS

MORE GREAT BOOKS FROM

Even the things that go *Bump* in the night
will learn that you <u>DON'T</u> mess with...
Terrorbelle.

"Thomas certainly brings the goods to the table
 when it comes to writing urban fiction...I promise, you will love...
Terrorbelle: Fairy With a Gun. Who doesn't love a well-stacked,
ass-kicking, gun-toting, woman with bullet-proof, razor-sharp wings
that investigates all manner of supernatural spookiness? I know I do,
and Thomas's humor shows through in every tale. Jim Butcher and
Laurell K Hamilton have nothing on Thomas." The Raven's Barrow

From The Murphy's Lore Universe Of

PATRICK THOMAS

www. padwolf.com & www.terrorbelle.com

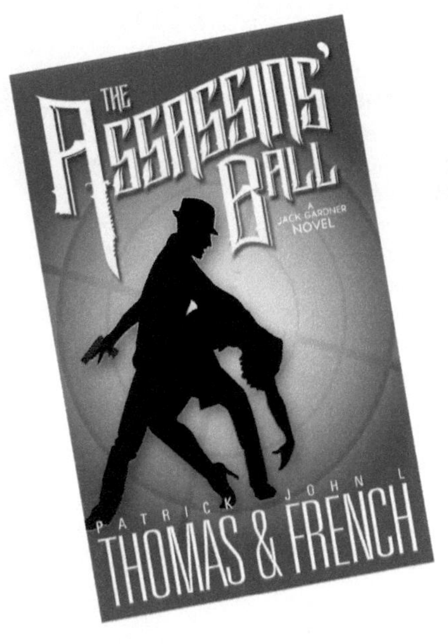

THE ASSASSINS' BALL

When there's a murder at a convention of killers... everyone's a suspect.

Coming soon from
PATRICK THOMAS & JOHN L. FRENCH

IT'S A CRIME TO MISS OUT ON THESE OTHER GREAT BOOKS FROM

JOHN L. FRENCH

John L. French is a crime scene supervisor with the Baltimore Police Department Crime Laboratory. In 1992 he began writing crime fiction, basing his stories on his experiences on the streets of what some have called one of the most dangerous cities in the country. His books include THE DEVIL OF HARBOR CITY, SOULS ON FIRE, PAST SINS, BULLETS AND BRIMSTONE and HERE THERE BE MONSTERS. He is the editor of BAD COP, NO DONUT which features tales of police behaving badly.

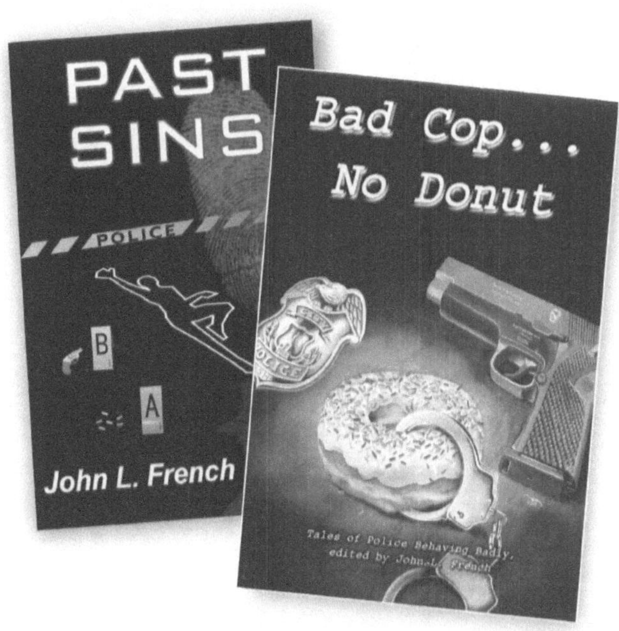

More GREAT Science Fiction!

THE STARSCAPE PROJECT

As his quest begins, an artificial intelligence life form enters the galaxy and launches a series of covert attacks against the Empire. The Teconeans assume that the Federation is responsible, and galactic peace is about to unravel. As Stryker chases his nemesis into Teconean space, he finds himself thrown into the middle of the battle. Knowing that Earth will be the aliens' next target, Stryker must decide whether to let them destroy the Empire, or to join forces with his Teconean enemies against the invaders. The key to the mysterious aliens lies buried on the moon of Kennedy Prime, and it's up to Stryker to solve the puzzle before war begins. The fate of the galaxy is at stake.

ZONE OF THE TENTH DGREE

In 1912, an alien ship crash lands in the Atlantic ocean, setting up a secret colony that remains undetected for centuries, allowing them to manipulate some of the most important events in human history -- from the sinking of the Titanic to the Bermuda triangle to global warming. Now, the technology of the 26th century has discovered the aliens' distress beacon, and it's a race against time as the Navy tries to stop a terrorist armed with a nuclear weapon from destroying the colony and triggering an all-out war as the mother-ship approaches

Now available from

PADWOLF®
PUBLISHING

visit padwolf.com

YOUR NEXT FAVORITE BOOK
IS JUST A MOUSE CLICK AWAY
AT PADWOLF.COM!

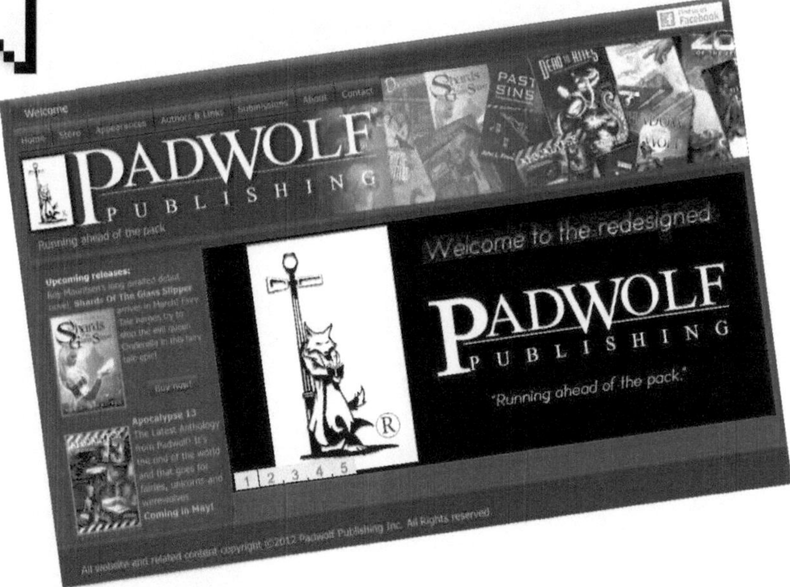

- **Buy books!** Novels, anthologies and more! Urban Fantasy, Horror, Mystery, Science Fiction, Epic Fantasy, Young Adult, just to name a few. From vampires to gun toting fairies, we've got all of your favorites in one place. Check out our newest releases and e-books or browse through our extensive catalog—including the Murphy's Lore series by Patrick Thomas!
- Find out the **latest news** about our authors!
- Location! Location! Location! Get the scoop on upcoming **author appearances** & booth shows!
- **Get social!** Padwolf Publishing is on Facebook! Follow your favorite padwolf authors on Twitter!
- Check out the **Padwolf blog**! Where our authors and editors contribute thoughts, rants, tips and tidbits!

VISIT THE NEWLY RENOVATED
WWW.PADWOLF.COM